COMICS SQUAD

SQUAD

DETENTION!

★ COMICS BY ★

JARRETT J. KROSOCZKA

GEORGE O'CONNOR

VICTORIA JAMIESON

BEN HATKE

RAFAEL ROSADO & JORGE AGUIRRE

LARK PIEN

MATT PHELAN

JENNIFER L. HOLM & MATTHEW HOLM

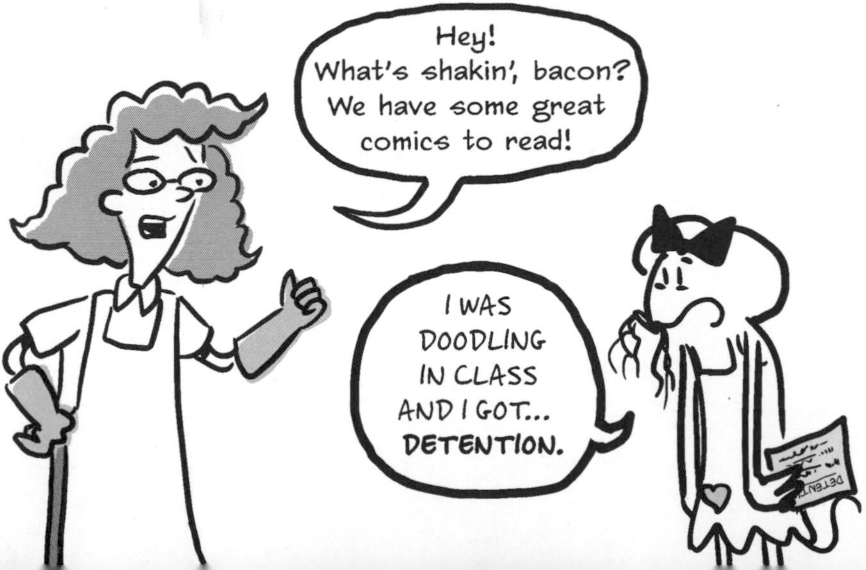
Hey! What's shakin', bacon? We have some great comics to read!
I WAS DOODLING IN CLASS AND I GOT... DETENTION.

COMICS SQUAD

SQUAD

DETENTION!

· EDITED BY ·

JENNIFER L. HOLM, MATTHEW HOLM & JARRETT J. KROSOCZKA

Oh no! Here. Take a cookie.

NO CUPCAKES?

RANDOM HOUSE 🏠 NEW YORK

For anyone who has ever been caught drawing in class.

I KNOW YOUR PAIN.

Compilation copyright © 2017 by Jennifer L. Holm, Matthew Holm, and Jarrett J. Krosoczka

"The Breakfast Bunch in . . . Detention Disaster" copyright © 2017 by Jarrett J. Krosoczka. "Cheating Death w/ Sisyphus" copyright © 2017 by George O'Connor. "Worse Than Detention" copyright © 2017 by Victoria Jamieson. "Milo's Journey" copyright © 2017 by Ben Hatke. "Too Nice!" copyright © 2017 by Rafael Rosado and Jorge Aguirre. "Cyclopean Kid: Detention Is Forever!" copyright © 2017 by Lark Pien. "Think About What You've Done!" copyright © 2017 by Matt Phelan. "Squish: Leave No Cell Behind!" copyright © 2017 by Jennifer L. Holm and Matthew Holm.

Cover art copyright © 2017 by Jennifer L. Holm and Matthew Holm, Jarrett J. Krosoczka, George O'Connor, Victoria Jamieson, Ben Hatke, Rafael Rosado, Jorge Aguirre, Lark Pien, and Matt Phelan

All rights reserved. Published in the United States by Random House Children's Books, a division of Penguin Random House LLC, New York.

Random House and the colophon are registered trademarks of Penguin Random House LLC.

Visit us on the Web! randomhousekids.com

Educators and librarians, for a variety of teaching tools, visit us at RHTeachersLibrarians.com

Library of Congress Cataloging-in-Publication Data is available upon request.

ISBN 978-0-553-51267-0 (tr. pbk.) — ISBN 978-0-553-51268-7 (lib. bdg.) — ISBN 978-0-553-51269-4 (ebook)

MANUFACTURED IN CHINA

10 9 8 7 6 5 4 3 2 1

First Edition

Random House Children's Books supports
the First Amendment and celebrates the right to read.

★ CONTENTS ★

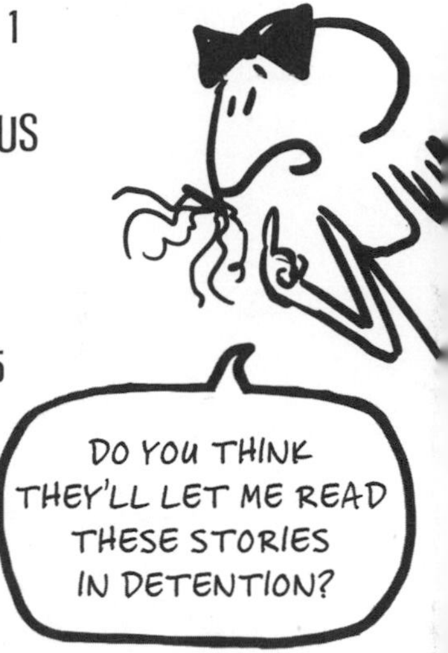
DO YOU THINK THEY'LL LET ME READ THESE STORIES IN DETENTION?

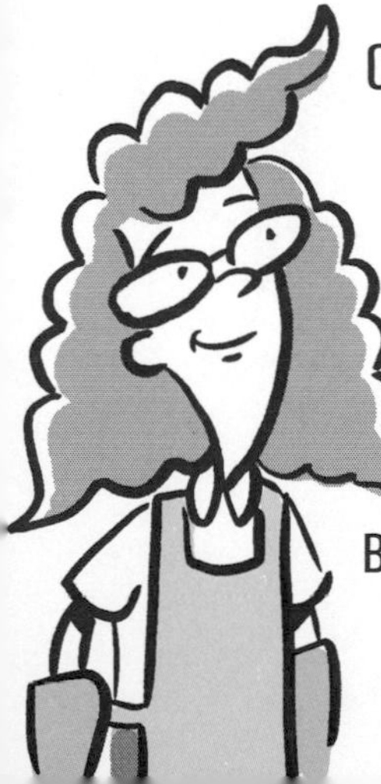

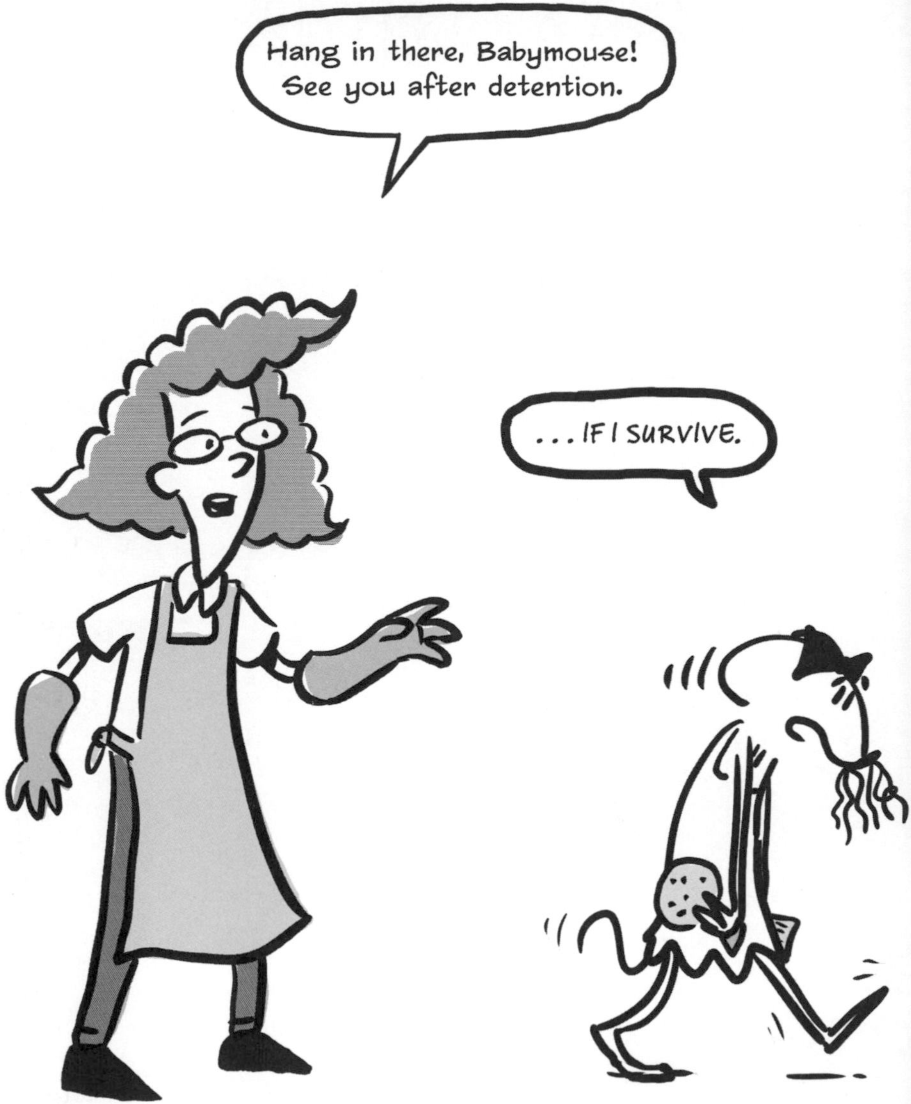
Hang in there, Babymouse!
See you after detention.
. . . IF I SURVIVE.

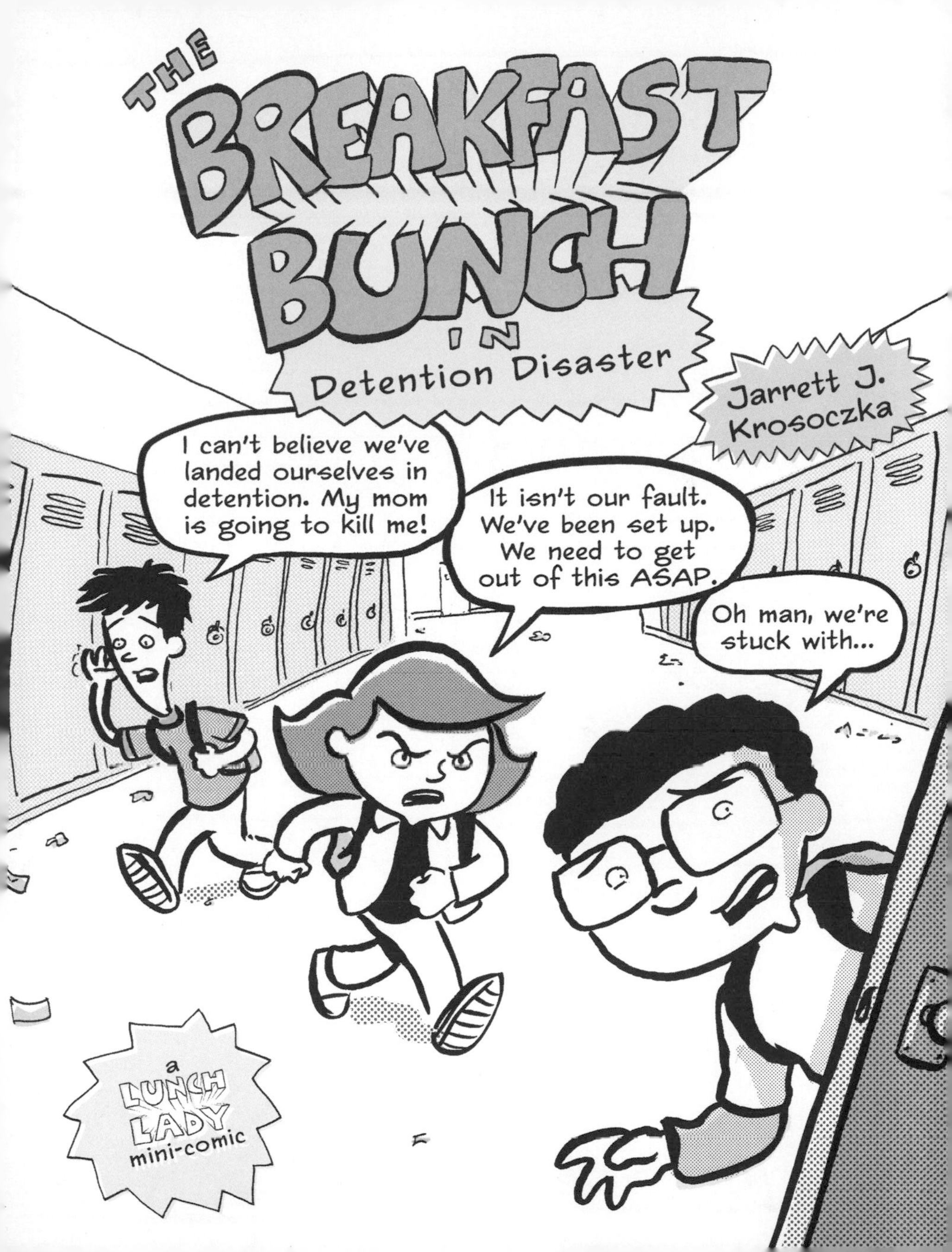
THE BREAKFAST BUNCH IN
Detention Disaster
Jarrett J. Krosoczka
I can't believe we've landed ourselves in detention. My mom is going to kill me!
It isn't our fault. We've been set up. We need to get out of this ASAP.
Oh man, we're stuck with...
a LUNCH LADY mini-comic

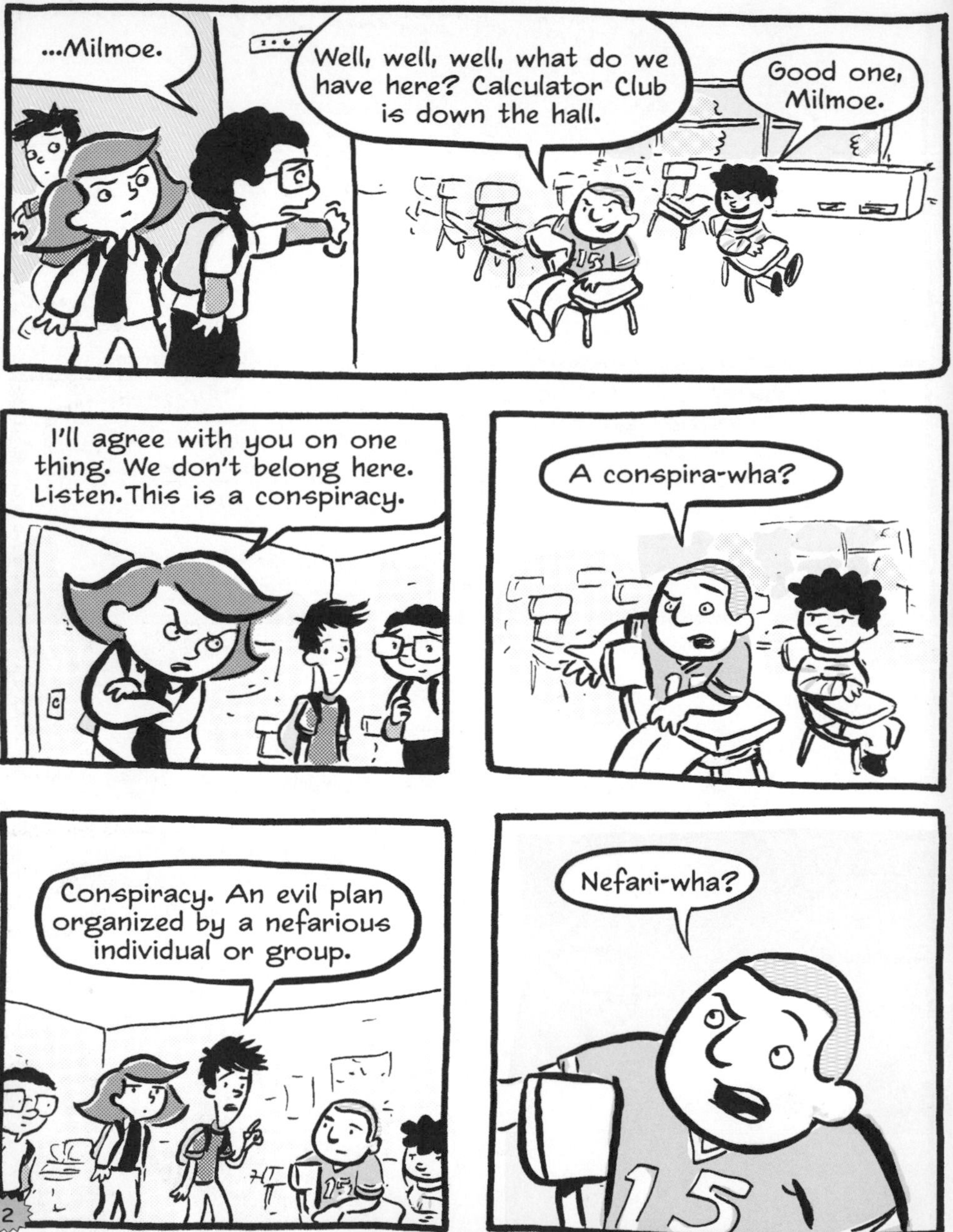
...Milmoe.
Well, well, well, what do we have here? Calculator Club is down the hall.
Good one, Milmoe.
I'll agree with you on one thing. We don't belong here. Listen. This is a conspiracy.
A conspira-wha?
Conspiracy. An evil plan organized by a nefarious individual or group.
Nefari-wha?

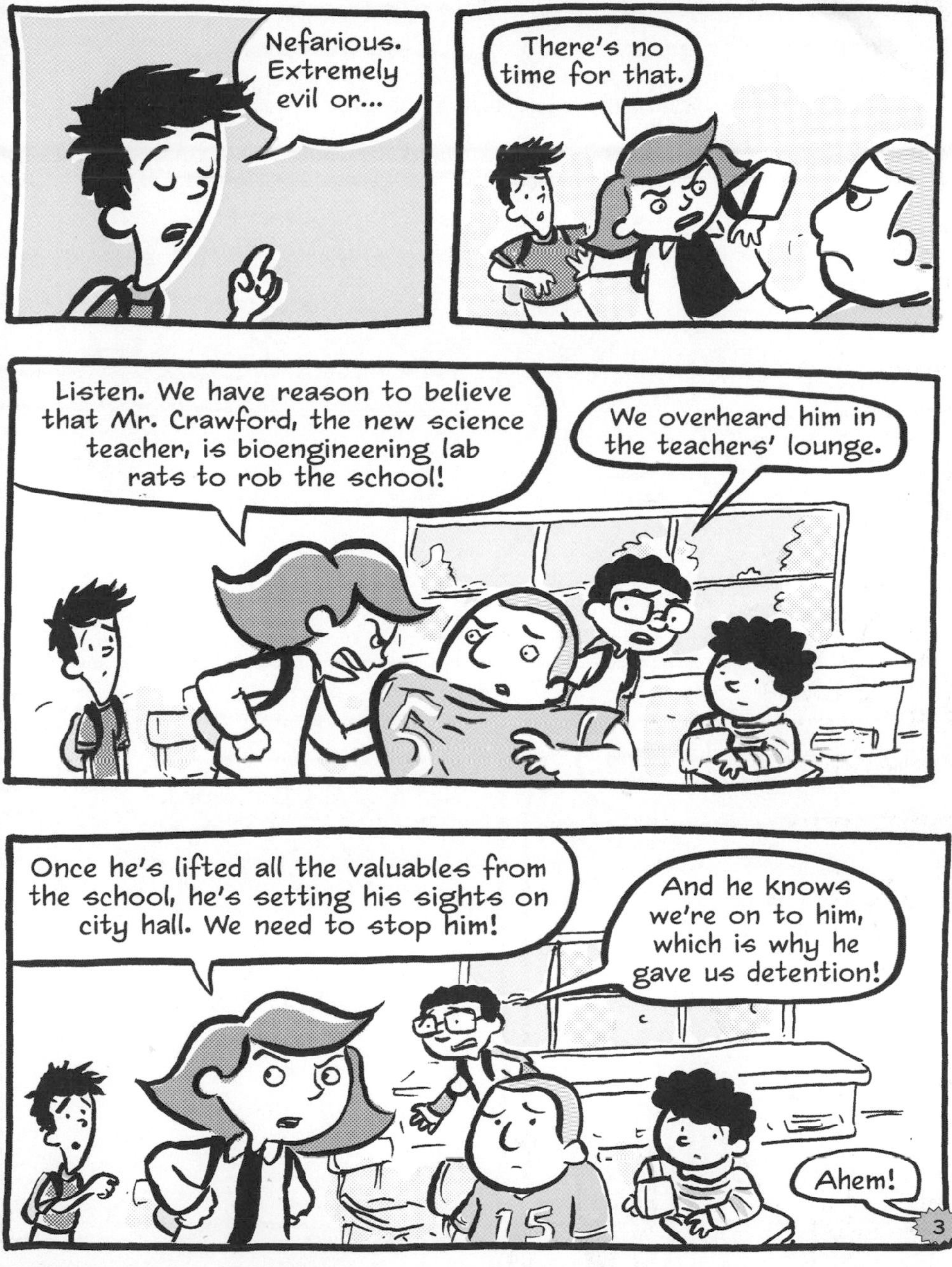

Nefarious. Extremely evil or...
There's no time for that.
Listen. We have reason to believe that Mr. Crawford, the new science teacher, is bioengineering lab rats to rob the school!
We overheard him in the teachers' lounge.
Once he's lifted all the valuables from the school, he's setting his sights on city hall. We need to stop him!
And he knows we're on to him, which is why he gave us detention!
Ahem!
15

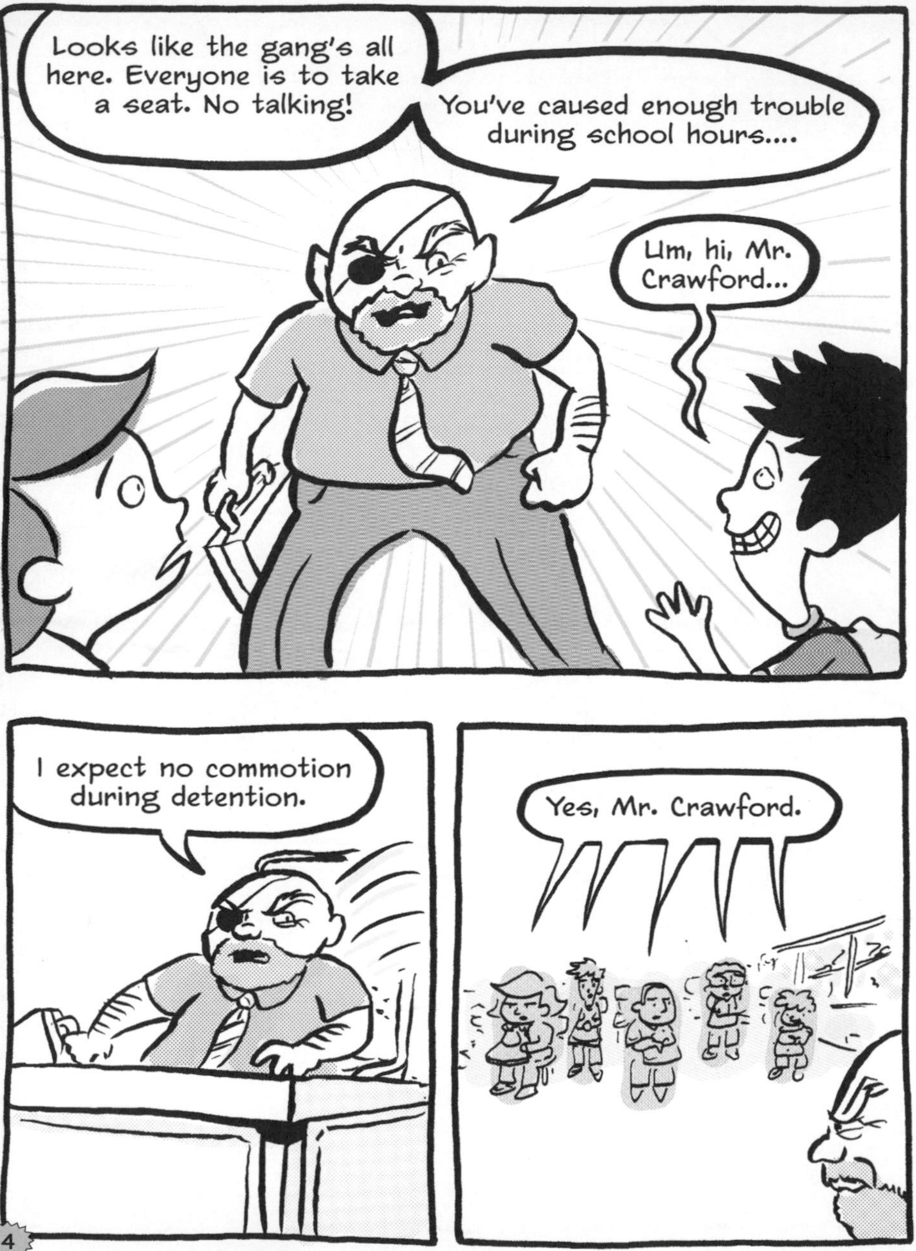
Looks like the gang's all here. Everyone is to take a seat. No talking!
You've caused enough trouble during school hours....
Um, hi, Mr. Crawford...
I expect no commotion during detention.
Yes, Mr. Crawford.

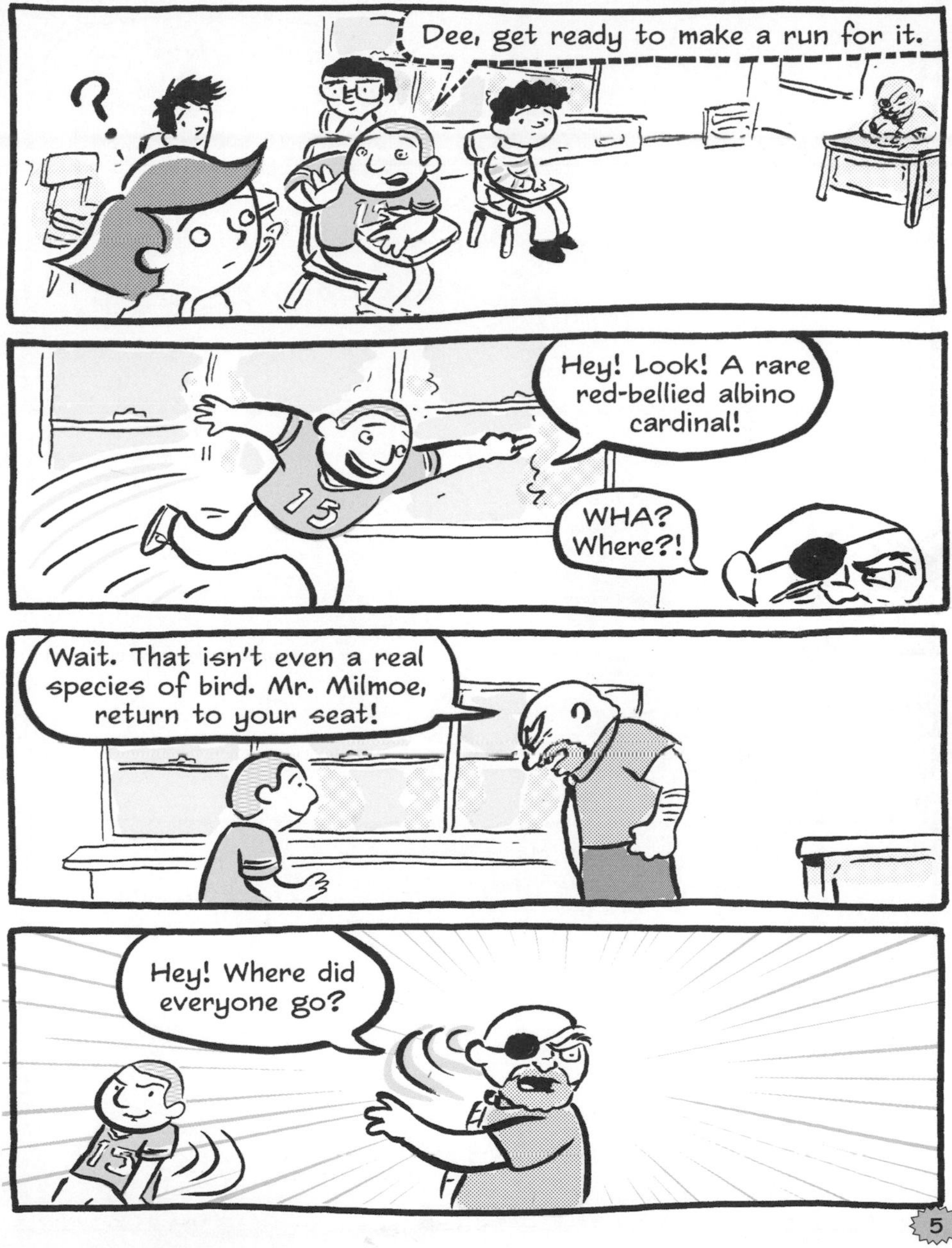
?
Dee, get ready to make a run for it.
15
Hey! Look! A rare red-bellied albino cardinal!
15
WHA? Where?!
Wait. That isn't even a real species of bird. Mr. Milmoe, return to your seat!
Hey! Where did everyone go?
15

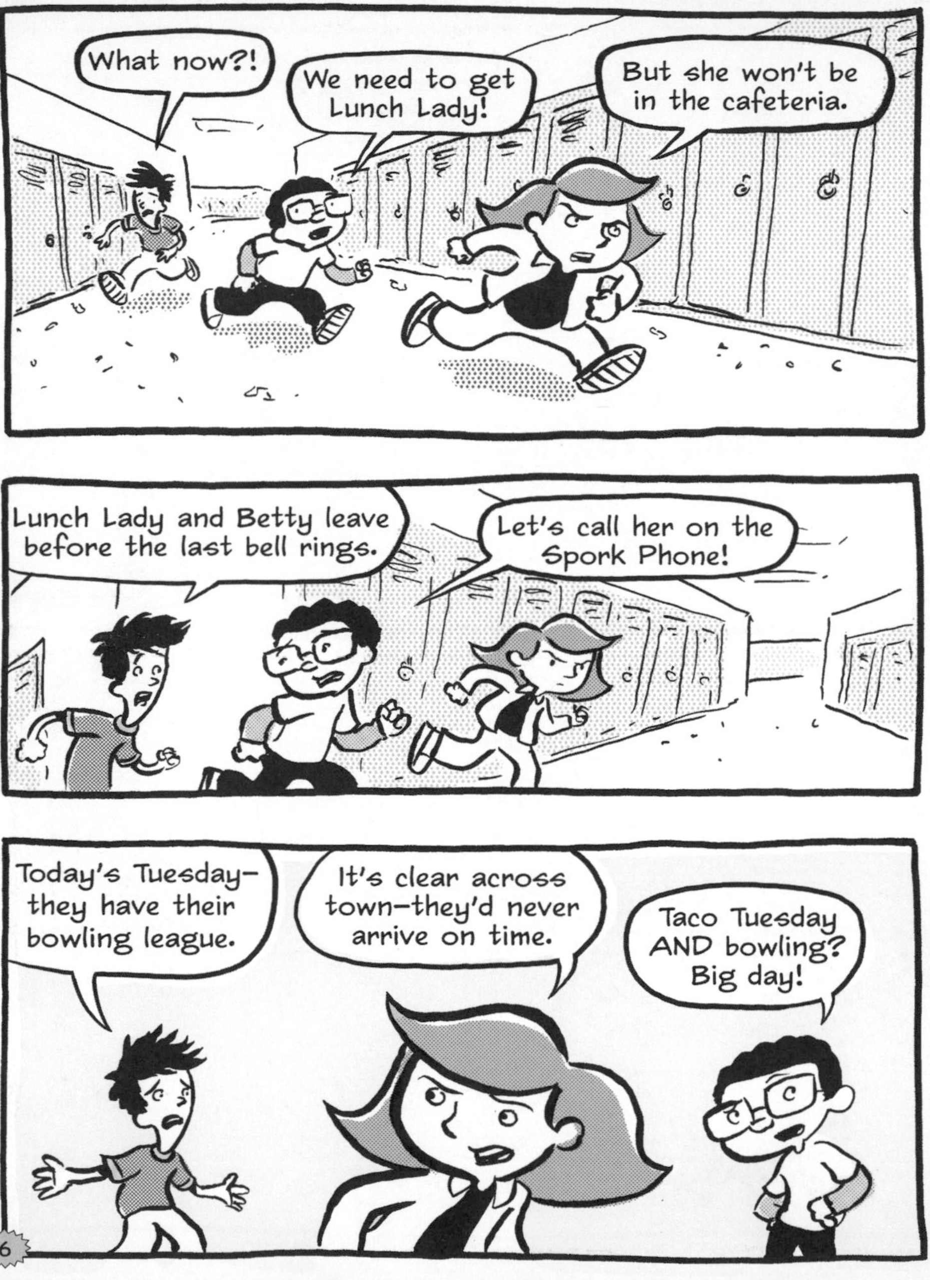
What now?!
We need to get Lunch Lady!
But she won't be in the cafeteria.
Lunch Lady and Betty leave before the last bell rings.
Let's call her on the Spork Phone!
Today's Tuesday— they have their bowling league.
It's clear across town—they'd never arrive on time.
Taco Tuesday AND bowling? Big day!

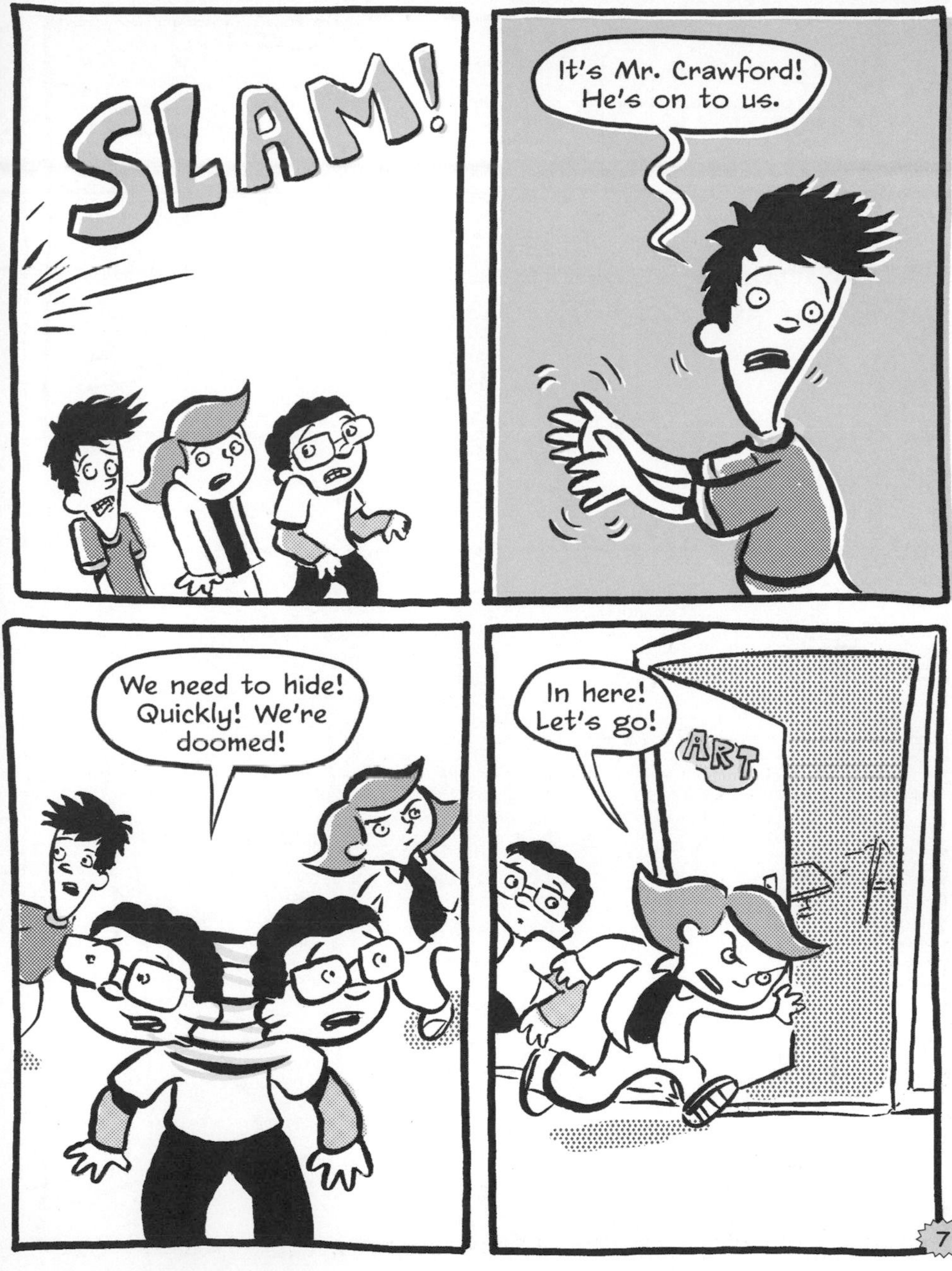
SLAM!
It's Mr. Crawford! He's on to us.
We need to hide! Quickly! We're doomed!
In here! Let's go!
ART

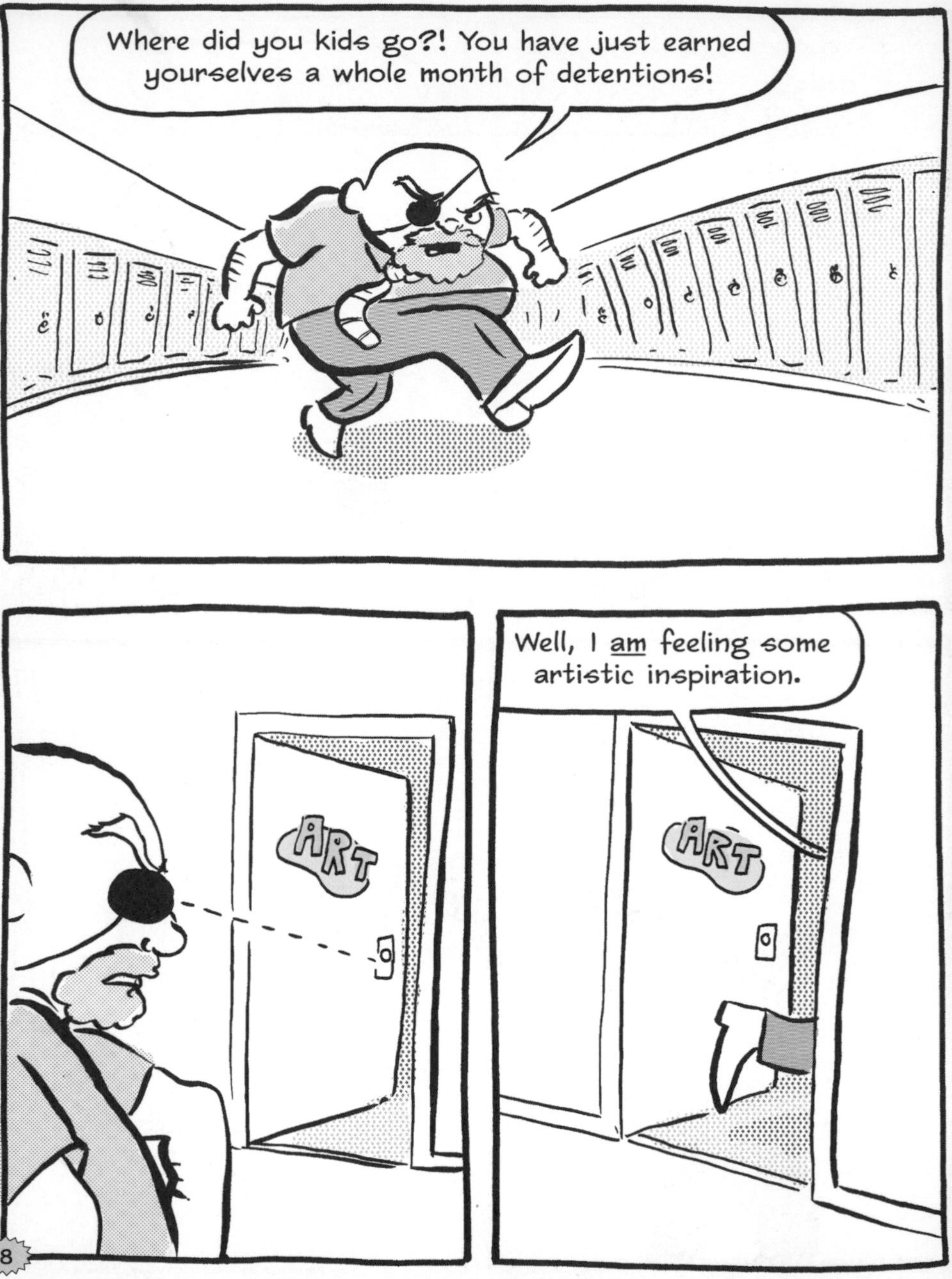
Where did you kids go?! You have just earned yourselves a whole month of detentions!
ART
ART
Well, I am feeling some artistic inspiration.

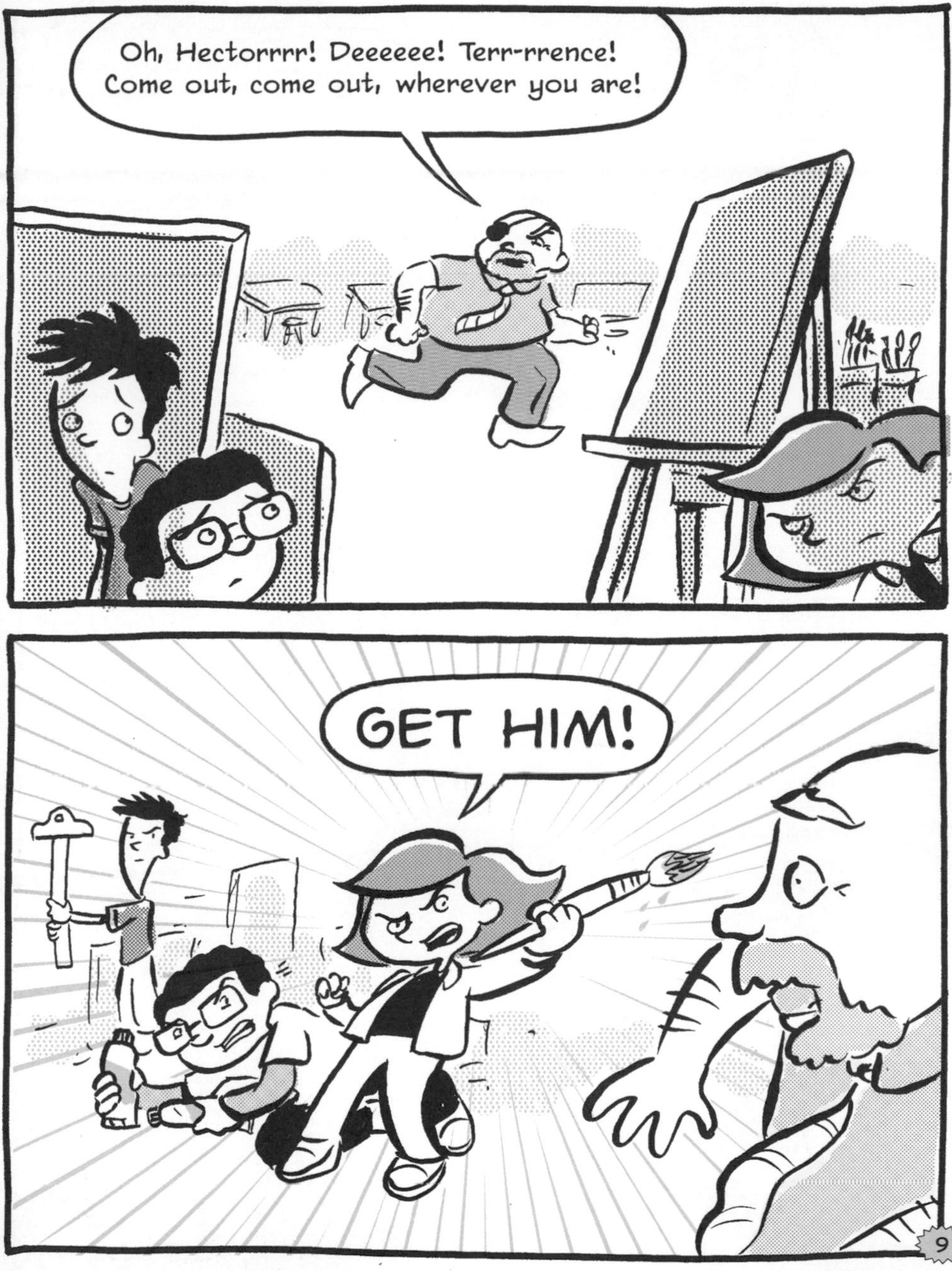
Oh, Hectorrrr! Deeeeee! Terr-rrence! Come out, come out, wherever you are!
GET HIM!

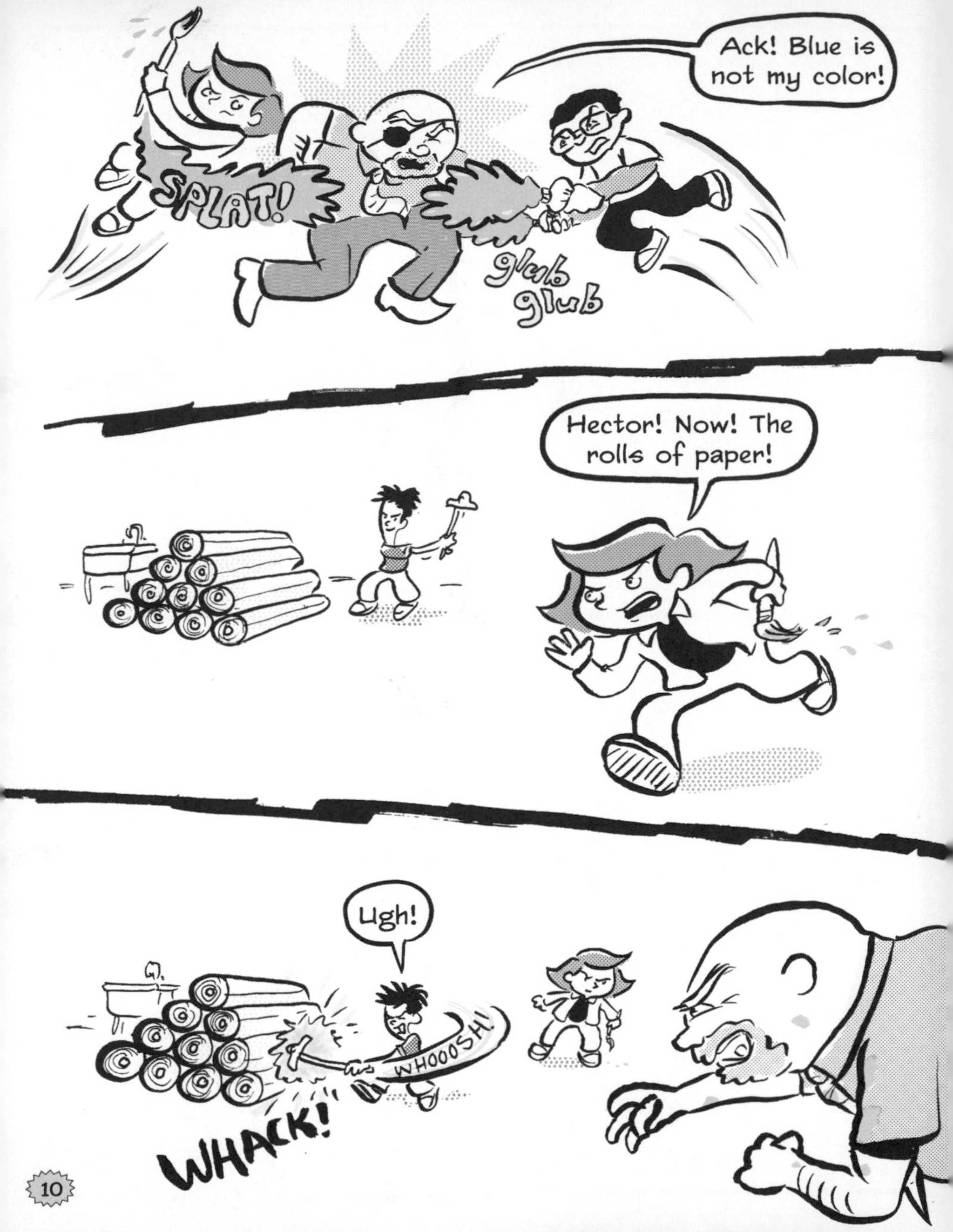
Ack! Blue is not my color!
SPLAT!
glub glub
Hector! Now! The rolls of paper!
Ugh!
WHOOOSH!
WHACK!

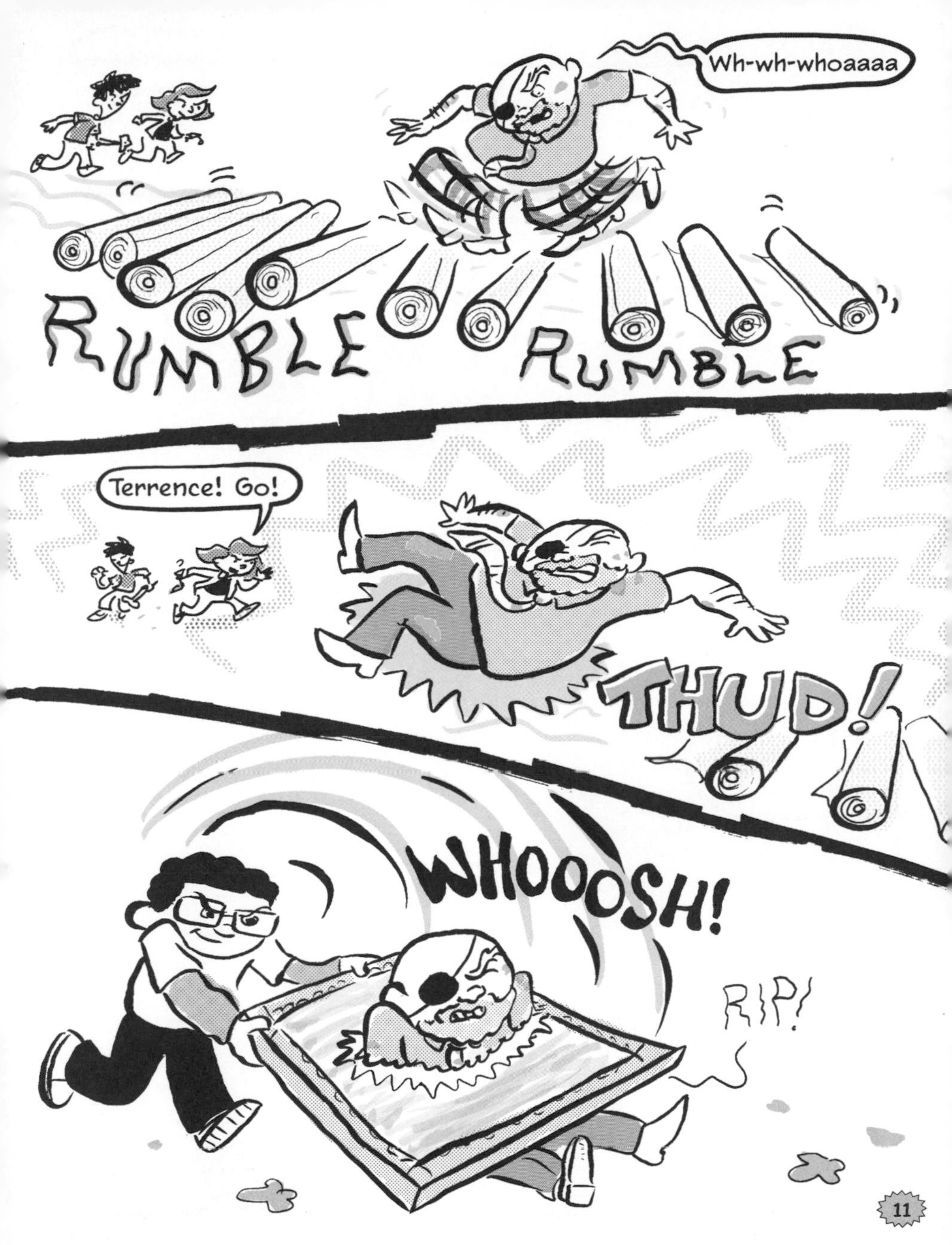
Wh-wh-whoaaaa
RUMBLE RUMBLE
Terrence! Go!
THUD!
WHOOOSH!
RIP!

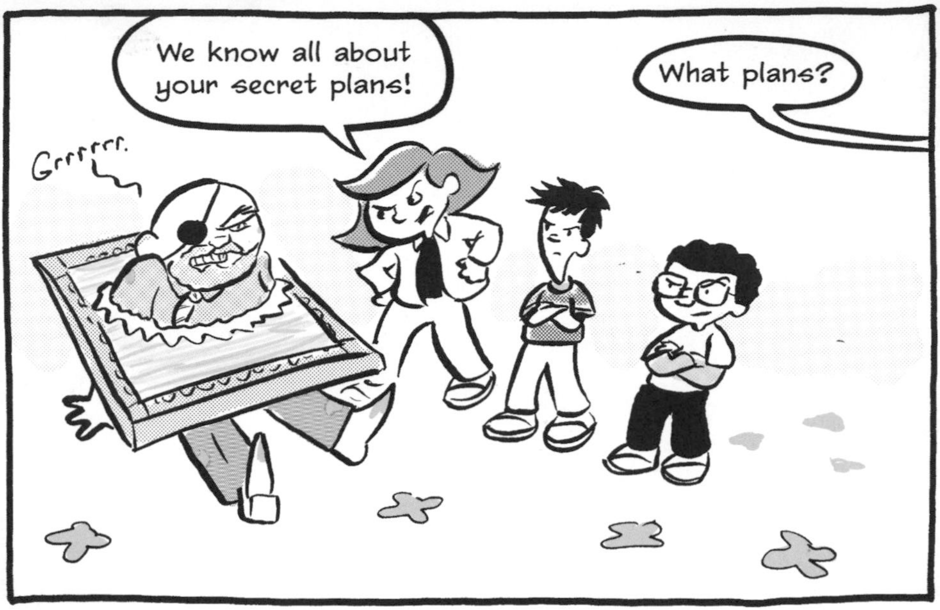
We know all about your secret plans!
What plans?
Grrrrrr.

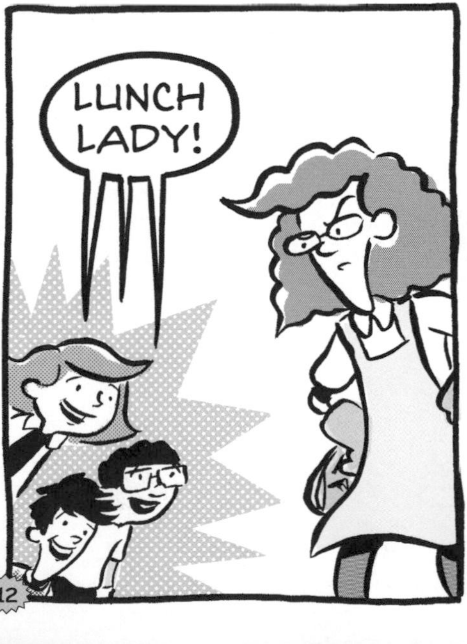
LUNCH LADY!

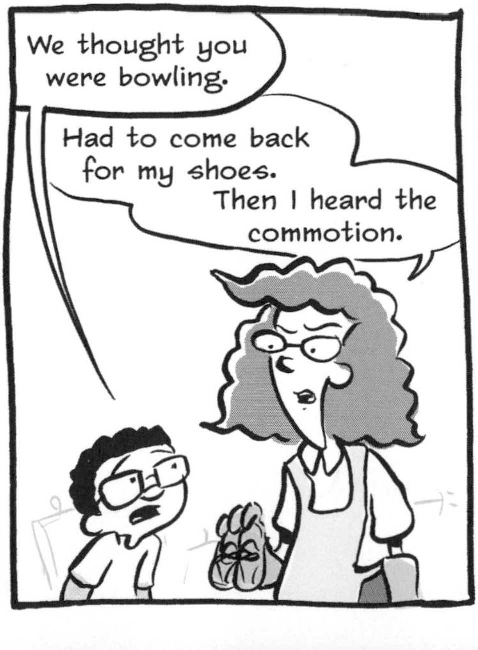
We thought you were bowling.
Had to come back for my shoes.
Then I heard the commotion.

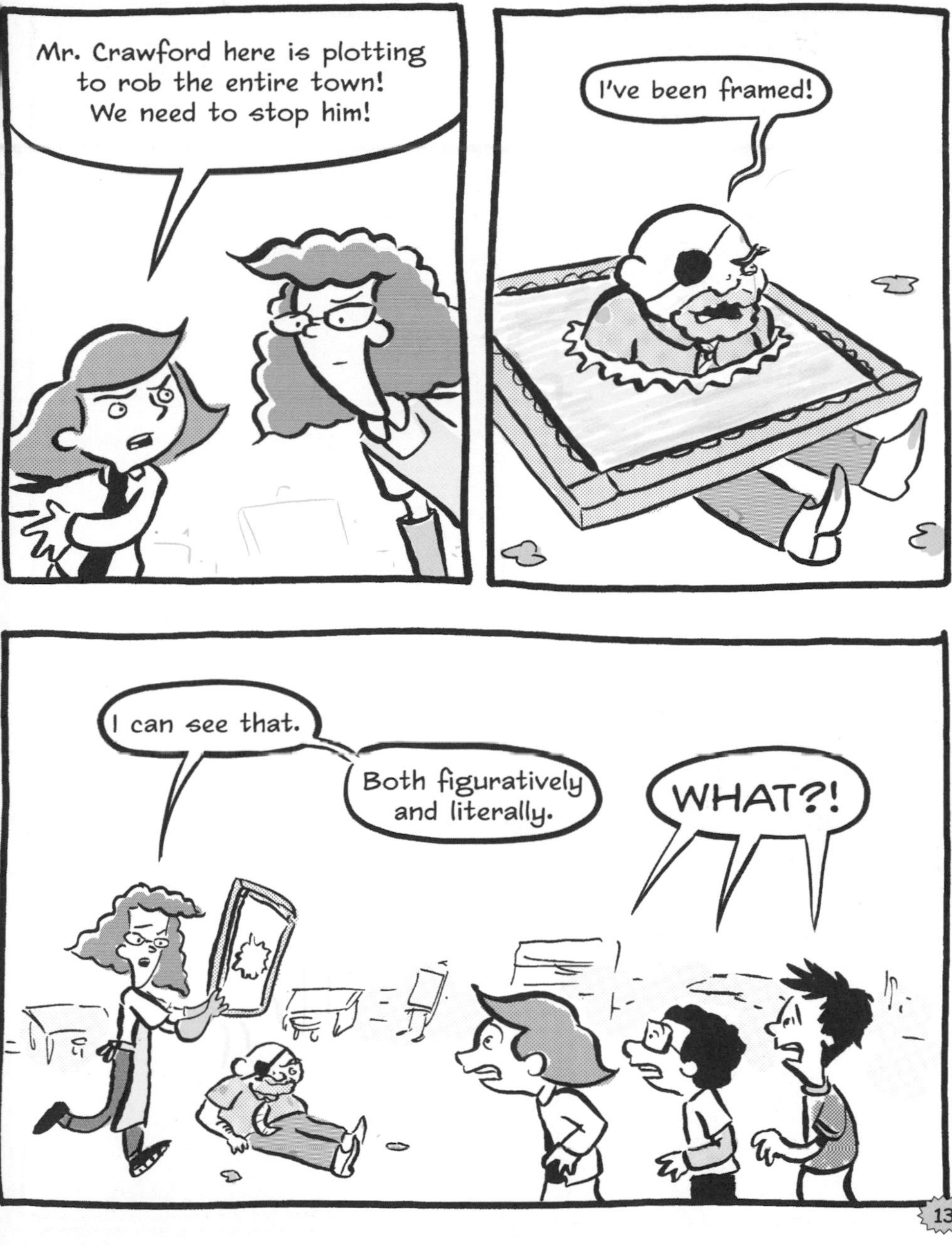
Mr. Crawford here is plotting to rob the entire town! We need to stop him!
I've been framed!
I can see that.
Both figuratively and literally.
WHAT?!

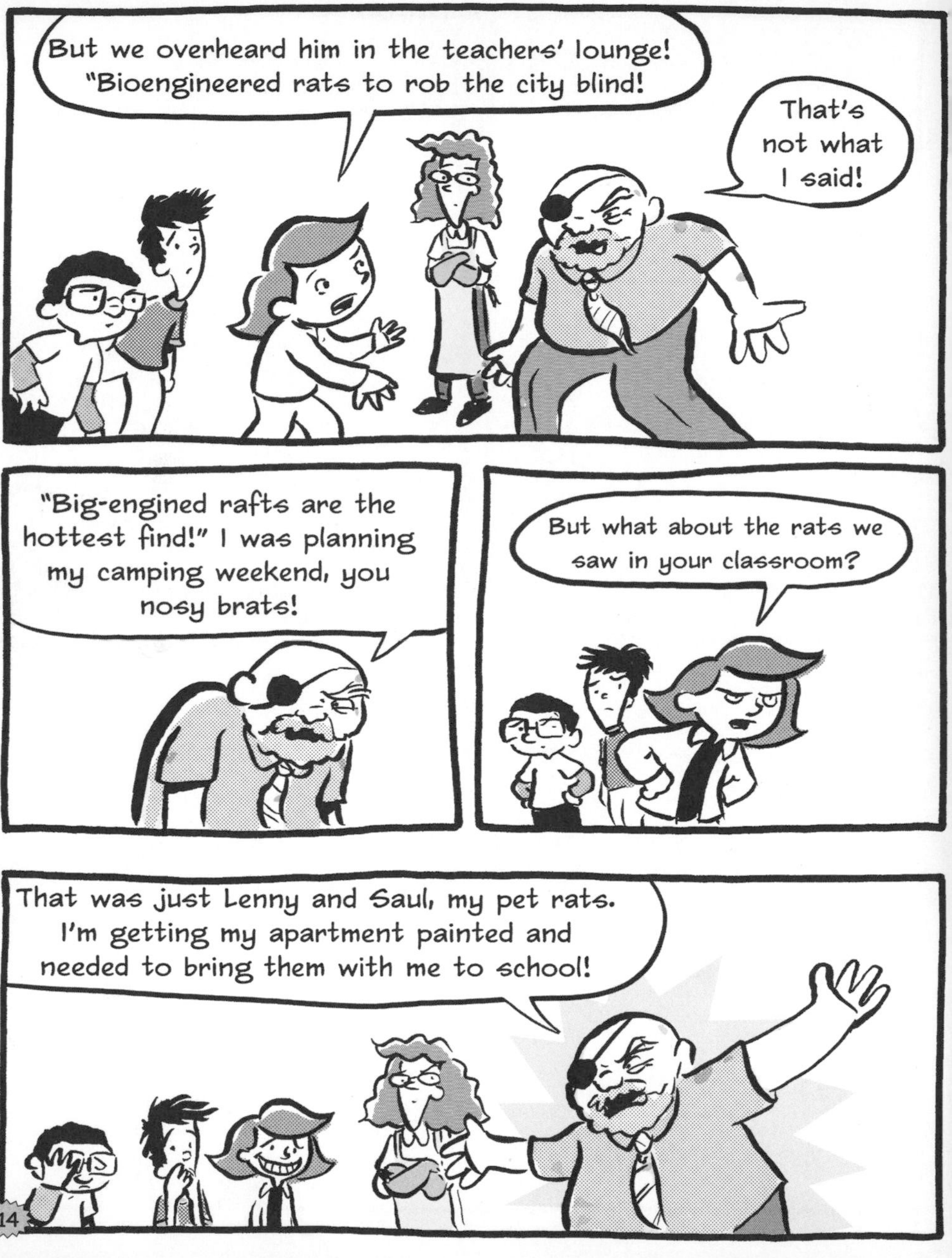

But we overheard him in the teachers' lounge! "Bioengineered rats to rob the city blind!
That's not what I said!
"Big-engined rafts are the hottest find!" I was planning my camping weekend, you nosy brats!
But what about the rats we saw in your classroom?
That was just Lenny and Saul, my pet rats. I'm getting my apartment painted and needed to bring them with me to school!

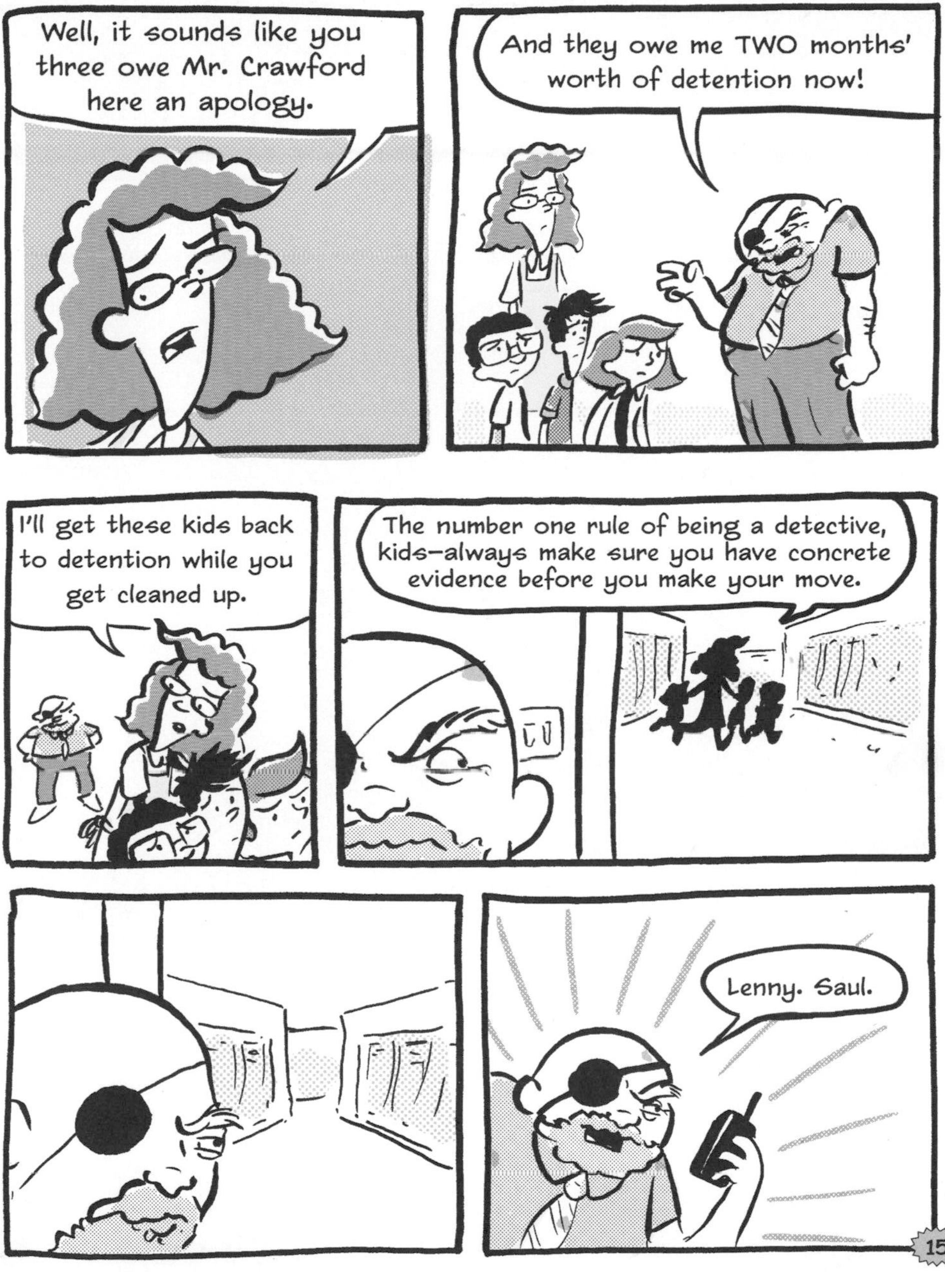

Well, it sounds like you three owe Mr. Crawford here an apology.
And they owe me TWO months' worth of detention now!
I'll get these kids back to detention while you get cleaned up.
The number one rule of being a detective, kids—always make sure you have concrete evidence before you make your move.
Lenny. Saul.

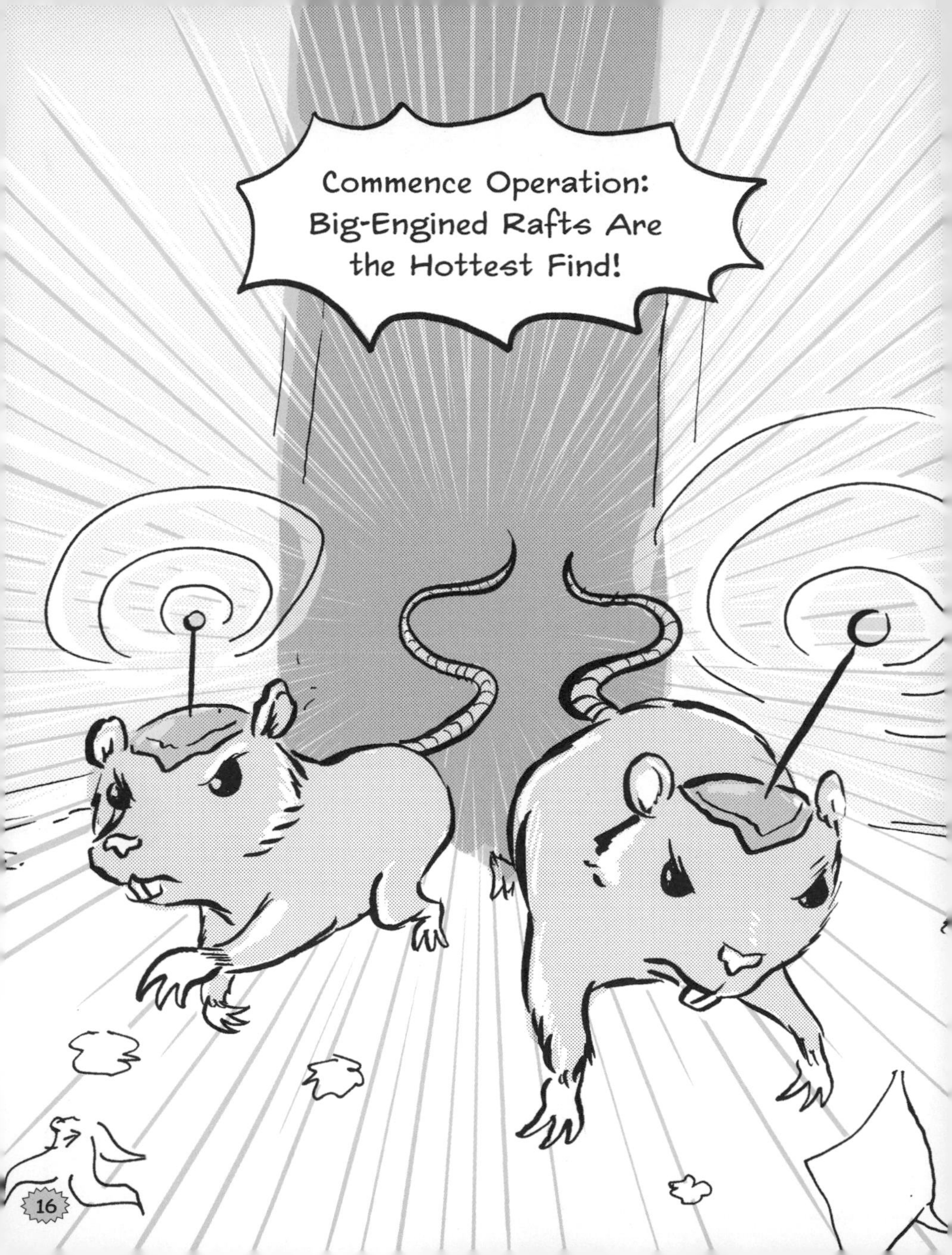
Commence Operation: Big-Engined Rafts Are the Hottest Find!

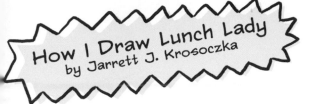

How I Draw Lunch Lady
by Jarrett J. Krosoczka

When I draw my comics, I sketch with a non-photo blue pencil and draw the final artwork with a brush dipped in India ink.

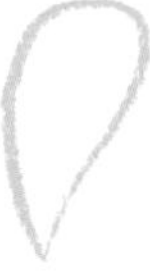

1) I draw an upside-down teardrop.

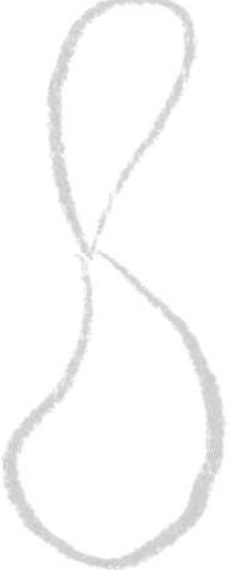

2) I draw a regular teardrop.

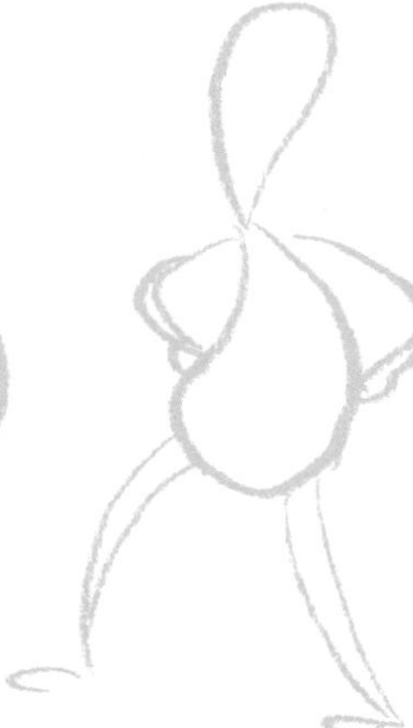

3) I sketch out her arms and legs.

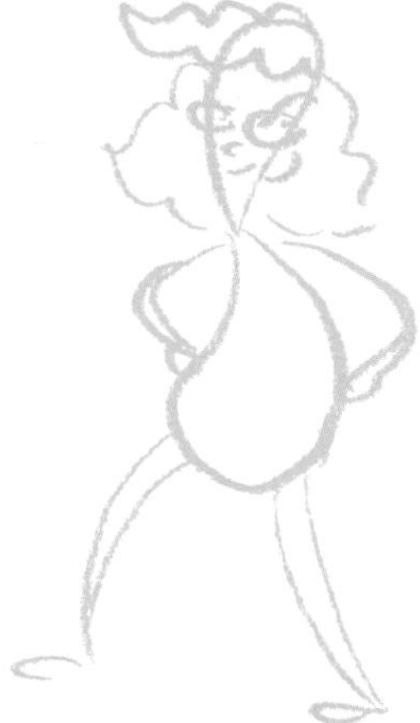

4) I draw her perm and facial features.

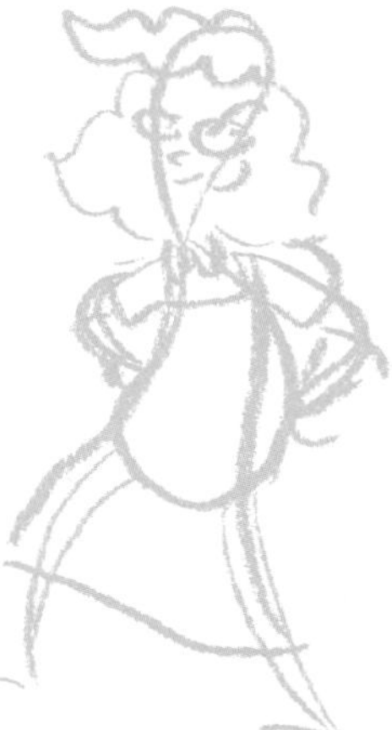

5) I sketch out her apron, gloves and clothes.

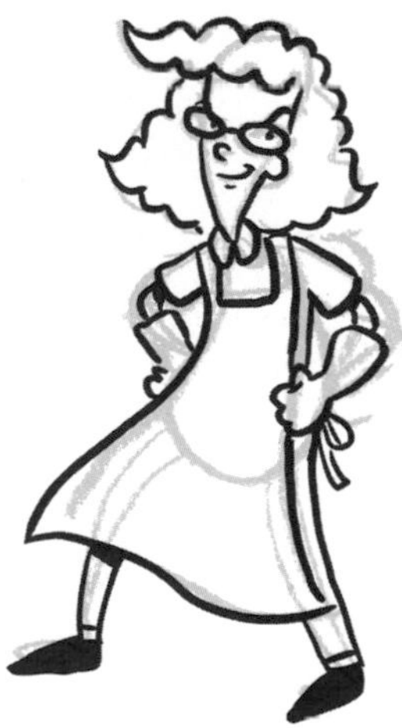

6) I go over the pencil sketch with ink.

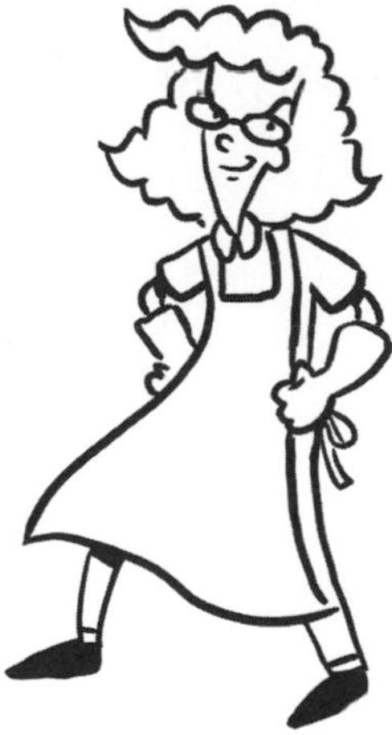

7) Then I scan in the artwork as black-and-white.
(The computer can't see the non-photo blue color.)

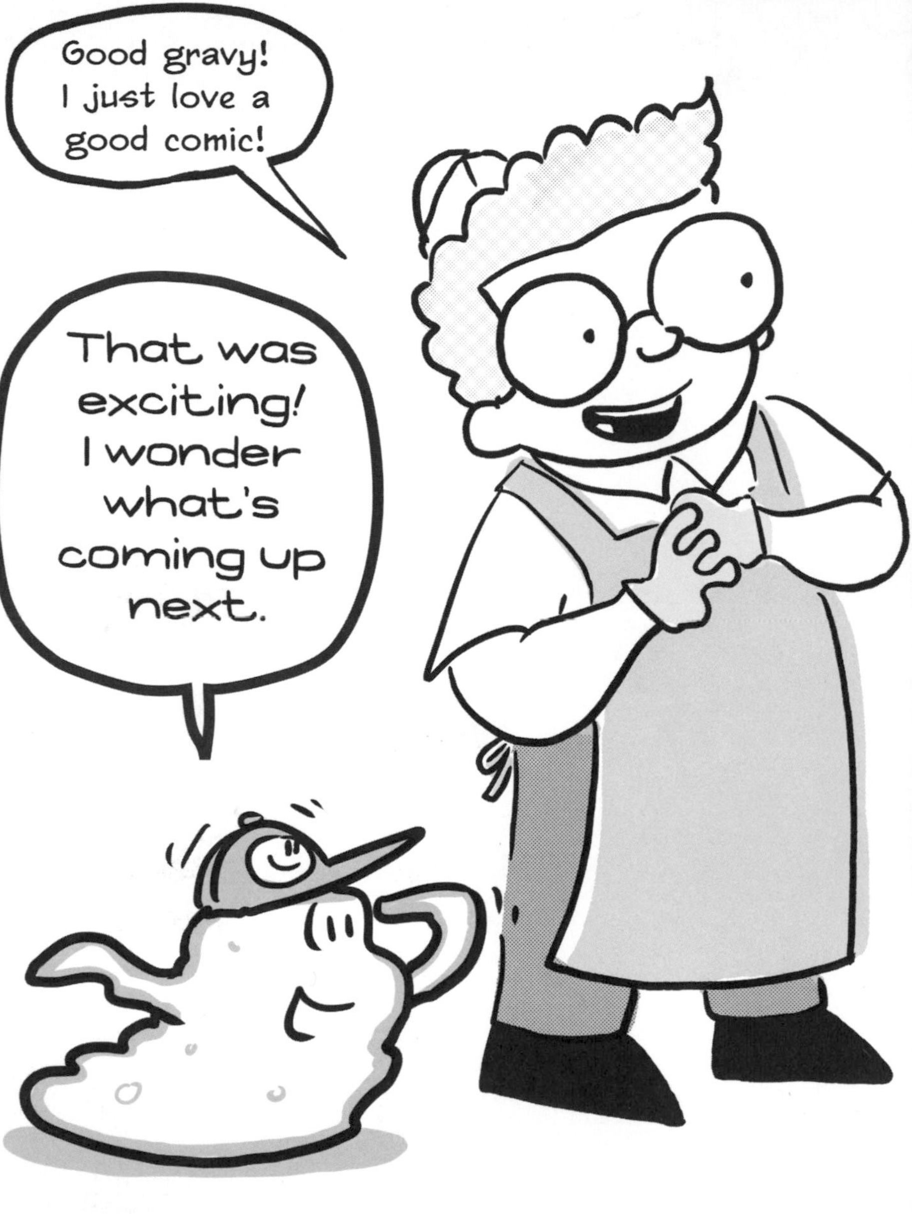
Good gravy! I just love a good comic!
That was exciting! I wonder what's coming up next.

CHEATING DEATH W/ SISYPHUS

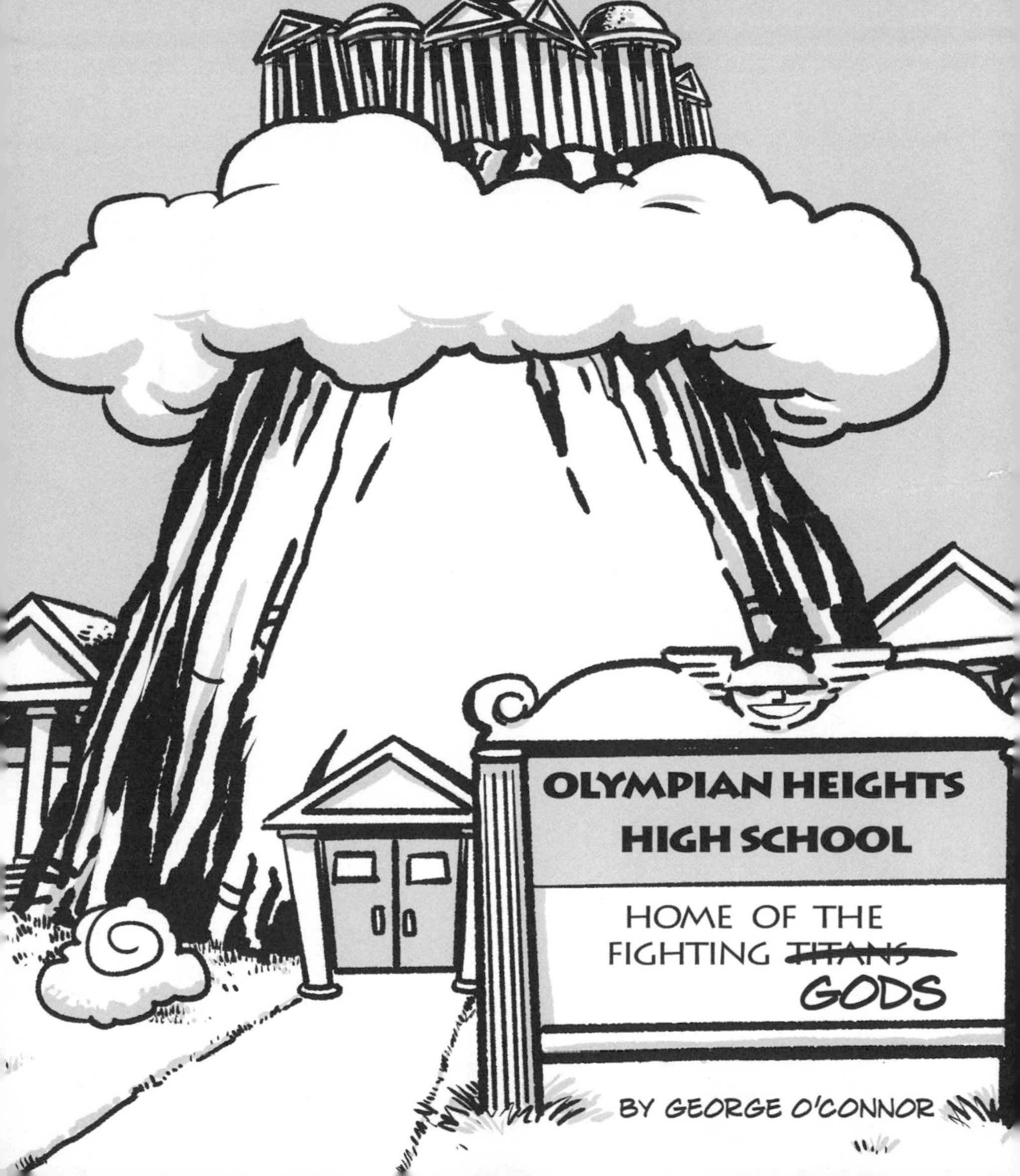

OLYMPIAN HEIGHTS
HIGH SCHOOL
HOME OF THE
FIGHTING ~~TITANS~~
GODS
BY GEORGE O'CONNOR

CHEATING DEATH W/ SISYPHUS

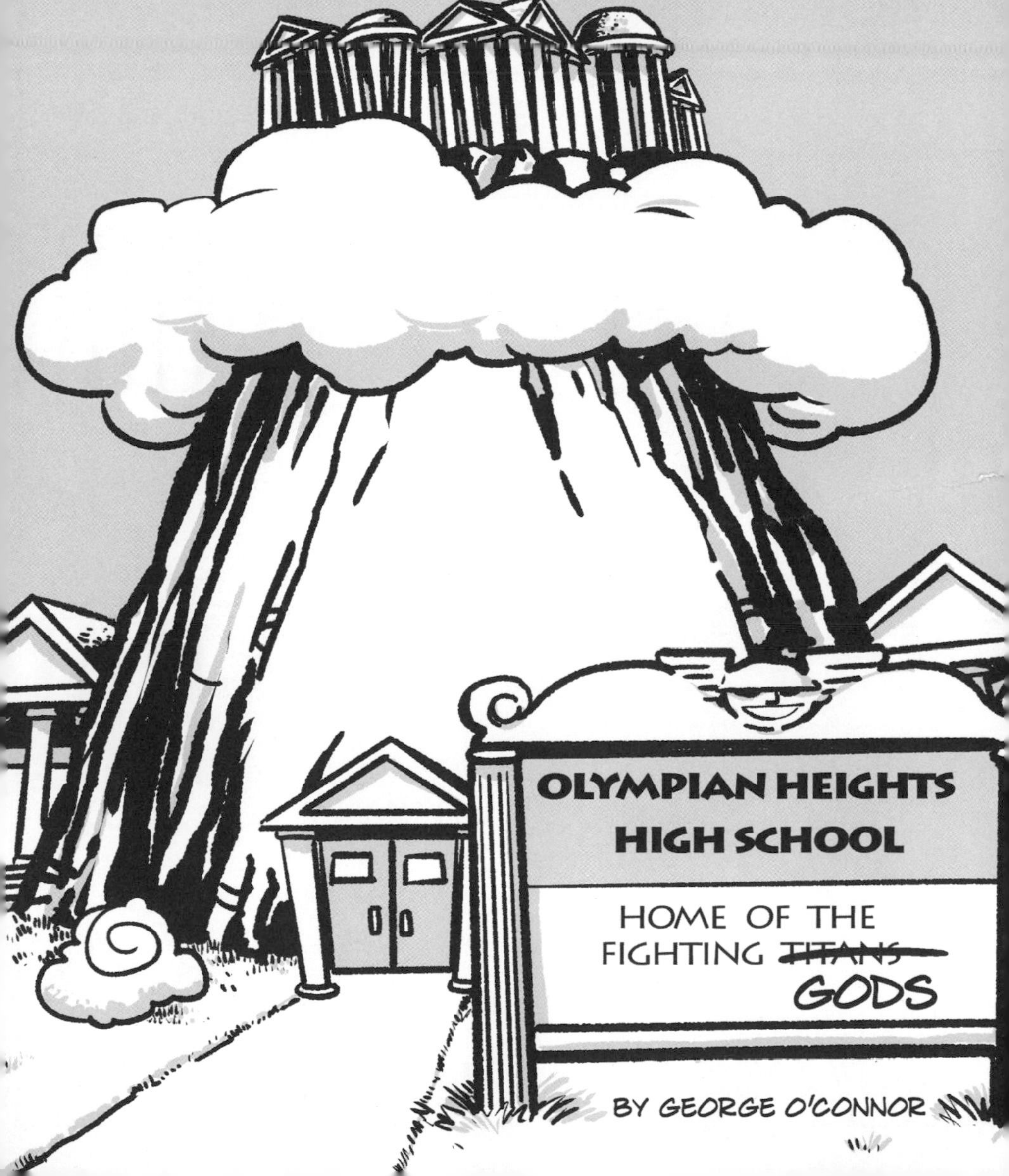
OLYMPIAN HEIGHTS
HIGH SCHOOL
HOME OF THE
FIGHTING ~~TITANS~~
GODS
BY GEORGE O'CONNOR

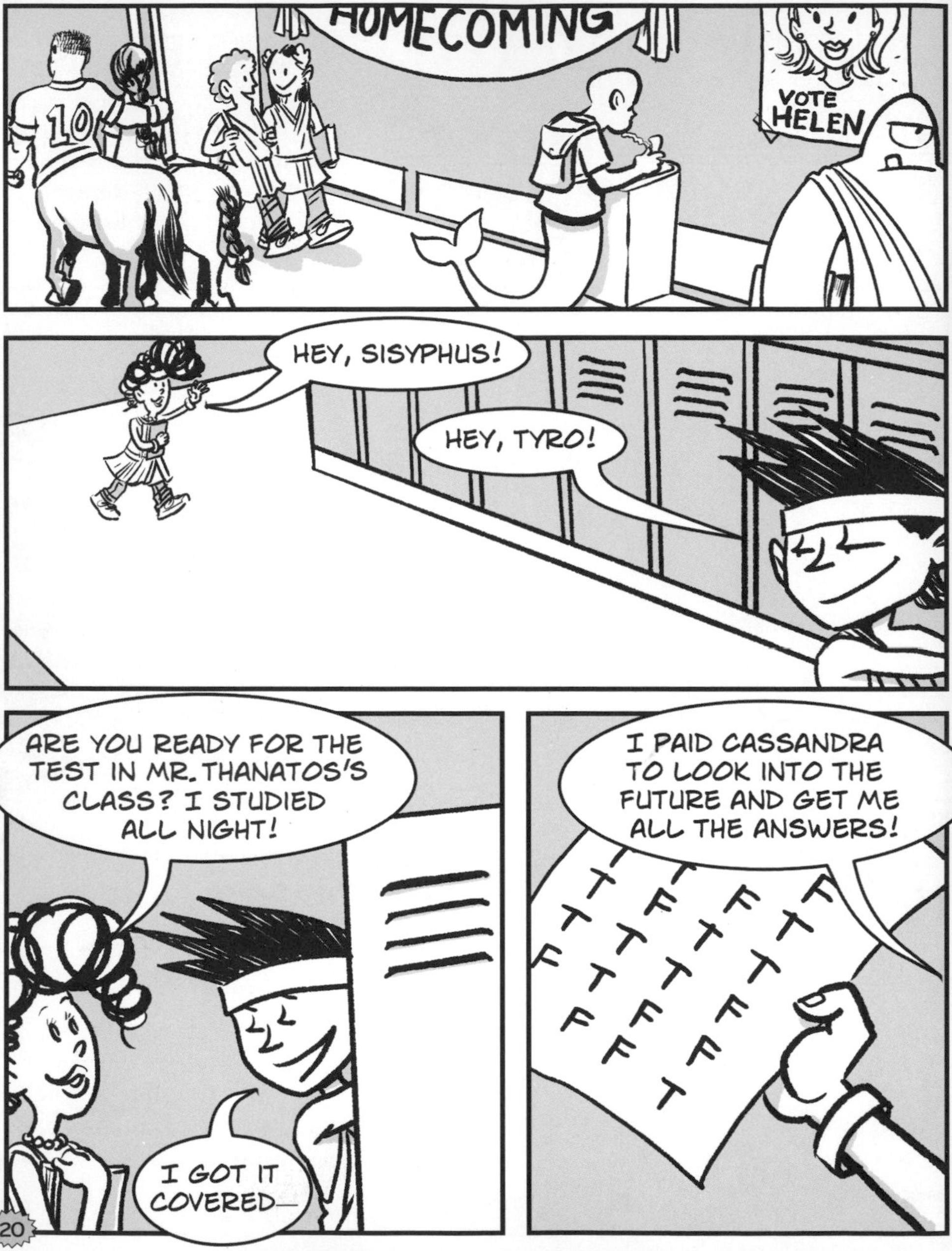
HOMECOMING
VOTE HELEN
HEY, SISYPHUS!
HEY, TYRO!
ARE YOU READY FOR THE TEST IN MR. THANATOS'S CLASS? I STUDIED ALL NIGHT!
I GOT IT COVERED—
I PAID CASSANDRA TO LOOK INTO THE FUTURE AND GET ME ALL THE ANSWERS!

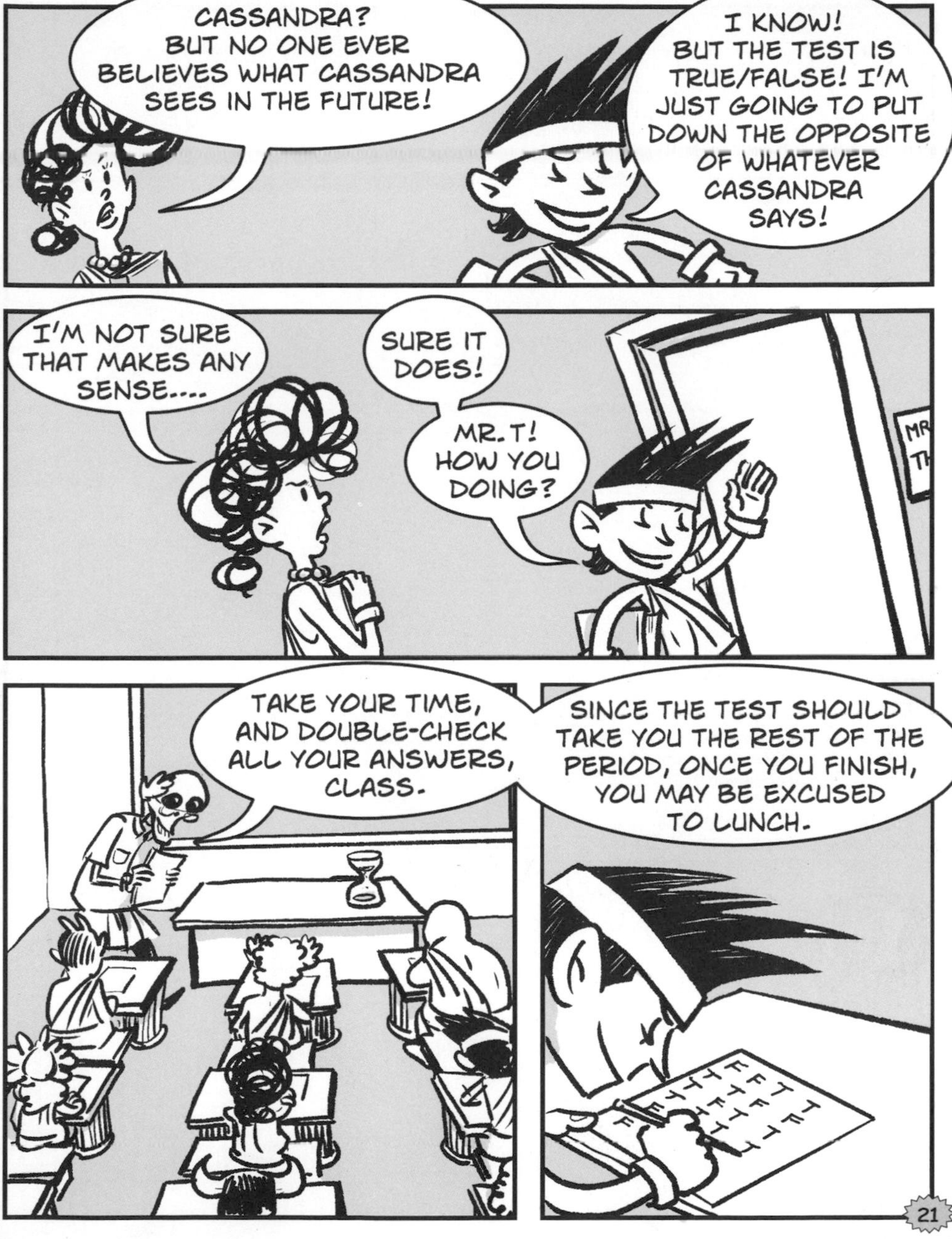
CASSANDRA? BUT NO ONE EVER BELIEVES WHAT CASSANDRA SEES IN THE FUTURE!
I KNOW! BUT THE TEST IS TRUE/FALSE! I'M JUST GOING TO PUT DOWN THE OPPOSITE OF WHATEVER CASSANDRA SAYS!
I'M NOT SURE THAT MAKES ANY SENSE....
SURE IT DOES!
MR. T! HOW YOU DOING?
TAKE YOUR TIME, AND DOUBLE-CHECK ALL YOUR ANSWERS, CLASS.
SINCE THE TEST SHOULD TAKE YOU THE REST OF THE PERIOD, ONCE YOU FINISH, YOU MAY BE EXCUSED TO LUNCH.

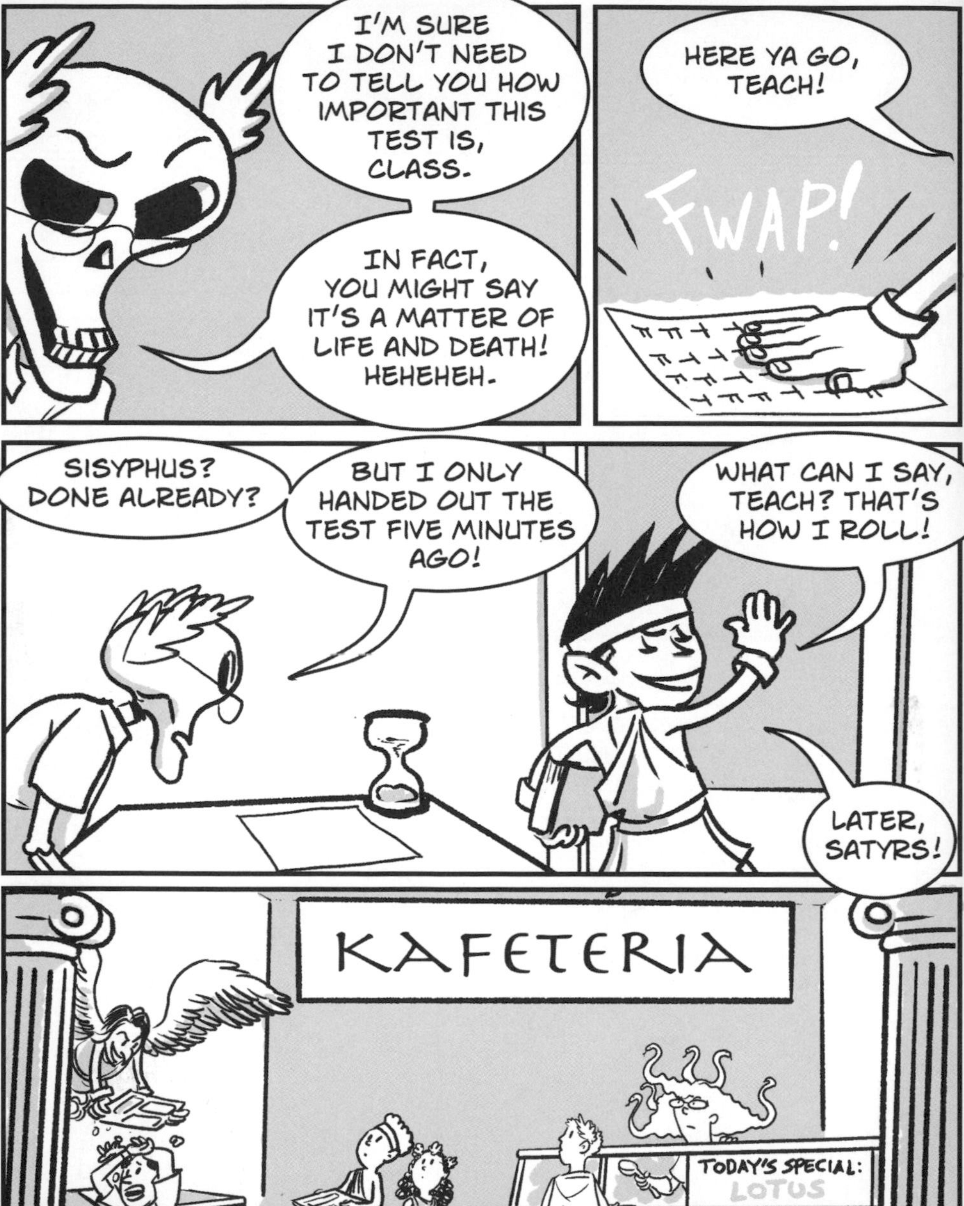
I'M SURE I DON'T NEED TO TELL YOU HOW IMPORTANT THIS TEST IS, CLASS.
IN FACT, YOU MIGHT SAY IT'S A MATTER OF LIFE AND DEATH! HEHEHEH.
HERE YA GO, TEACH!
FWAP!
SISYPHUS? DONE ALREADY?
BUT I ONLY HANDED OUT THE TEST FIVE MINUTES AGO!
WHAT CAN I SAY, TEACH? THAT'S HOW I ROLL!
LATER, SATYRS!
KAFETERIA
TODAY'S SPECIAL:
LOTUS

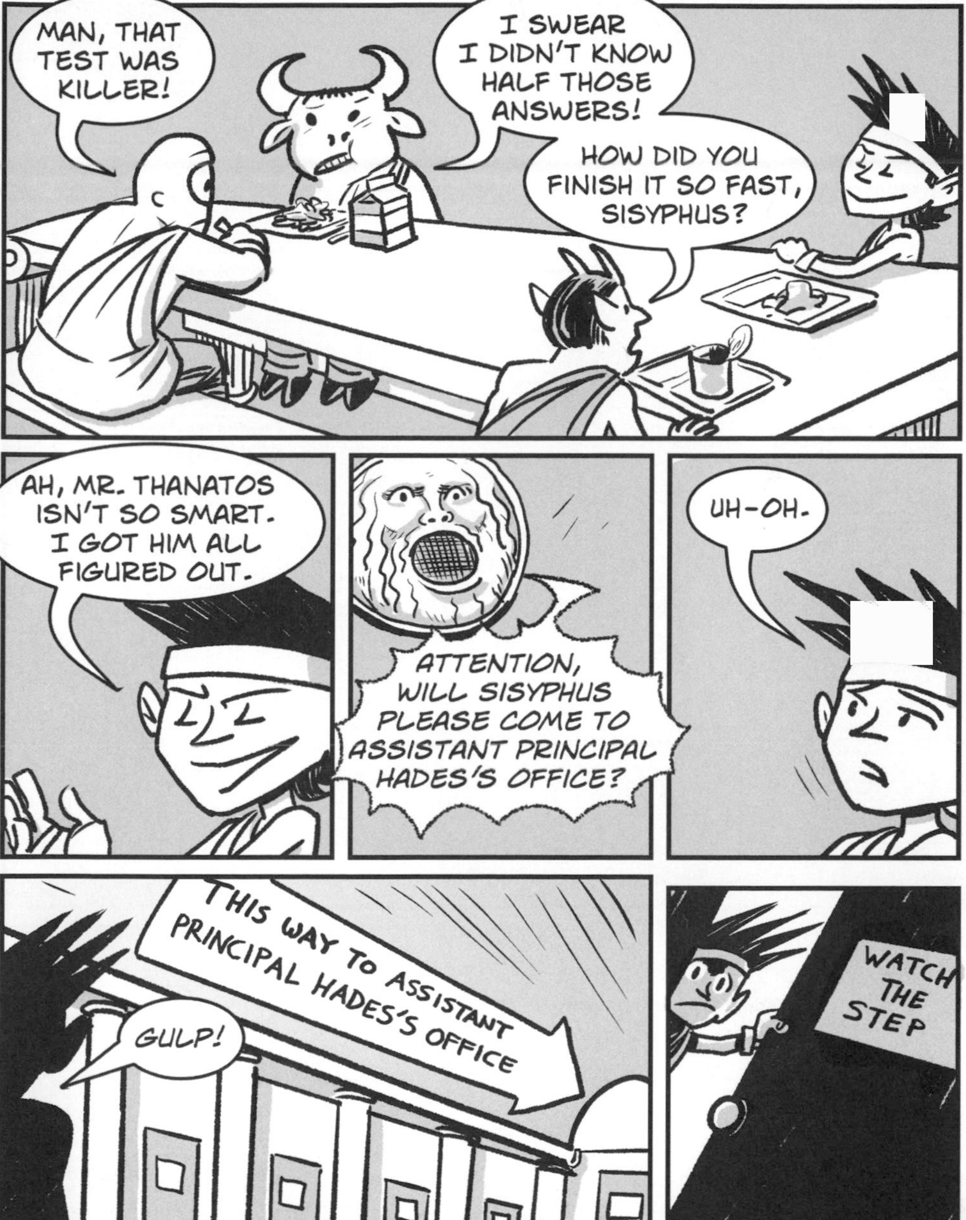

MAN, THAT TEST WAS KILLER!
I SWEAR I DIDN'T KNOW HALF THOSE ANSWERS!
HOW DID YOU FINISH IT SO FAST, SISYPHUS?
AH, MR. THANATOS ISN'T SO SMART. I GOT HIM ALL FIGURED OUT.
ATTENTION, WILL SISYPHUS PLEASE COME TO ASSISTANT PRINCIPAL HADES'S OFFICE?
UH-OH.
THIS WAY TO ASSISTANT PRINCIPAL HADES'S OFFICE
GULP!
WATCH THE STEP

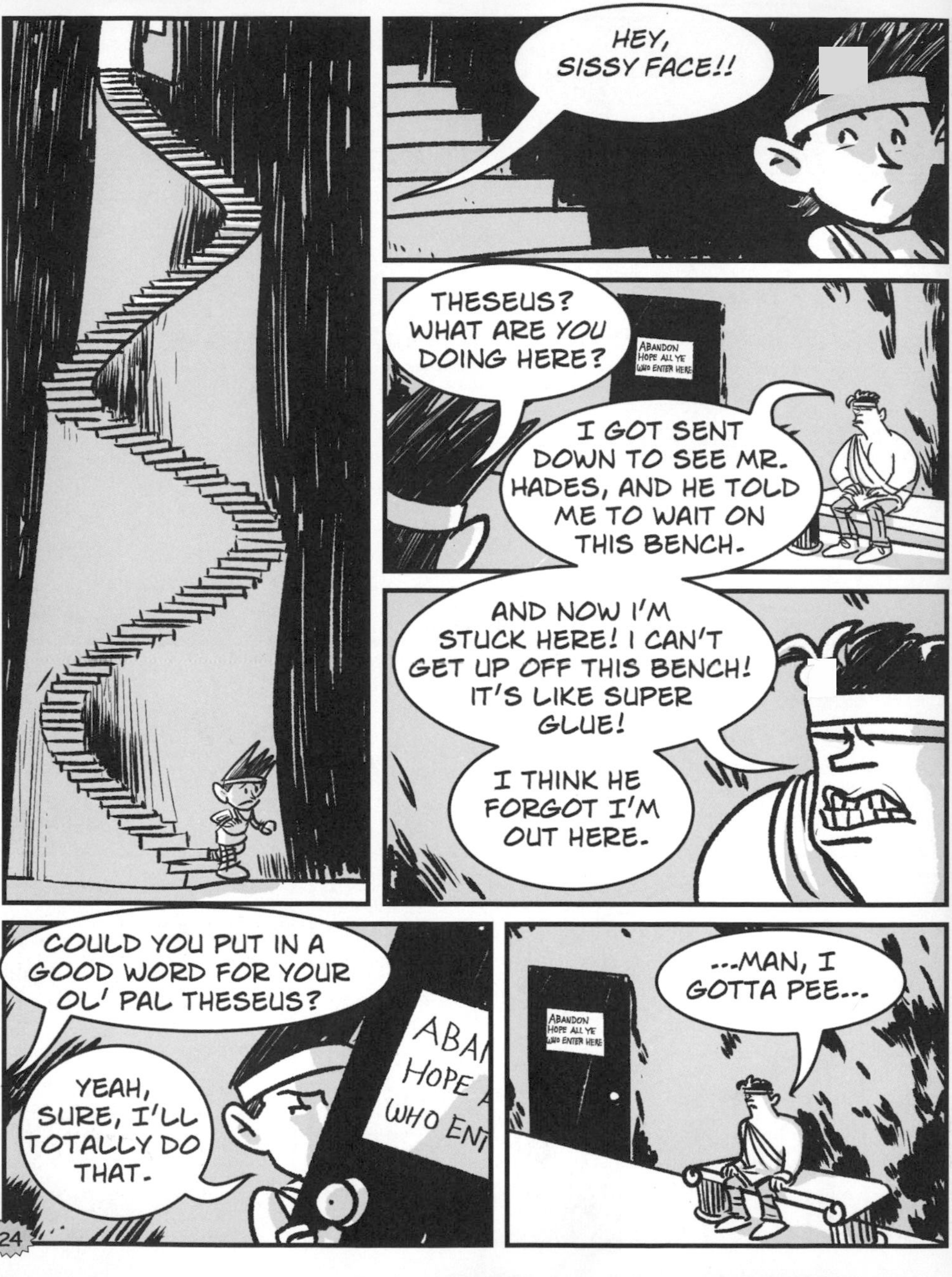
HEY, SISSY FACE!!
THESEUS? WHAT ARE YOU DOING HERE?
ABANDON HOPE ALL YE WHO ENTER HERE
I GOT SENT DOWN TO SEE MR. HADES, AND HE TOLD ME TO WAIT ON THIS BENCH.
AND NOW I'M STUCK HERE! I CAN'T GET UP OFF THIS BENCH! IT'S LIKE SUPER GLUE!
I THINK HE FORGOT I'M OUT HERE.
COULD YOU PUT IN A GOOD WORD FOR YOUR OL' PAL THESEUS?
YEAH, SURE, I'LL TOTALLY DO THAT.
...MAN, I GOTTA PEE...
ABANDON HOPE ALL YE WHO ENTER HERE

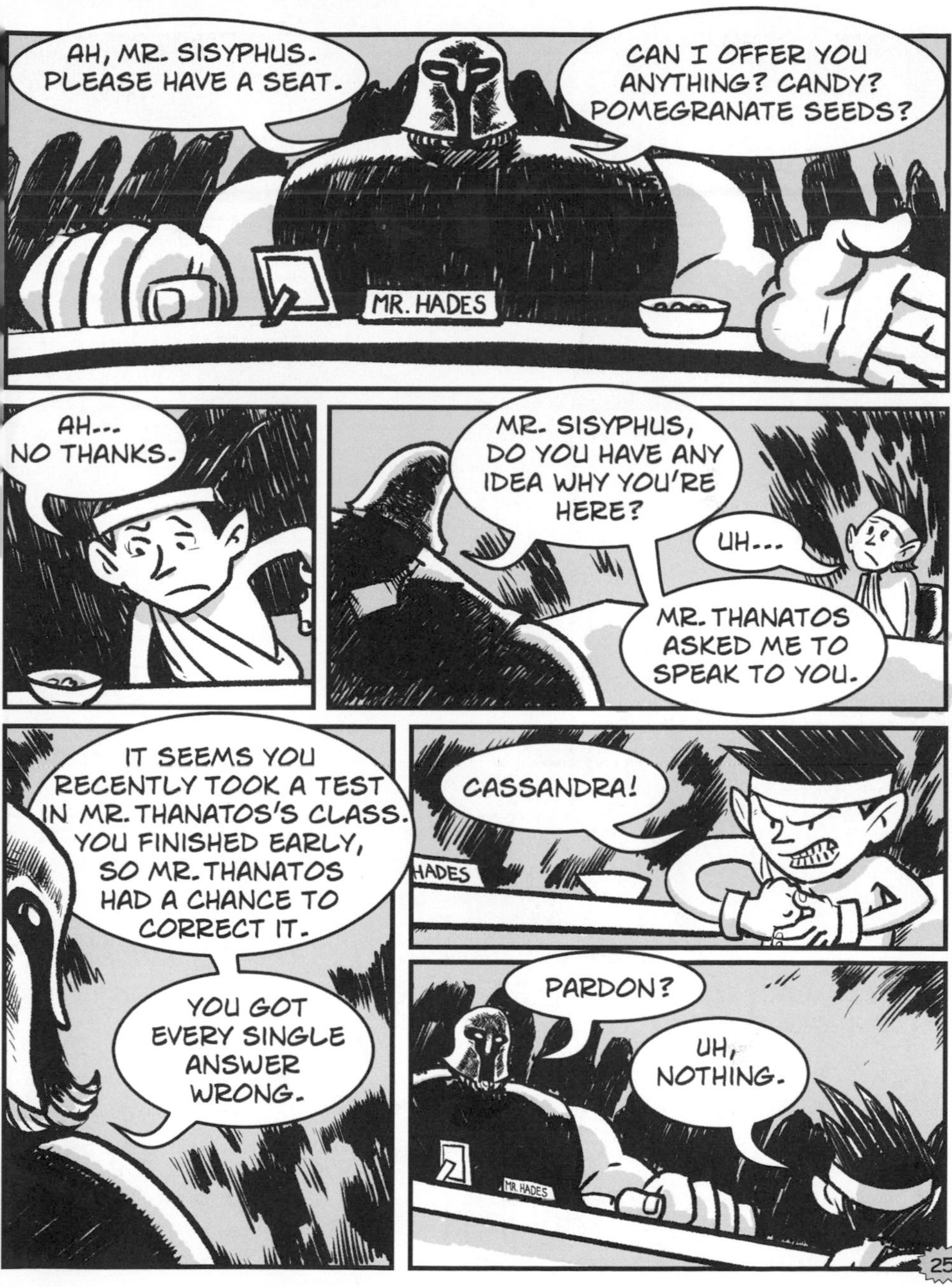
AH, MR. SISYPHUS. PLEASE HAVE A SEAT.
CAN I OFFER YOU ANYTHING? CANDY? POMEGRANATE SEEDS?
MR. HADES
AH... NO THANKS.
MR. SISYPHUS, DO YOU HAVE ANY IDEA WHY YOU'RE HERE?
UH...
MR. THANATOS ASKED ME TO SPEAK TO YOU.
IT SEEMS YOU RECENTLY TOOK A TEST IN MR. THANATOS'S CLASS. YOU FINISHED EARLY, SO MR. THANATOS HAD A CHANCE TO CORRECT IT.
YOU GOT EVERY SINGLE ANSWER WRONG.
CASSANDRA!
HADES
PARDON?
UH, NOTHING.
MR. HADES

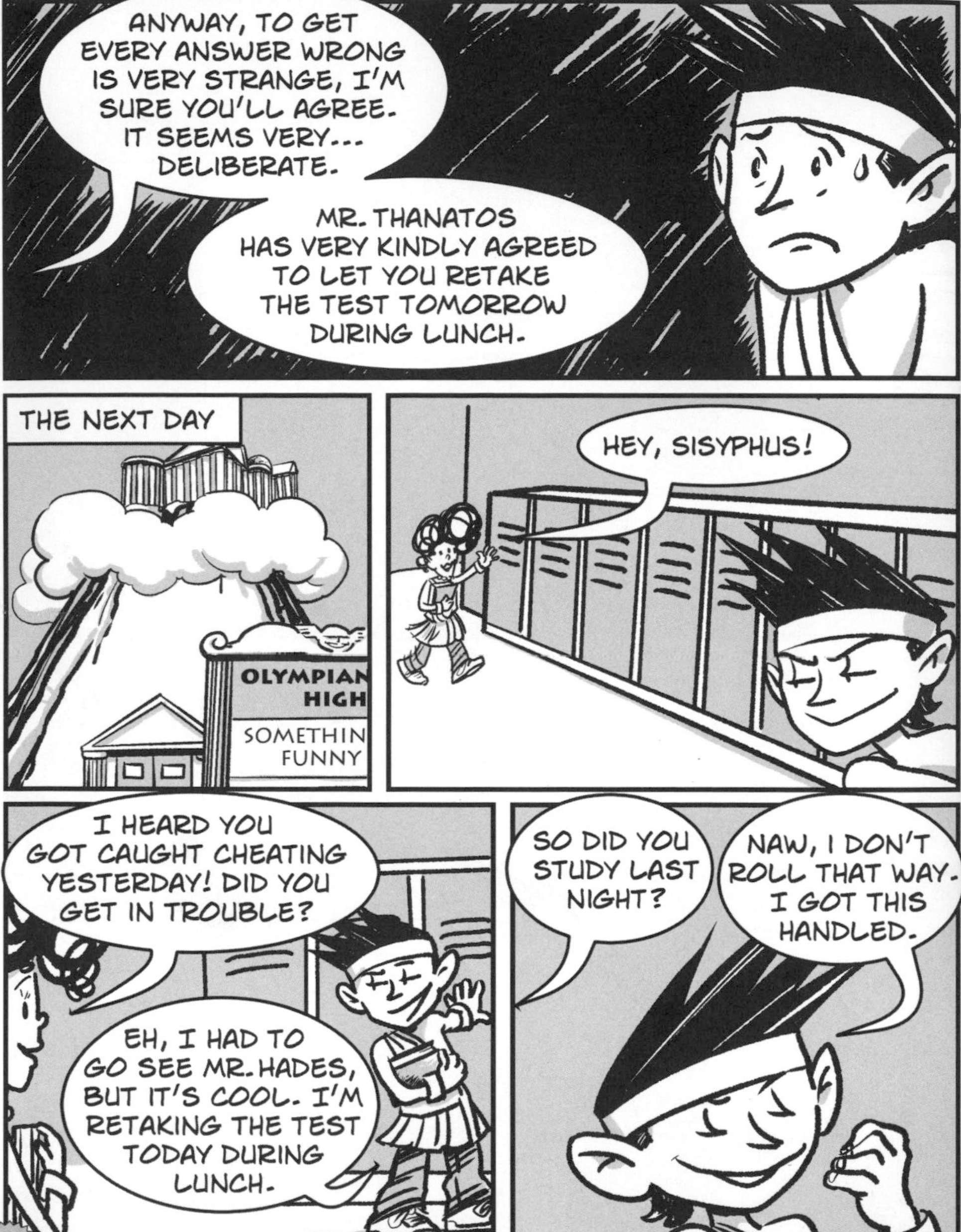
ANYWAY, TO GET EVERY ANSWER WRONG IS VERY STRANGE, I'M SURE YOU'LL AGREE. IT SEEMS VERY... DELIBERATE.
MR. THANATOS HAS VERY KINDLY AGREED TO LET YOU RETAKE THE TEST TOMORROW DURING LUNCH.
THE NEXT DAY
OLYMPIAN HIGH
SOMETHIN FUNNY
HEY, SISYPHUS!
I HEARD YOU GOT CAUGHT CHEATING YESTERDAY! DID YOU GET IN TROUBLE?
EH, I HAD TO GO SEE MR. HADES, BUT IT'S COOL. I'M RETAKING THE TEST TODAY DURING LUNCH.
SO DID YOU STUDY LAST NIGHT?
NAW, I DON'T ROLL THAT WAY. I GOT THIS HANDLED.

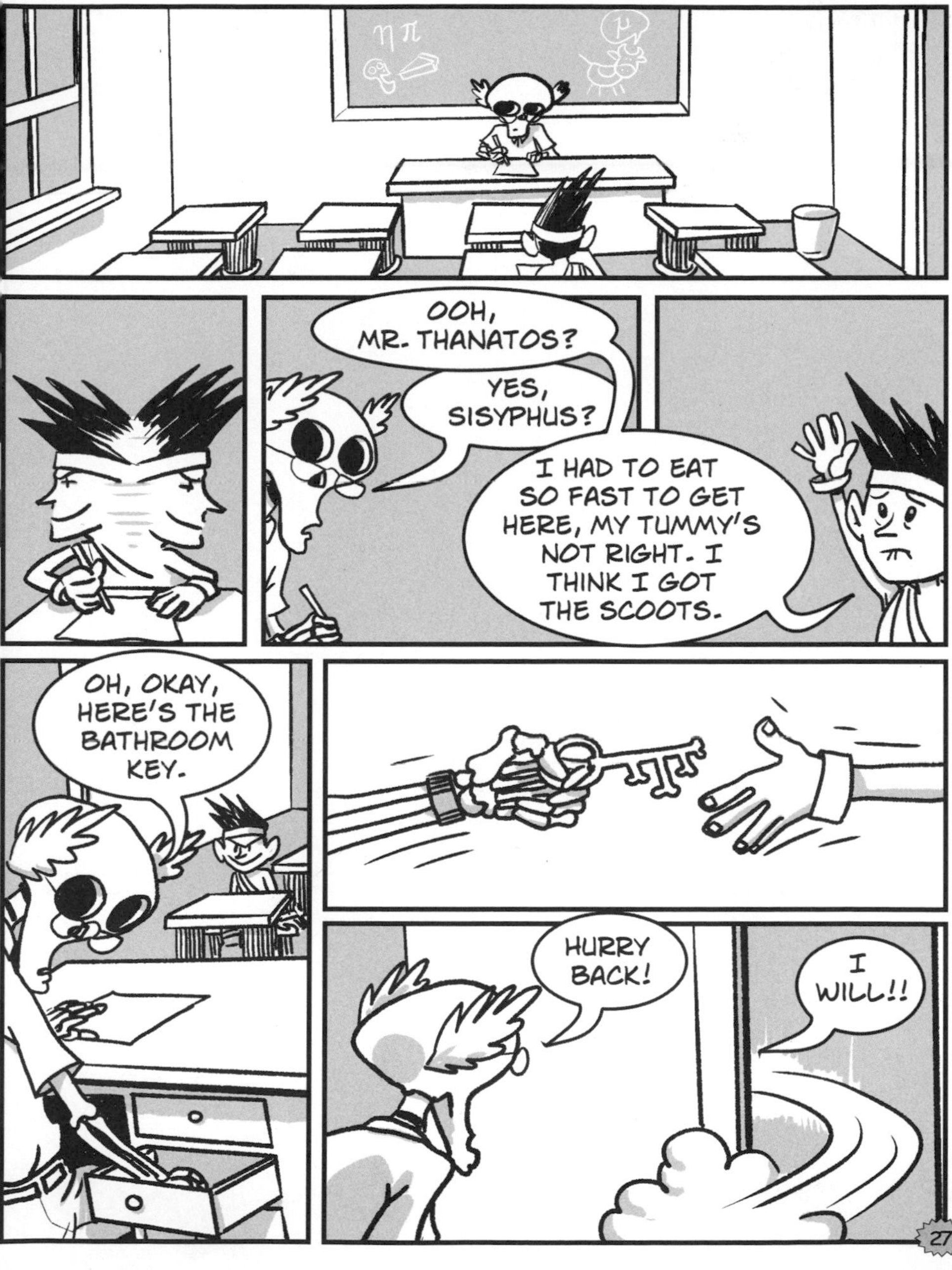
OOH, MR. THANATOS?
YES, SISYPHUS?
I HAD TO EAT SO FAST TO GET HERE, MY TUMMY'S NOT RIGHT. I THINK I GOT THE SCOOTS.
OH, OKAY, HERE'S THE BATHROOM KEY.
HURRY BACK!
I WILL!!

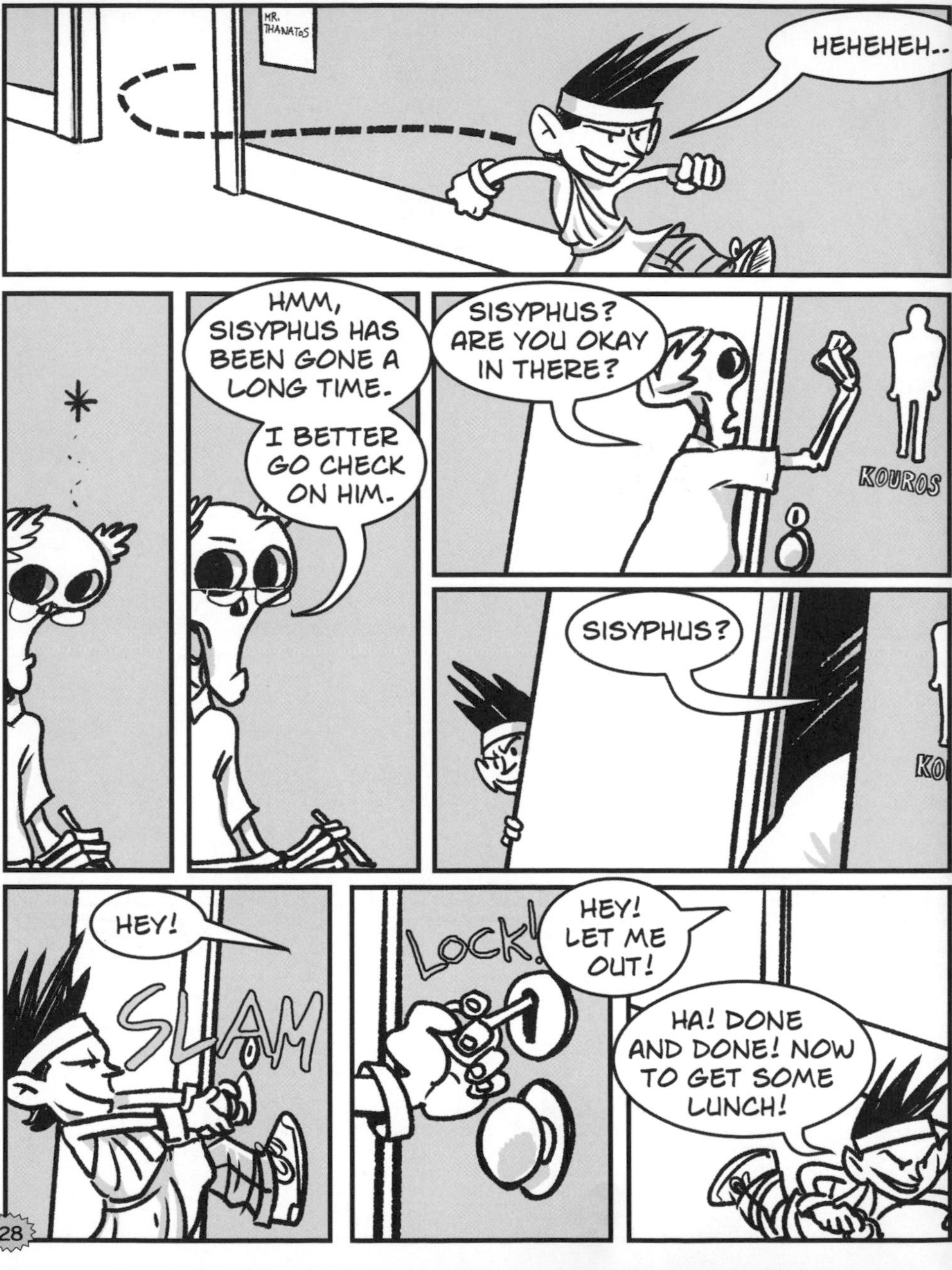
MR. THANATOS
HEHEHEH..
HMM, SISYPHUS HAS BEEN GONE A LONG TIME.
I BETTER GO CHECK ON HIM.
SISYPHUS? ARE YOU OKAY IN THERE?
KOUROS
SISYPHUS?
HEY!
SLAM
LOCK!
HEY! LET ME OUT!
HA! DONE AND DONE! NOW TO GET SOME LUNCH!

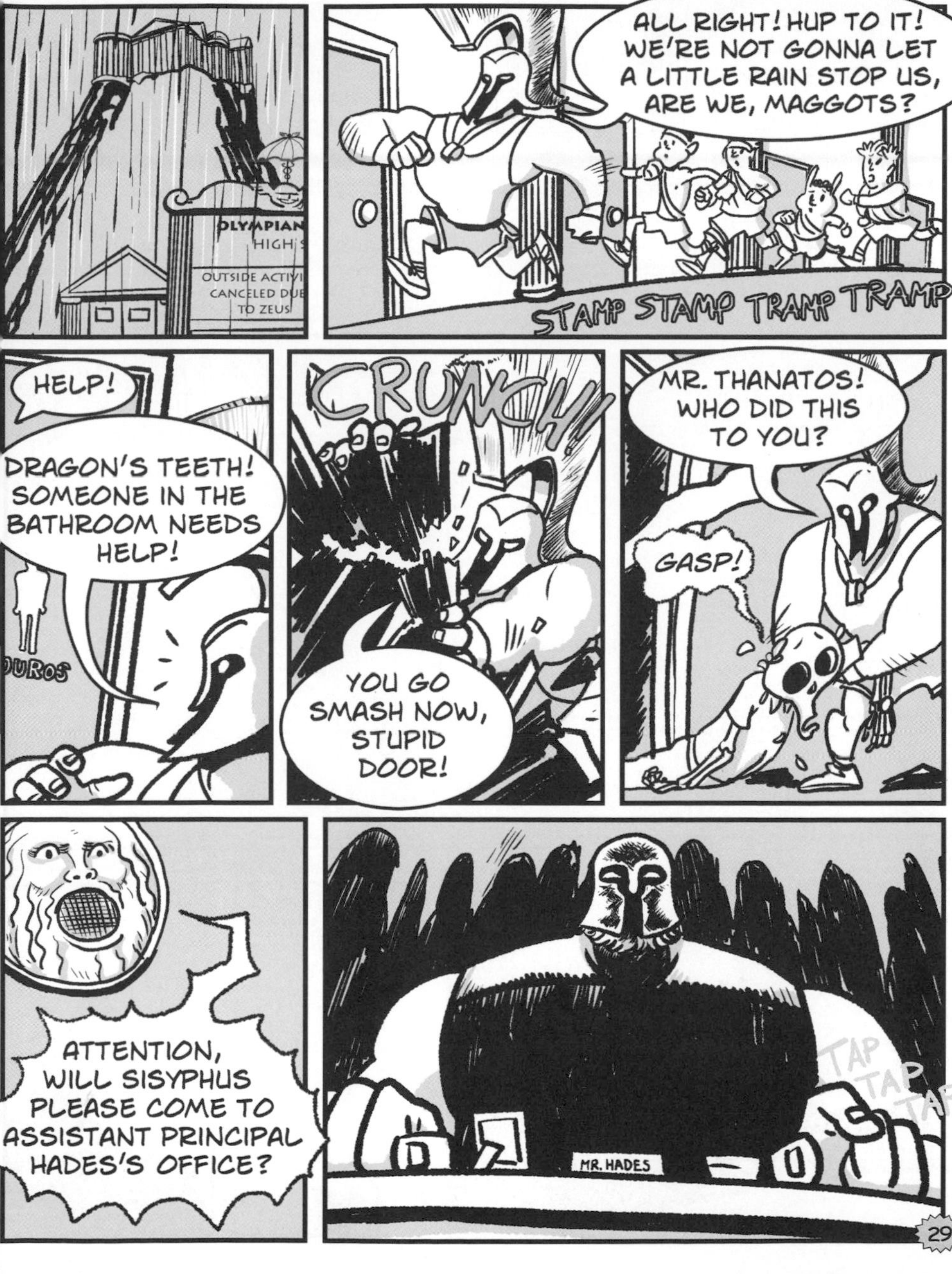
OLYMPIAN
HIGH S
OUTSIDE ACTIVI
CANCELED DUE
TO ZEUS
ALL RIGHT! HUP TO IT! WE'RE NOT GONNA LET A LITTLE RAIN STOP US, ARE WE, MAGGOTS?
STAMP STAMP TRAMP TRAMP
HELP!
DRAGON'S TEETH! SOMEONE IN THE BATHROOM NEEDS HELP!
OUROS
CRUNCH!
YOU GO SMASH NOW, STUPID DOOR!
MR. THANATOS! WHO DID THIS TO YOU?
GASP!
ATTENTION, WILL SISYPHUS PLEASE COME TO ASSISTANT PRINCIPAL HADES'S OFFICE?
TAP TAP TAP
MR. HADES

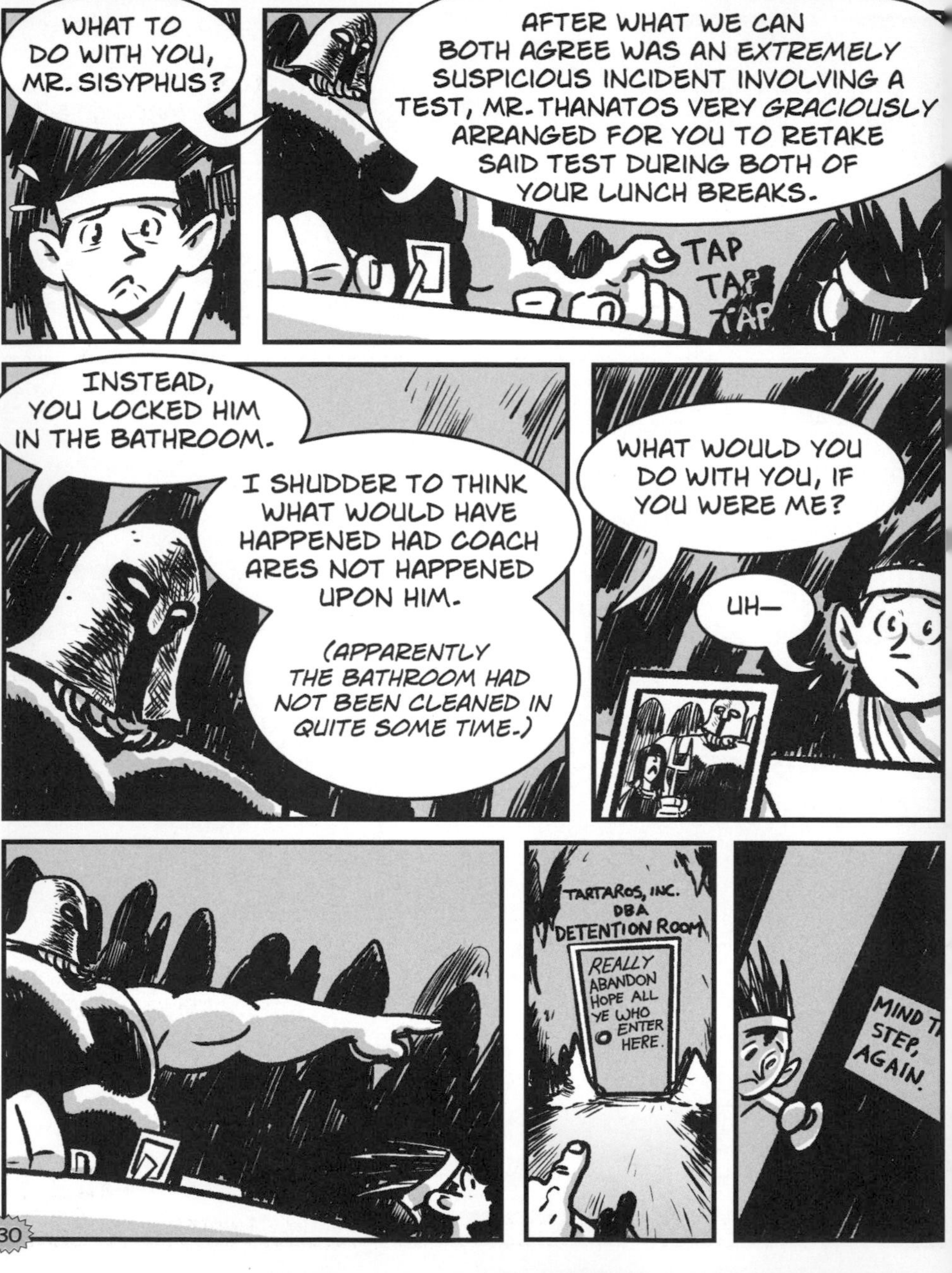
WHAT TO DO WITH YOU, MR. SISYPHUS?
AFTER WHAT WE CAN BOTH AGREE WAS AN EXTREMELY SUSPICIOUS INCIDENT INVOLVING A TEST, MR. THANATOS VERY GRACIOUSLY ARRANGED FOR YOU TO RETAKE SAID TEST DURING BOTH OF YOUR LUNCH BREAKS.
TAP TAP TAP
INSTEAD, YOU LOCKED HIM IN THE BATHROOM.
I SHUDDER TO THINK WHAT WOULD HAVE HAPPENED HAD COACH ARES NOT HAPPENED UPON HIM.
(APPARENTLY THE BATHROOM HAD NOT BEEN CLEANED IN QUITE SOME TIME.)
WHAT WOULD YOU DO WITH YOU, IF YOU WERE ME?
UH—
TARTAROS, INC. DBA DETENTION ROOM
REALLY ABANDON HOPE ALL YE WHO ENTER HERE.
MIND T STEP, AGAIN.

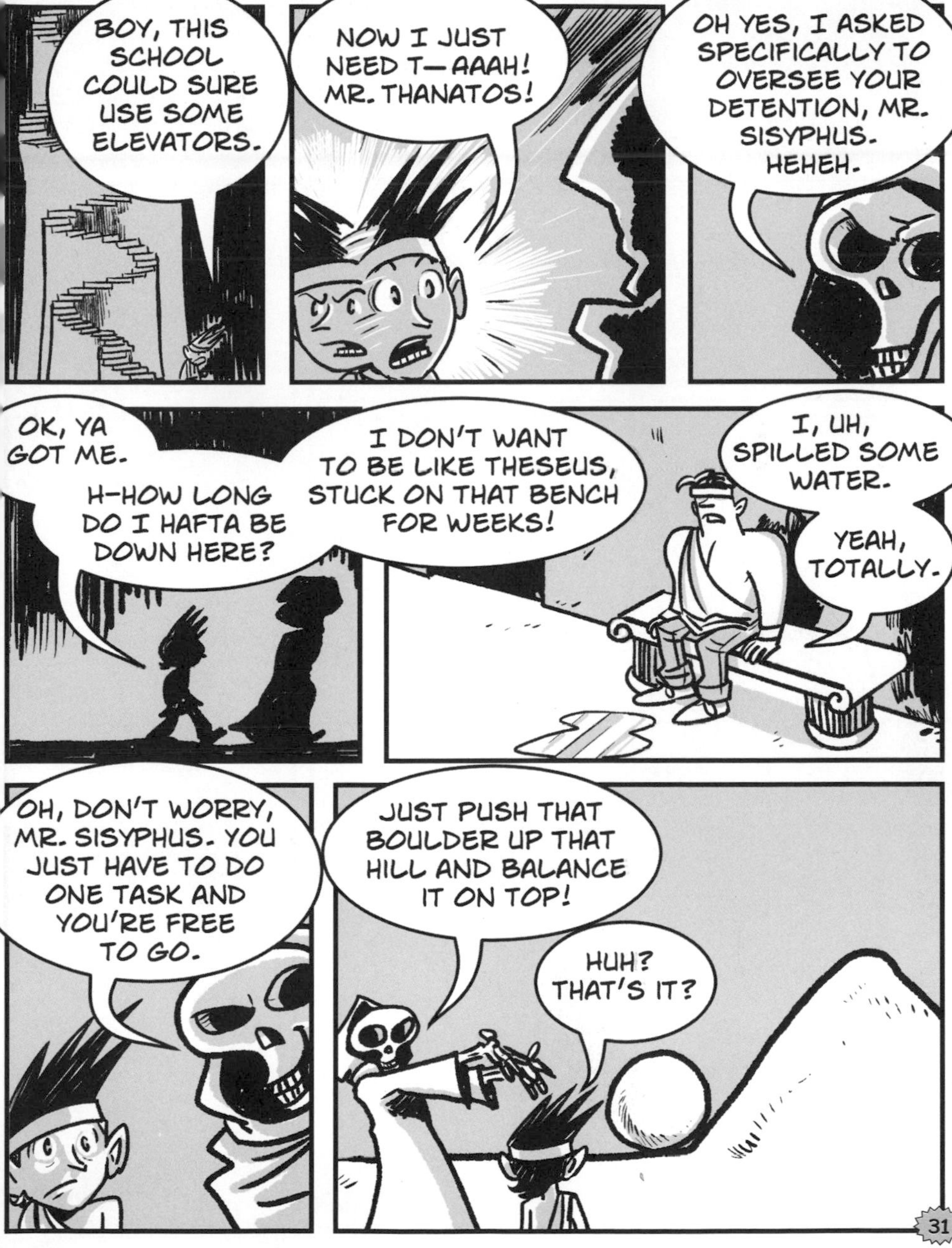
BOY, THIS SCHOOL COULD SURE USE SOME ELEVATORS.
NOW I JUST NEED T— AAAH! MR. THANATOS!
OH YES, I ASKED SPECIFICALLY TO OVERSEE YOUR DETENTION, MR. SISYPHUS. HEHEH.
OK, YA GOT ME.
H-HOW LONG DO I HAFTA BE DOWN HERE?
I DON'T WANT TO BE LIKE THESEUS, STUCK ON THAT BENCH FOR WEEKS!
I, UH, SPILLED SOME WATER.
YEAH, TOTALLY.
OH, DON'T WORRY, MR. SISYPHUS. YOU JUST HAVE TO DO ONE TASK AND YOU'RE FREE TO GO.
JUST PUSH THAT BOULDER UP THAT HILL AND BALANCE IT ON TOP!
HUH? THAT'S IT?

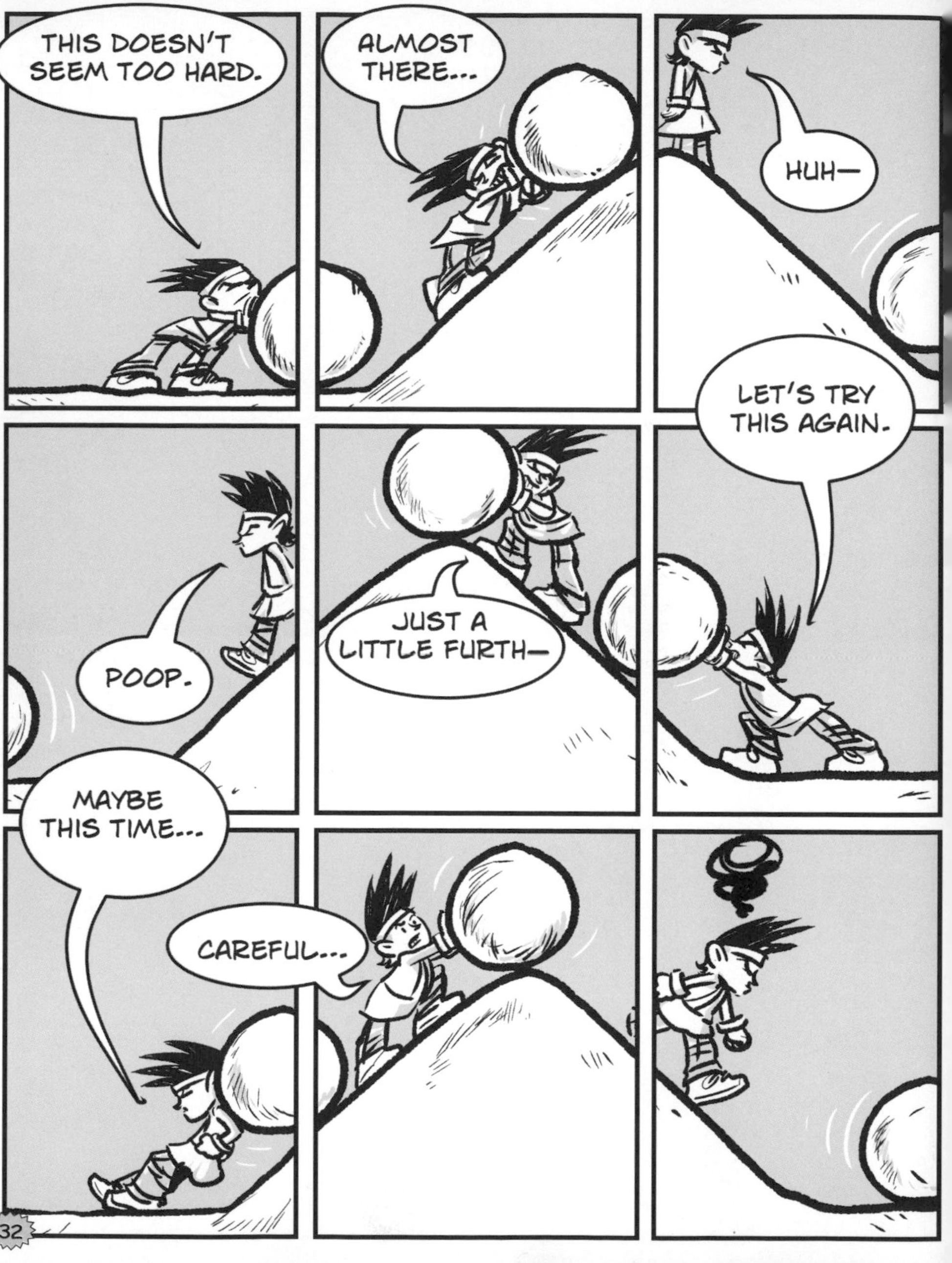
THIS DOESN'T SEEM TOO HARD.
ALMOST THERE...
HUH—
LET'S TRY THIS AGAIN.
POOP.
JUST A LITTLE FURTH—
MAYBE THIS TIME...
CAREFUL...

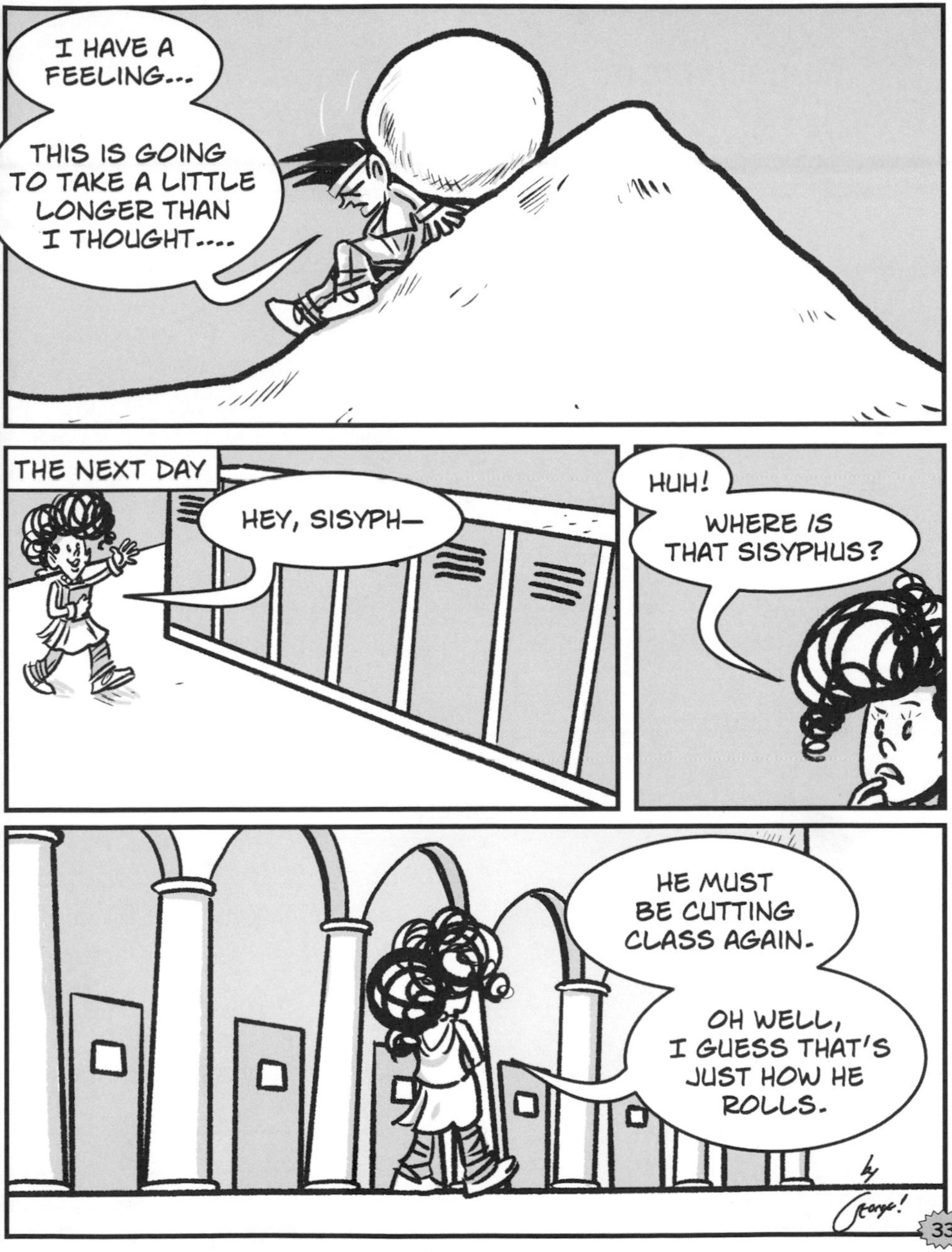

I HAVE A FEELING...
THIS IS GOING TO TAKE A LITTLE LONGER THAN I THOUGHT....
THE NEXT DAY
HEY, SISYPH—
HUH!
WHERE IS THAT SISYPHUS?
HE MUST BE CUTTING CLASS AGAIN.
OH WELL, I GUESS THAT'S JUST HOW HE ROLLS.
by George!

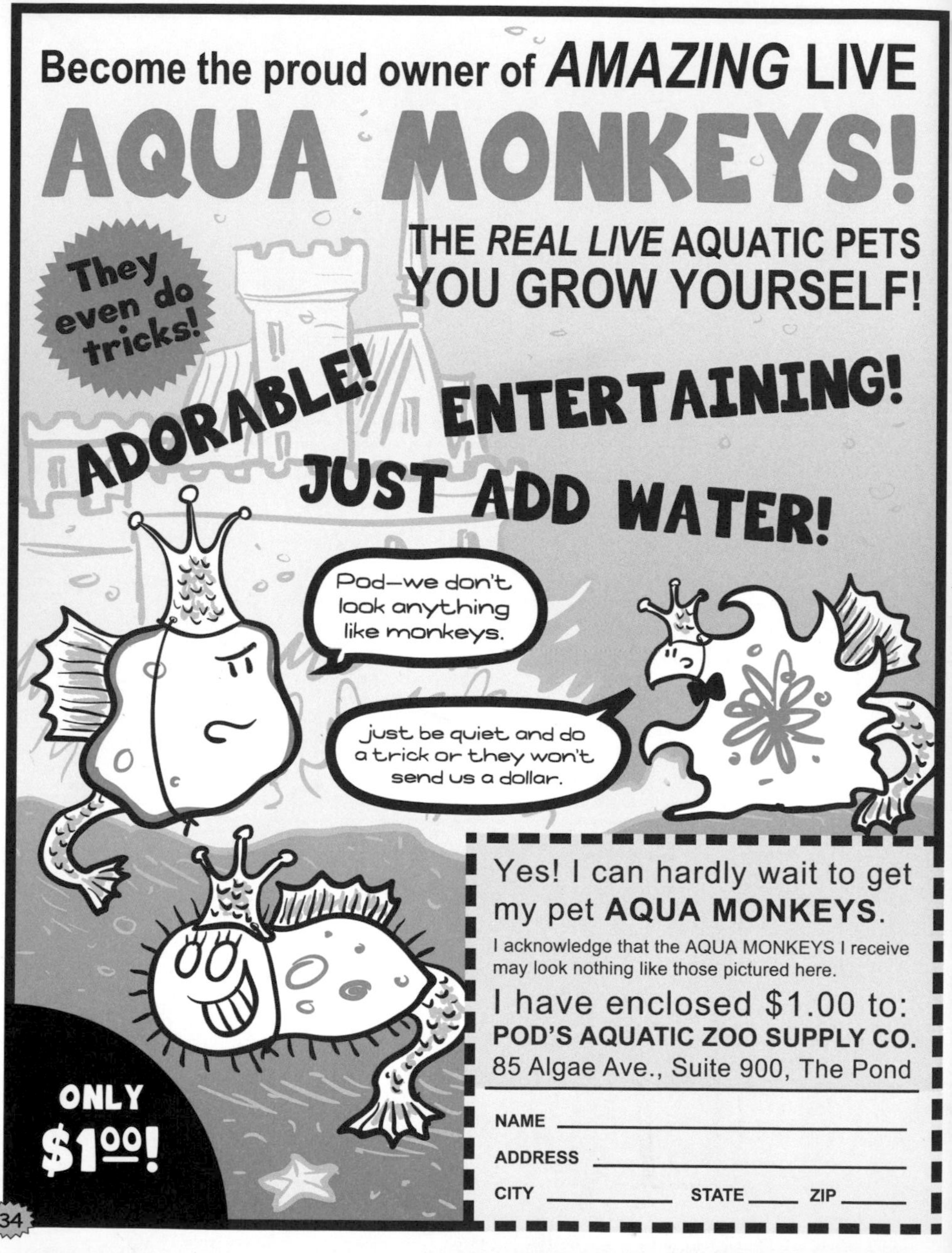
Become the proud owner of AMAZING LIVE
AQUA MONKEYS!
THE REAL LIVE AQUATIC PETS
YOU GROW YOURSELF!
They even do tricks!
ADORABLE!
ENTERTAINING!
JUST ADD WATER!
Pod—we don't look anything like monkeys.
just be quiet and do a trick or they won't send us a dollar.
Yes! I can hardly wait to get my pet AQUA MONKEYS.
I acknowledge that the AQUA MONKEYS I receive may look nothing like those pictured here.
I have enclosed $1.00 to:
POD'S AQUATIC ZOO SUPPLY CO.
85 Algae Ave., Suite 900, The Pond
NAME
ADDRESS
CITY
STATE
ZIP
ONLY $1.00!

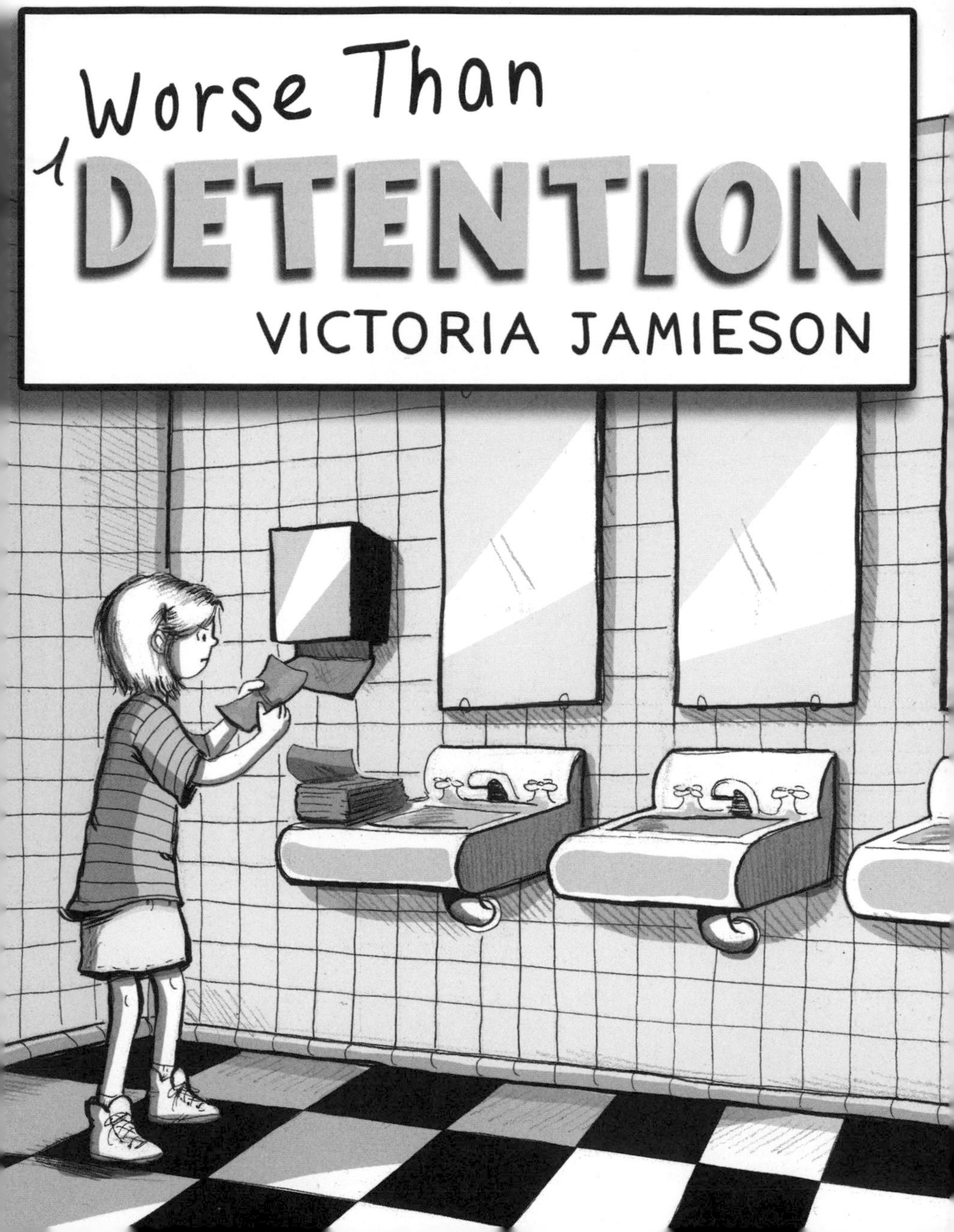
Worse Than
DETENTION
VICTORIA JAMIESON

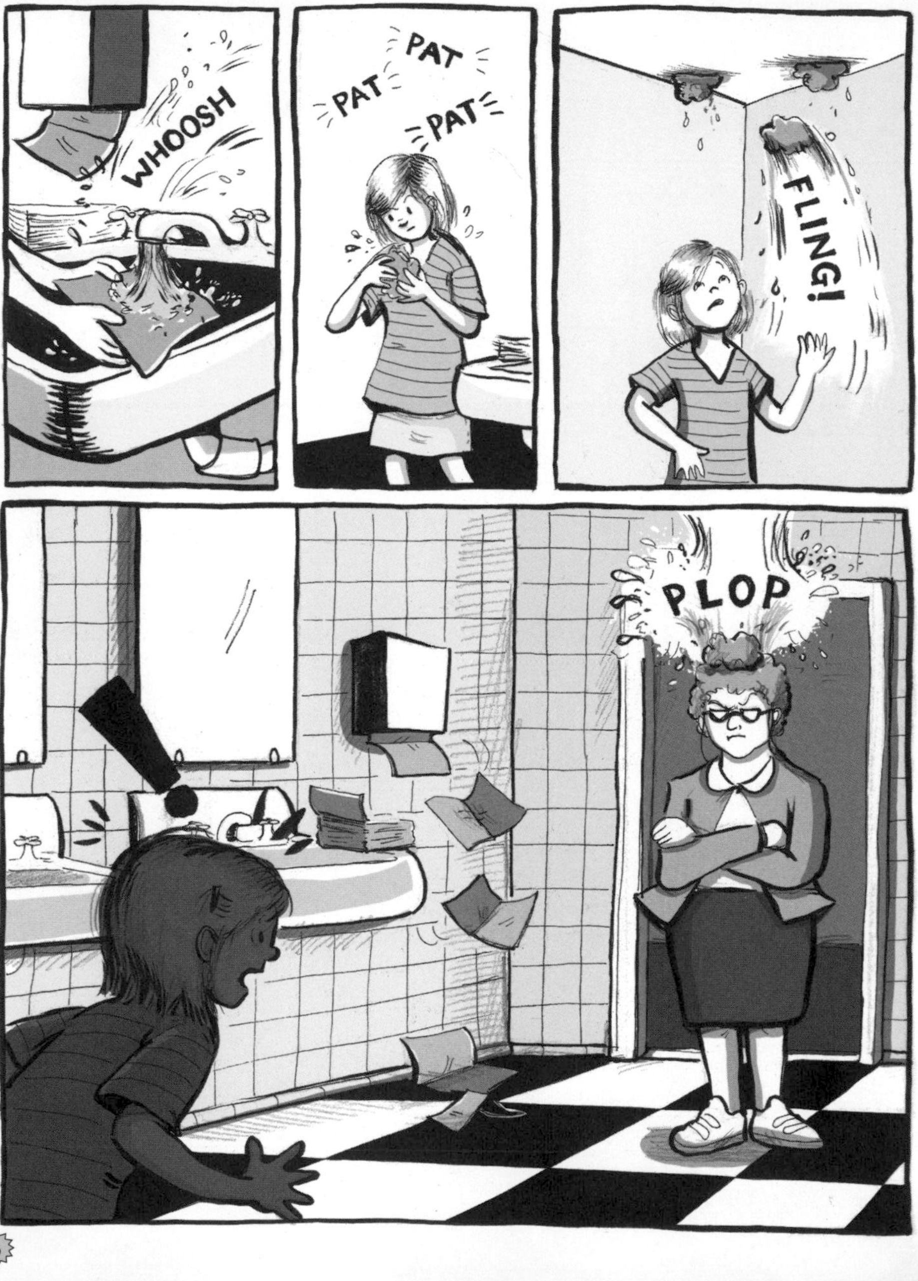
WHOOSH
PAT
PAT
PAT
FLING!
PLOP

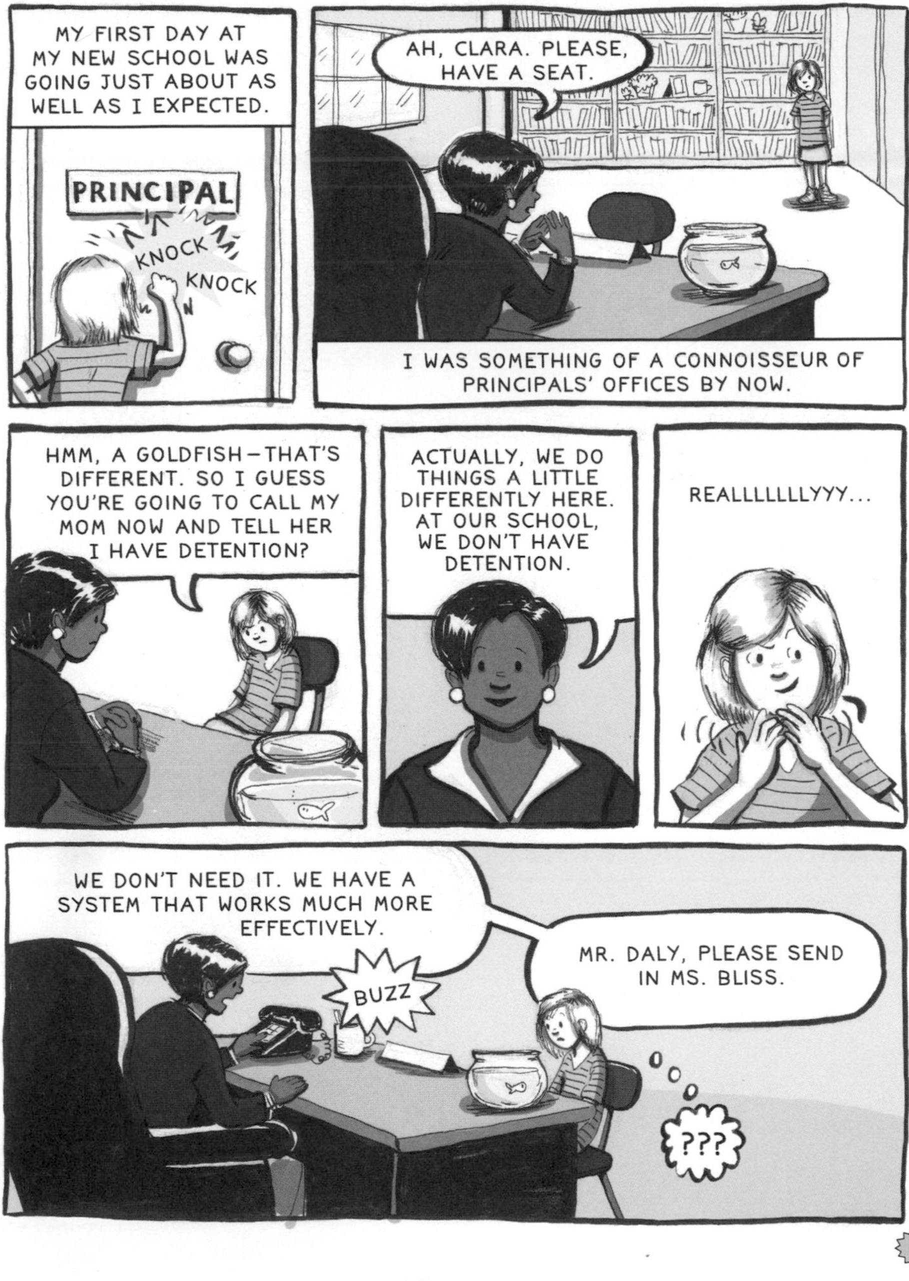

MY FIRST DAY AT MY NEW SCHOOL WAS GOING JUST ABOUT AS WELL AS I EXPECTED.
PRINCIPAL
KNOCK
KNOCK
AH, CLARA. PLEASE, HAVE A SEAT.
I WAS SOMETHING OF A CONNOISSEUR OF PRINCIPALS' OFFICES BY NOW.
HMM, A GOLDFISH—THAT'S DIFFERENT. SO I GUESS YOU'RE GOING TO CALL MY MOM NOW AND TELL HER I HAVE DETENTION?
ACTUALLY, WE DO THINGS A LITTLE DIFFERENTLY HERE. AT OUR SCHOOL, WE DON'T HAVE DETENTION.
REALLLLLLLYYY...
WE DON'T NEED IT. WE HAVE A SYSTEM THAT WORKS MUCH MORE EFFECTIVELY.
BUZZ
MR. DALY, PLEASE SEND IN MS. BLISS.
???

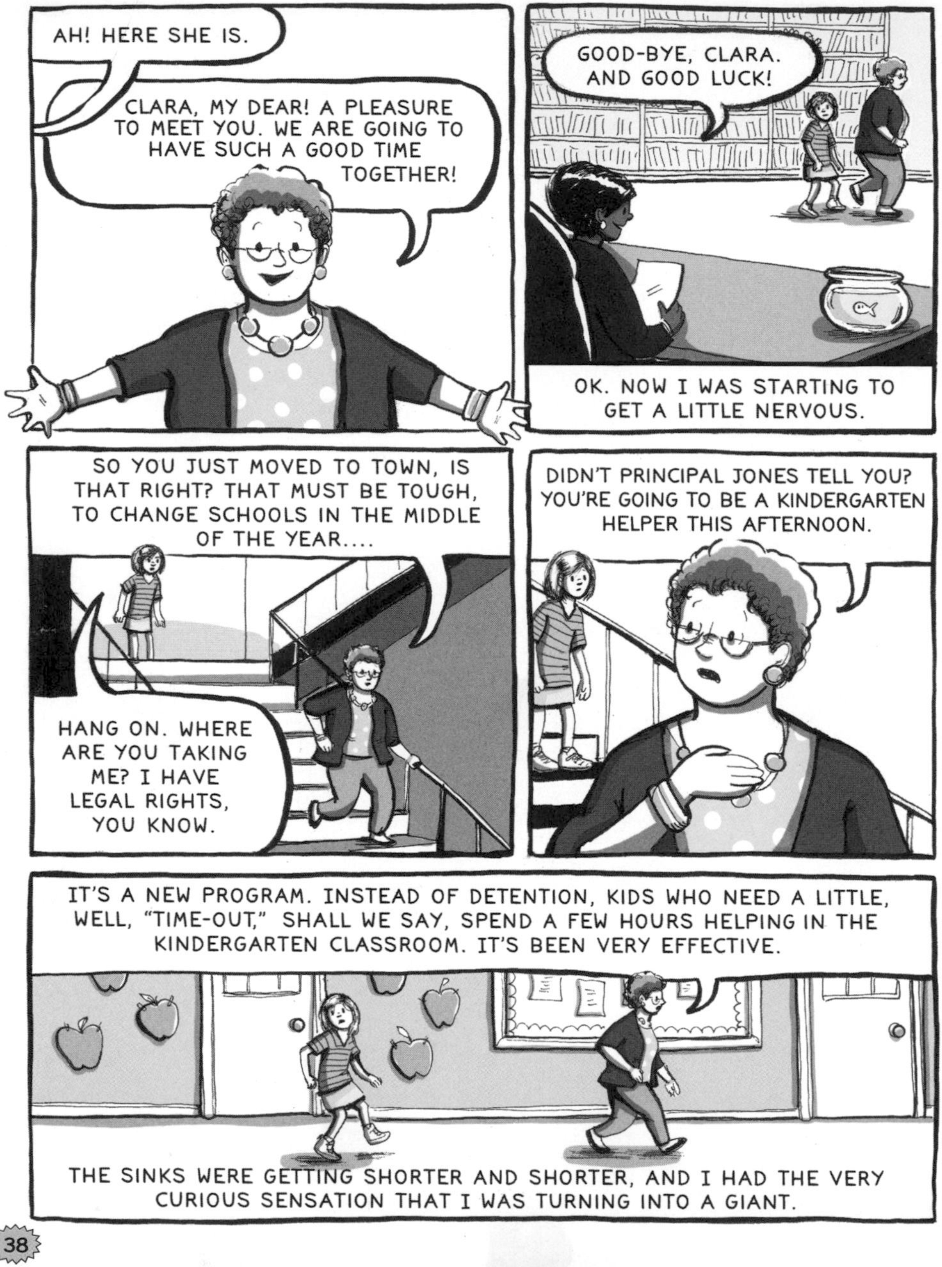

AH! HERE SHE IS.
CLARA, MY DEAR! A PLEASURE TO MEET YOU. WE ARE GOING TO HAVE SUCH A GOOD TIME TOGETHER!
GOOD-BYE, CLARA. AND GOOD LUCK!
OK. NOW I WAS STARTING TO GET A LITTLE NERVOUS.
SO YOU JUST MOVED TO TOWN, IS THAT RIGHT? THAT MUST BE TOUGH, TO CHANGE SCHOOLS IN THE MIDDLE OF THE YEAR....
HANG ON. WHERE ARE YOU TAKING ME? I HAVE LEGAL RIGHTS, YOU KNOW.
DIDN'T PRINCIPAL JONES TELL YOU? YOU'RE GOING TO BE A KINDERGARTEN HELPER THIS AFTERNOON.
IT'S A NEW PROGRAM. INSTEAD OF DETENTION, KIDS WHO NEED A LITTLE, WELL, "TIME-OUT," SHALL WE SAY, SPEND A FEW HOURS HELPING IN THE KINDERGARTEN CLASSROOM. IT'S BEEN VERY EFFECTIVE.
THE SINKS WERE GETTING SHORTER AND SHORTER, AND I HAD THE VERY CURIOUS SENSATION THAT I WAS TURNING INTO A GIANT.

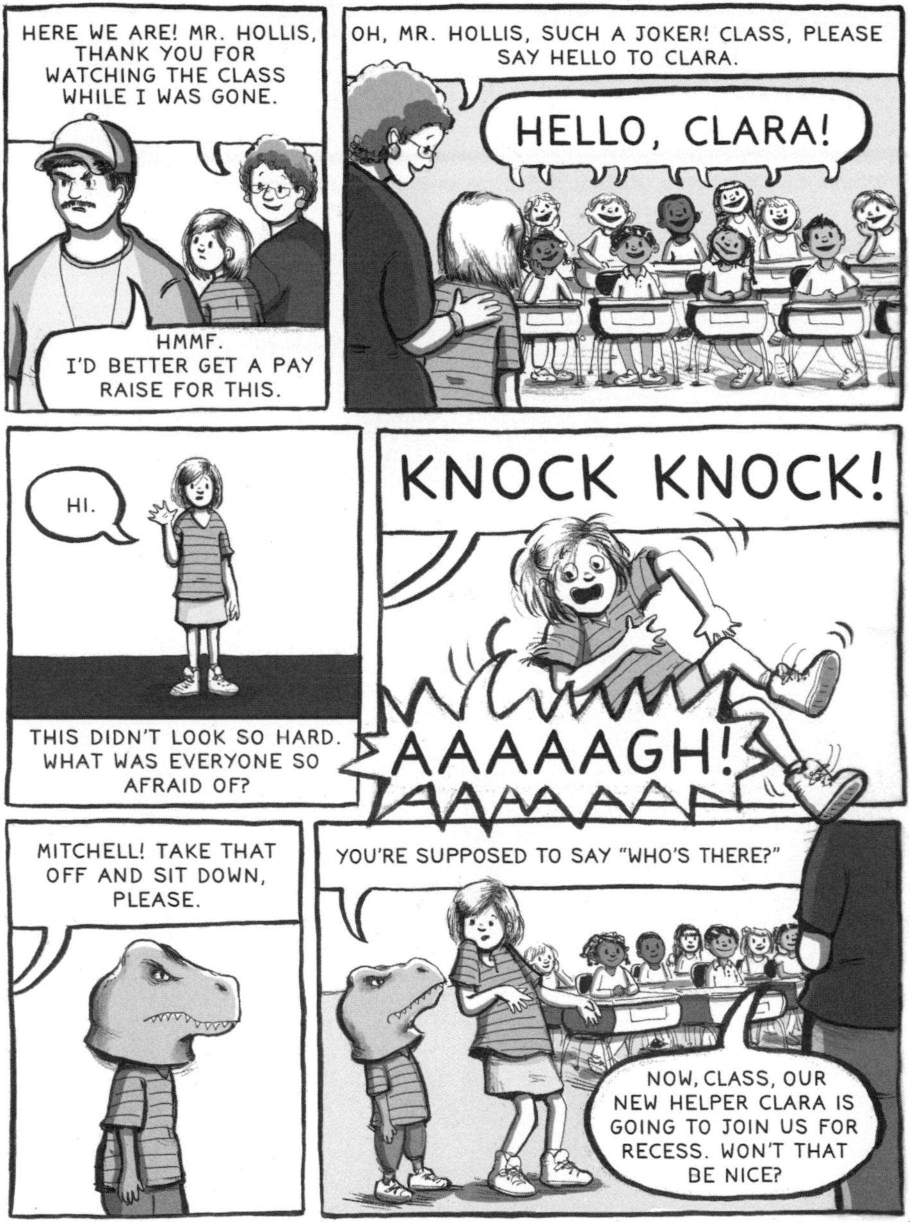
HERE WE ARE! MR. HOLLIS, THANK YOU FOR WATCHING THE CLASS WHILE I WAS GONE.
HMMF. I'D BETTER GET A PAY RAISE FOR THIS.
OH, MR. HOLLIS, SUCH A JOKER! CLASS, PLEASE SAY HELLO TO CLARA.
HELLO, CLARA!
HI.
THIS DIDN'T LOOK SO HARD. WHAT WAS EVERYONE SO AFRAID OF?
KNOCK KNOCK!
AAAAAGH!
MITCHELL! TAKE THAT OFF AND SIT DOWN, PLEASE.
YOU'RE SUPPOSED TO SAY "WHO'S THERE?"
NOW, CLASS, OUR NEW HELPER CLARA IS GOING TO JOIN US FOR RECESS. WON'T THAT BE NICE?

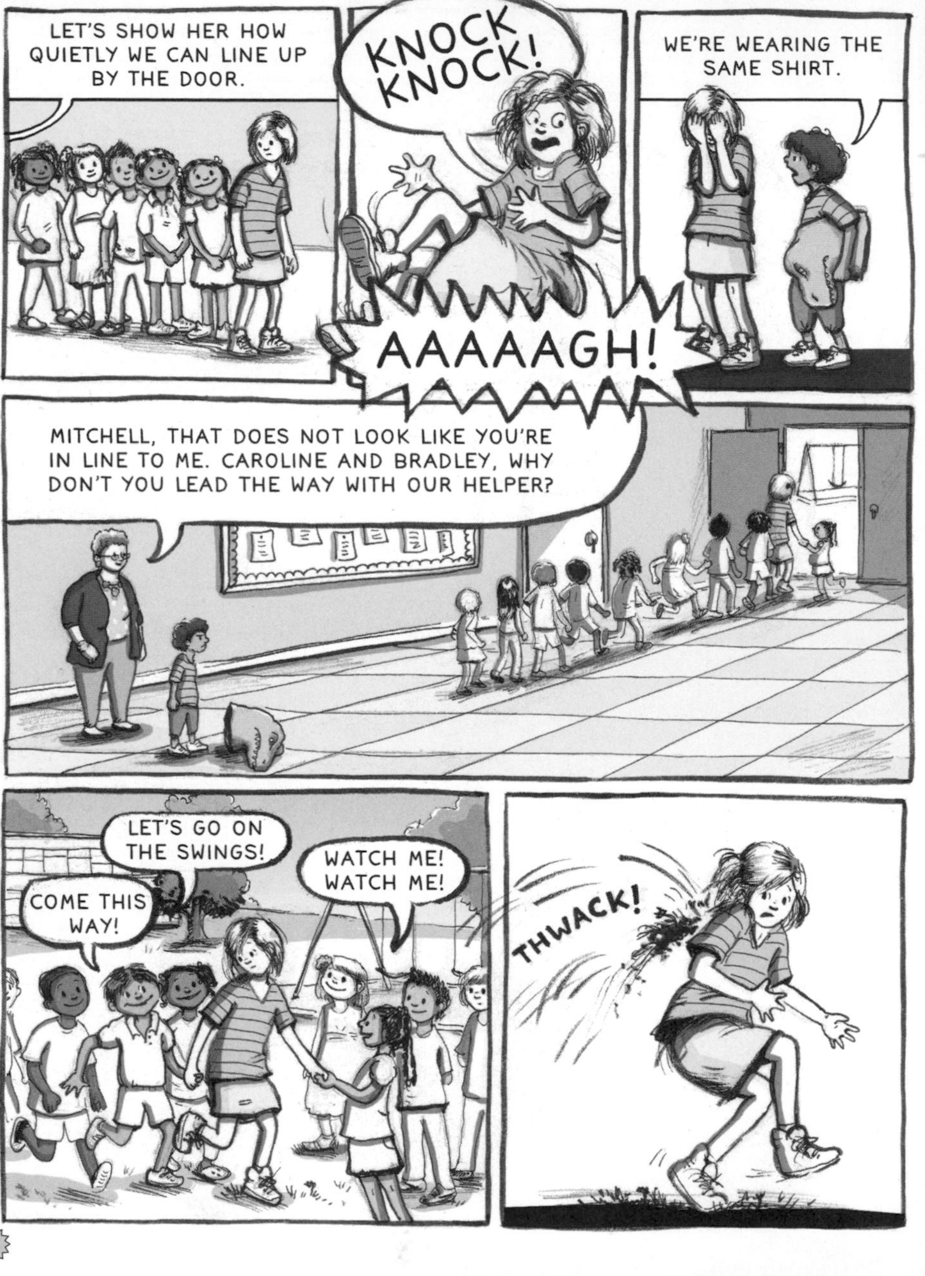

LET'S SHOW HER HOW QUIETLY WE CAN LINE UP BY THE DOOR.
KNOCK KNOCK!
AAAAAGH!
WE'RE WEARING THE SAME SHIRT.
MITCHELL, THAT DOES NOT LOOK LIKE YOU'RE IN LINE TO ME. CAROLINE AND BRADLEY, WHY DON'T YOU LEAD THE WAY WITH OUR HELPER?
LET'S GO ON THE SWINGS!
COME THIS WAY!
WATCH ME! WATCH ME!
THWACK!

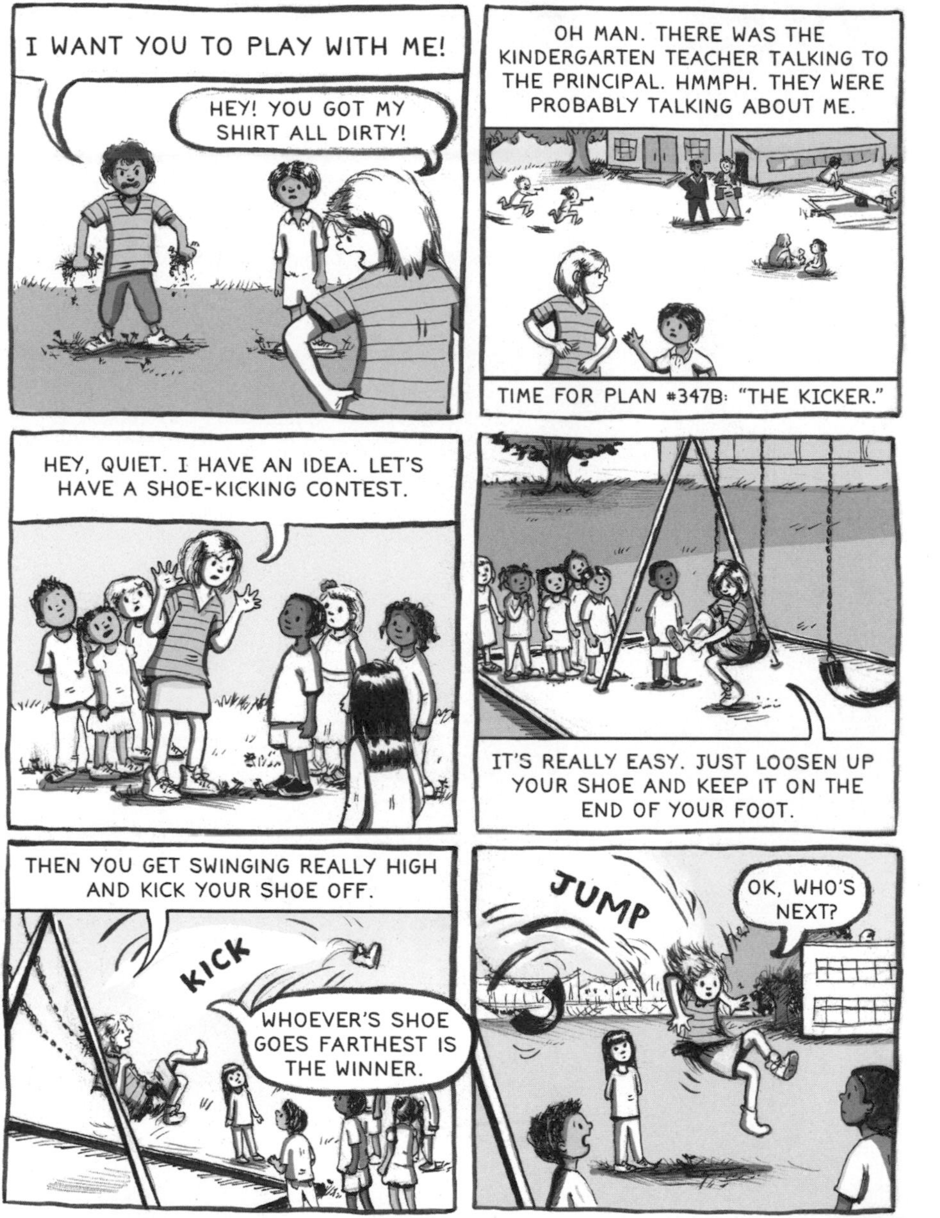
I WANT YOU TO PLAY WITH ME!
HEY! YOU GOT MY SHIRT ALL DIRTY!
OH MAN. THERE WAS THE KINDERGARTEN TEACHER TALKING TO THE PRINCIPAL. HMMPH. THEY WERE PROBABLY TALKING ABOUT ME.
TIME FOR PLAN #347B: "THE KICKER."
HEY, QUIET. I HAVE AN IDEA. LET'S HAVE A SHOE-KICKING CONTEST.
IT'S REALLY EASY. JUST LOOSEN UP YOUR SHOE AND KEEP IT ON THE END OF YOUR FOOT.
THEN YOU GET SWINGING REALLY HIGH AND KICK YOUR SHOE OFF.
KICK
WHOEVER'S SHOE GOES FARTHEST IS THE WINNER.
JUMP
OK, WHO'S NEXT?

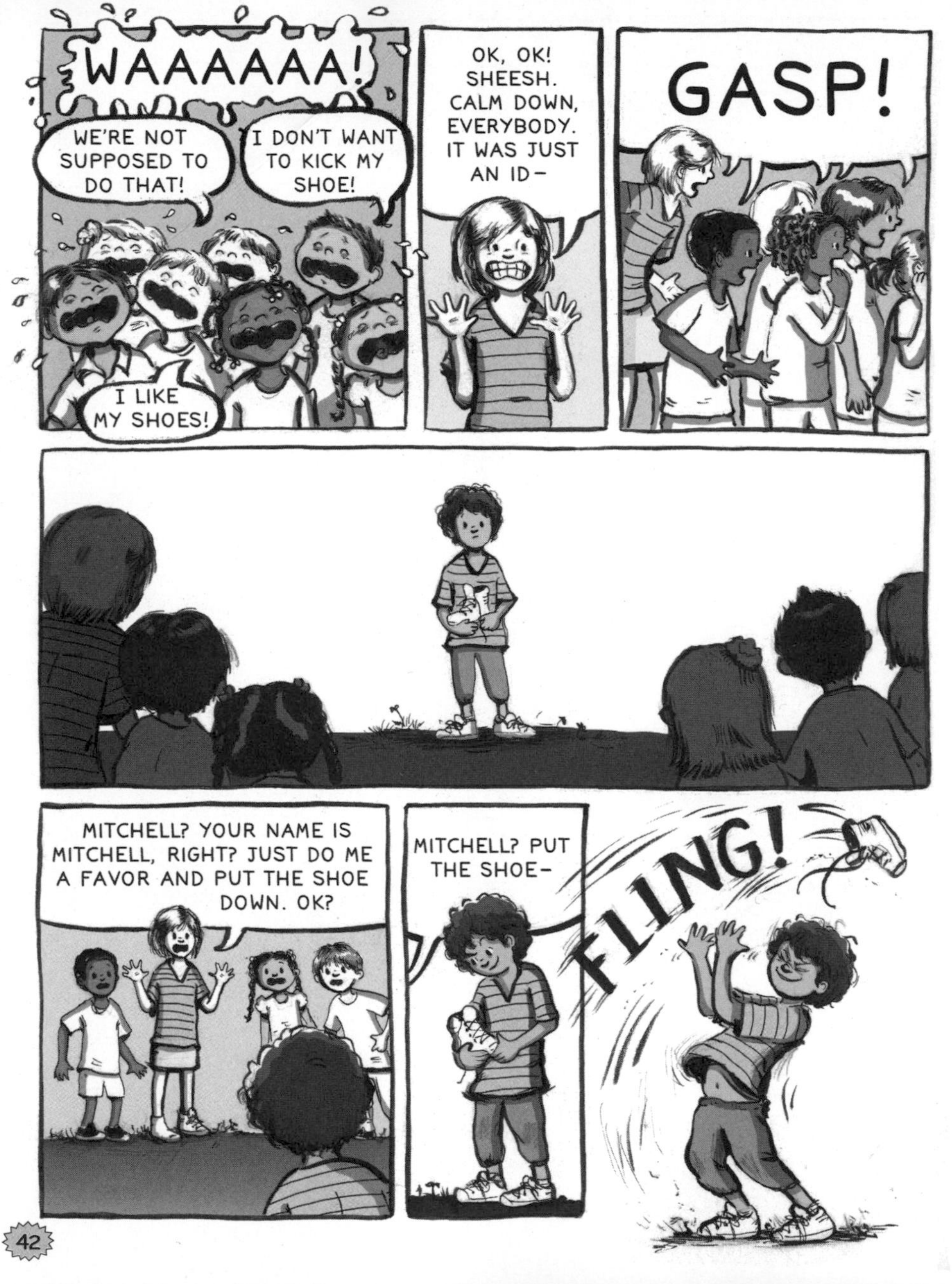

WAAAAAA!
WE'RE NOT SUPPOSED TO DO THAT!
I DON'T WANT TO KICK MY SHOE!
I LIKE MY SHOES!
OK, OK! SHEESH. CALM DOWN, EVERYBODY. IT WAS JUST AN ID–
GASP!
MITCHELL? YOUR NAME IS MITCHELL, RIGHT? JUST DO ME A FAVOR AND PUT THE SHOE DOWN. OK?
MITCHELL? PUT THE SHOE–
FLING!

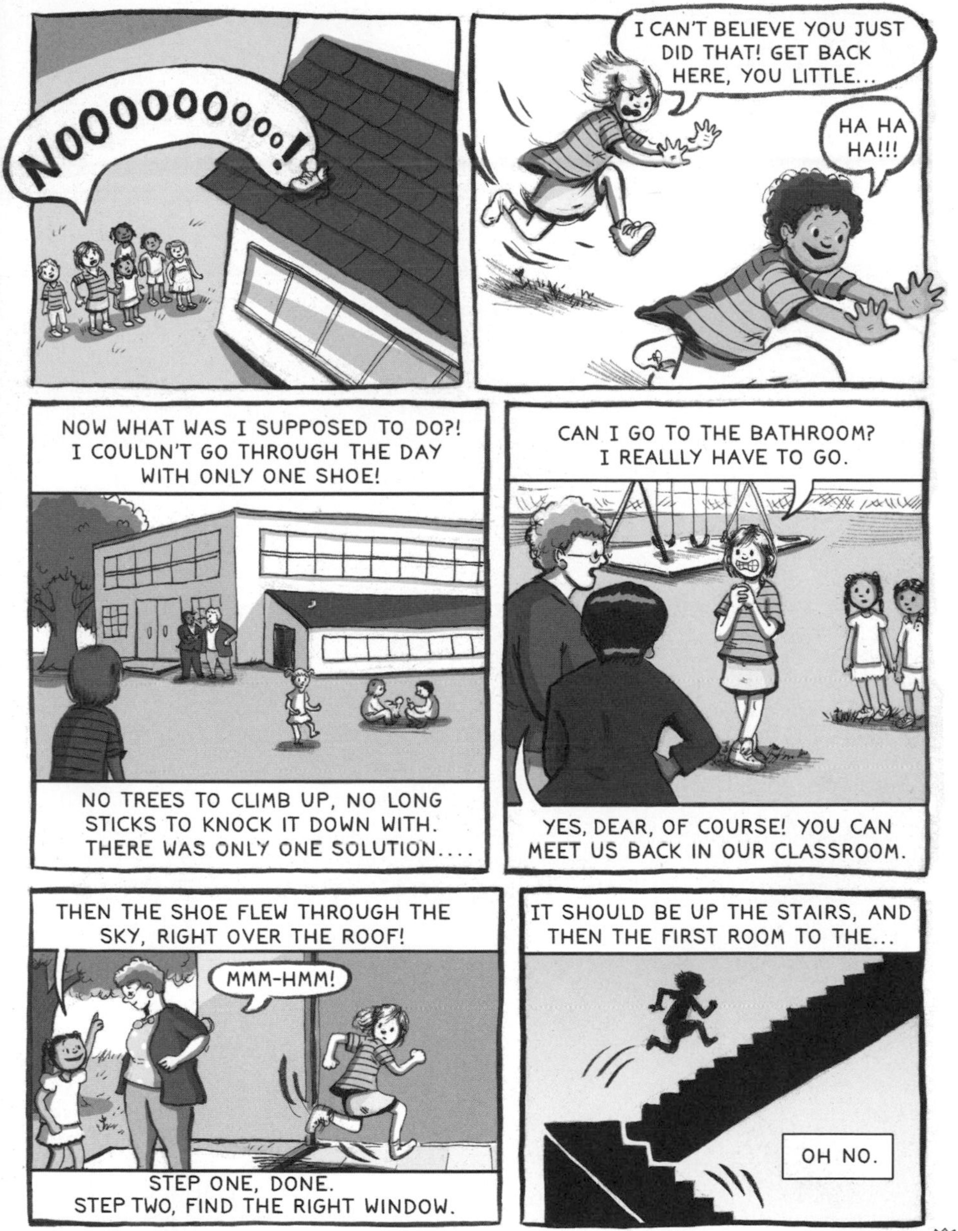
NOOOOOOooo!
I CAN'T BELIEVE YOU JUST DID THAT! GET BACK HERE, YOU LITTLE...
HA HA HA!!!
NOW WHAT WAS I SUPPOSED TO DO?! I COULDN'T GO THROUGH THE DAY WITH ONLY ONE SHOE!
NO TREES TO CLIMB UP, NO LONG STICKS TO KNOCK IT DOWN WITH. THERE WAS ONLY ONE SOLUTION....
CAN I GO TO THE BATHROOM? I REALLLY HAVE TO GO.
YES, DEAR, OF COURSE! YOU CAN MEET US BACK IN OUR CLASSROOM.
THEN THE SHOE FLEW THROUGH THE SKY, RIGHT OVER THE ROOF!
MMM-HMM!
STEP ONE, DONE.
STEP TWO, FIND THE RIGHT WINDOW.
IT SHOULD BE UP THE STAIRS, AND THEN THE FIRST ROOM TO THE...
OH NO.

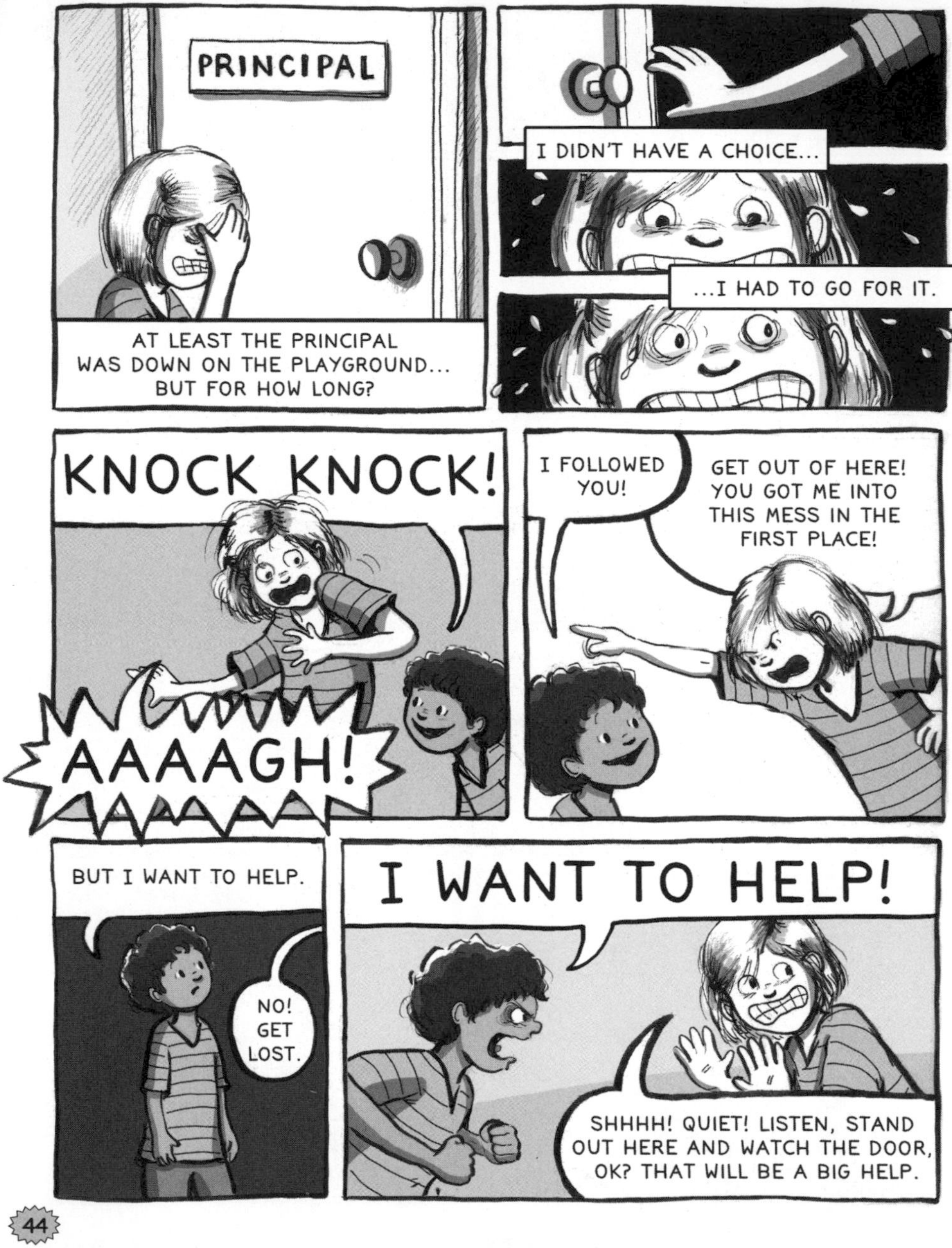
PRINCIPAL
AT LEAST THE PRINCIPAL WAS DOWN ON THE PLAYGROUND... BUT FOR HOW LONG?
I DIDN'T HAVE A CHOICE...
...I HAD TO GO FOR IT.
KNOCK KNOCK!
AAAAGH!
I FOLLOWED YOU!
GET OUT OF HERE! YOU GOT ME INTO THIS MESS IN THE FIRST PLACE!
BUT I WANT TO HELP.
NO! GET LOST.
I WANT TO HELP!
SHHHH! QUIET! LISTEN, STAND OUT HERE AND WATCH THE DOOR, OK? THAT WILL BE A BIG HELP.

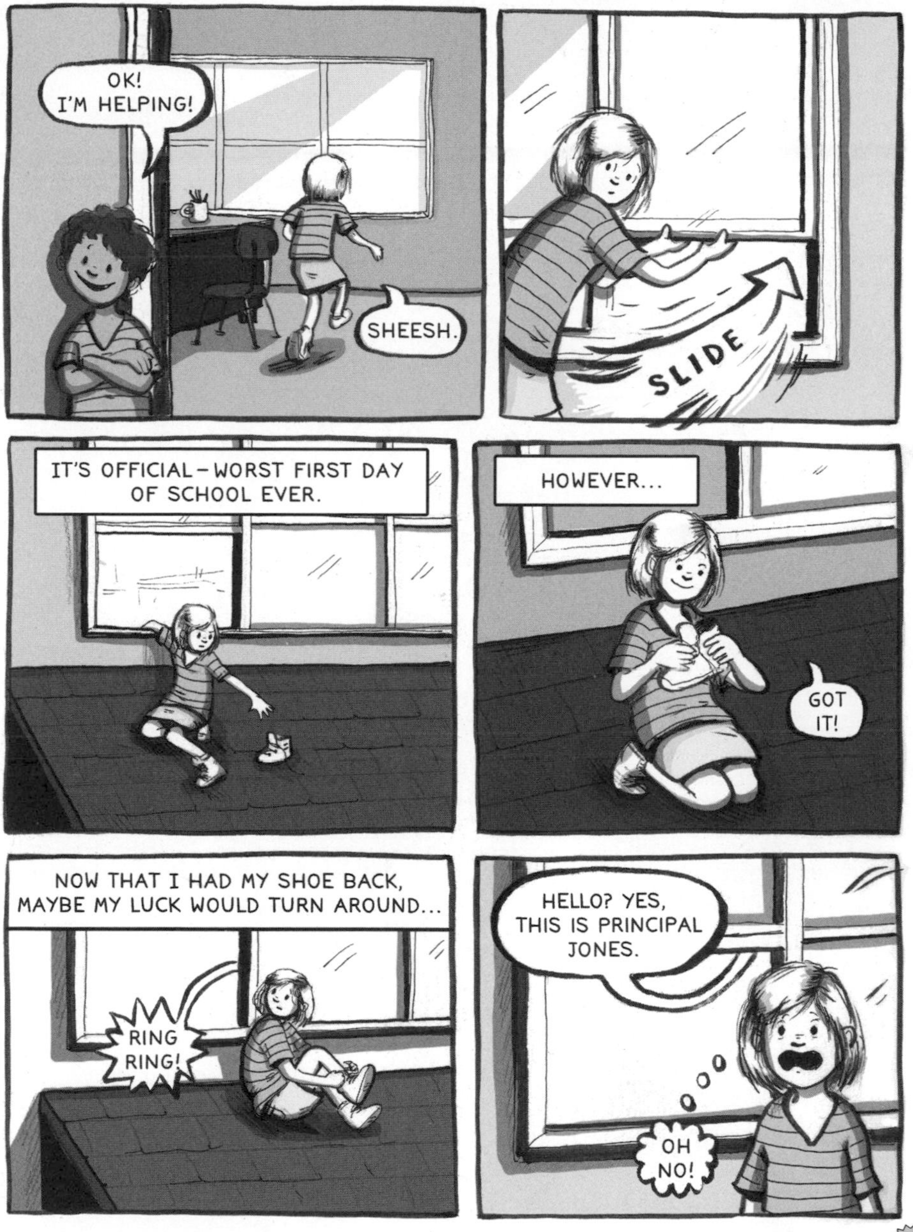
OK! I'M HELPING!
SHEESH.
SLIDE
IT'S OFFICIAL—WORST FIRST DAY OF SCHOOL EVER.
HOWEVER...
GOT IT!
NOW THAT I HAD MY SHOE BACK, MAYBE MY LUCK WOULD TURN AROUND...
RING RING!
HELLO? YES, THIS IS PRINCIPAL JONES.
OH NO!

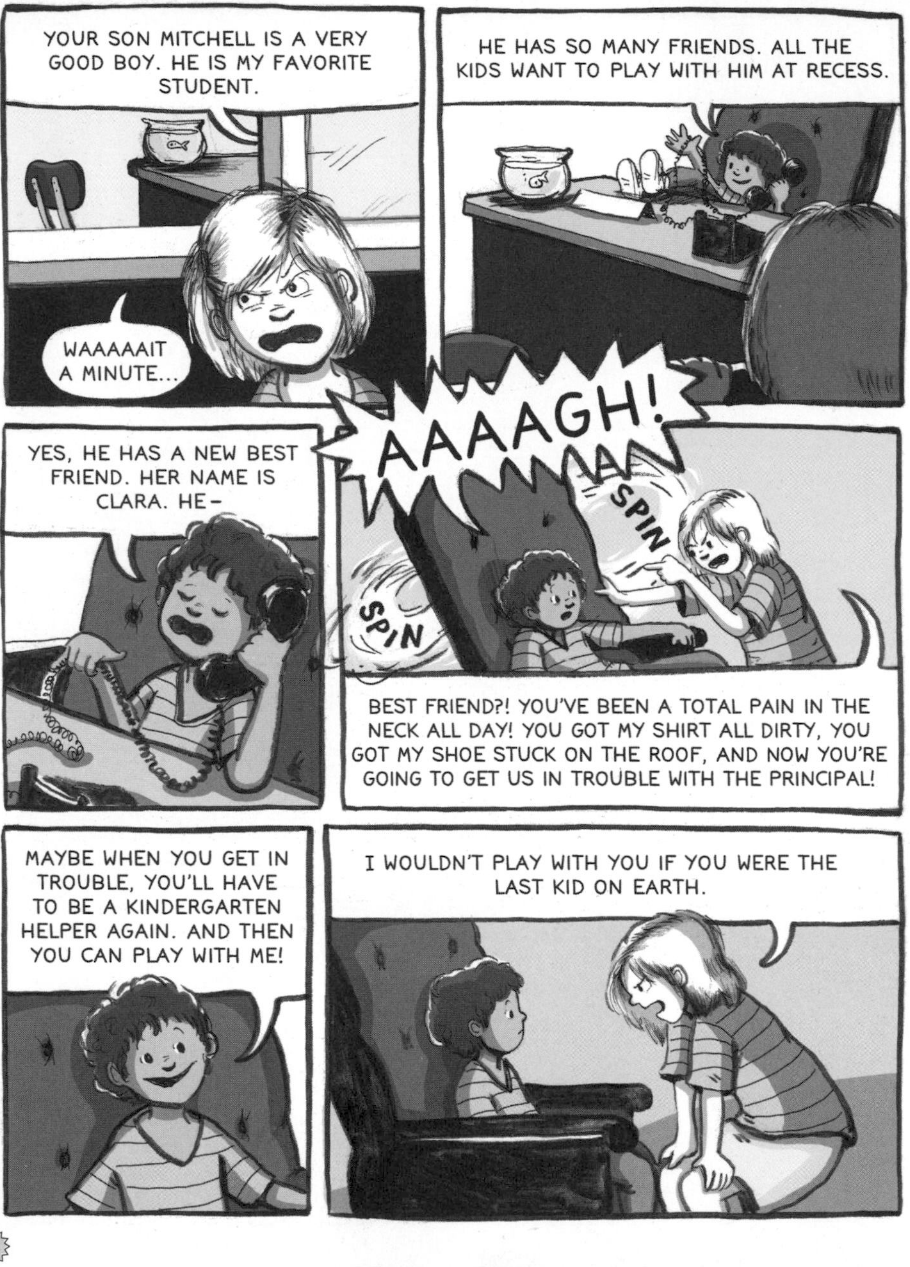

YOUR SON MITCHELL IS A VERY GOOD BOY. HE IS MY FAVORITE STUDENT.
WAAAAAIT A MINUTE...
HE HAS SO MANY FRIENDS. ALL THE KIDS WANT TO PLAY WITH HIM AT RECESS.
YES, HE HAS A NEW BEST FRIEND. HER NAME IS CLARA. HE–
AAAAGH!
SPIN
SPIN
BEST FRIEND?! YOU'VE BEEN A TOTAL PAIN IN THE NECK ALL DAY! YOU GOT MY SHIRT ALL DIRTY, YOU GOT MY SHOE STUCK ON THE ROOF, AND NOW YOU'RE GOING TO GET US IN TROUBLE WITH THE PRINCIPAL!
MAYBE WHEN YOU GET IN TROUBLE, YOU'LL HAVE TO BE A KINDERGARTEN HELPER AGAIN. AND THEN YOU CAN PLAY WITH ME!
I WOULDN'T PLAY WITH YOU IF YOU WERE THE LAST KID ON EARTH.

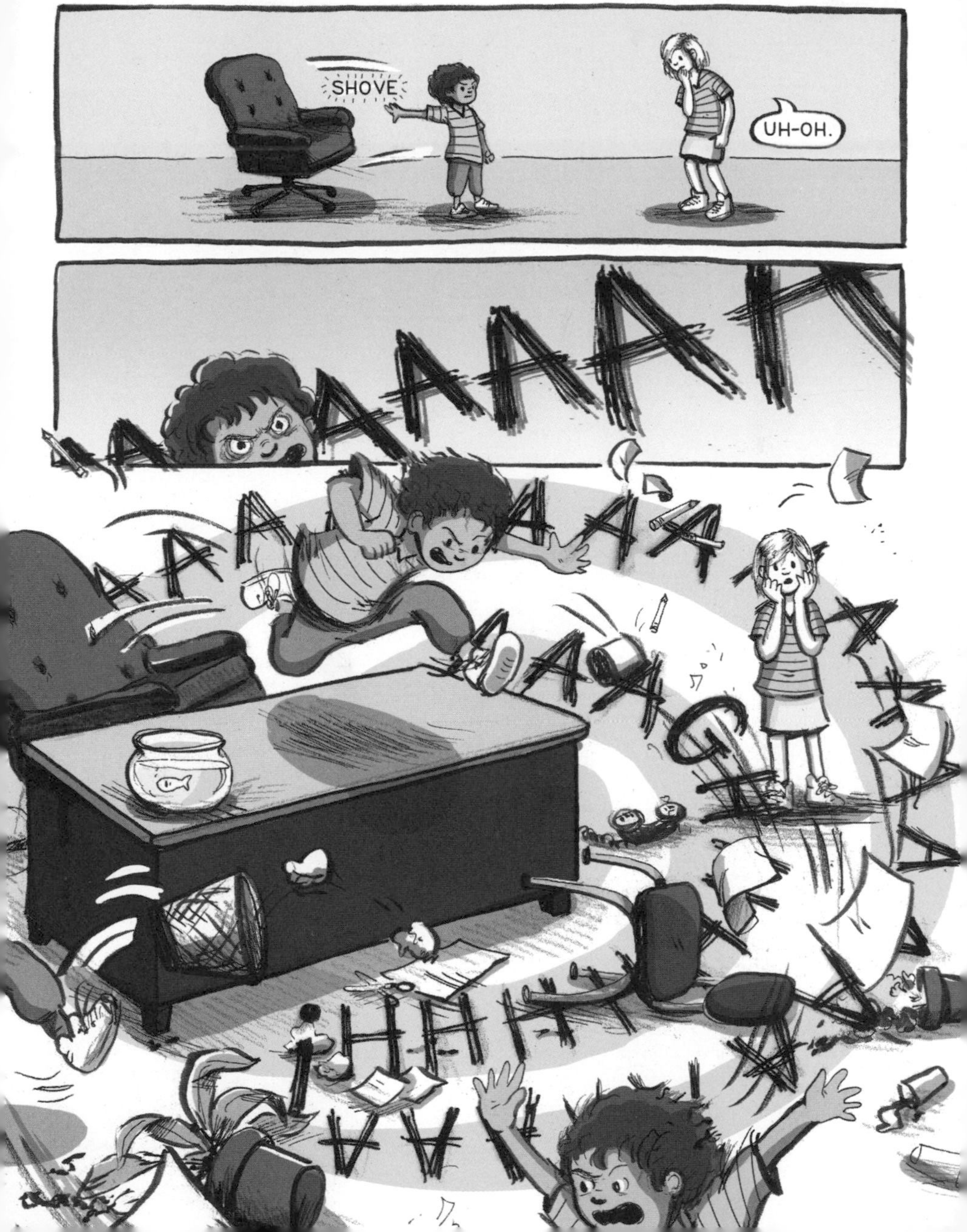
SHOVE
UH-OH.

MITCHELL, STOP!

MITCHELL, STOP!

MITCHELL, STOP!

MITCHELL, PLEASE PUT THE FISH DOWN. HE DIDN'T DO ANYTHING WRONG.

NO!

MITCHELL, BE A GOOD BOY AND PUT THE FISH DOWN.

I'M NOT A GOOD BOY! I'M A BAD BOY!

I'M GOING TO COUNT TO THREE, AND YOU'RE GOING TO PUT THAT GOLDFISH DOWN. ONE...TWO...

HE WAS GOING TO DROP IT. I KNEW IT. I KNEW THAT LOOK IN HIS EYE.

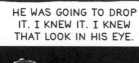

TWO AND THREE-QUARTERS...

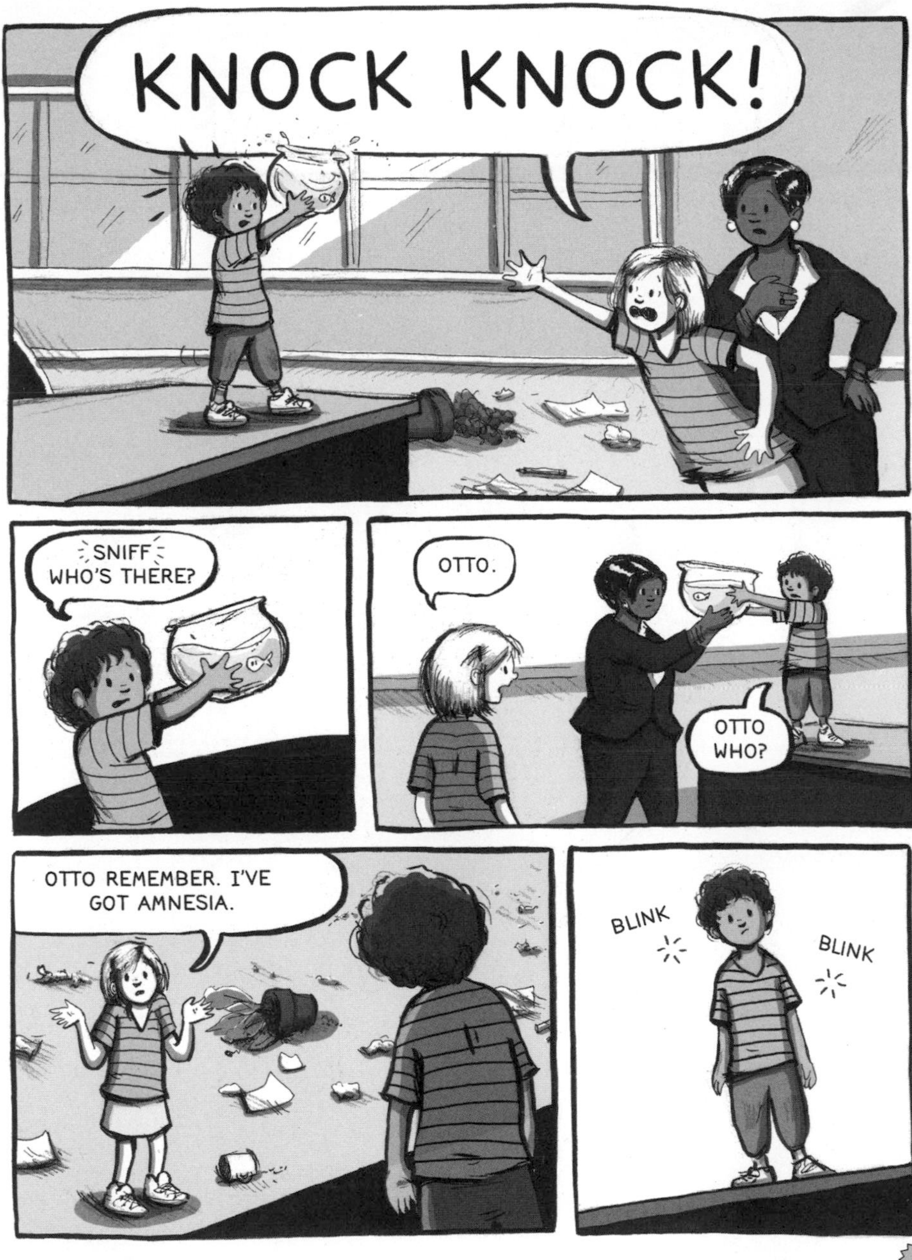
KNOCK KNOCK!
SNIFF WHO'S THERE?
OTTO.
OTTO WHO?
OTTO REMEMBER. I'VE GOT AMNESIA.
BLINK
BLINK

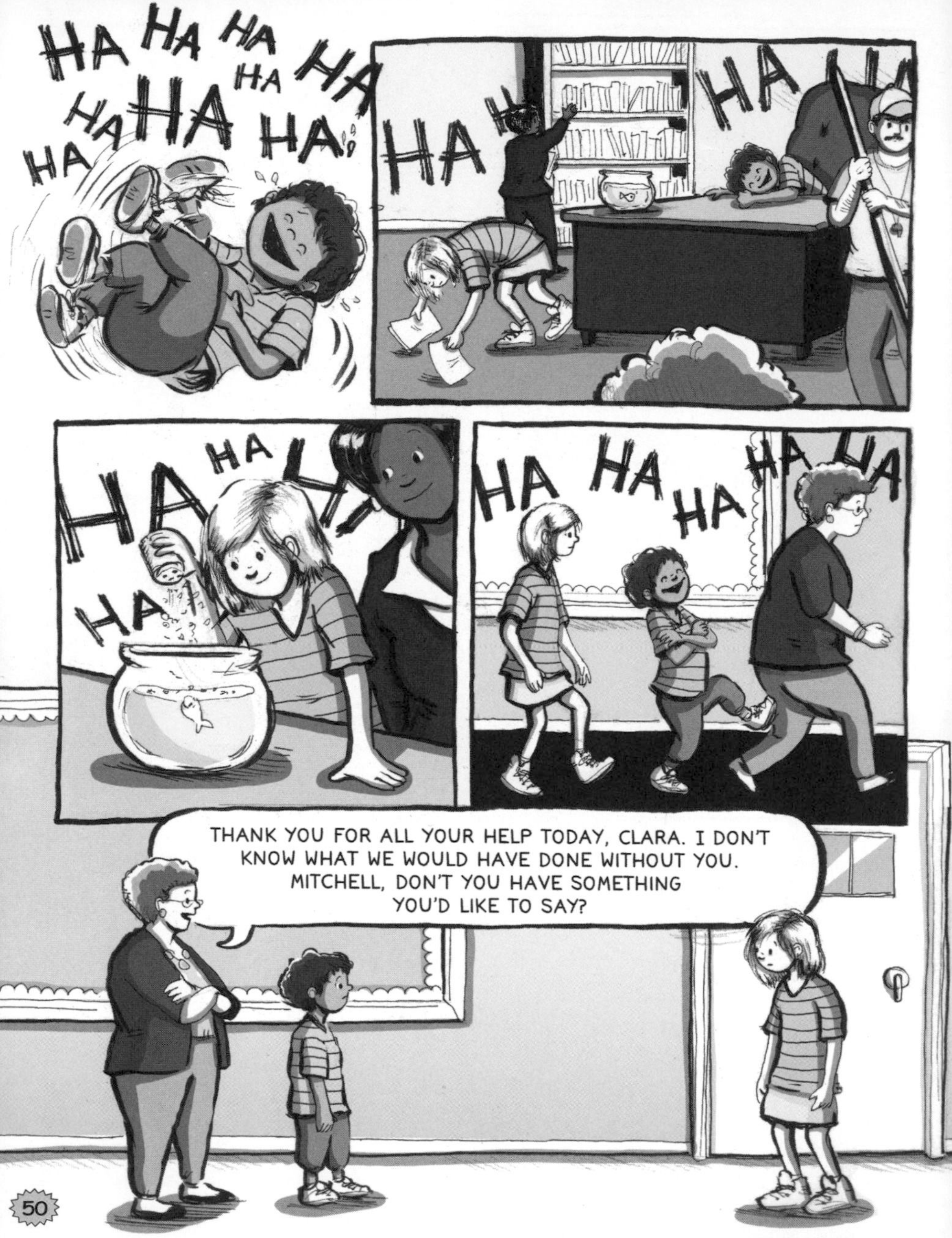
HA HA HA HA HA HA HA HA HA HA
HA HA HA
HA HA HA
HA HA HA HA HA HA
THANK YOU FOR ALL YOUR HELP TODAY, CLARA. I DON'T KNOW WHAT WE WOULD HAVE DONE WITHOUT YOU. MITCHELL, DON'T YOU HAVE SOMETHING YOU'D LIKE TO SAY?

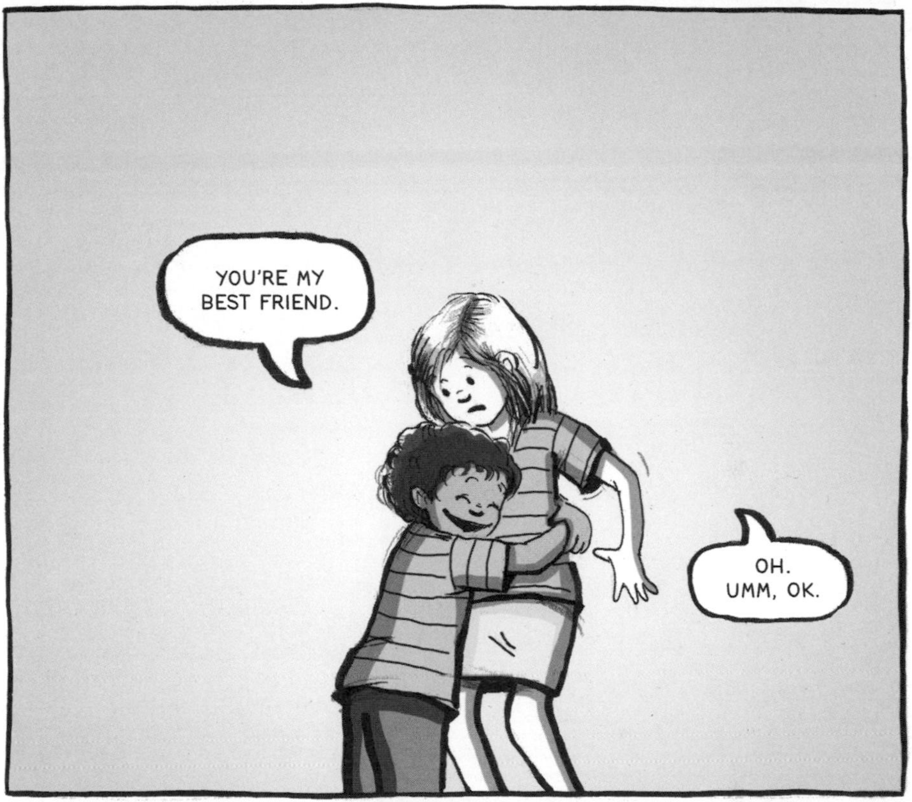
YOU'RE MY BEST FRIEND.
OH. UMM, OK.

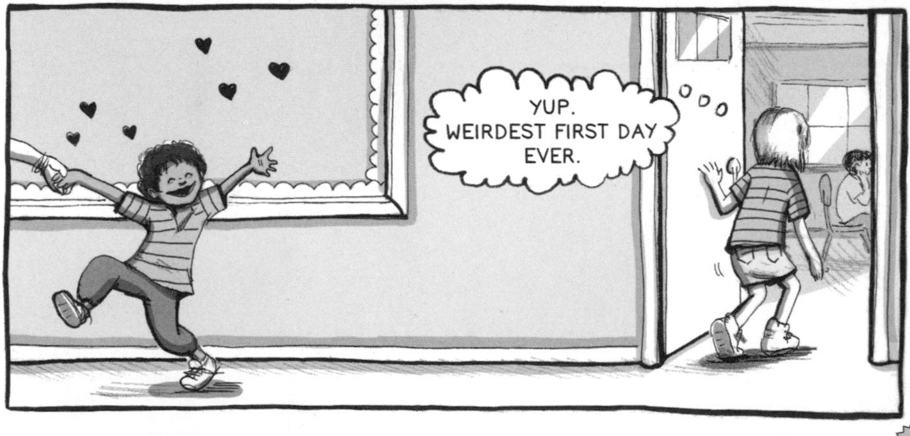
YUP. WEIRDEST FIRST DAY EVER.

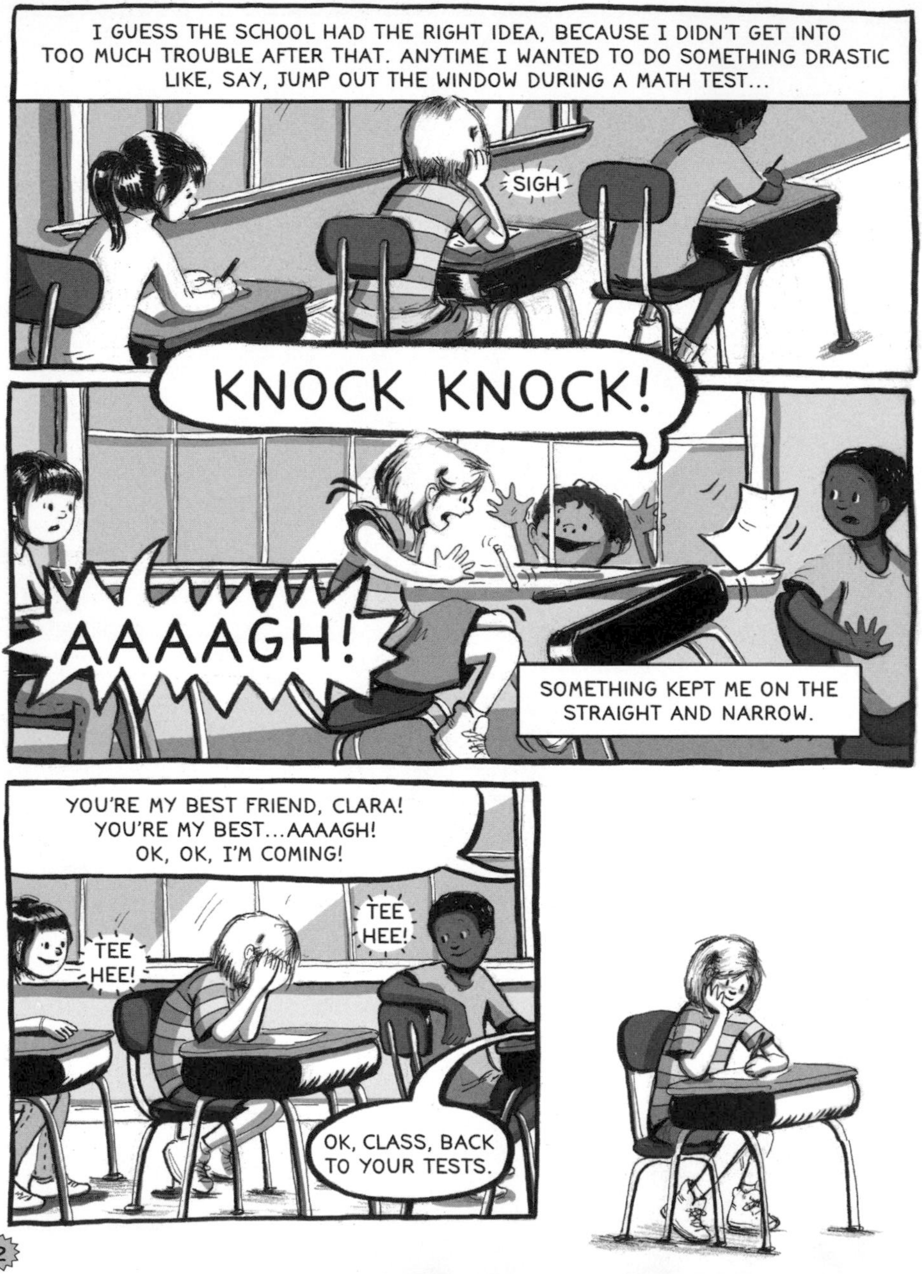
I GUESS THE SCHOOL HAD THE RIGHT IDEA, BECAUSE I DIDN'T GET INTO TOO MUCH TROUBLE AFTER THAT. ANYTIME I WANTED TO DO SOMETHING DRASTIC LIKE, SAY, JUMP OUT THE WINDOW DURING A MATH TEST...
SIGH
KNOCK KNOCK!
AAAAGH!
SOMETHING KEPT ME ON THE STRAIGHT AND NARROW.
YOU'RE MY BEST FRIEND, CLARA! YOU'RE MY BEST...AAAAGH! OK, OK, I'M COMING!
TEE HEE!
TEE HEE!
OK, CLASS, BACK TO YOUR TESTS.

THE END

MILO'S JOURNEY

BY BEN HATKE

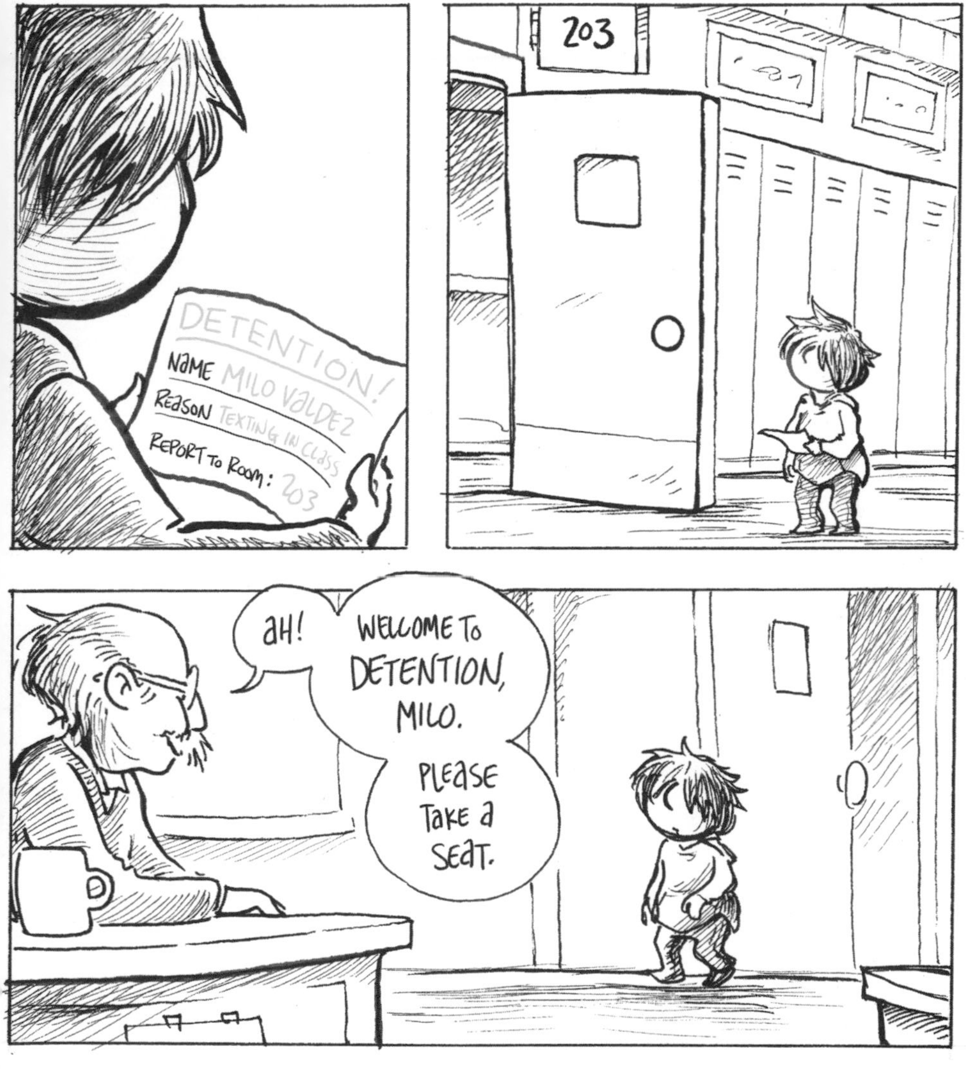
DETENTION!
NAME MILO VALDEZ
REASON TEXTING IN CLASS
REPORT TO ROOM: 203
203
AH!
WELCOME TO DETENTION, MILO.
PLEASE TAKE A SEAT.

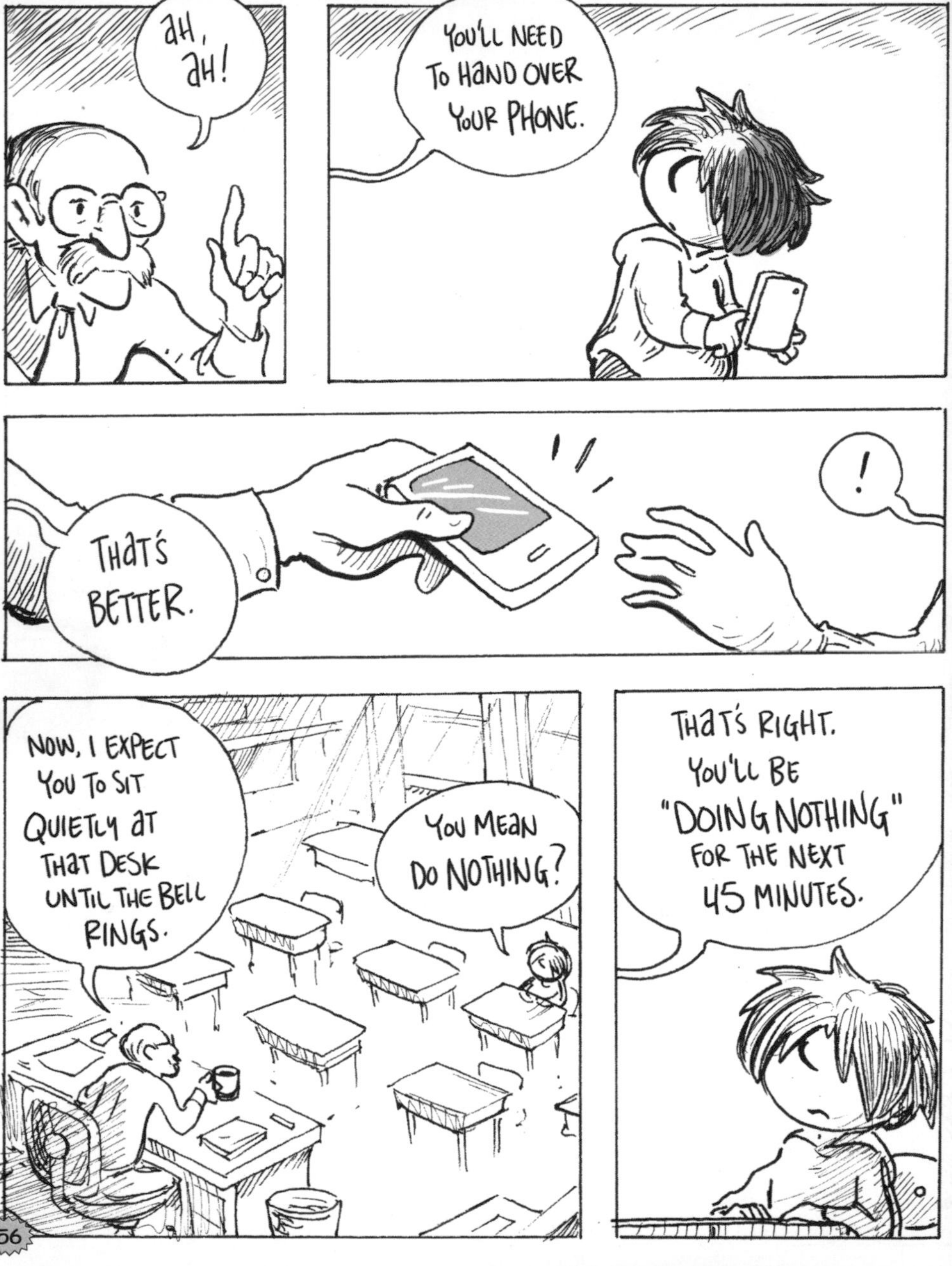
AH, AH!
YOU'LL NEED TO HAND OVER YOUR PHONE.
THAT'S BETTER.
!
NOW, I EXPECT YOU TO SIT QUIETLY AT THAT DESK UNTIL THE BELL RINGS.
YOU MEAN DO NOTHING?
THAT'S RIGHT. YOU'LL BE "DOING NOTHING" FOR THE NEXT 45 MINUTES.

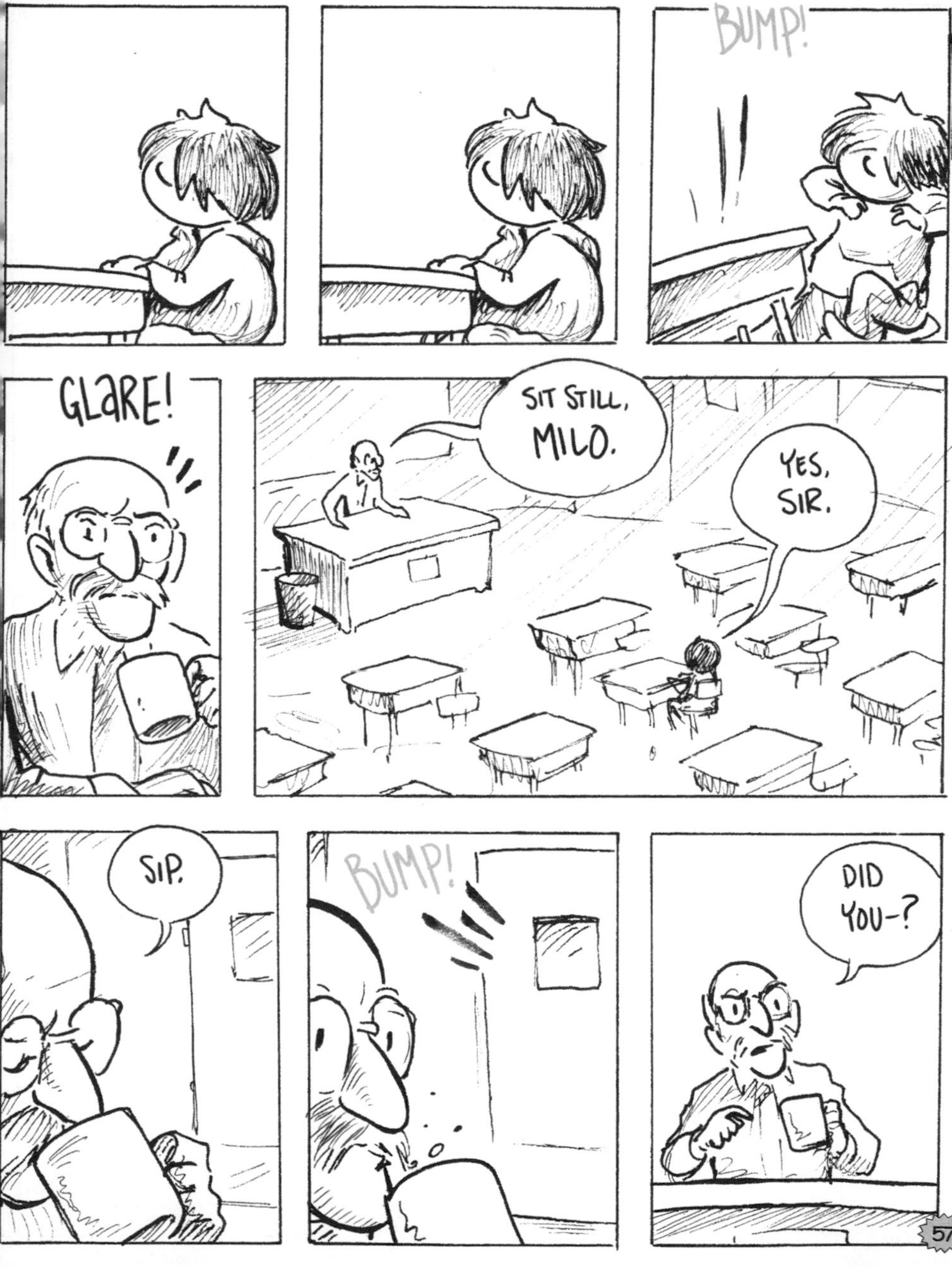

BUMP!
GLARE!
SIT STILL, MILO.
YES, SIR.
SIP.
BUMP!
DID YOU-?

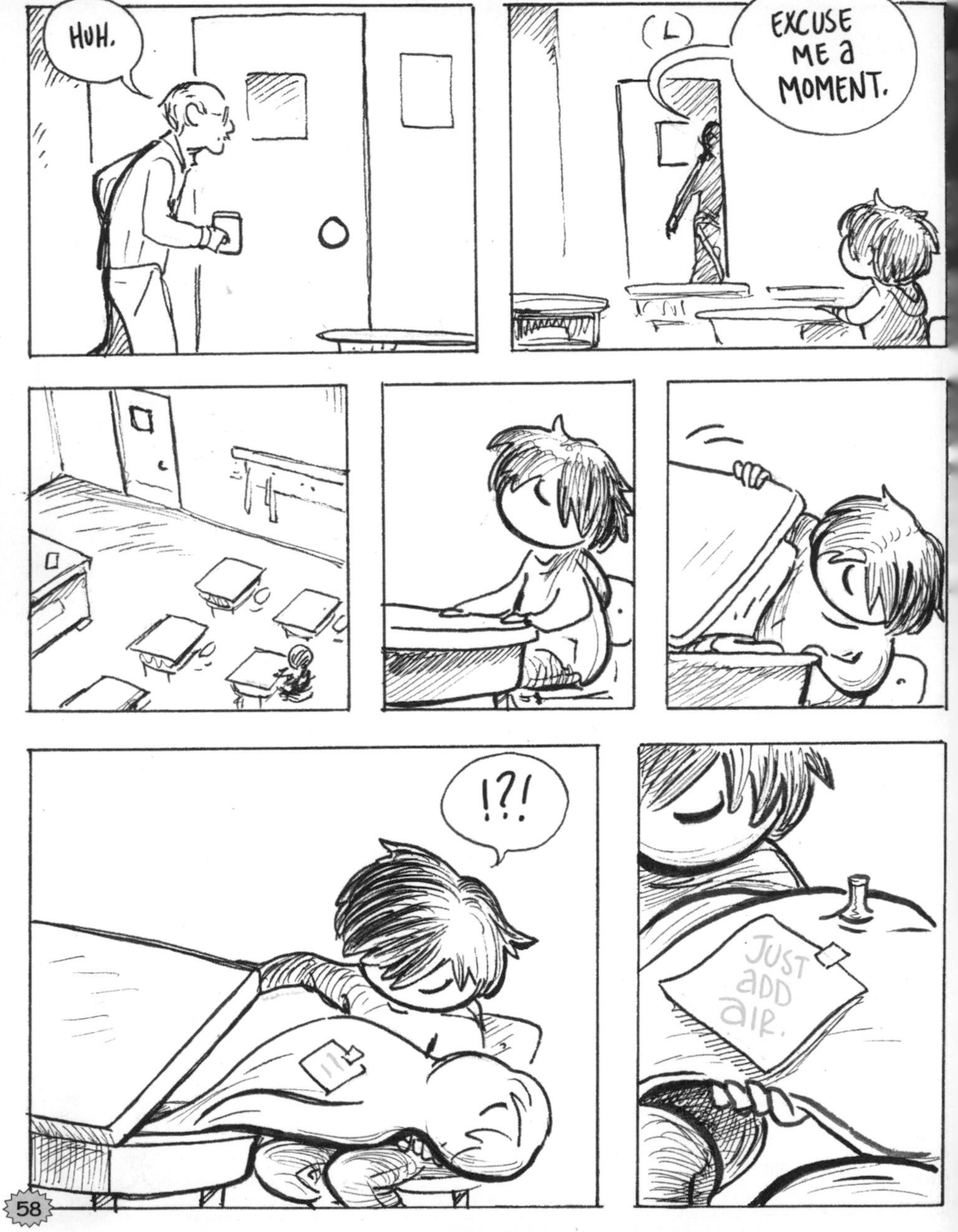
HUH.
EXCUSE ME a MOMENT.
!?!
JUST add air.

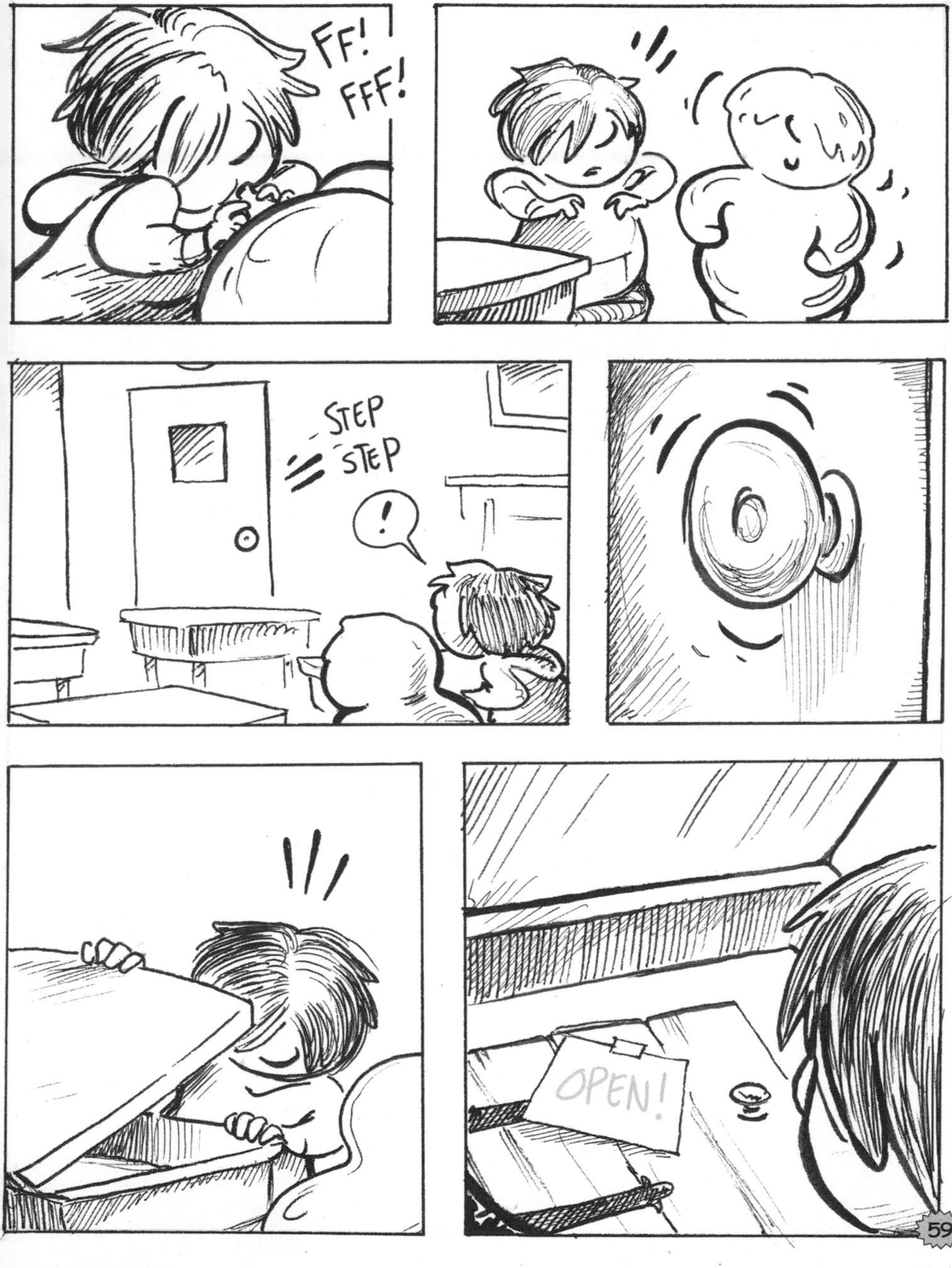
FF!
FFF!
STEP
STEP
!
OPEN!

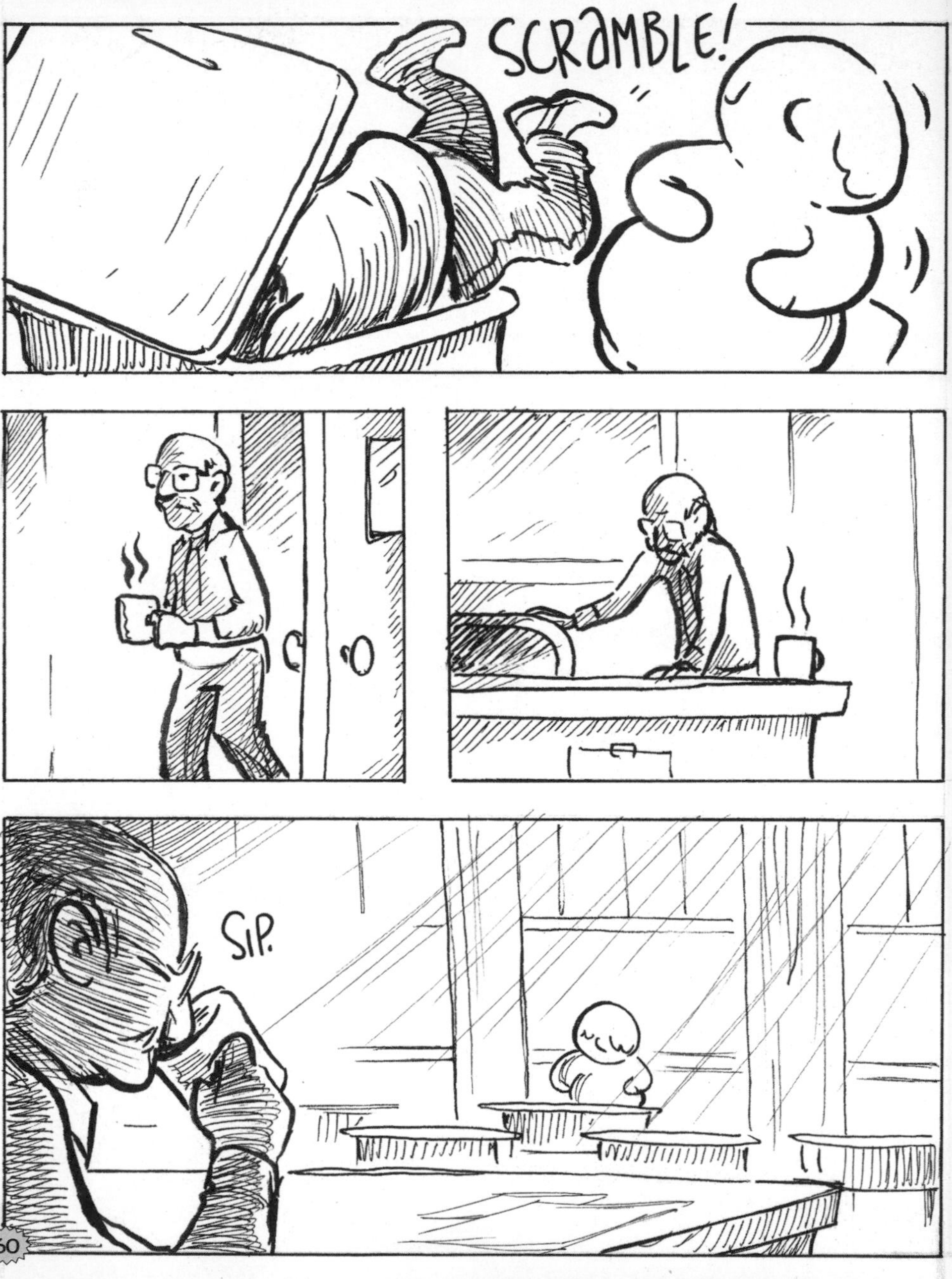
SCRAMBLE!
SIP.

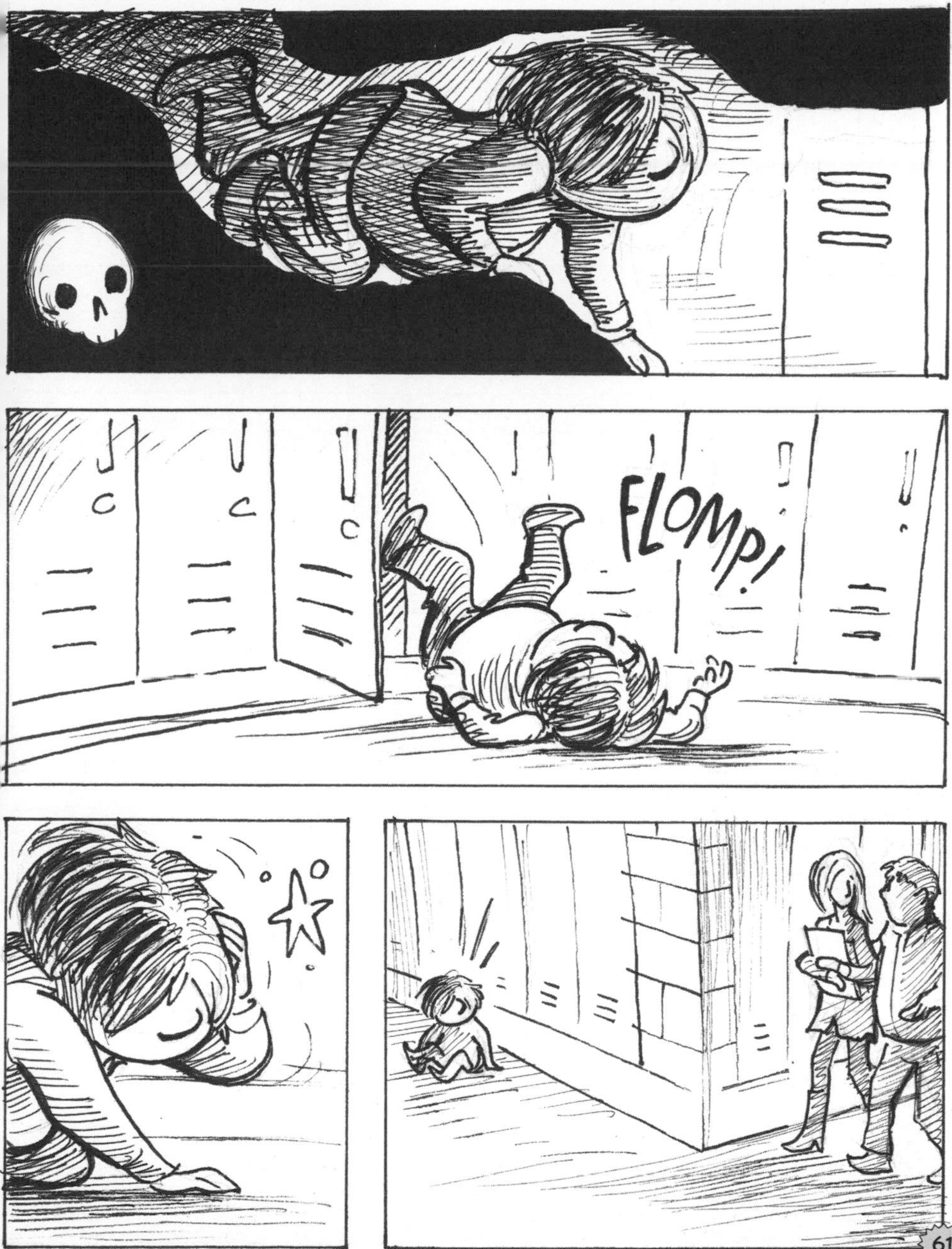
FLOMP!

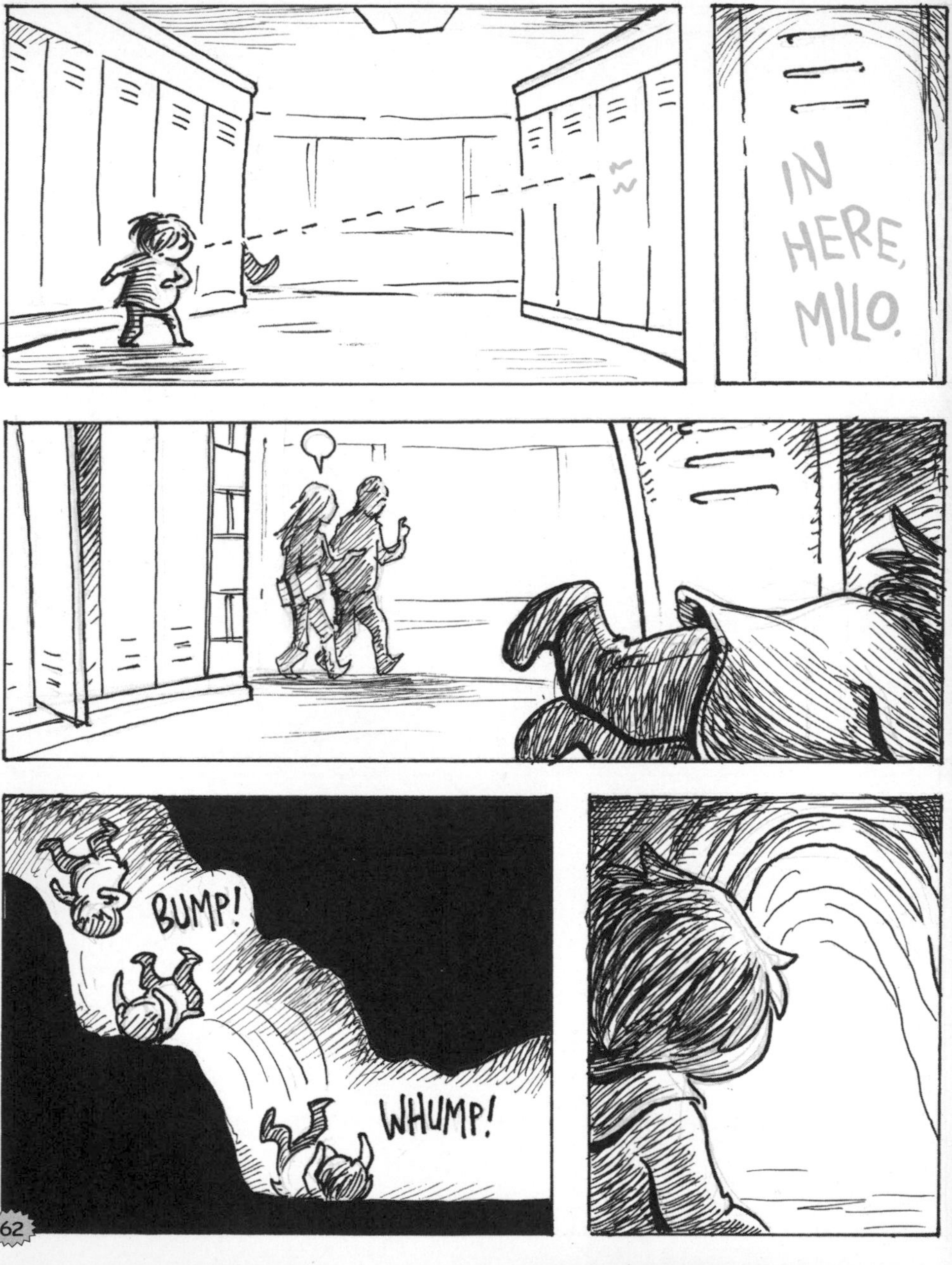
IN HERE, MILO.
BUMP!
WHUMP!

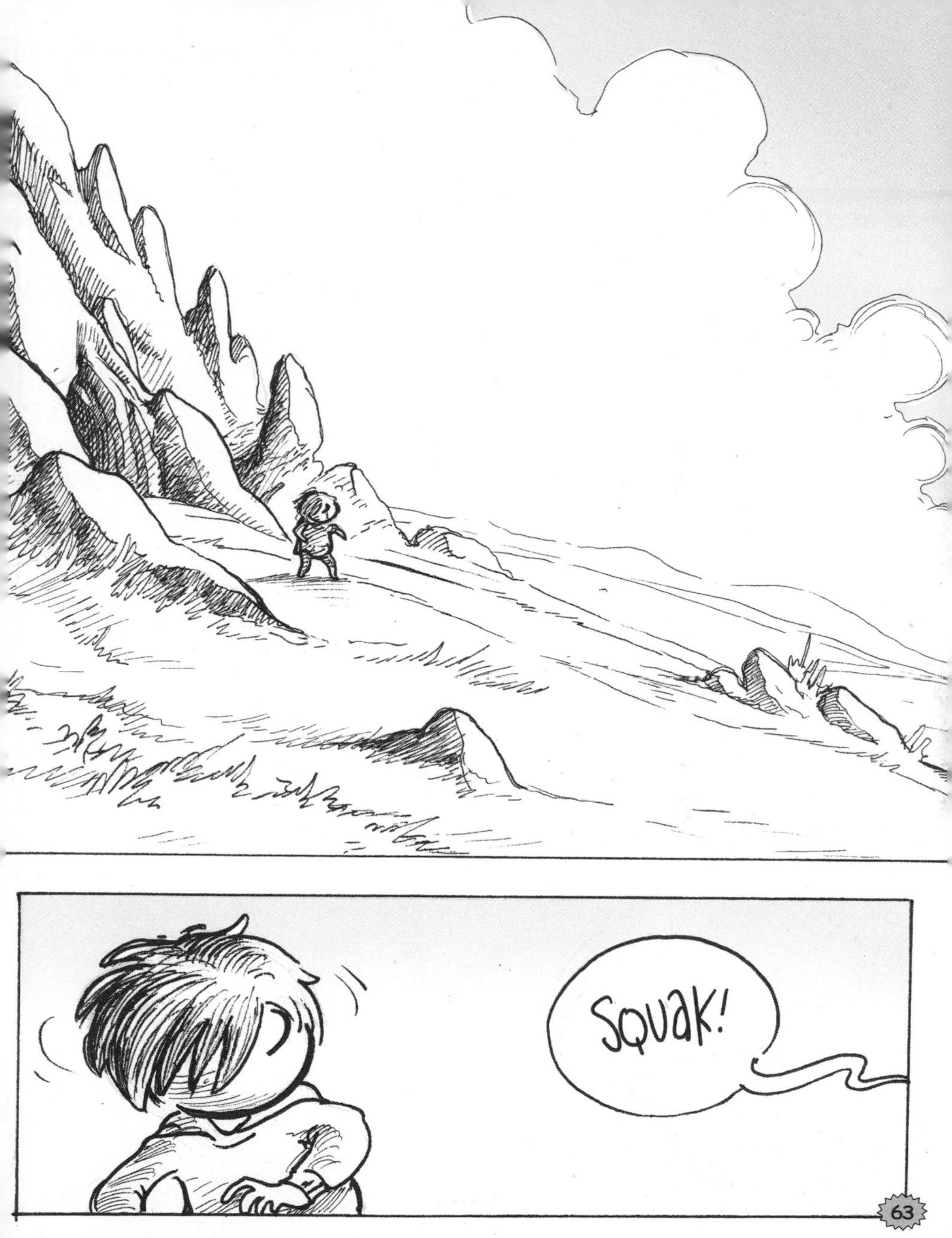
SQUAK!

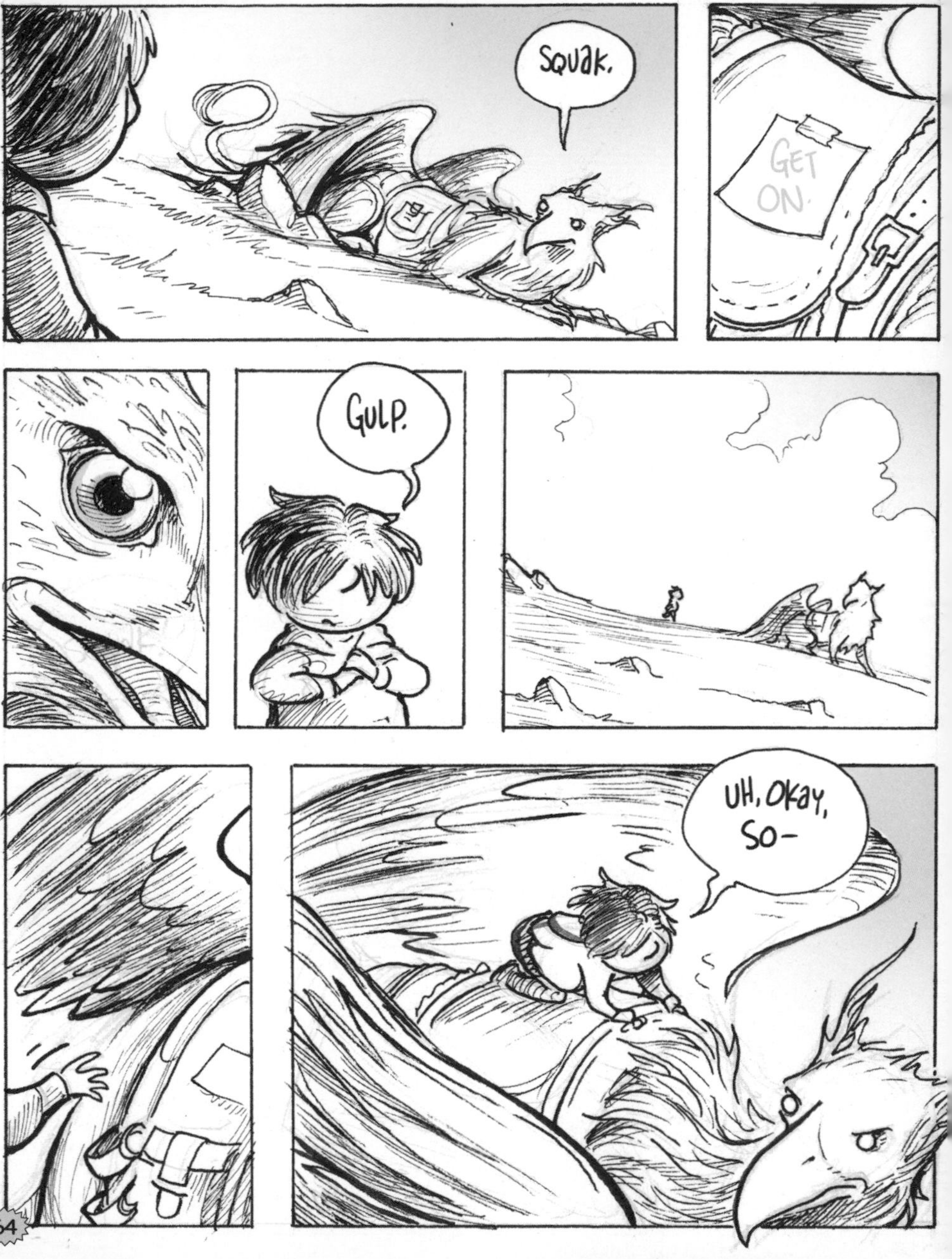
SQUAK.
GET ON.
GULP.
UH, OKAY, SO-

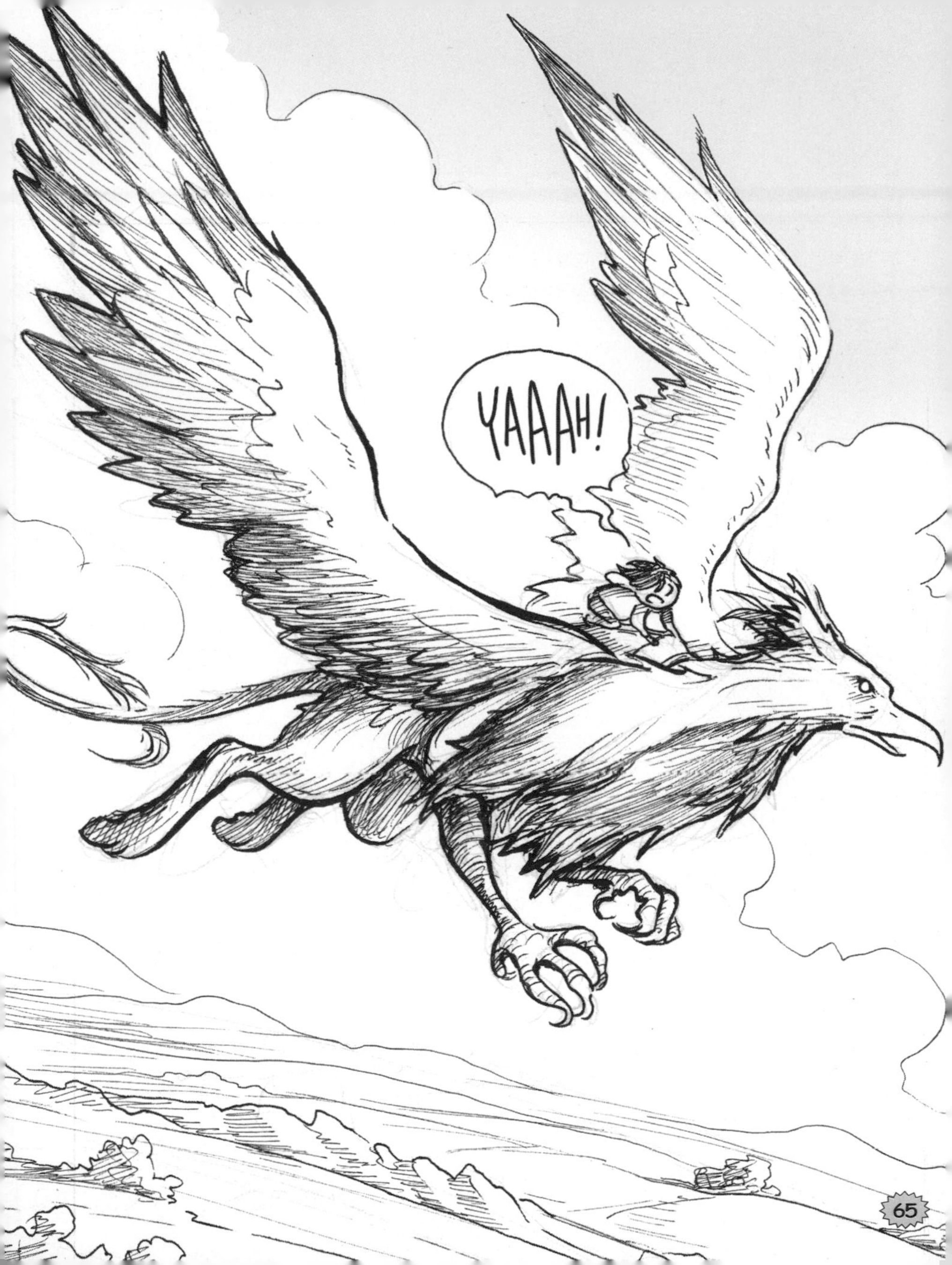
YAAAH!

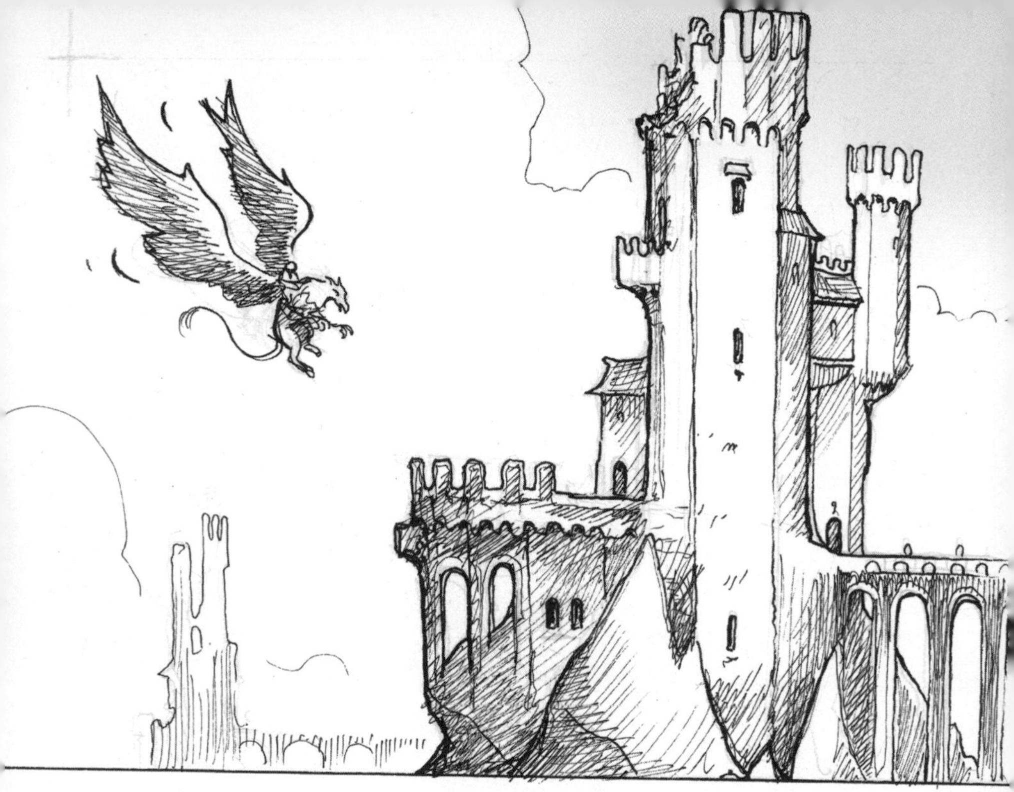

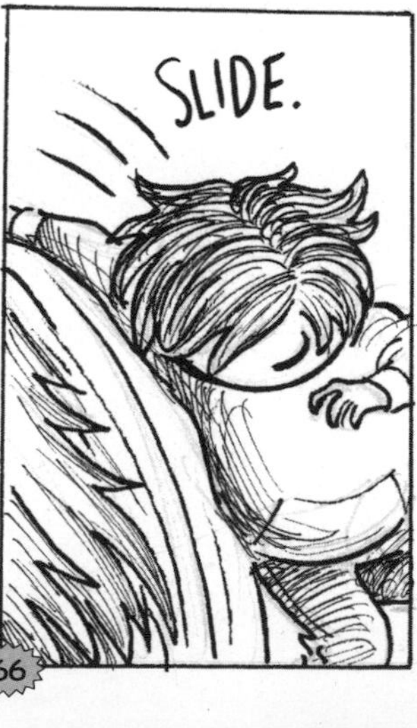
SLIDE.

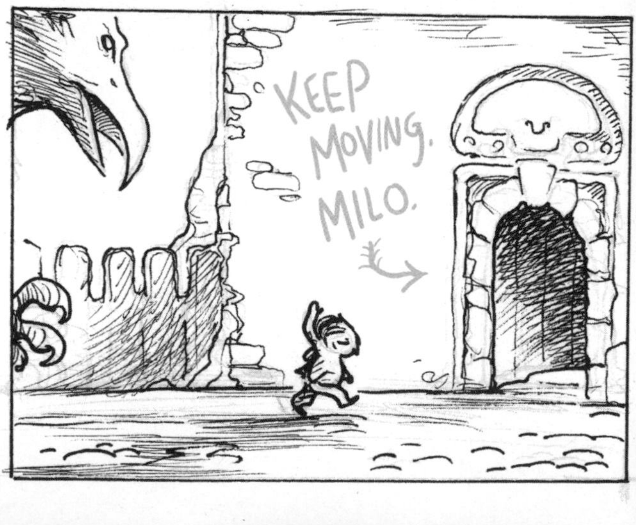
KEEP MOVING. MILO.

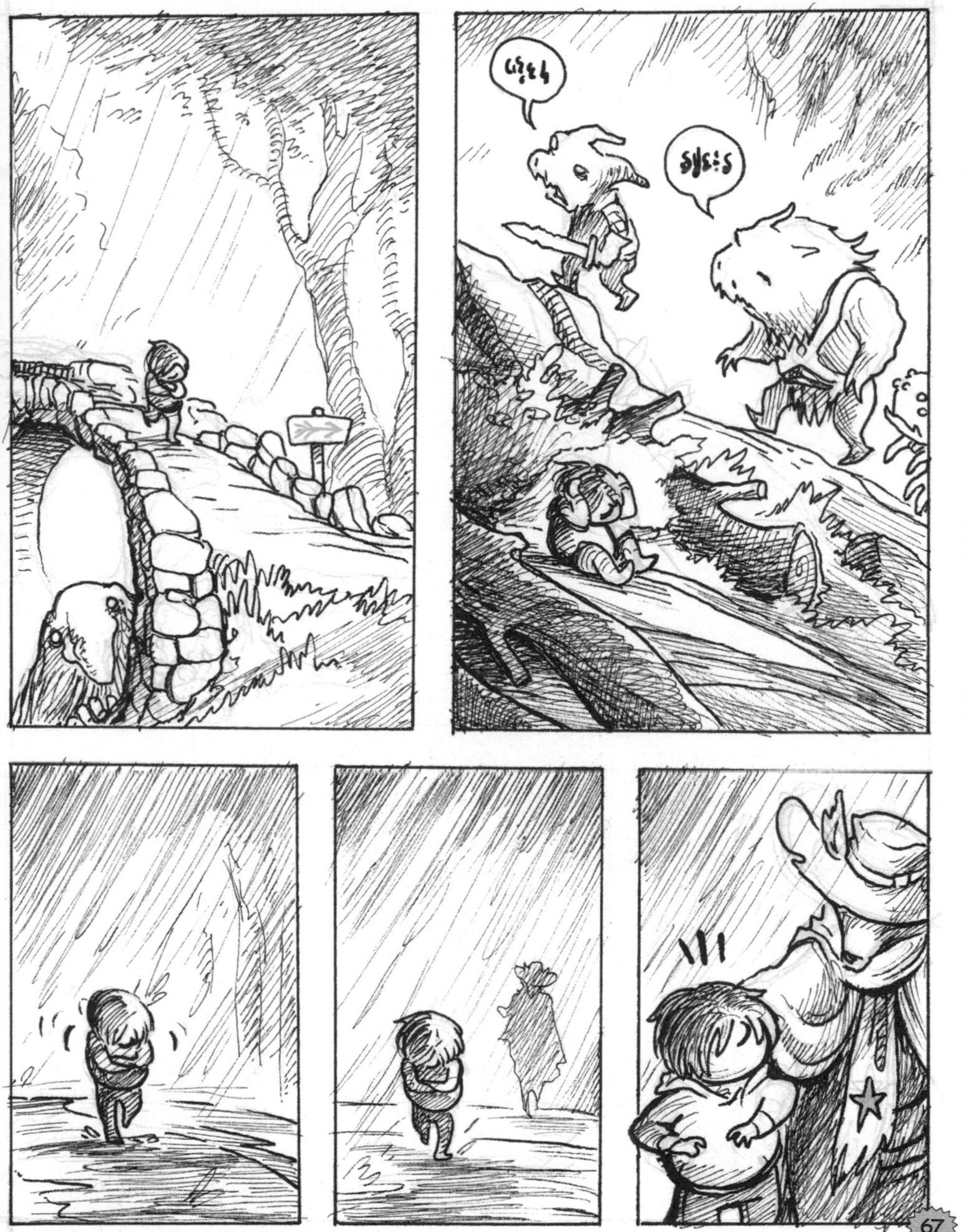

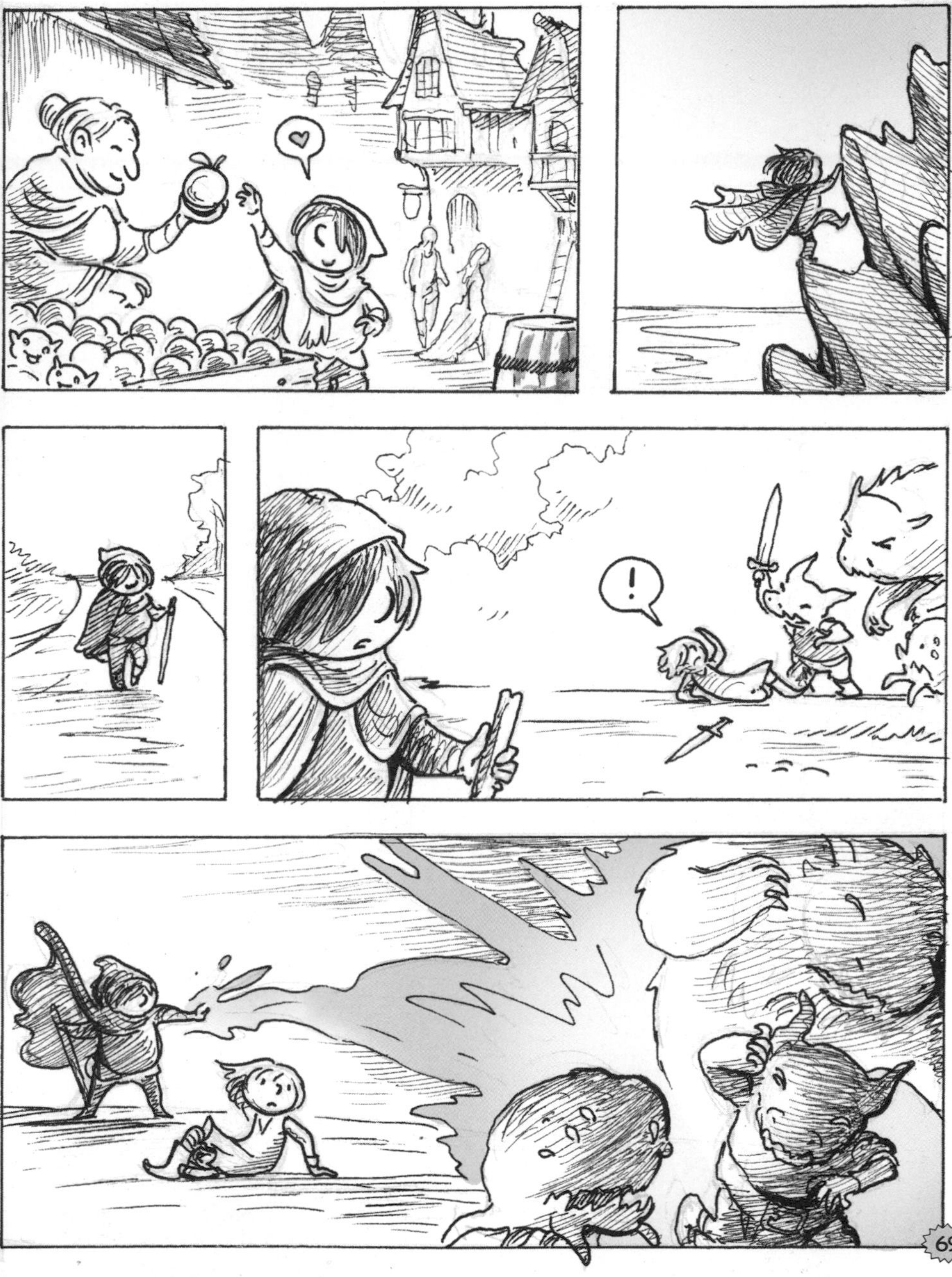
!

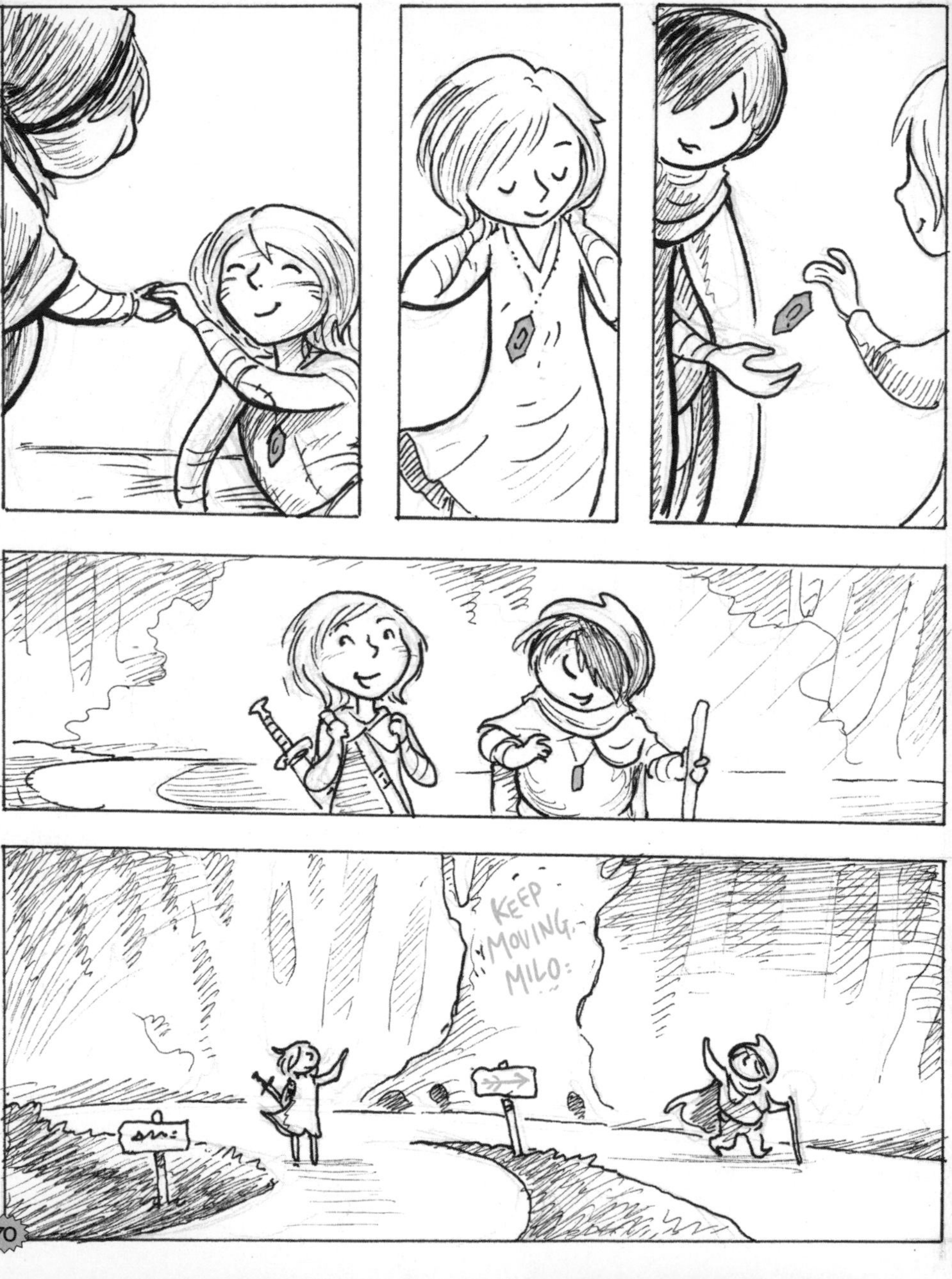
KEEP MOVING, MILO:

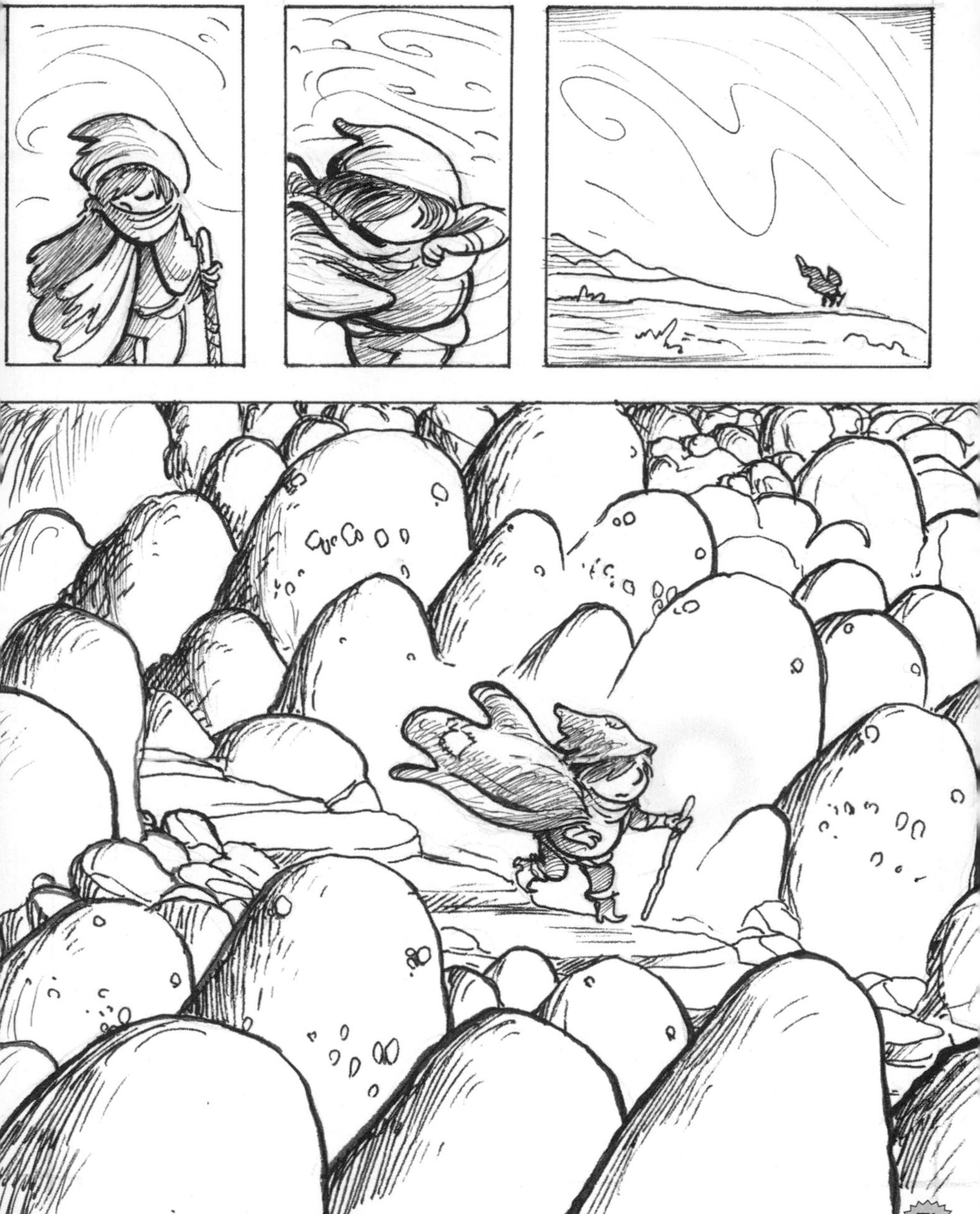

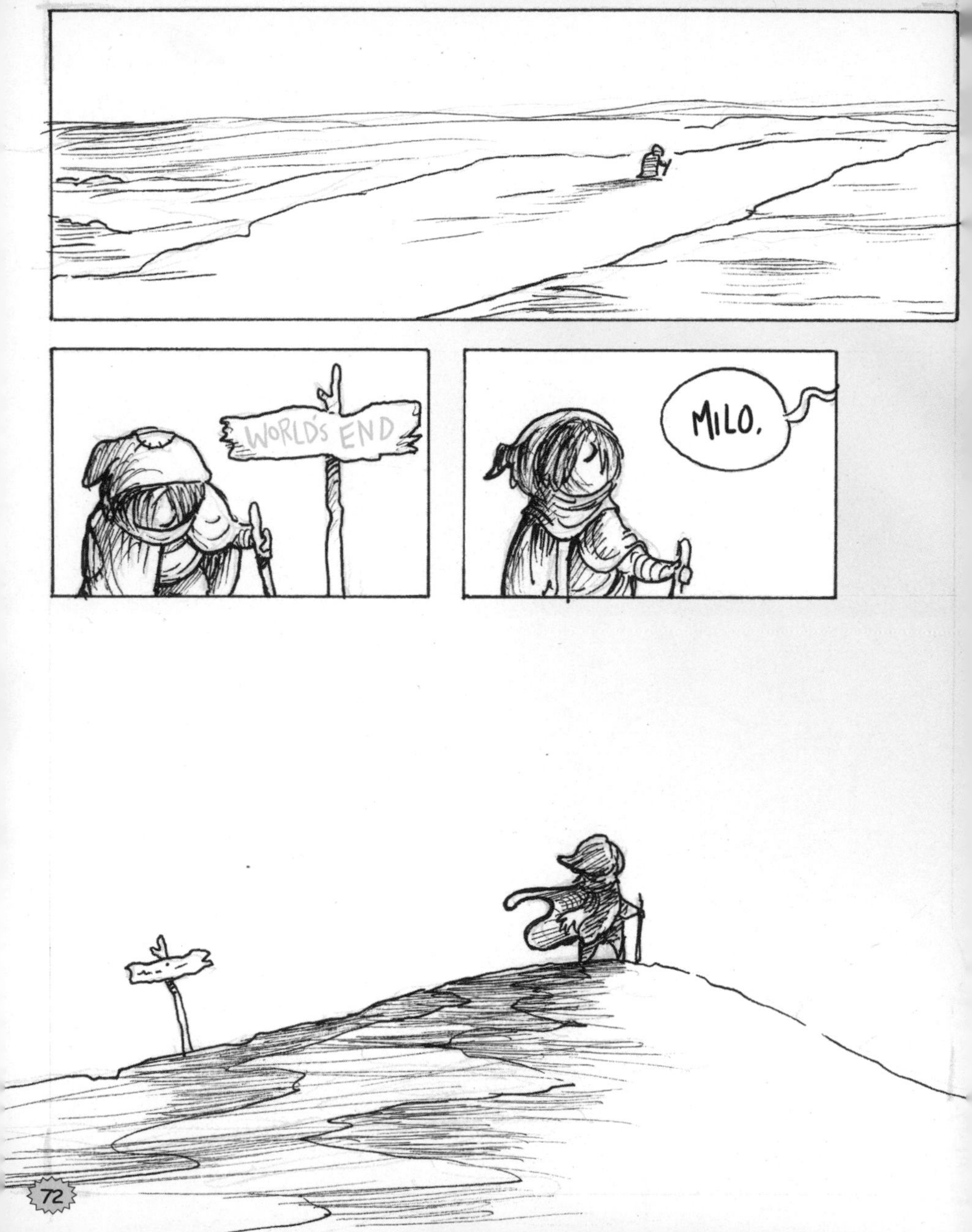
WORLD'S END
MILO.

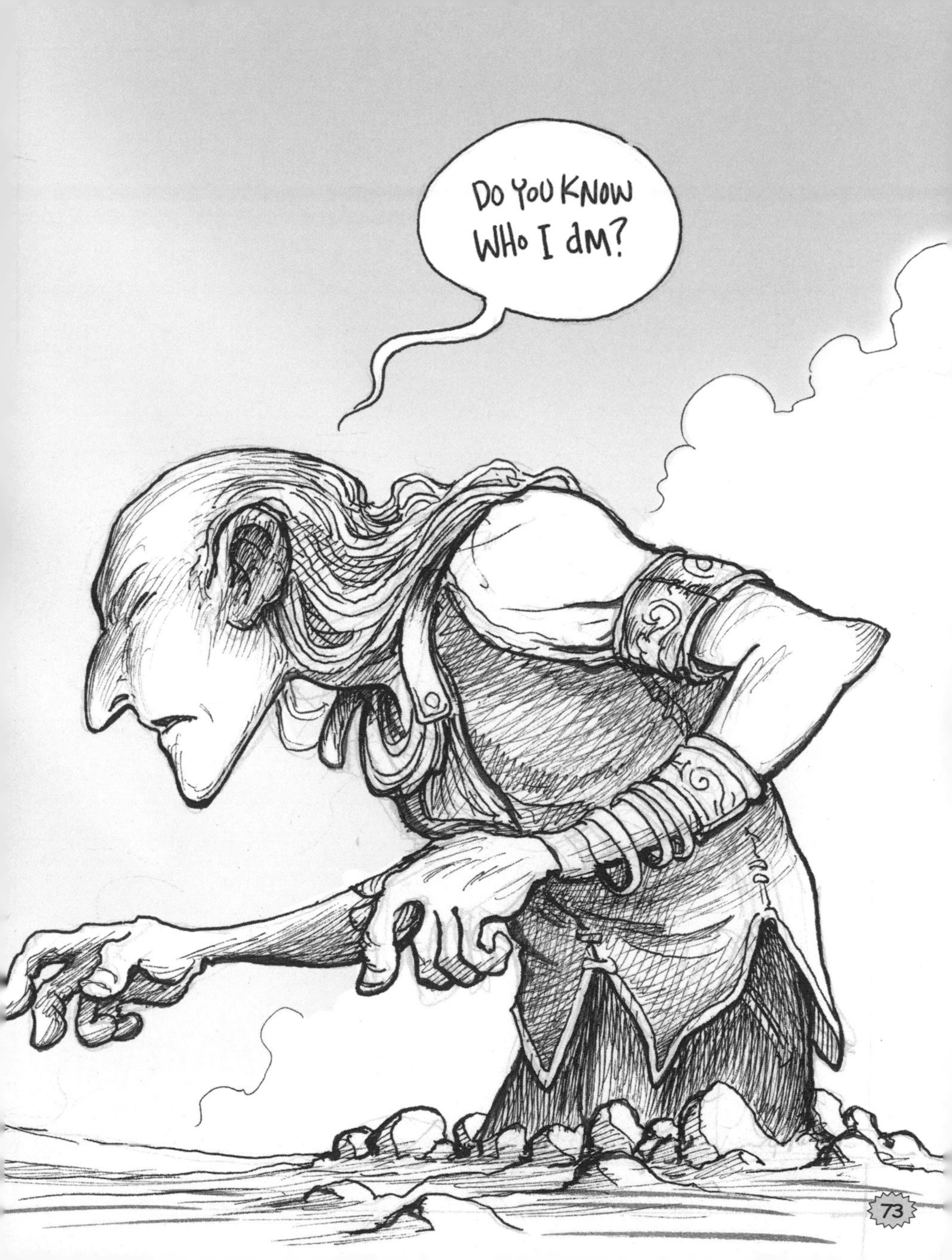
DO YOU KNOW WHO I AM?

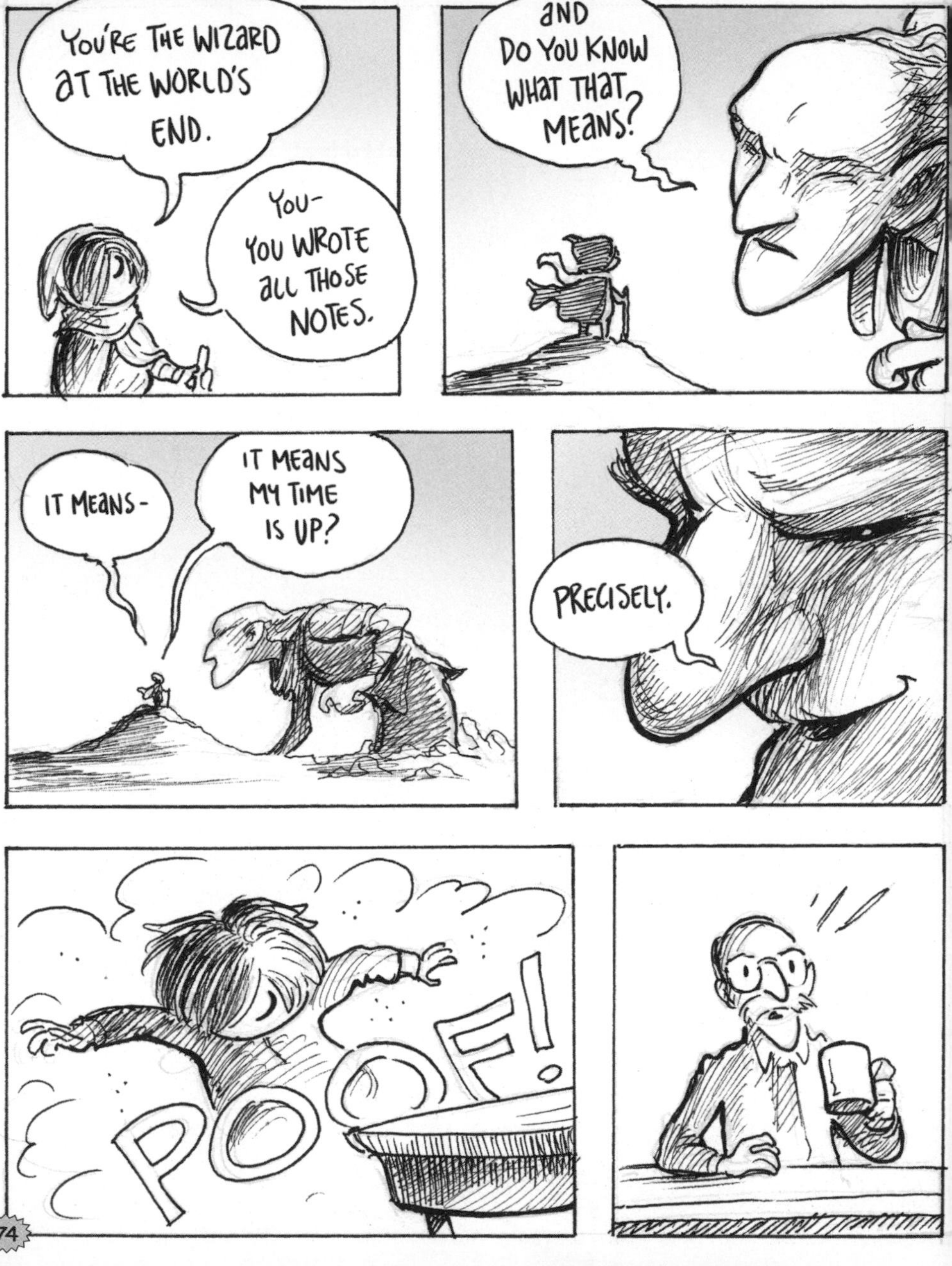
YOU'RE THE WIZARD AT THE WORLD'S END.
YOU- YOU WROTE ALL THOSE NOTES.
AND DO YOU KNOW WHAT THAT MEANS?
IT MEANS-
IT MEANS MY TIME IS UP?
PRECISELY.
POOF!

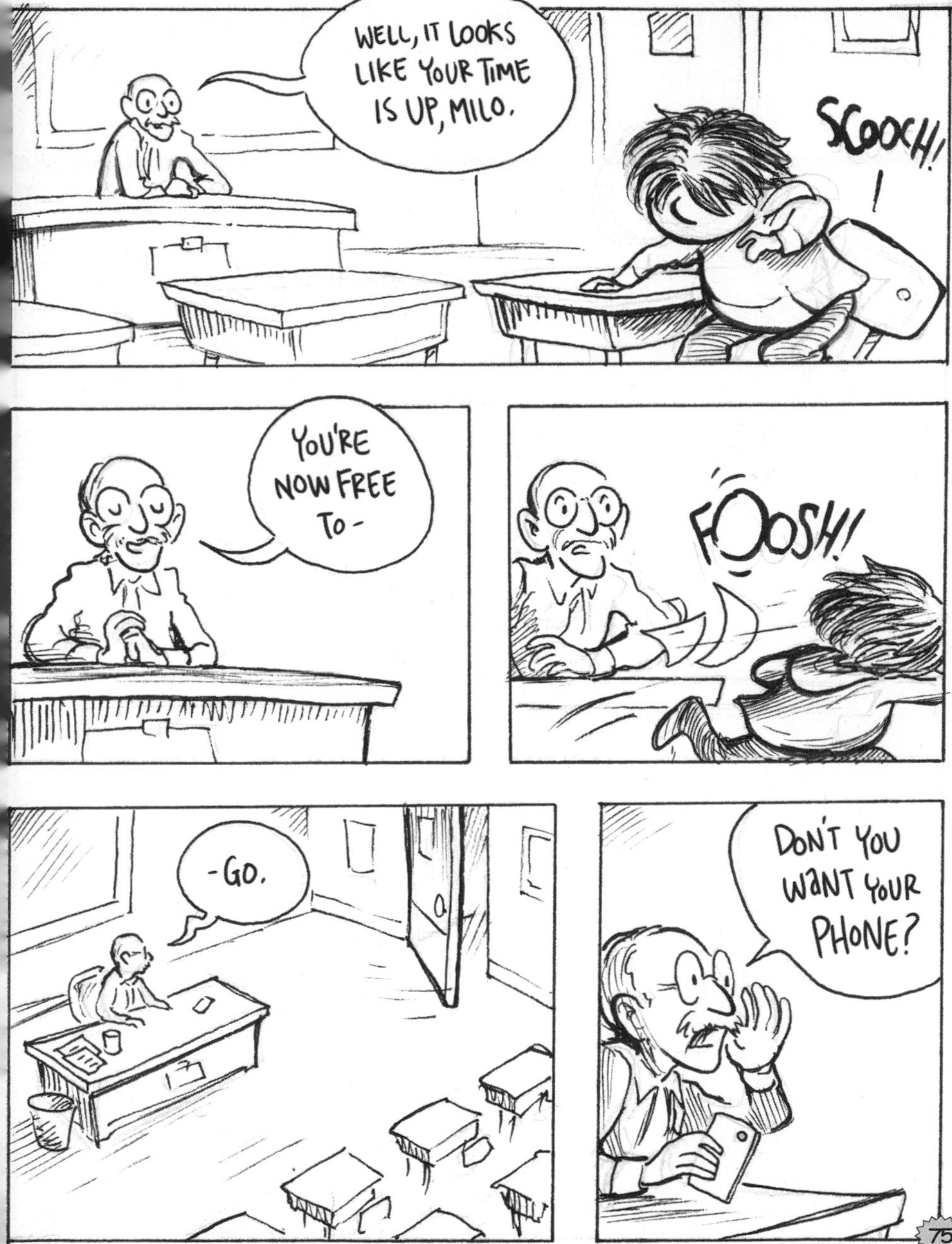
WELL, IT LOOKS LIKE YOUR TIME IS UP, MILO.
SCOOCH!
YOU'RE NOW FREE TO-
FOOSH!
-GO.
DON'T YOU WANT YOUR PHONE?

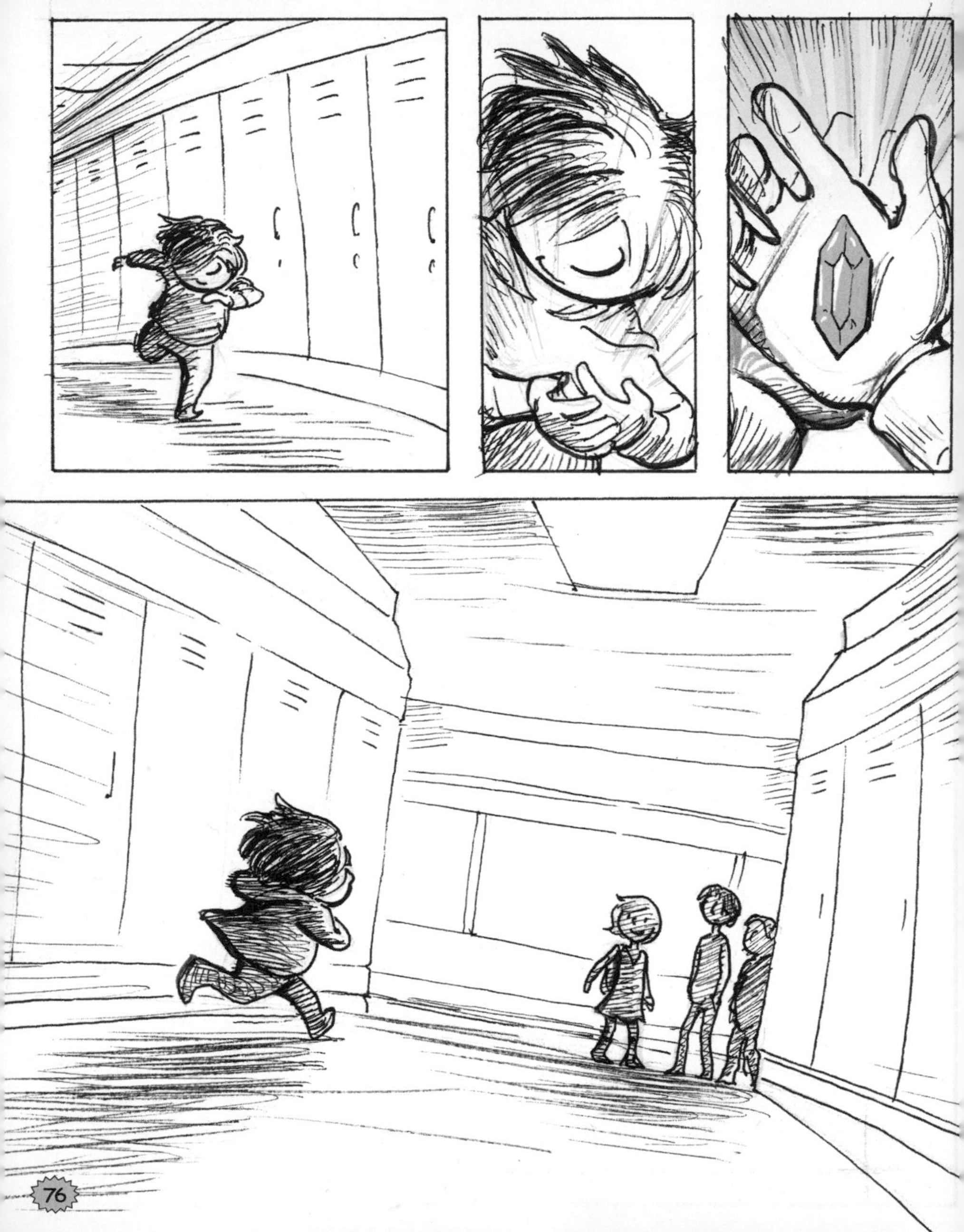

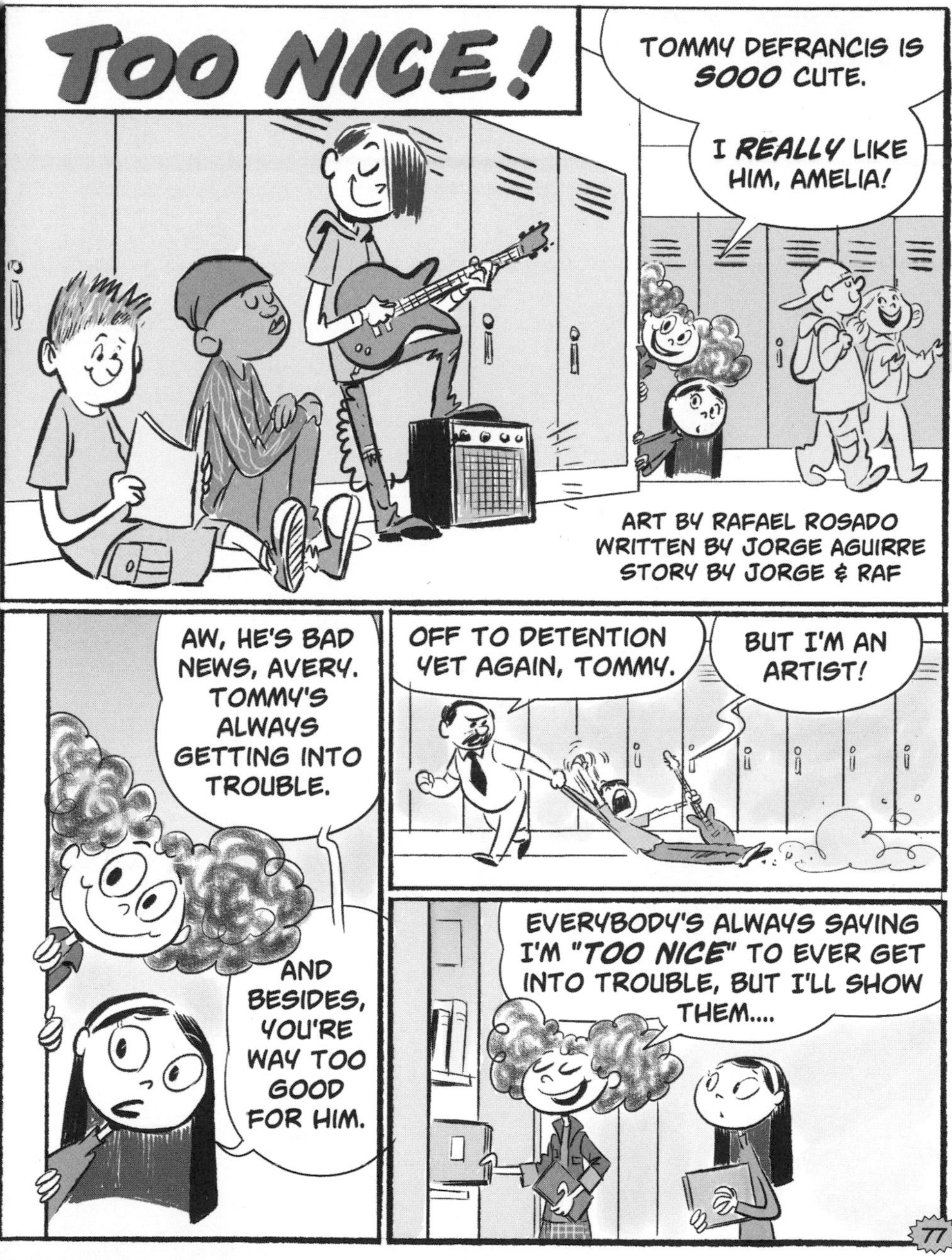
TOO NICE!
TOMMY DEFRANCIS IS SOOO CUTE.
I REALLY LIKE HIM, AMELIA!
ART BY RAFAEL ROSADO
WRITTEN BY JORGE AGUIRRE
STORY BY JORGE & RAF
AW, HE'S BAD NEWS, AVERY. TOMMY'S ALWAYS GETTING INTO TROUBLE.
AND BESIDES, YOU'RE WAY TOO GOOD FOR HIM.
OFF TO DETENTION YET AGAIN, TOMMY.
BUT I'M AN ARTIST!
EVERYBODY'S ALWAYS SAYING I'M "TOO NICE" TO EVER GET INTO TROUBLE, BUT I'LL SHOW THEM....

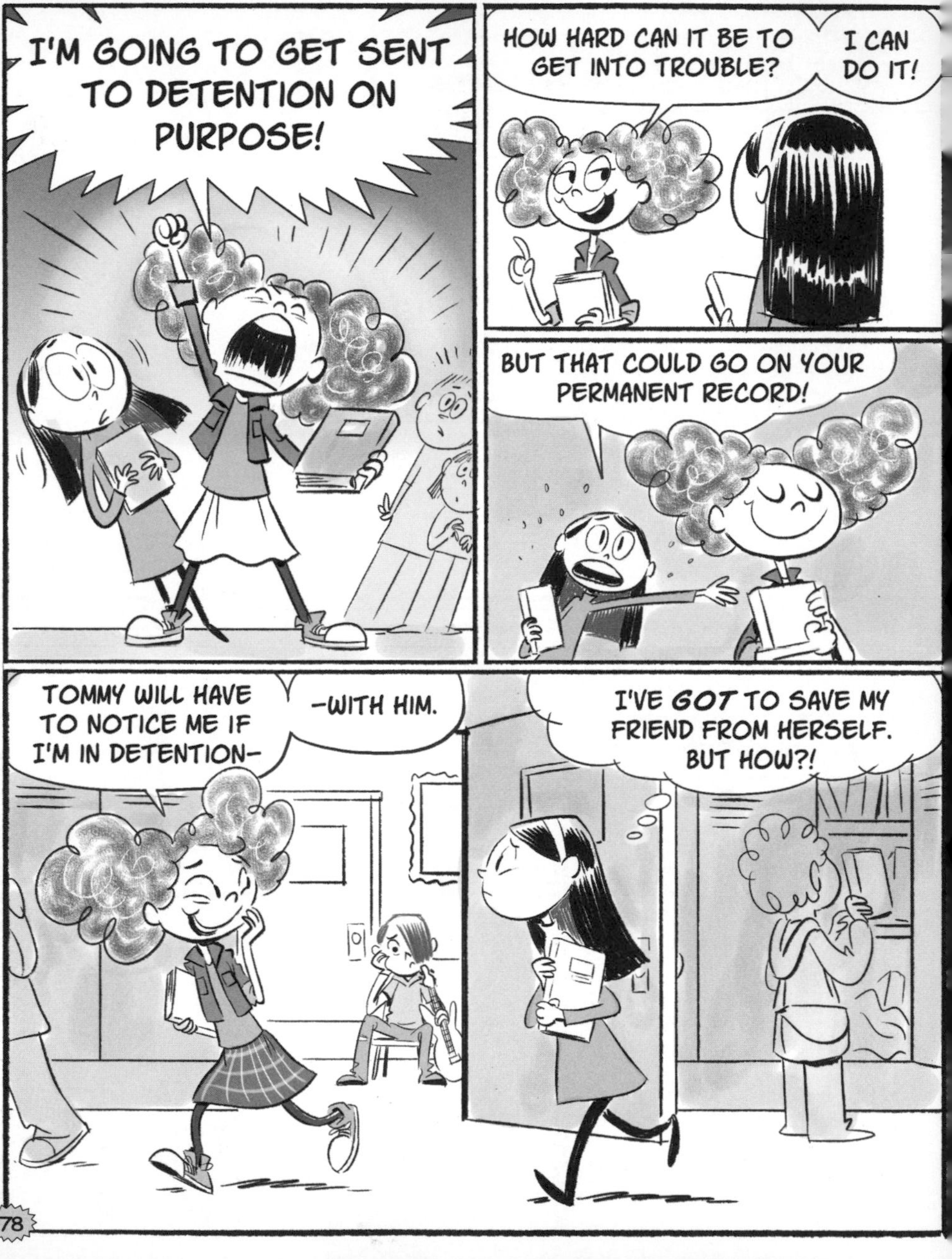
I'M GOING TO GET SENT TO DETENTION ON PURPOSE!
HOW HARD CAN IT BE TO GET INTO TROUBLE?
I CAN DO IT!
BUT THAT COULD GO ON YOUR PERMANENT RECORD!
TOMMY WILL HAVE TO NOTICE ME IF I'M IN DETENTION-
-WITH HIM.
I'VE *GOT* TO SAVE MY FRIEND FROM HERSELF. BUT HOW?!

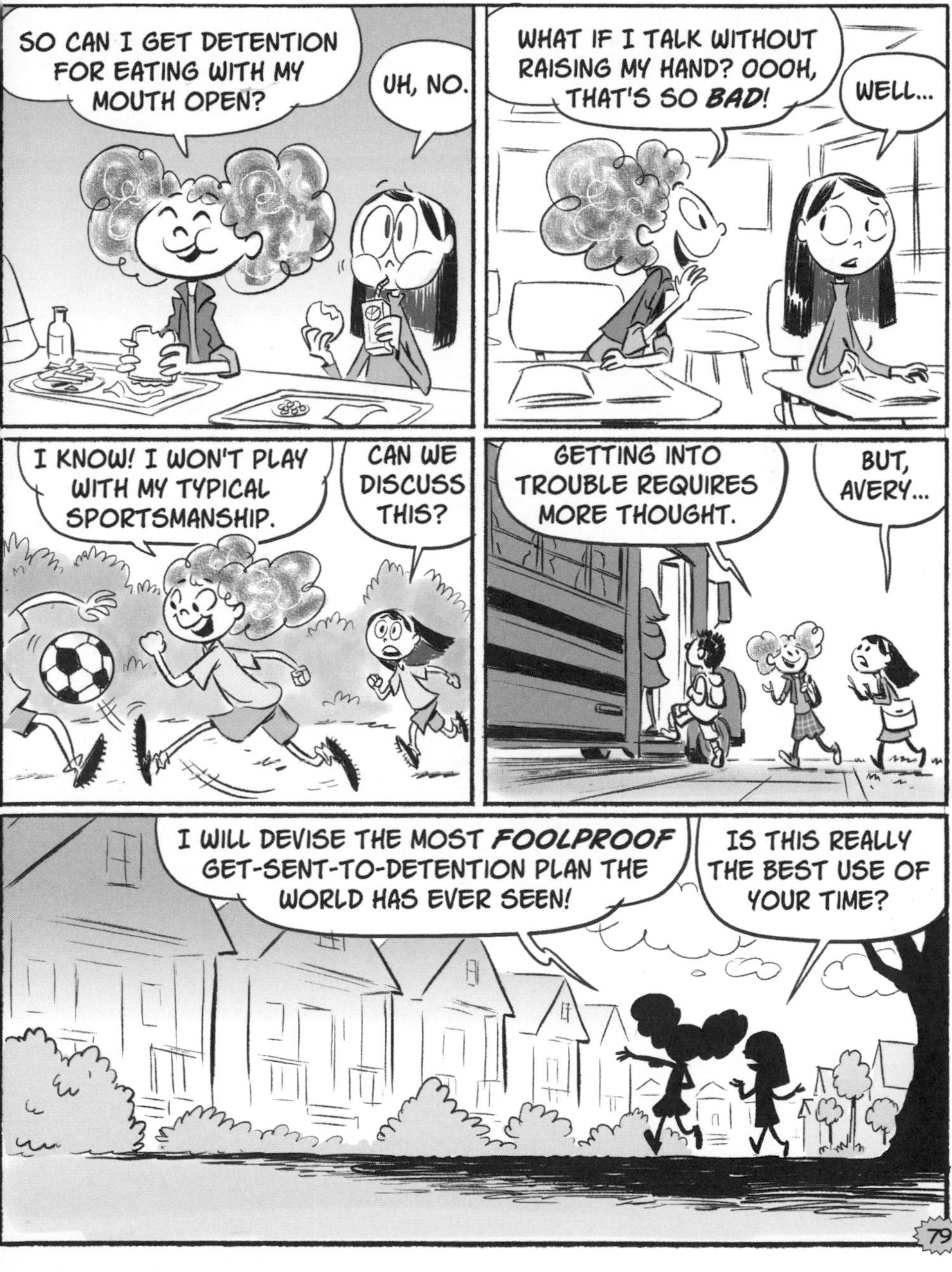
SO CAN I GET DETENTION FOR EATING WITH MY MOUTH OPEN?
UH, NO.
WHAT IF I TALK WITHOUT RAISING MY HAND? OOOH, THAT'S SO *BAD*!
WELL...
I KNOW! I WON'T PLAY WITH MY TYPICAL SPORTSMANSHIP.
CAN WE DISCUSS THIS?
GETTING INTO TROUBLE REQUIRES MORE THOUGHT.
BUT, AVERY...
I WILL DEVISE THE MOST *FOOLPROOF* GET-SENT-TO-DETENTION PLAN THE WORLD HAS EVER SEEN!
IS THIS REALLY THE BEST USE OF YOUR TIME?

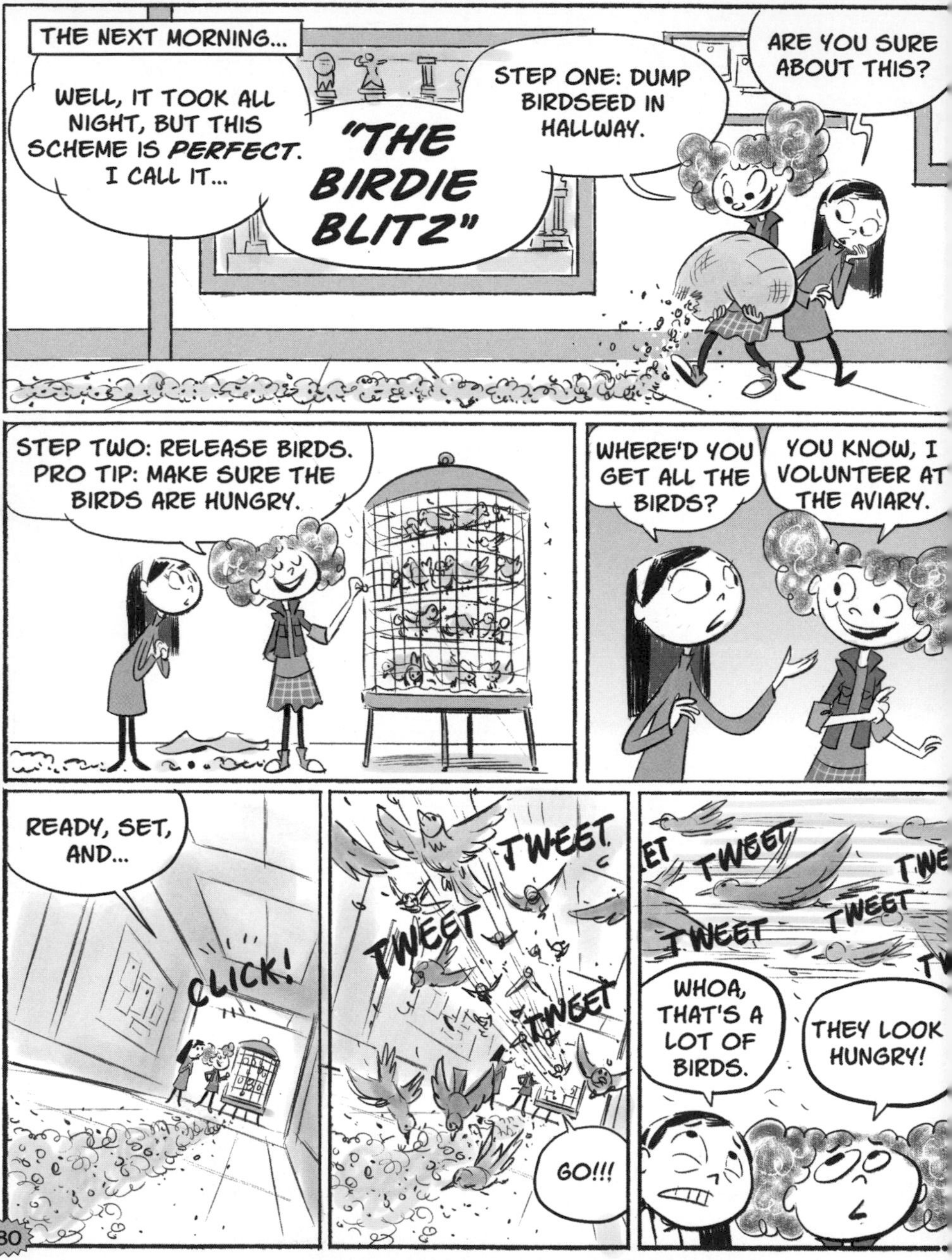
THE NEXT MORNING...
WELL, IT TOOK ALL NIGHT, BUT THIS SCHEME IS PERFECT. I CALL IT...
"THE BIRDIE BLITZ"
STEP ONE: DUMP BIRDSEED IN HALLWAY.
ARE YOU SURE ABOUT THIS?
STEP TWO: RELEASE BIRDS. PRO TIP: MAKE SURE THE BIRDS ARE HUNGRY.
WHERE'D YOU GET ALL THE BIRDS?
YOU KNOW, I VOLUNTEER AT THE AVIARY.
READY, SET, AND...
CLICK!
TWEET
TWEET
TWEET
GO!!!
TWEET
TWEET
TWEET
WHOA, THAT'S A LOT OF BIRDS.
THEY LOOK HUNGRY!

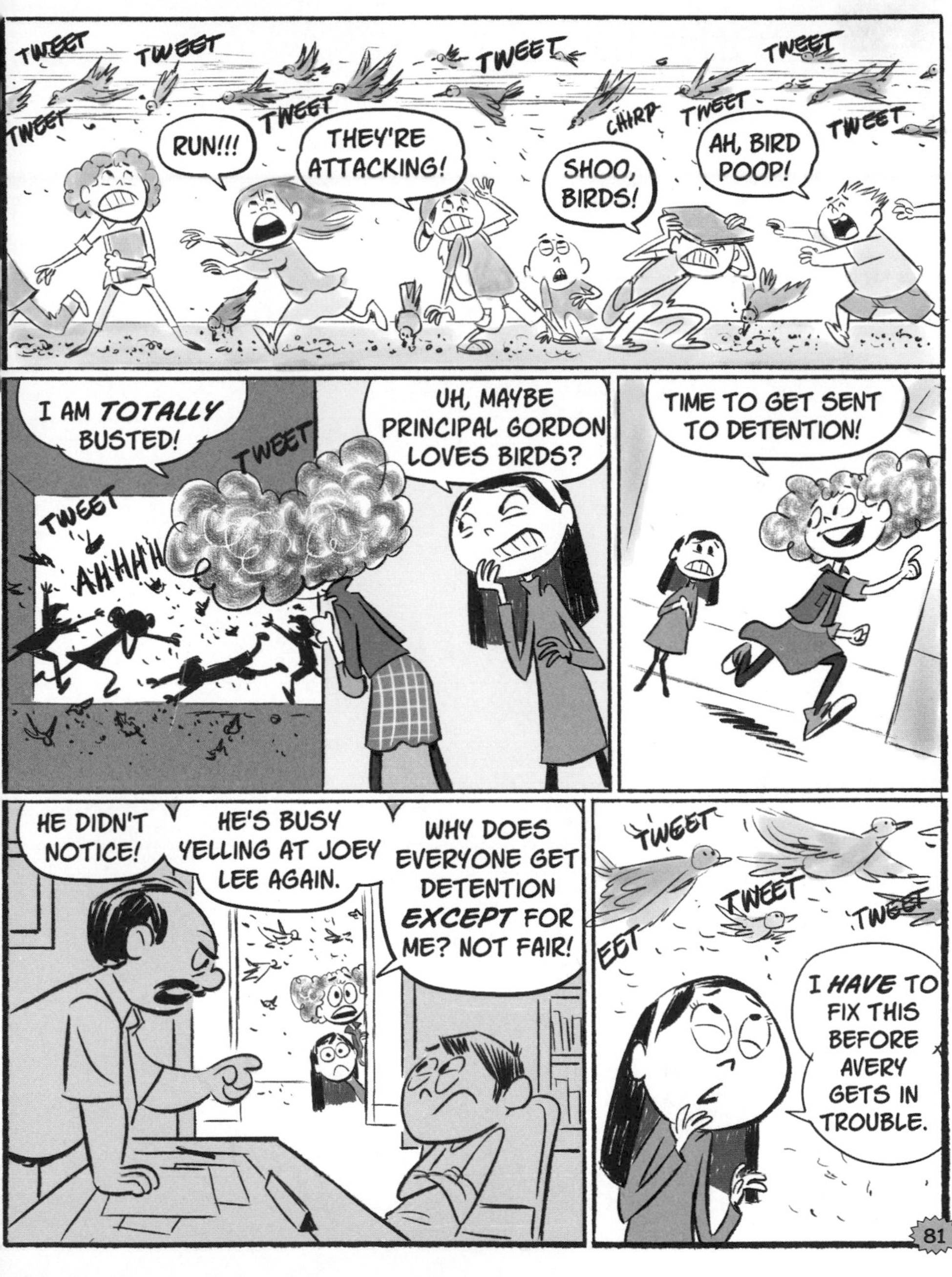
TWEET
TWEET
TWEET
TWEET
TWEET
TWEET
TWEET
RUN!!!
THEY'RE ATTACKING!
CHIRP
SHOO, BIRDS!
TWEET
AH, BIRD POOP!
TWEET
I AM *TOTALLY* BUSTED!
TWEET
TWEET
AHHHH
UH, MAYBE PRINCIPAL GORDON LOVES BIRDS?
TIME TO GET SENT TO DETENTION!
HE DIDN'T NOTICE!
HE'S BUSY YELLING AT JOEY LEE AGAIN.
WHY DOES EVERYONE GET DETENTION ***EXCEPT*** FOR ME? NOT FAIR!
TWEET
TWEET
TWEET
EET
I ***HAVE*** TO FIX THIS BEFORE AVERY GETS IN TROUBLE.

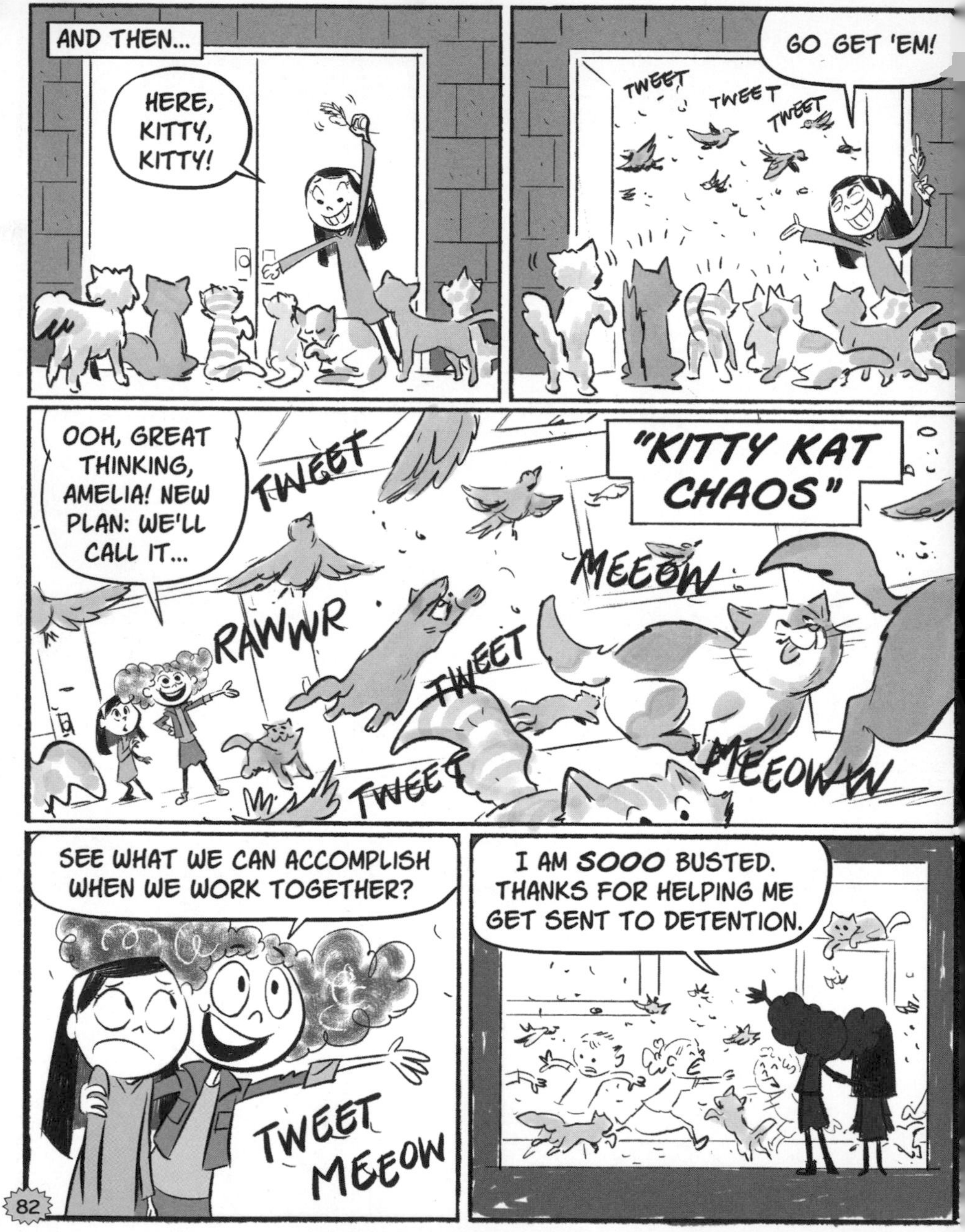
AND THEN...
HERE, KITTY, KITTY!
GO GET 'EM!
TWEET
TWEET
TWEET
OOH, GREAT THINKING, AMELIA! NEW PLAN: WE'LL CALL IT...
"KITTY KAT CHAOS"
TWEET
MEEOW
RAWWR
TWEET
TWEET
MEEOWW
SEE WHAT WE CAN ACCOMPLISH WHEN WE WORK TOGETHER?
TWEET
MEEOW
I AM *SOOO* BUSTED. THANKS FOR HELPING ME GET SENT TO DETENTION.

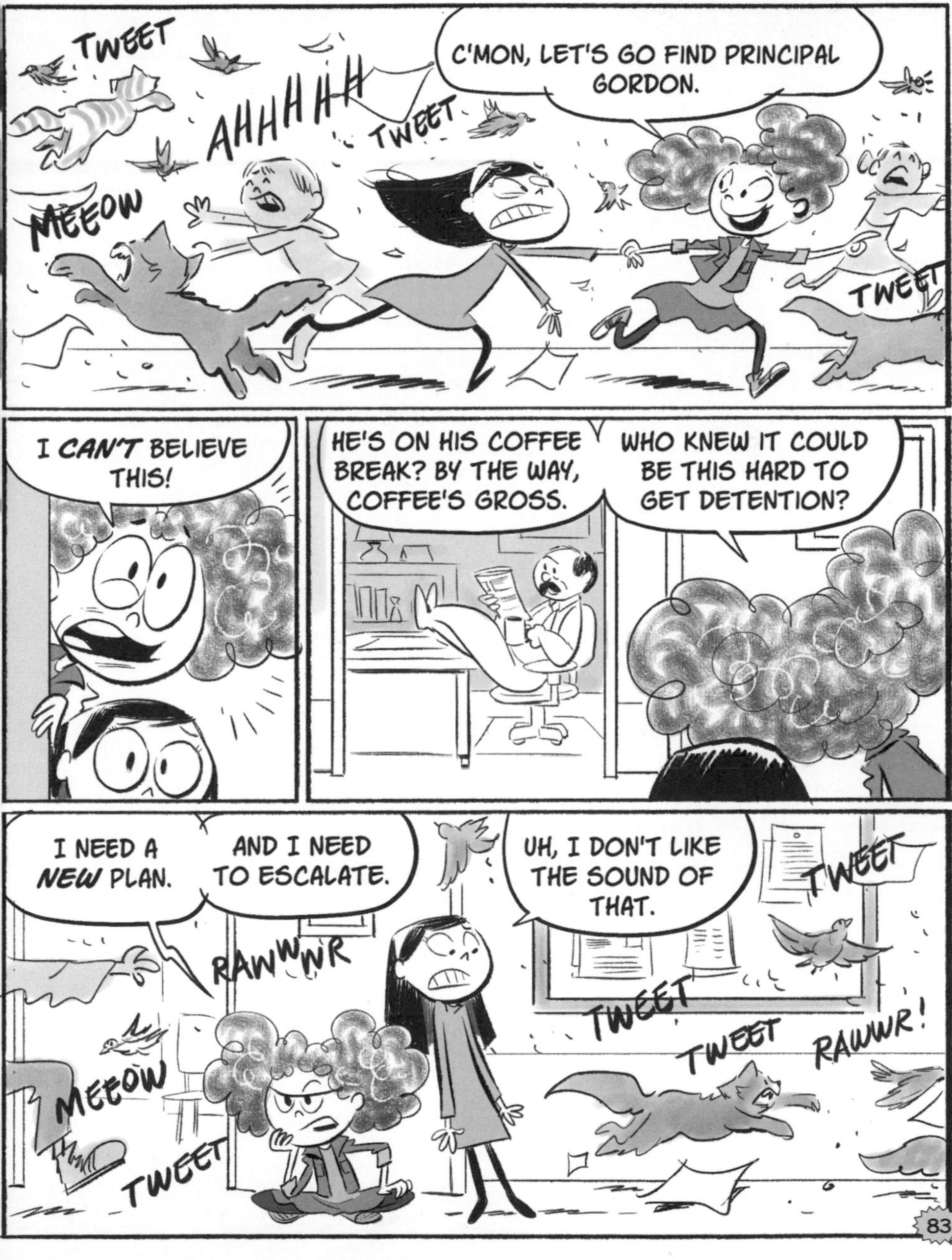
TWEET
AHHHHHH
TWEET
C'MON, LET'S GO FIND PRINCIPAL GORDON.
MEEOW
TWEET
I CAN'T BELIEVE THIS!
HE'S ON HIS COFFEE BREAK? BY THE WAY, COFFEE'S GROSS.
WHO KNEW IT COULD BE THIS HARD TO GET DETENTION?
I NEED A NEW PLAN.
AND I NEED TO ESCALATE.
UH, I DON'T LIKE THE SOUND OF THAT.
TWEET
RAWWWR
TWEET
TWEET
RAWWR!
MEEOW
TWEET

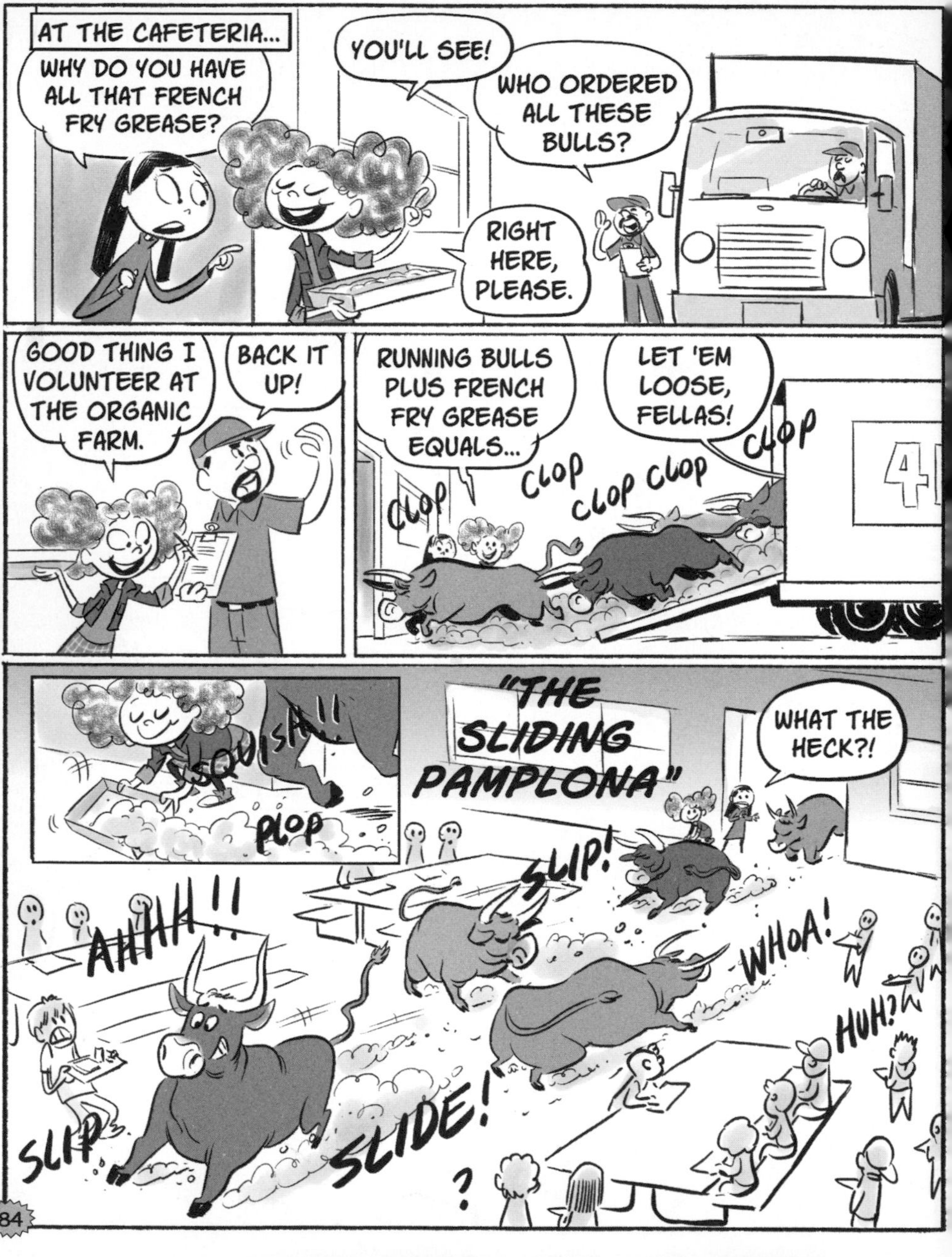
AT THE CAFETERIA...
WHY DO YOU HAVE ALL THAT FRENCH FRY GREASE?
YOU'LL SEE!
WHO ORDERED ALL THESE BULLS?
RIGHT HERE, PLEASE.
GOOD THING I VOLUNTEER AT THE ORGANIC FARM.
BACK IT UP!
RUNNING BULLS PLUS FRENCH FRY GREASE EQUALS...
LET 'EM LOOSE, FELLAS!
CLOP
CLOP
CLOP CLOP
CLOP
SQUISH!!
PLOP
"THE SLIDING PAMPLONA"
WHAT THE HECK?!
SLIP!
AHHH!!
WHOA!
HUH?
SLIP
SLIDE!
?

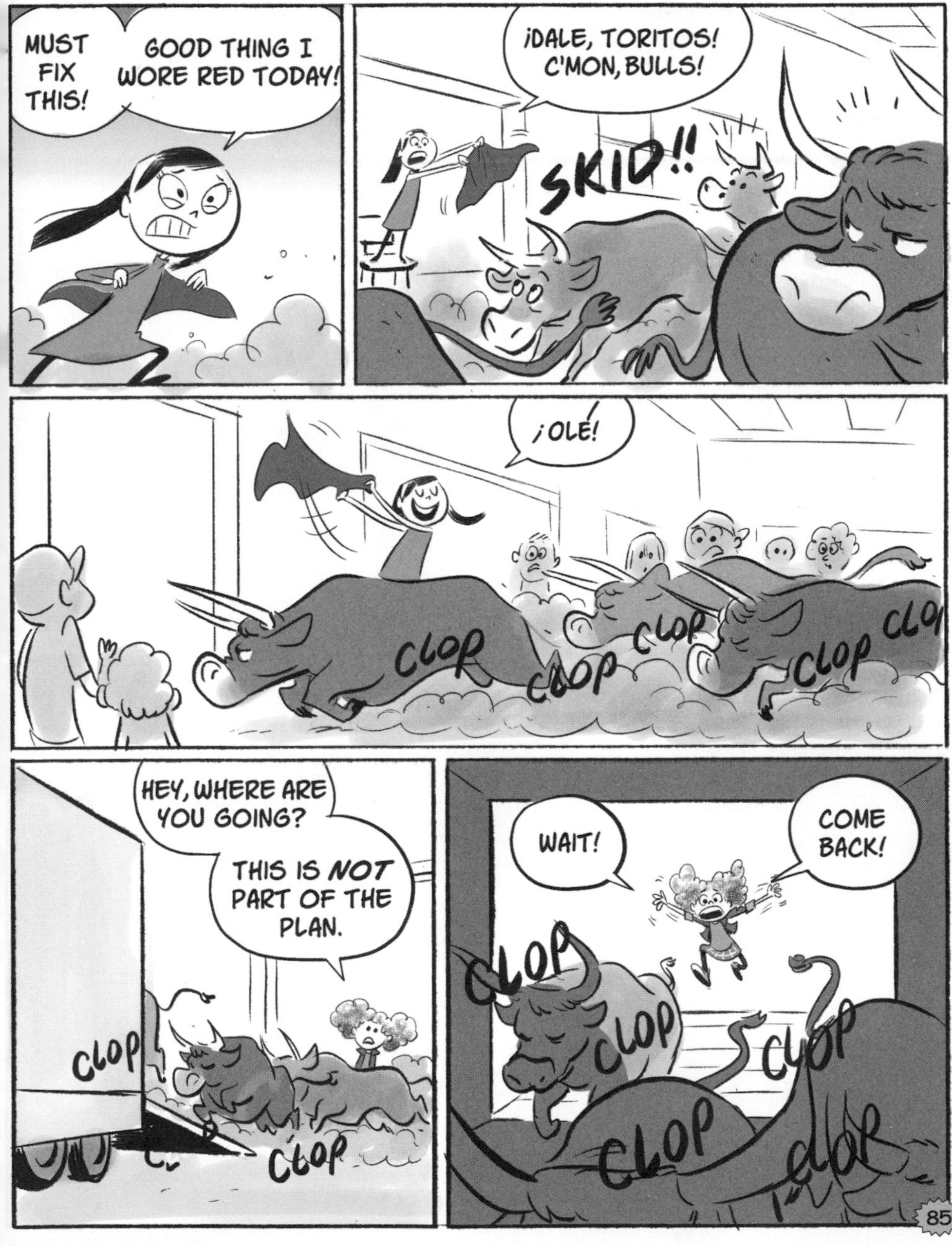
MUST FIX THIS!
GOOD THING I WORE RED TODAY!
¡DALE, TORITOS! C'MON, BULLS!
SKID!!
¡OLÉ!
CLOP
CLOP
CLOP
CLOP
CLOP
HEY, WHERE ARE YOU GOING?
THIS IS *NOT* PART OF THE PLAN.
CLOP
CLOP
WAIT!
COME BACK!
CLOP
CLOP
CLOP
CLOP

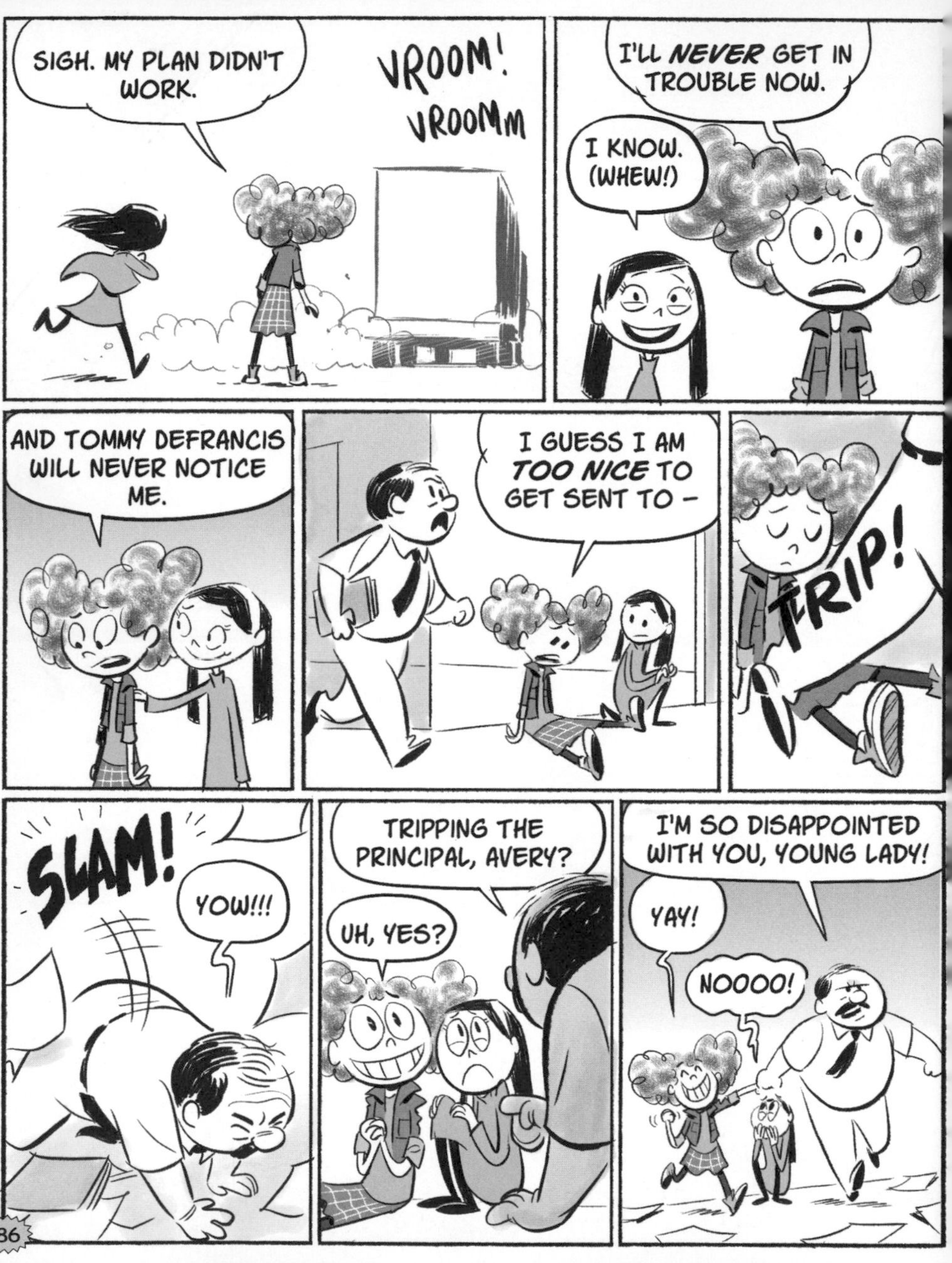
SIGH. MY PLAN DIDN'T WORK.
VROOM!
VROOMM
I'LL NEVER GET IN TROUBLE NOW.
I KNOW. (WHEW!)
AND TOMMY DEFRANCIS WILL NEVER NOTICE ME.
I GUESS I AM TOO NICE TO GET SENT TO –
TRIP!
SLAM!
YOW!!!
TRIPPING THE PRINCIPAL, AVERY?
UH, YES?
I'M SO DISAPPOINTED WITH YOU, YOUNG LADY!
YAY!
NOOOO!

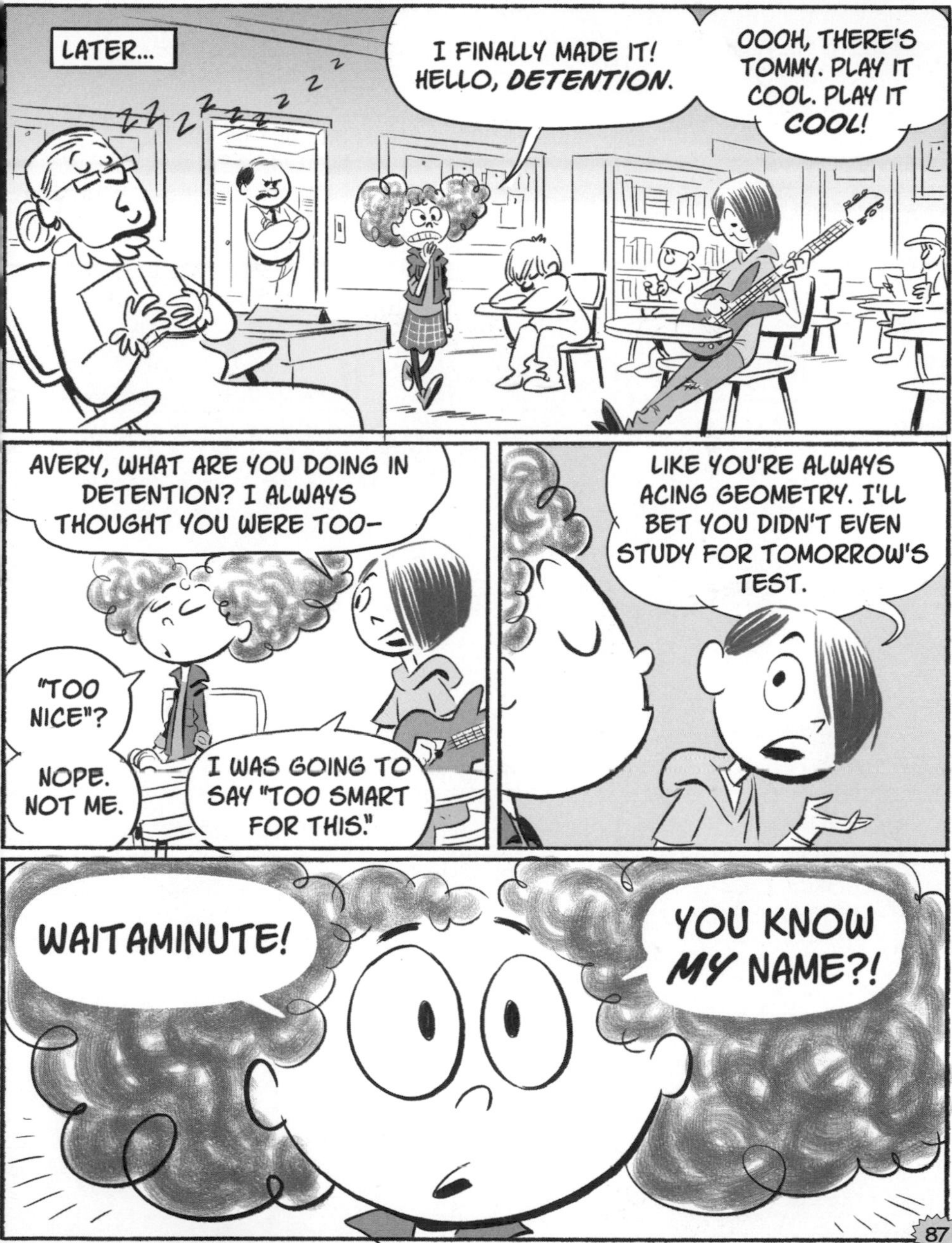
LATER...
I FINALLY MADE IT! HELLO, *DETENTION*.
OOOH, THERE'S TOMMY. PLAY IT COOL. PLAY IT *COOL*!
AVERY, WHAT ARE YOU DOING IN DETENTION? I ALWAYS THOUGHT YOU WERE TOO–
"TOO NICE"?
NOPE. NOT ME.
I WAS GOING TO SAY "TOO SMART FOR THIS."
LIKE YOU'RE ALWAYS ACING GEOMETRY. I'LL BET YOU DIDN'T EVEN STUDY FOR TOMORROW'S TEST.
WAITAMINUTE!
YOU KNOW *MY* NAME?!

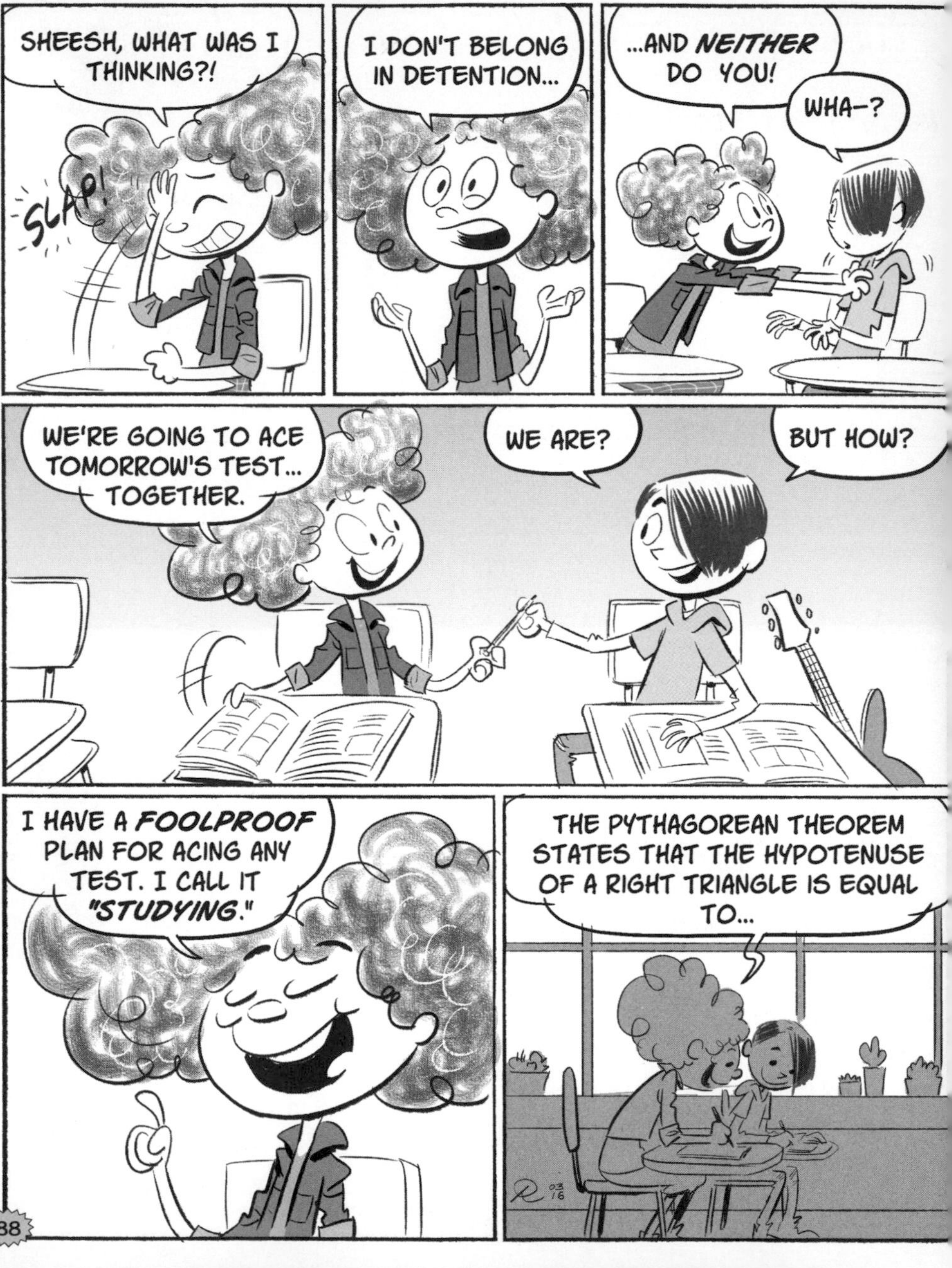

SHEESH, WHAT WAS I THINKING?!
SLAP!
I DON'T BELONG IN DETENTION...
...AND NEITHER DO YOU!
WHA-?
WE'RE GOING TO ACE TOMORROW'S TEST... TOGETHER.
WE ARE?
BUT HOW?
I HAVE A FOOLPROOF PLAN FOR ACING ANY TEST. I CALL IT "STUDYING."
THE PYTHAGOREAN THEOREM STATES THAT THE HYPOTENUSE OF A RIGHT TRIANGLE IS EQUAL TO...

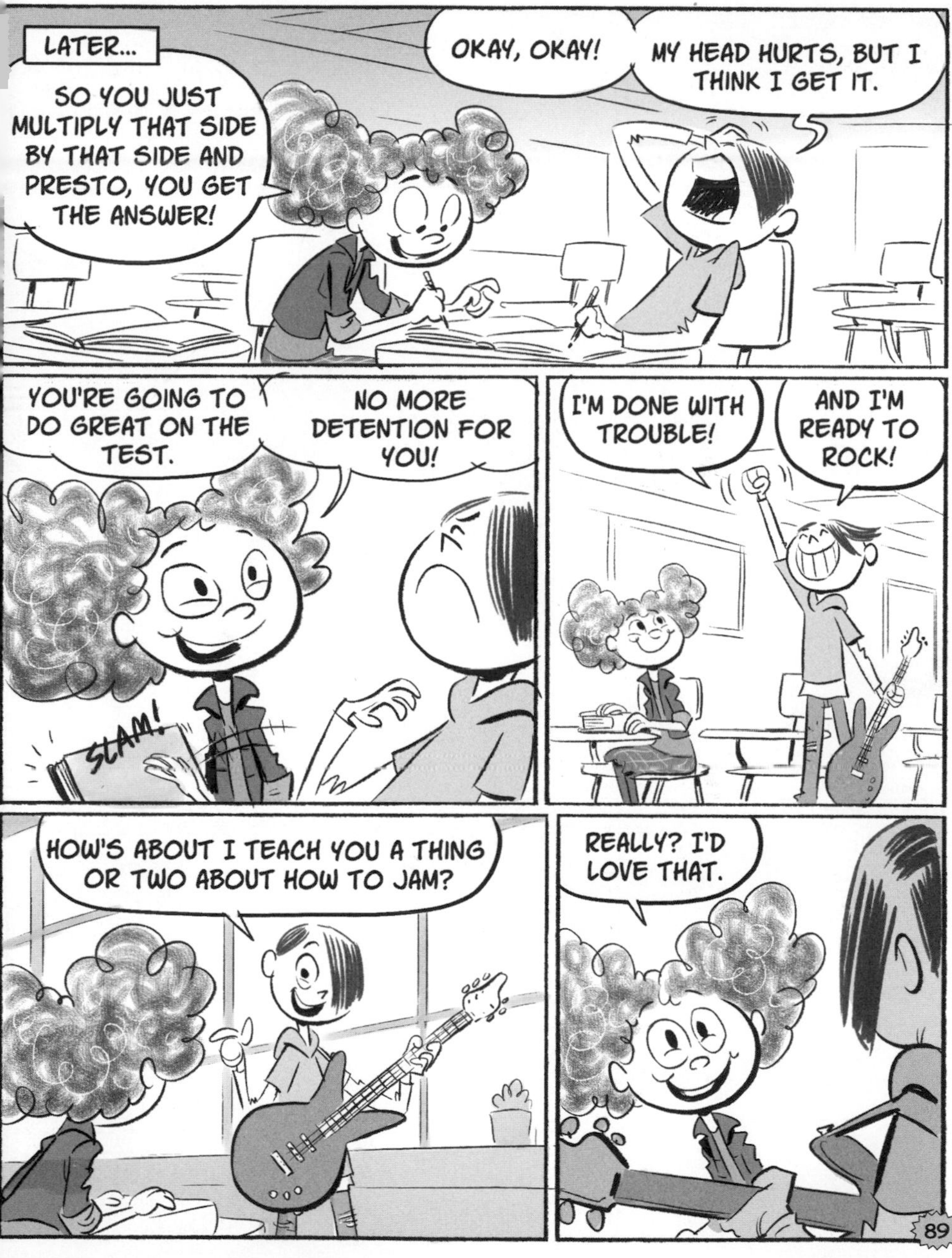
LATER...
SO YOU JUST MULTIPLY THAT SIDE BY THAT SIDE AND PRESTO, YOU GET THE ANSWER!
OKAY, OKAY!
MY HEAD HURTS, BUT I THINK I GET IT.
YOU'RE GOING TO DO GREAT ON THE TEST.
NO MORE DETENTION FOR YOU!
SLAM!
I'M DONE WITH TROUBLE!
AND I'M READY TO ROCK!
HOW'S ABOUT I TEACH YOU A THING OR TWO ABOUT HOW TO JAM?
REALLY? I'D LOVE THAT.

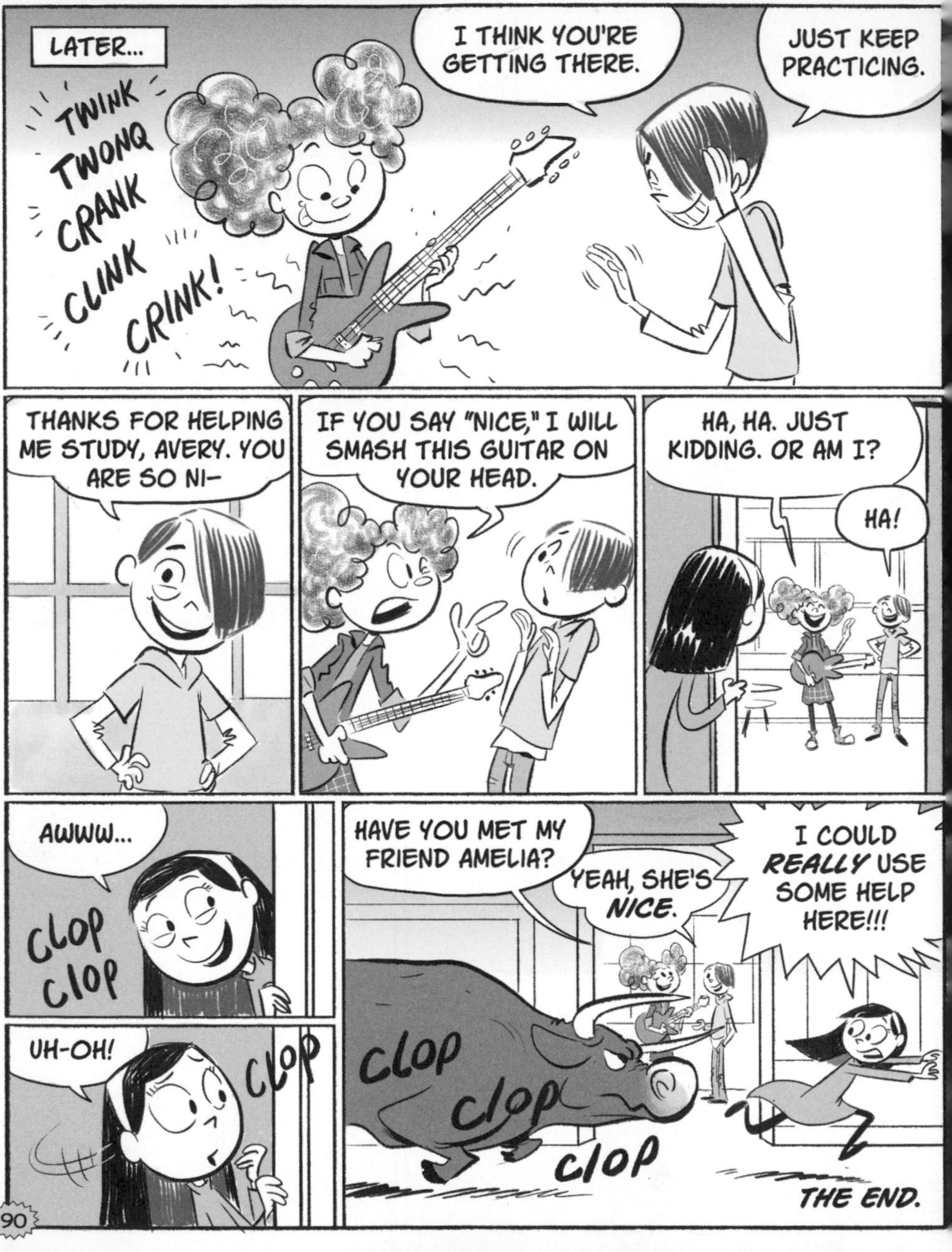

LATER...
TWINK
TWONQ
CRANK
CLINK
CRINK!
I THINK YOU'RE GETTING THERE.
JUST KEEP PRACTICING.
THANKS FOR HELPING ME STUDY, AVERY. YOU ARE SO NI–
IF YOU SAY "NICE," I WILL SMASH THIS GUITAR ON YOUR HEAD.
HA, HA. JUST KIDDING. OR AM I?
HA!
AWWW...
CLOP
CLOP
UH-OH!
CLOP
HAVE YOU MET MY FRIEND AMELIA?
YEAH, SHE'S *NICE*.
I COULD *REALLY* USE SOME HELP HERE!!!
CLOP
CLOP
CLOP
THE END.

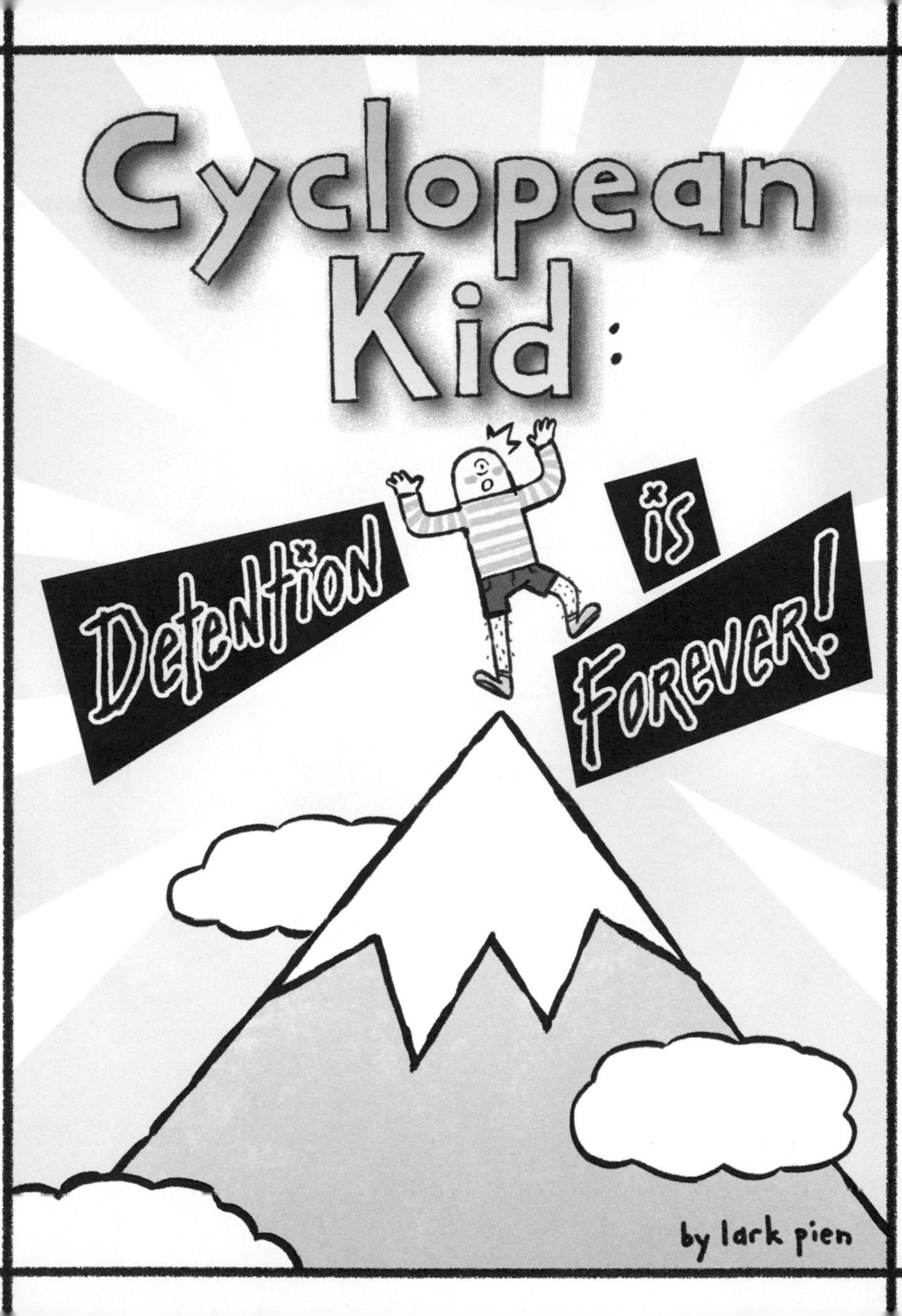
Cyclopean Kid:
Detention is Forever!
by lark pien

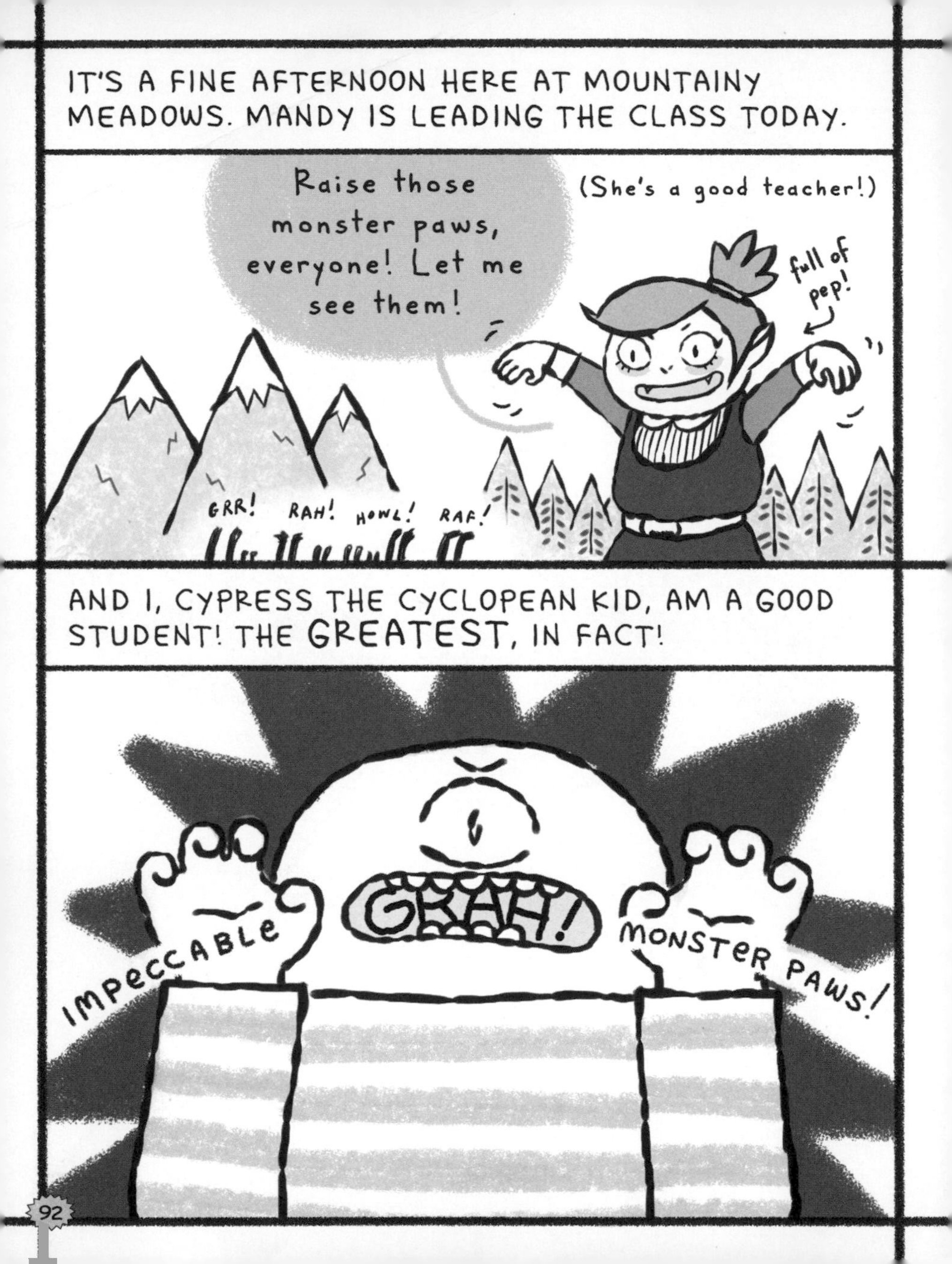

IT'S A FINE AFTERNOON HERE AT MOUNTAINY MEADOWS. MANDY IS LEADING THE CLASS TODAY.
Raise those monster paws, everyone! Let me see them!
(She's a good teacher!)
full of pep!
GRR! RAH! HOWL! RAF!
AND I, CYPRESS THE CYCLOPEAN KID, AM A GOOD STUDENT! THE GREATEST, IN FACT!
GRAH!
IMPECCABLE MONSTER PAWS!

THAT IS, I AM THE GREATEST IN MY DREAMS....

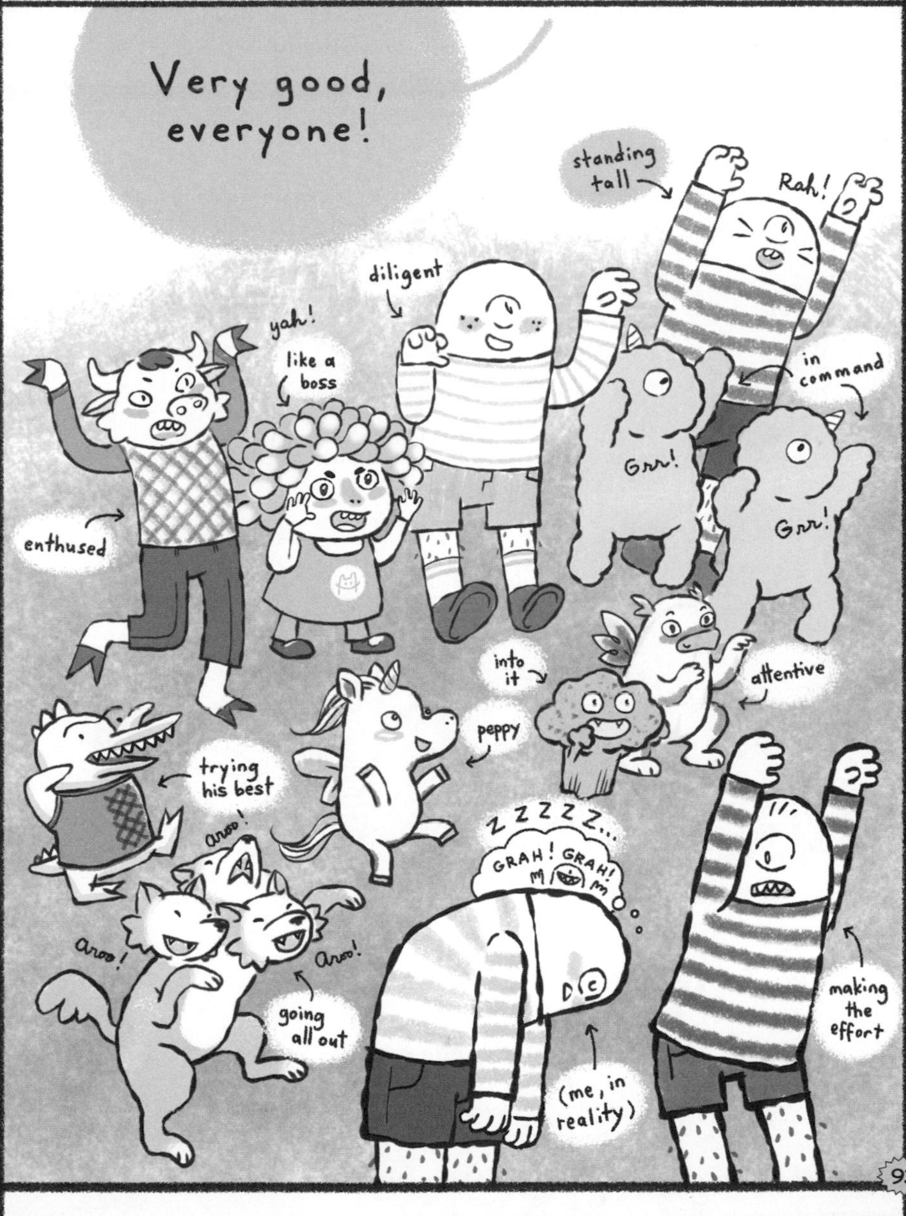
Very good, everyone!
standing tall
Rah!
diligent
yah!
like a boss
in command
Grr!
Grr!
enthused
into it
attentive
peppy
trying his best
Aroo!
Z Z Z Z Z...
GRAH! GRAH!
Aroo!
Aroo!
going all out
making the effort
(me, in reality)

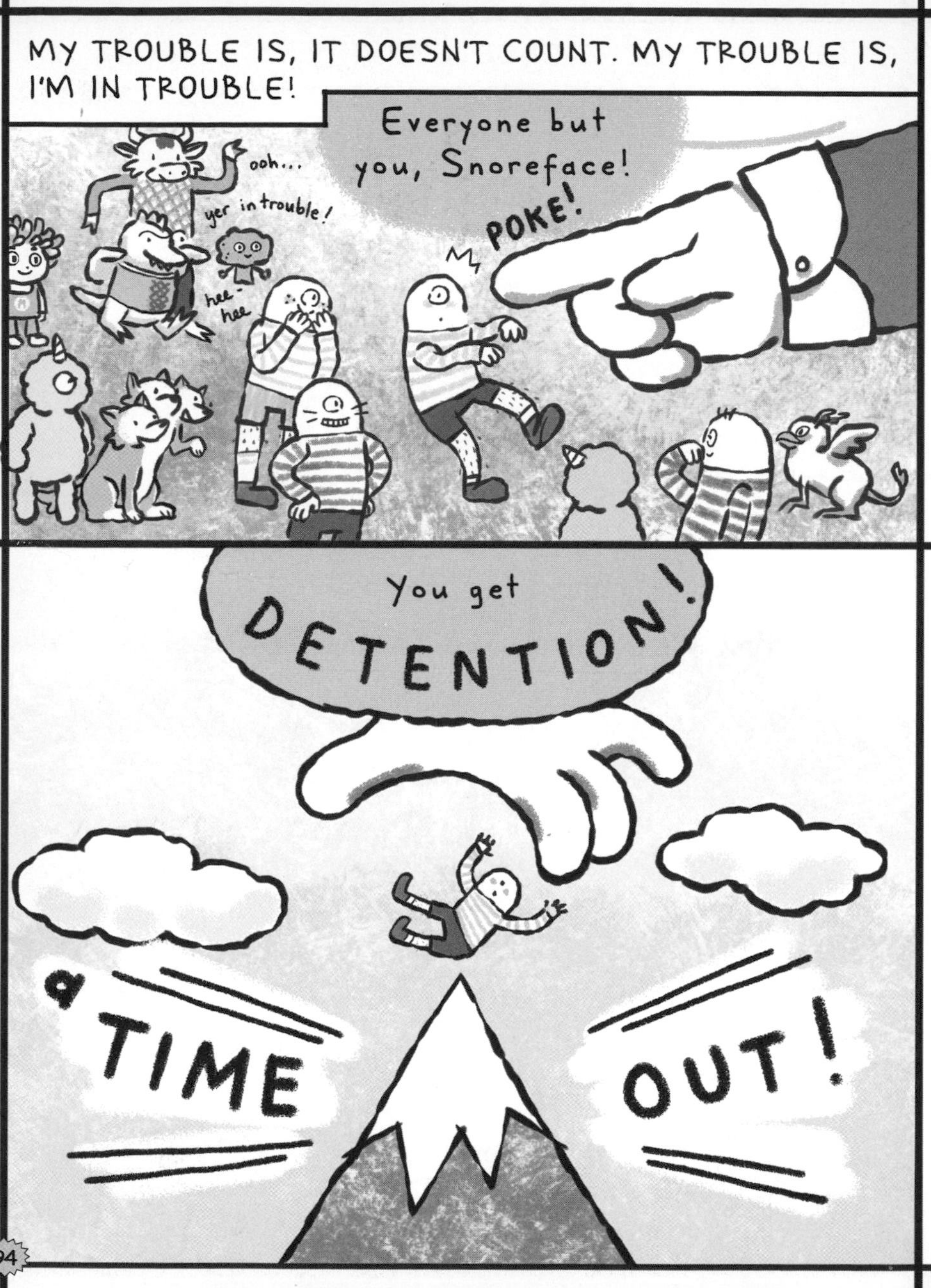
MY TROUBLE IS, IT DOESN'T COUNT. MY TROUBLE IS, I'M IN TROUBLE!
Everyone but you, Snoreface!
ooh...
yer in trouble!
hee-hee
POKE!
You get DETENTION!
a TIME OUT!

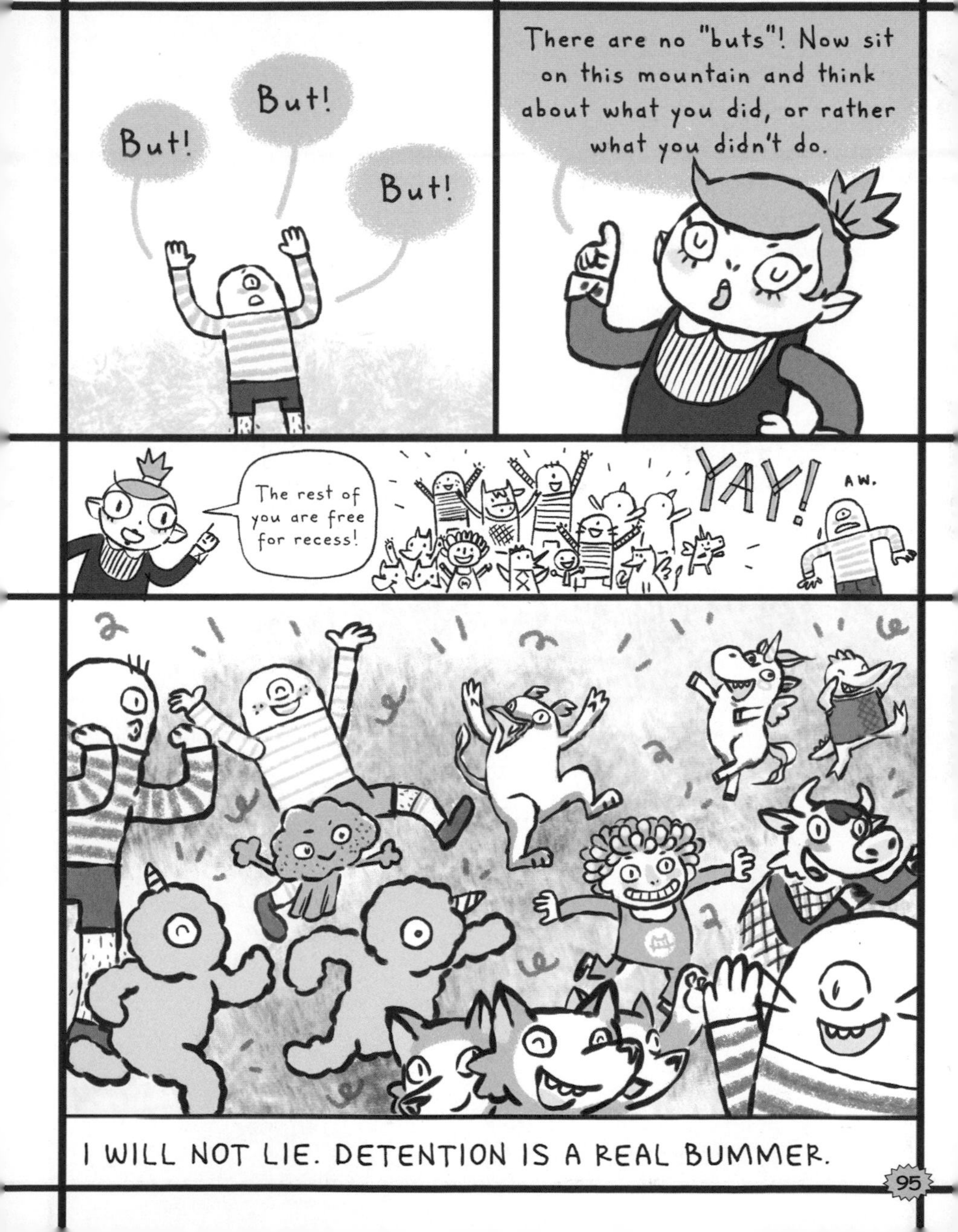

But!
But!
But!
There are no "buts"! Now sit on this mountain and think about what you did, or rather what you didn't do.
The rest of you are free for recess!
YAY!
AW.
I WILL NOT LIE. DETENTION IS A REAL BUMMER.

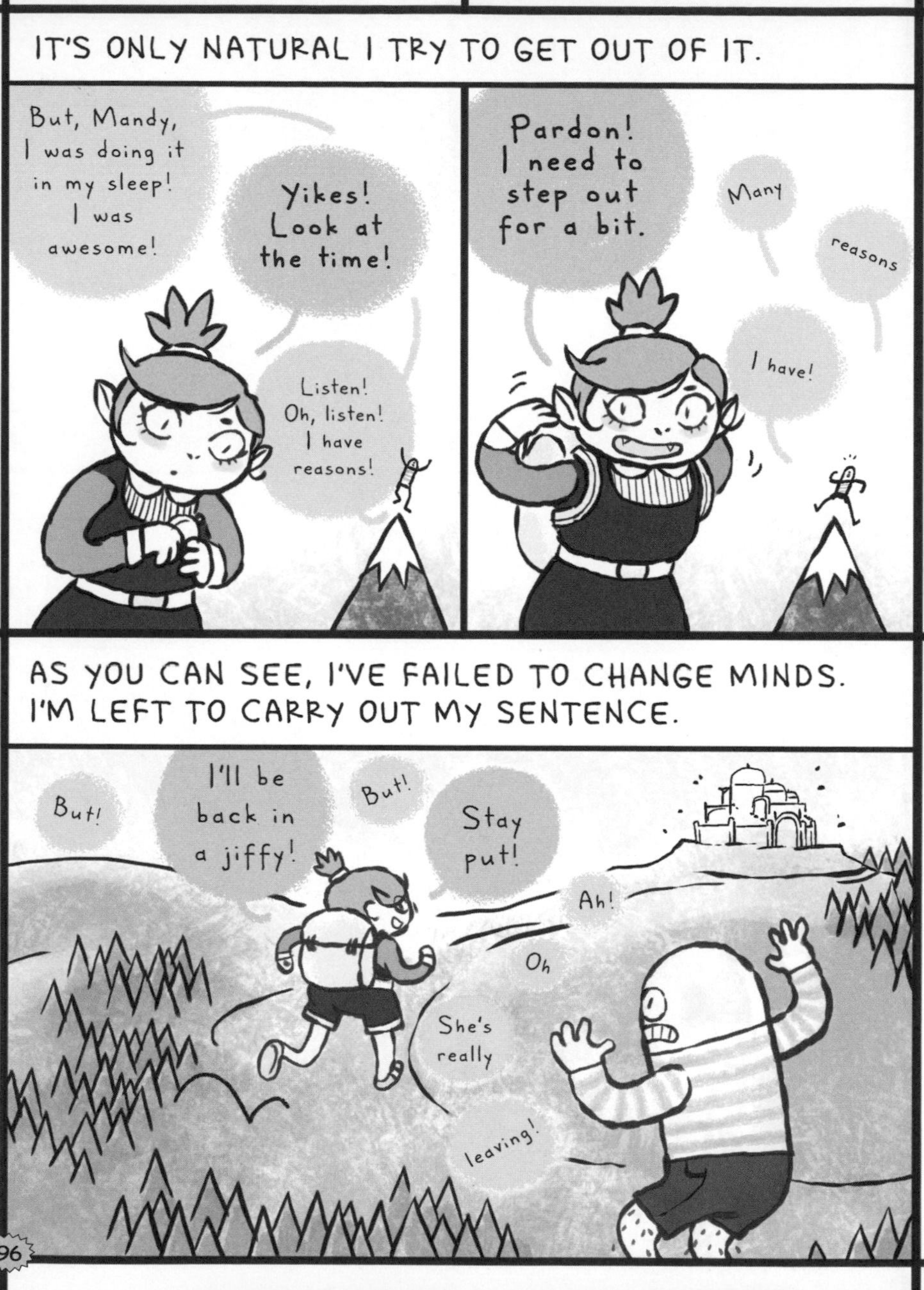

IT'S ONLY NATURAL I TRY TO GET OUT OF IT.
But, Mandy, I was doing it in my sleep! I was awesome!
Yikes! Look at the time!
Listen! Oh, listen! I have reasons!
Pardon! I need to step out for a bit.
Many
reasons
I have!
AS YOU CAN SEE, I'VE FAILED TO CHANGE MINDS. I'M LEFT TO CARRY OUT MY SENTENCE.
But!
I'll be back in a jiffy!
But!
Stay put!
Ah!
Oh
She's really
leaving!

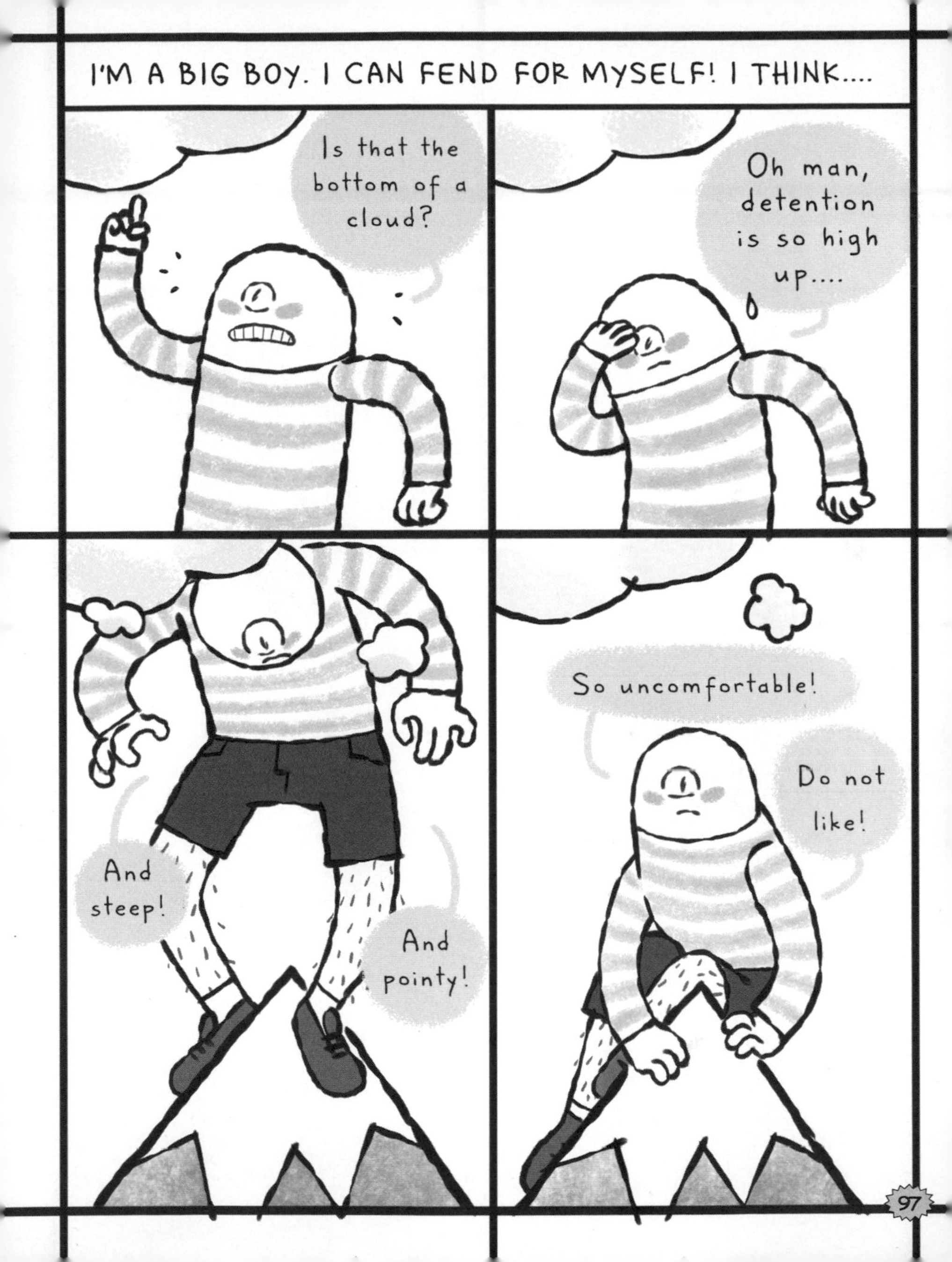
I'M A BIG BOY. I CAN FEND FOR MYSELF! I THINK....
Is that the bottom of a cloud?
Oh man, detention is so high up....
And steep!
And pointy!
So uncomfortable!
Do not like!

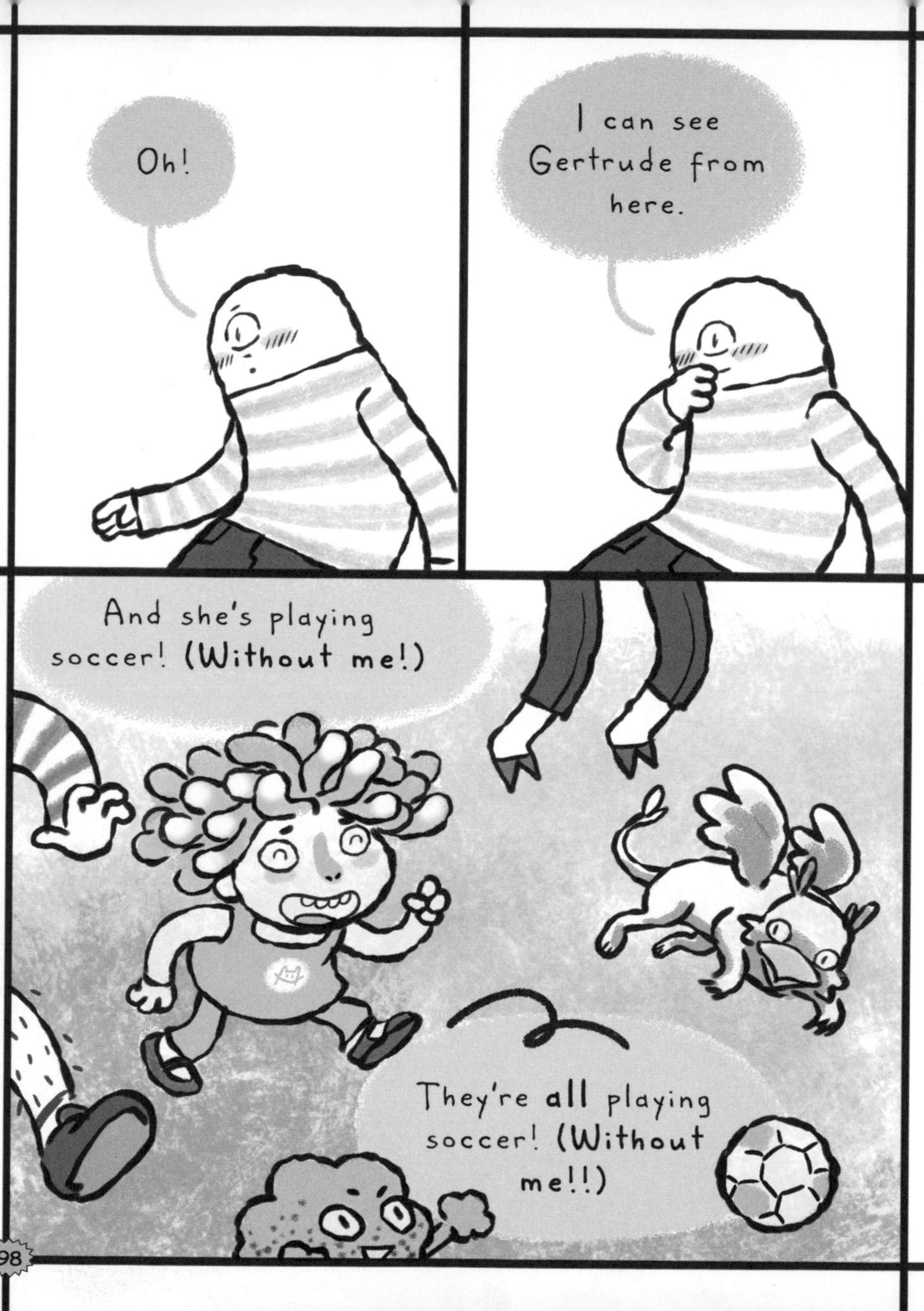
Oh!
I can see Gertrude from here.
And she's playing soccer! (Without me!)
They're all playing soccer! (Without me!!)

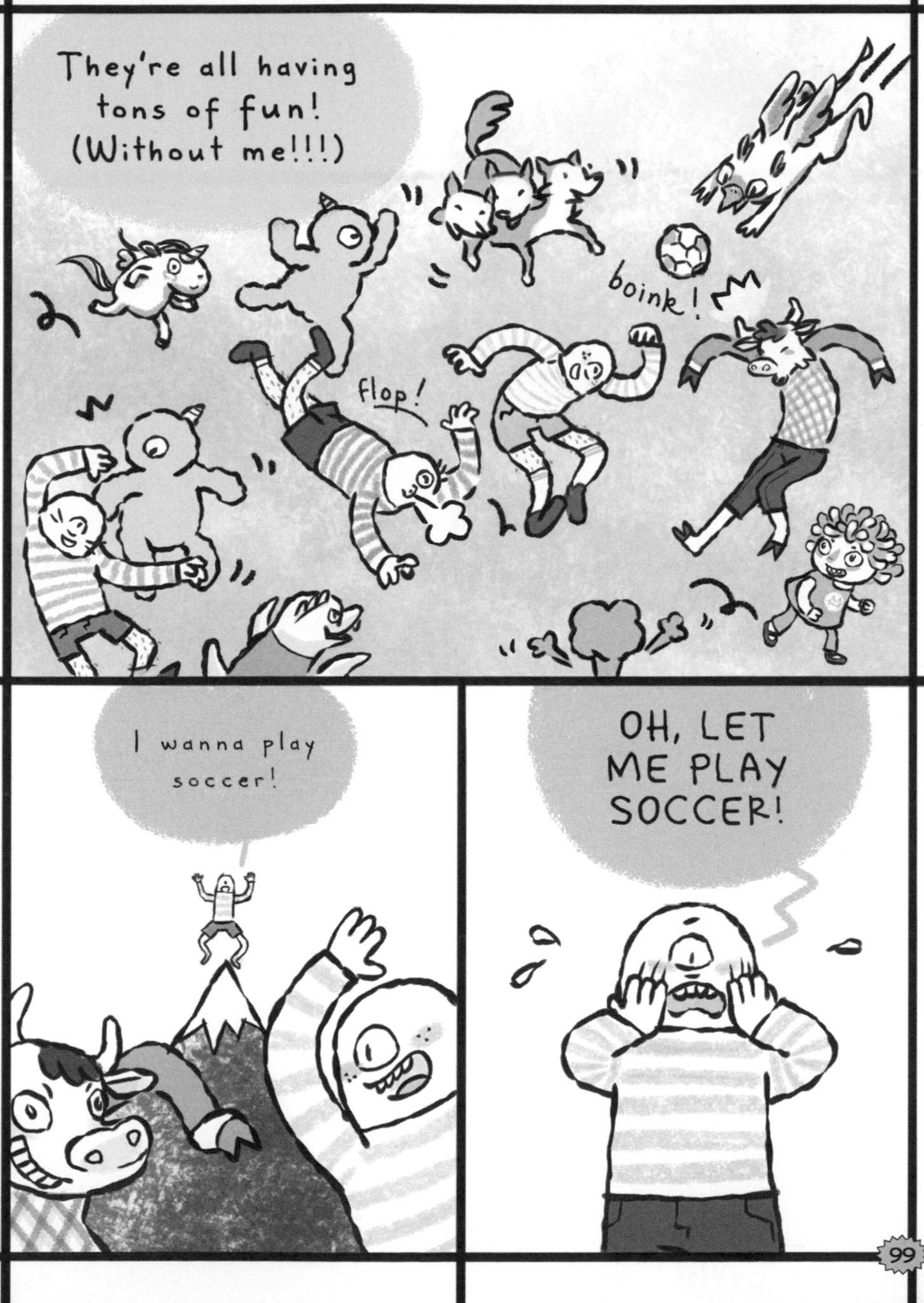
They're all having tons of fun! (Without me!!!)
boink!
flop!
I wanna play soccer!
OH, LET ME PLAY SOCCER!

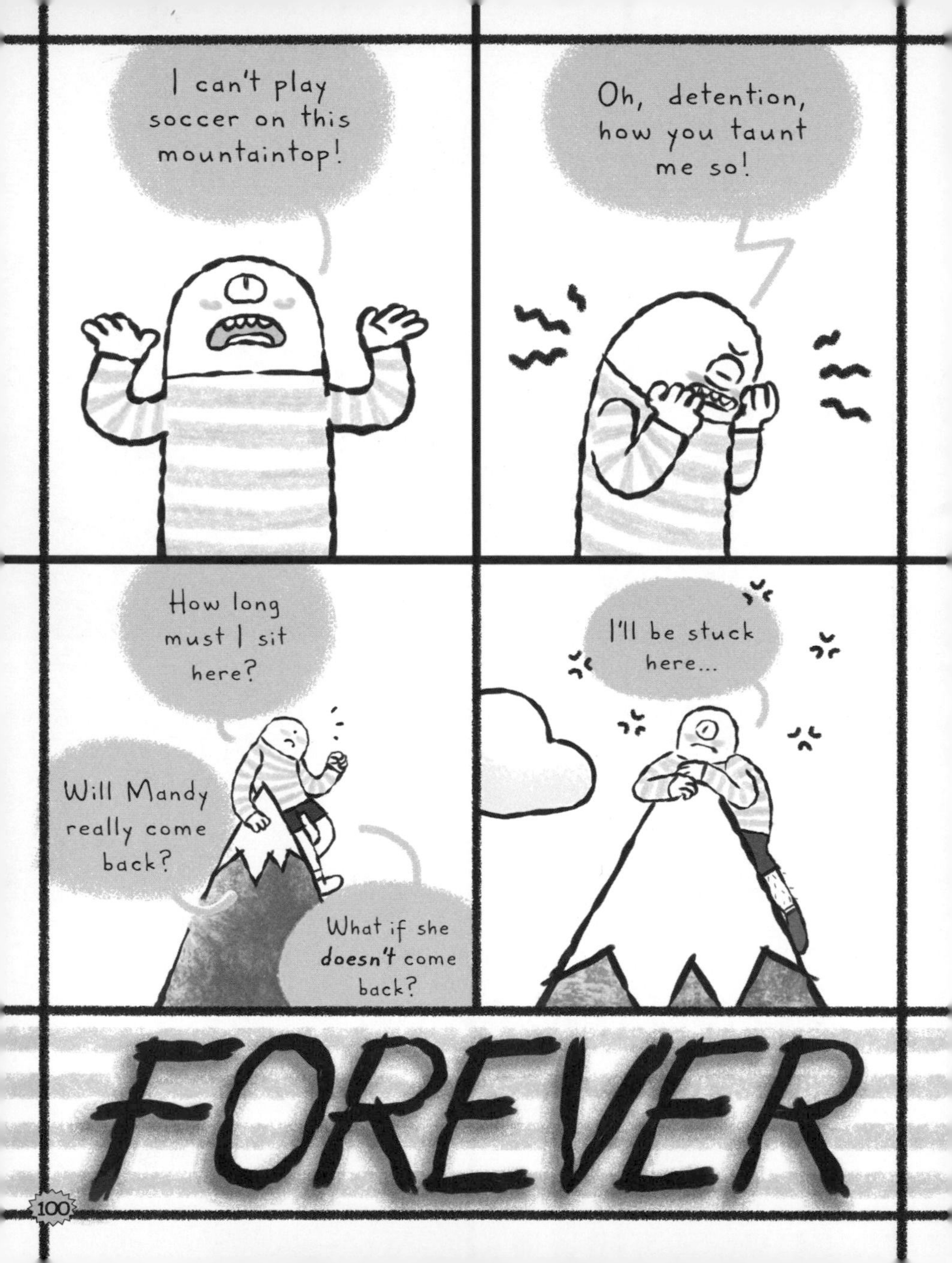
I can't play soccer on this mountaintop!
Oh, detention, how you taunt me so!
How long must I sit here?
Will Mandy really come back?
What if she **doesn't** come back?
I'll be stuck here...
FOREVER

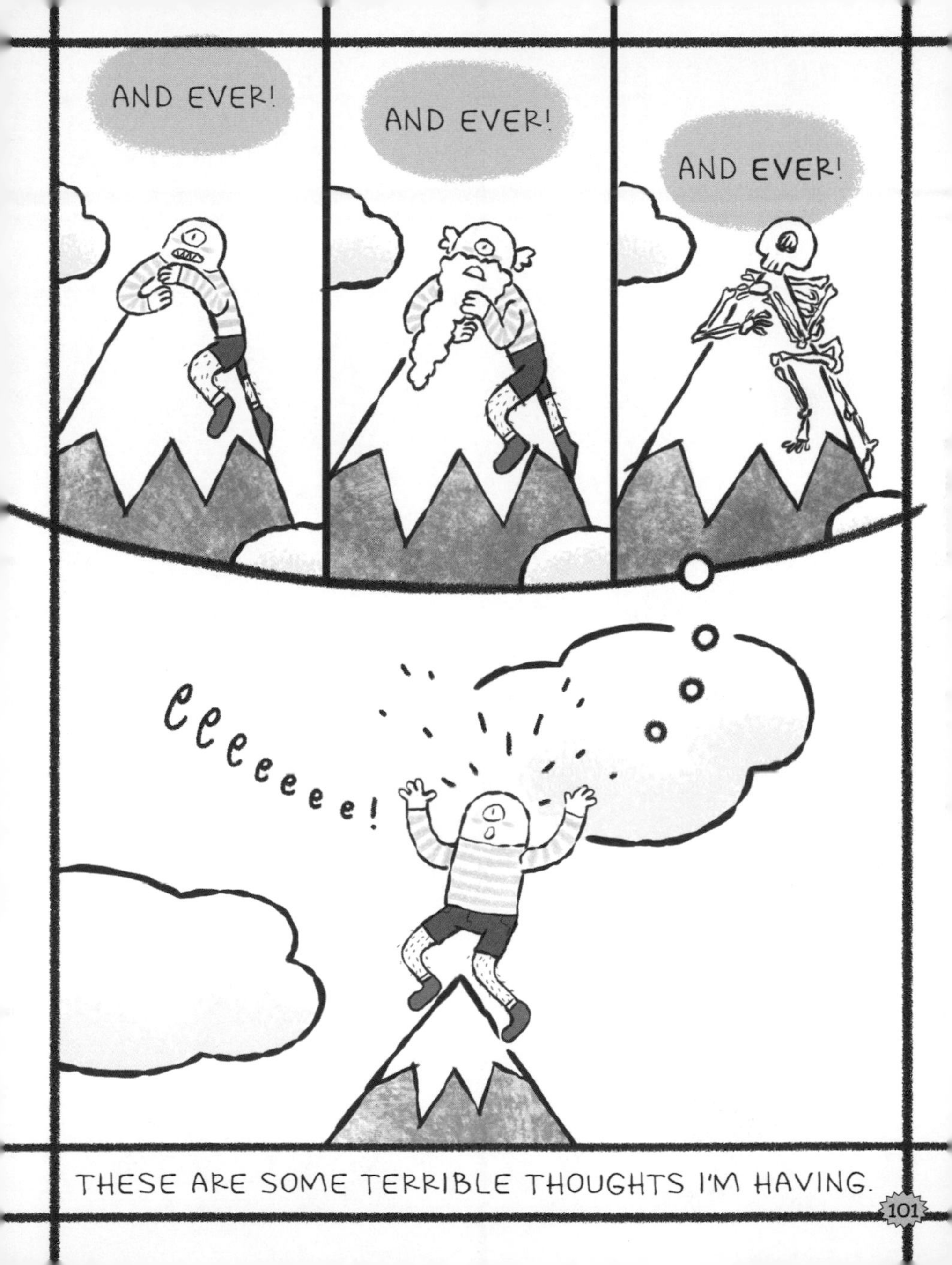
AND EVER!
AND EVER!
AND EVER!
eeeeeeeee!
THESE ARE SOME TERRIBLE THOUGHTS I'M HAVING.

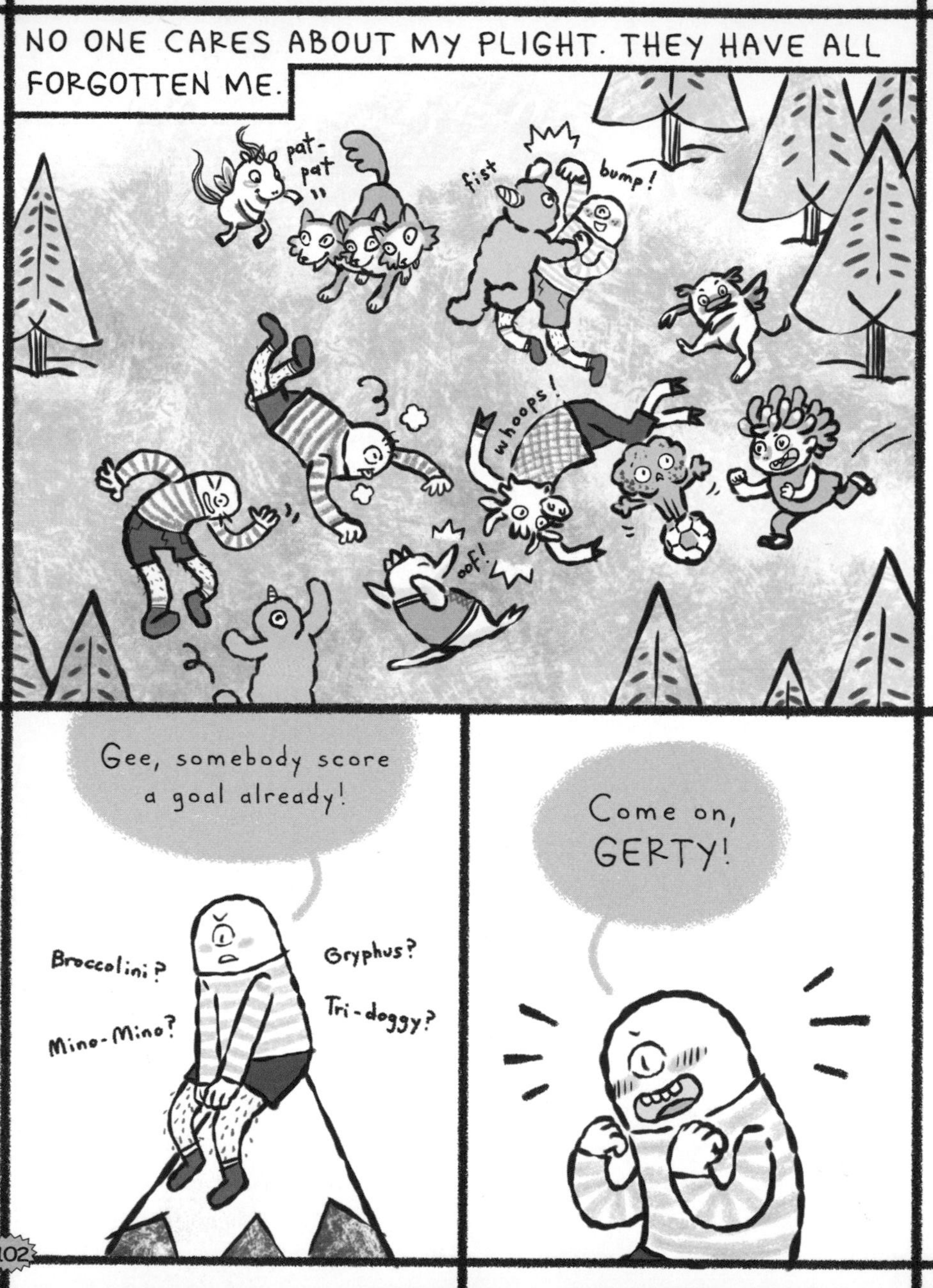
NO ONE CARES ABOUT MY PLIGHT. THEY HAVE ALL FORGOTTEN ME.
pat-pat
fist bump!
whoops!
oof!
Gee, somebody score a goal already!
Broccolini?
Gryphus?
Tri-doggy?
Mino-Mino?
Come on, GERTY!

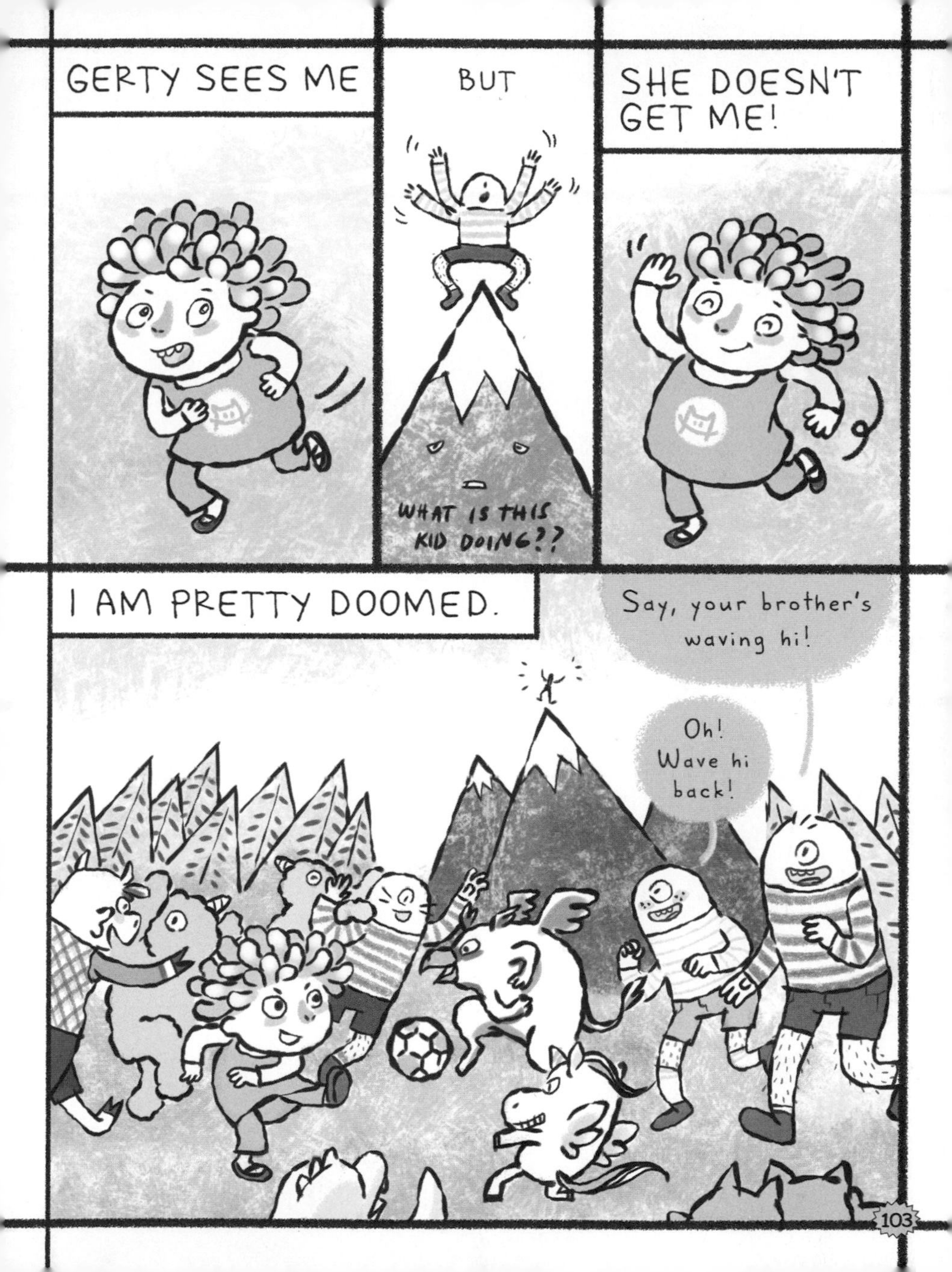

GERTY SEES ME
BUT
WHAT IS THIS KID DOING??
SHE DOESN'T GET ME!
I AM PRETTY DOOMED.
Say, your brother's waving hi!
Oh! Wave hi back!

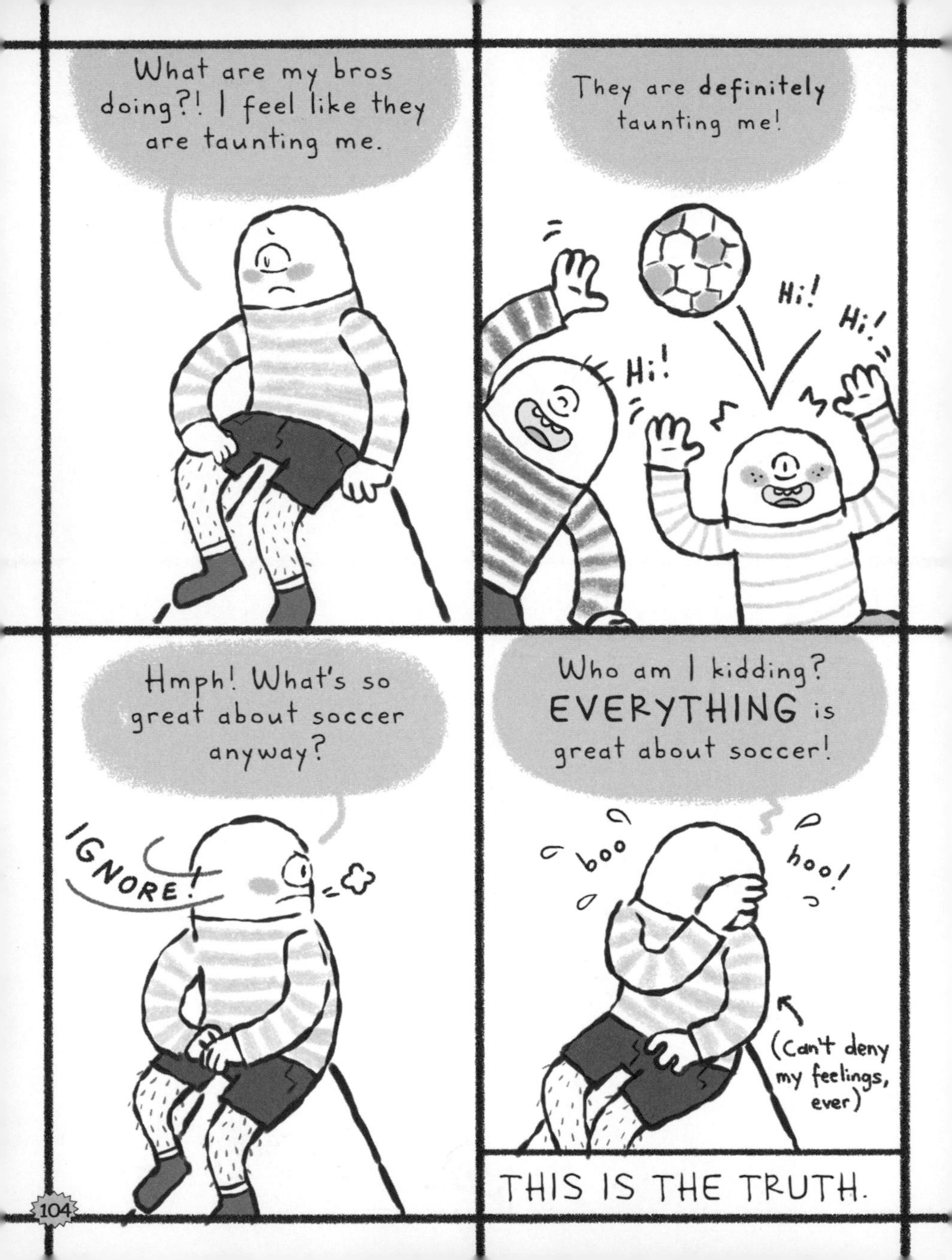

What are my bros doing?! I feel like they are taunting me.
They are definitely taunting me!
Hi!
Hi!
Hi!
Hmph! What's so great about soccer anyway?
IGNORE!
Who am I kidding? EVERYTHING is great about soccer!
boo
hoo!
(Can't deny my feelings, ever)
THIS IS THE TRUTH.

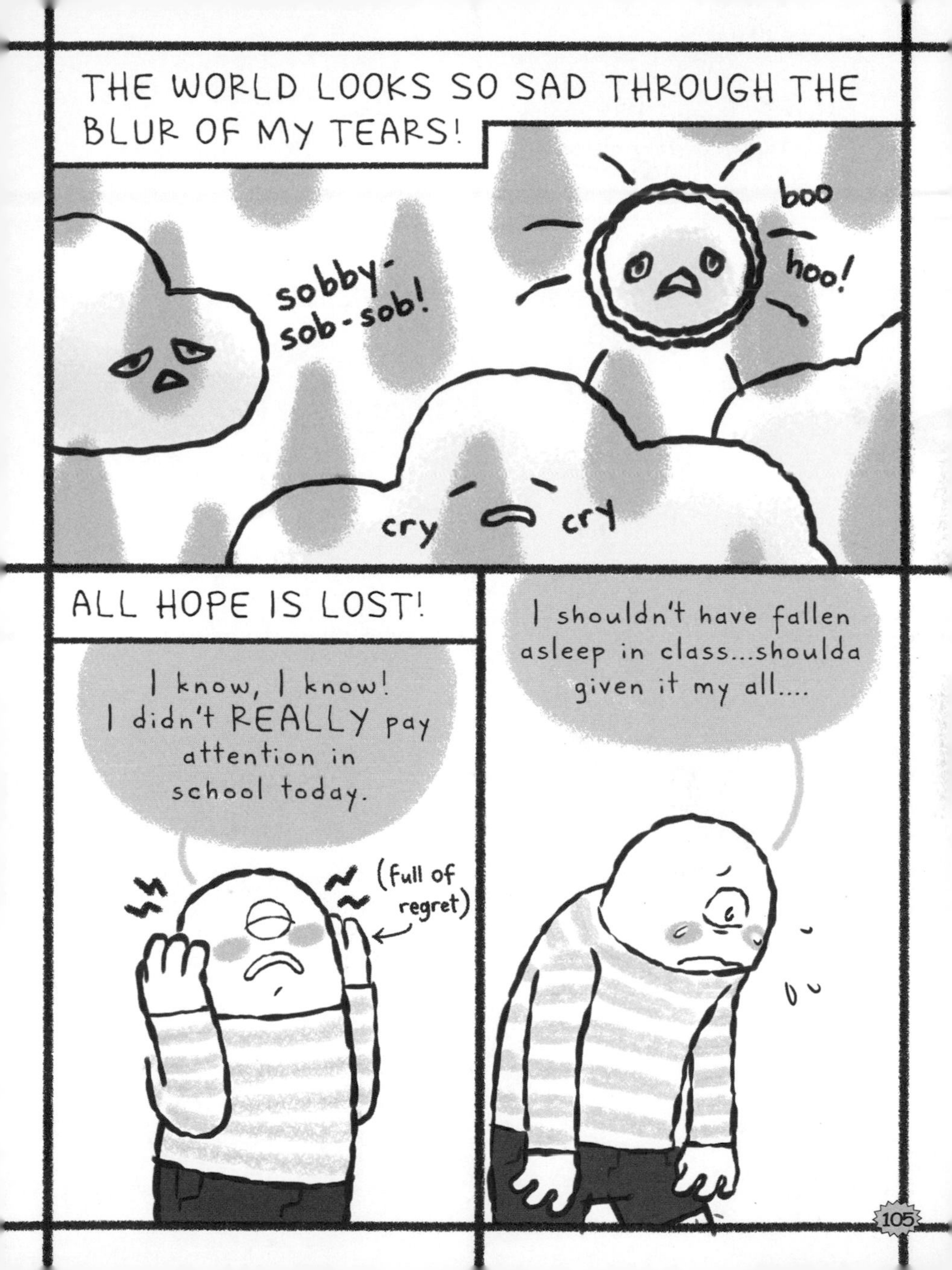
THE WORLD LOOKS SO SAD THROUGH THE BLUR OF MY TEARS!
sobby-sob-sob!
boo hoo!
cry cry
ALL HOPE IS LOST!
I know, I know! I didn't REALLY pay attention in school today.
(full of regret)
I shouldn't have fallen asleep in class...shoulda given it my all....

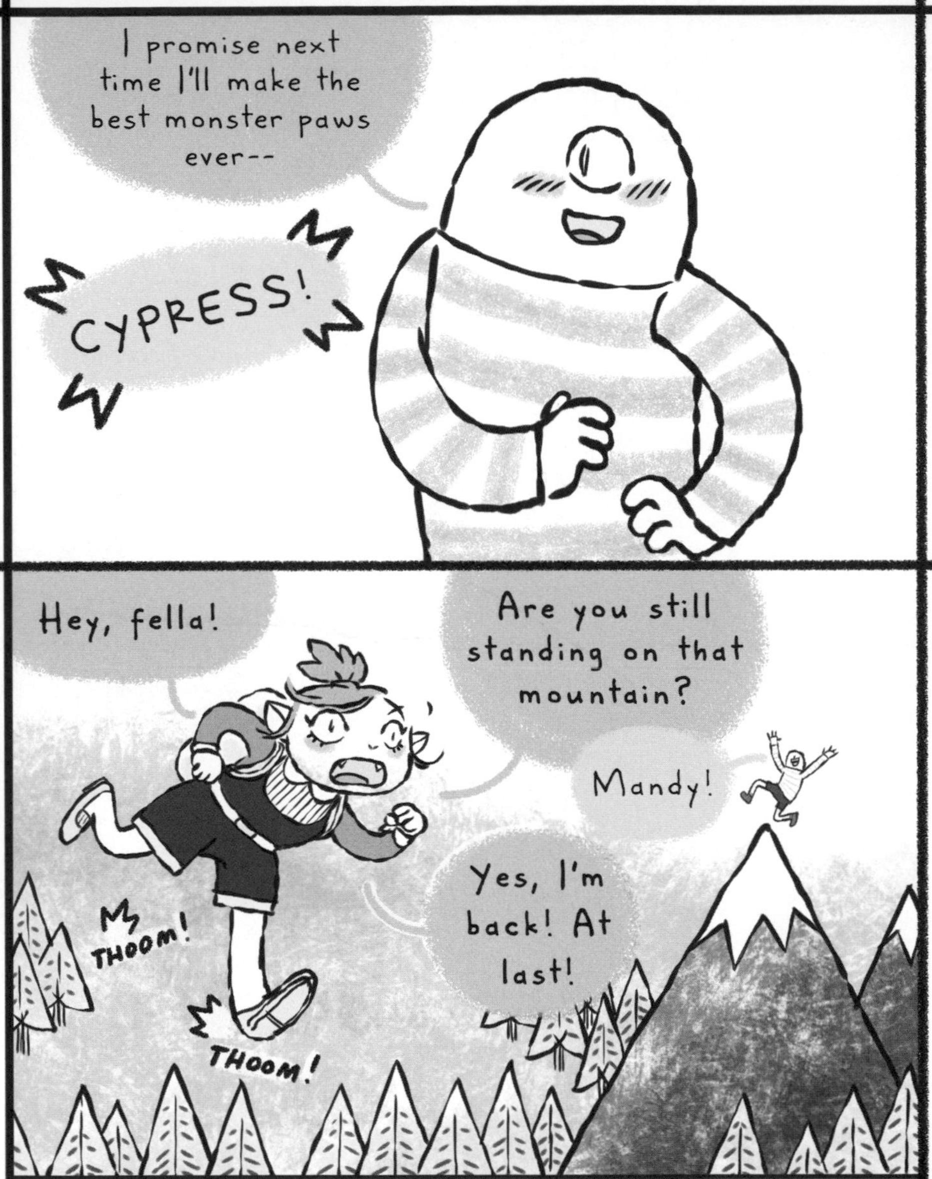
I promise next time I'll make the best monster paws ever--
CYPRESS!
Hey, fella!
Are you still standing on that mountain?
Mandy!
Yes, I'm back! At last!
THOOM!
THOOM!
AAAND...JUST LIKE THAT, I'M HAPPY AGAIN!

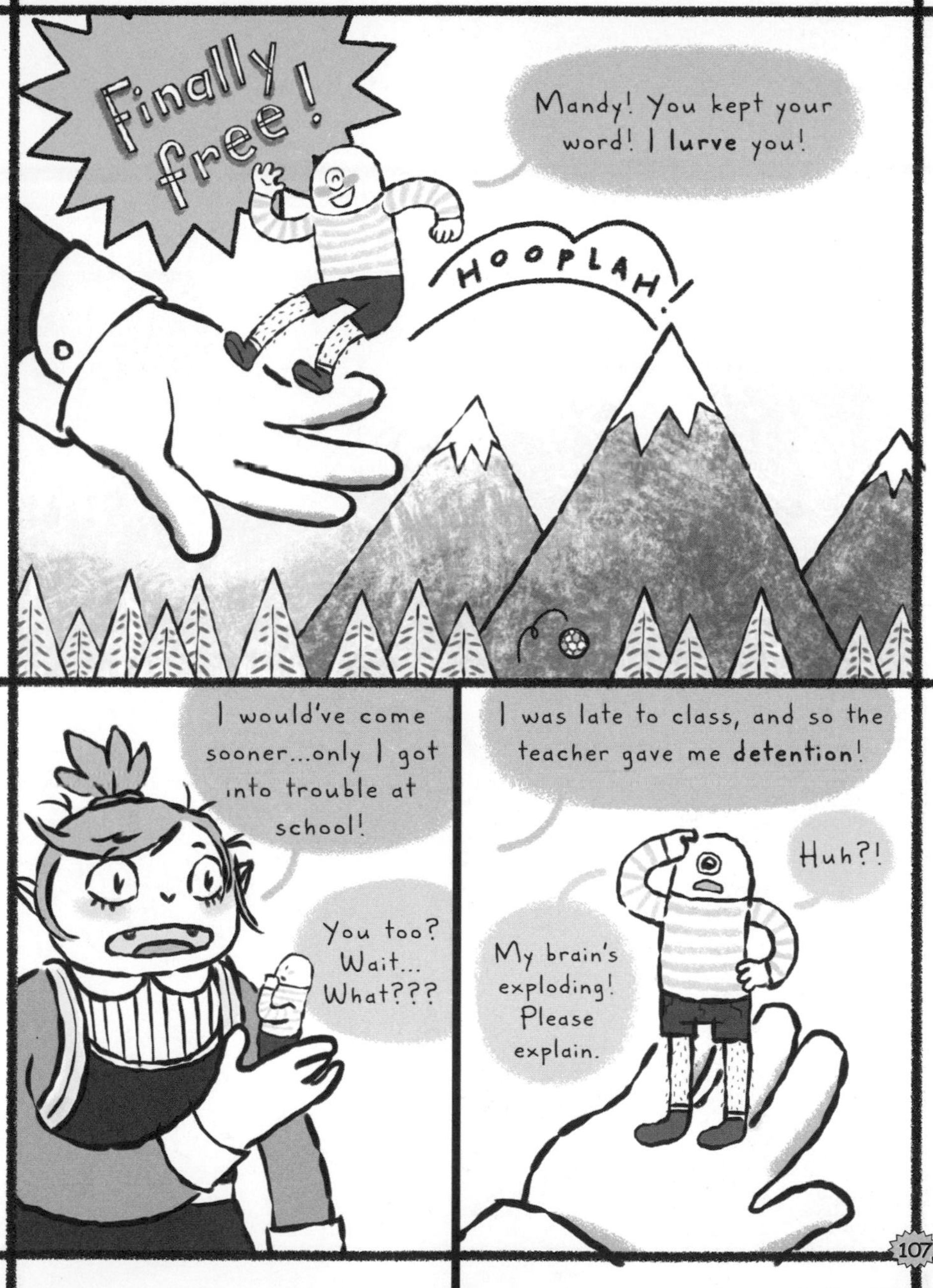
Finally free!
Mandy! You kept your word! I **lurve** you!
HOOPLAH!
I would've come sooner...only I got into trouble at school!
I was late to class, and so the teacher gave me **detention**!
Huh?!
You too? Wait... What???
My brain's exploding! Please explain.

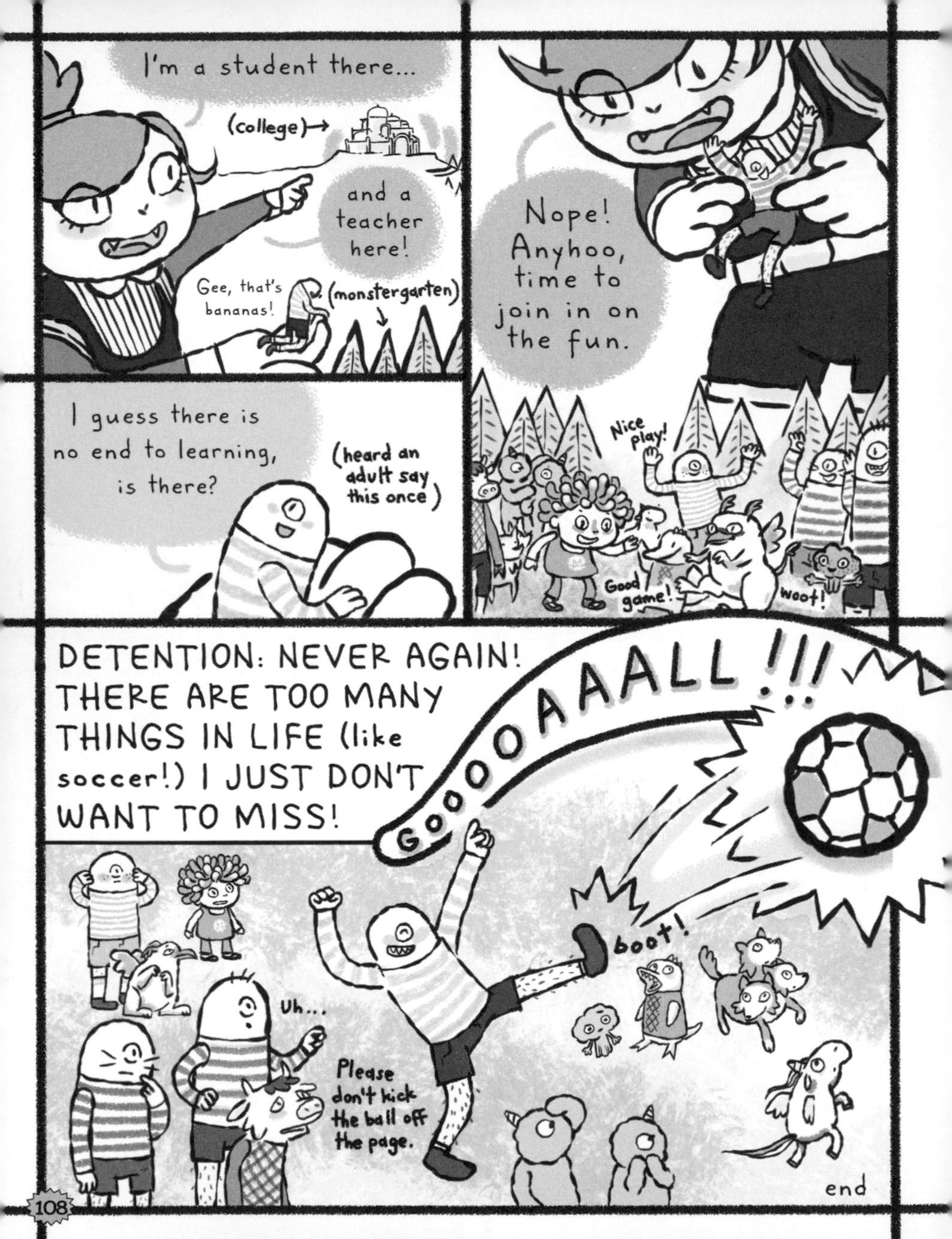
I'm a student there...
(college)→
and a teacher here!
Gee, that's bananas!
(monstergarten)
Nope! Anyhoo, time to join in on the fun.
I guess there is no end to learning, is there?
(heard an adult say this once)
Nice play!
Good game!
woot!
DETENTION: NEVER AGAIN! THERE ARE TOO MANY THINGS IN LIFE (like soccer!) I JUST DON'T WANT TO MISS!
GOOOOAAALL!!!
boot!
Uh...
Please don't kick the ball off the page.
end

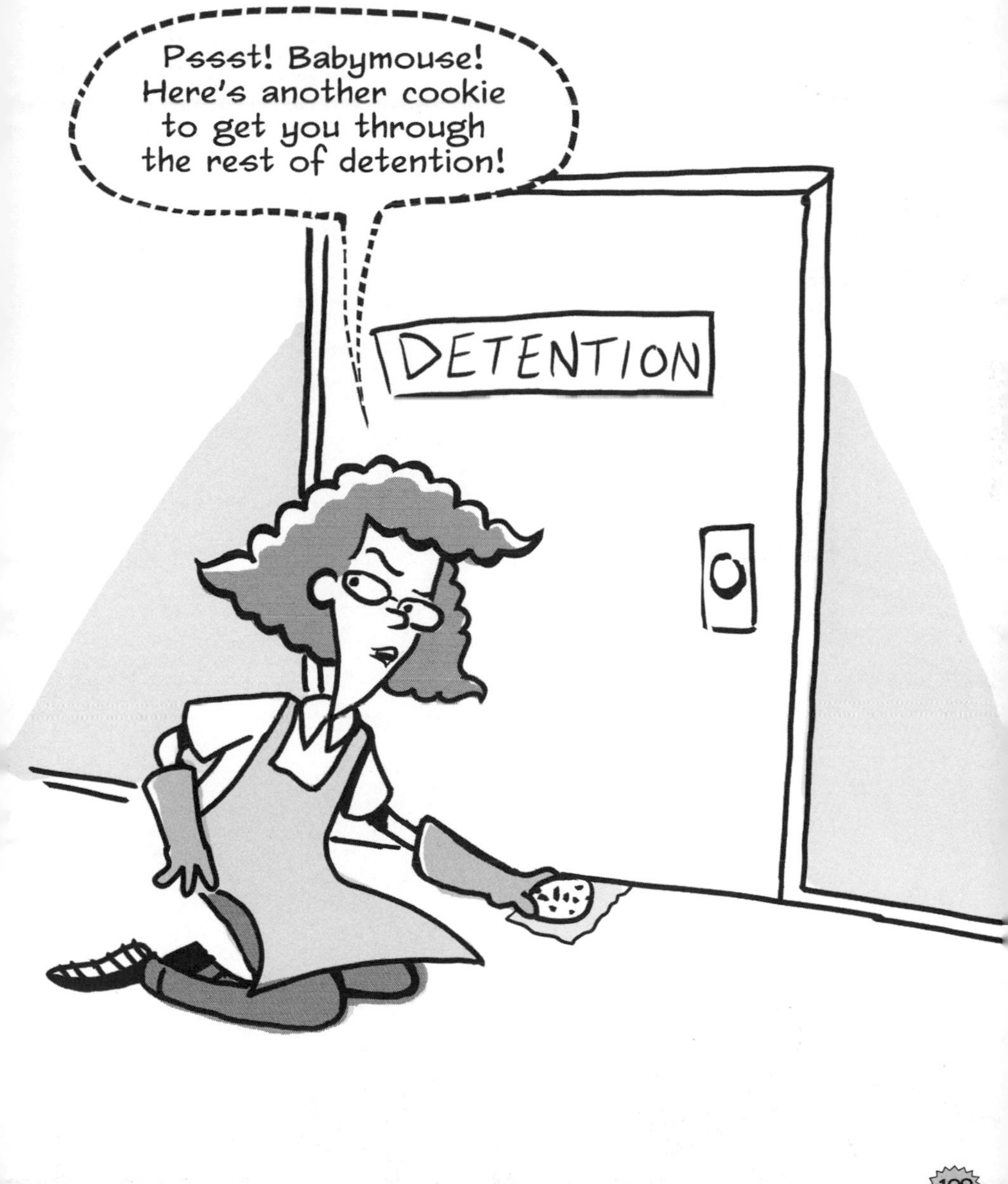
Pssst! Babymouse! Here's another cookie to get you through the rest of detention!
DETENTION

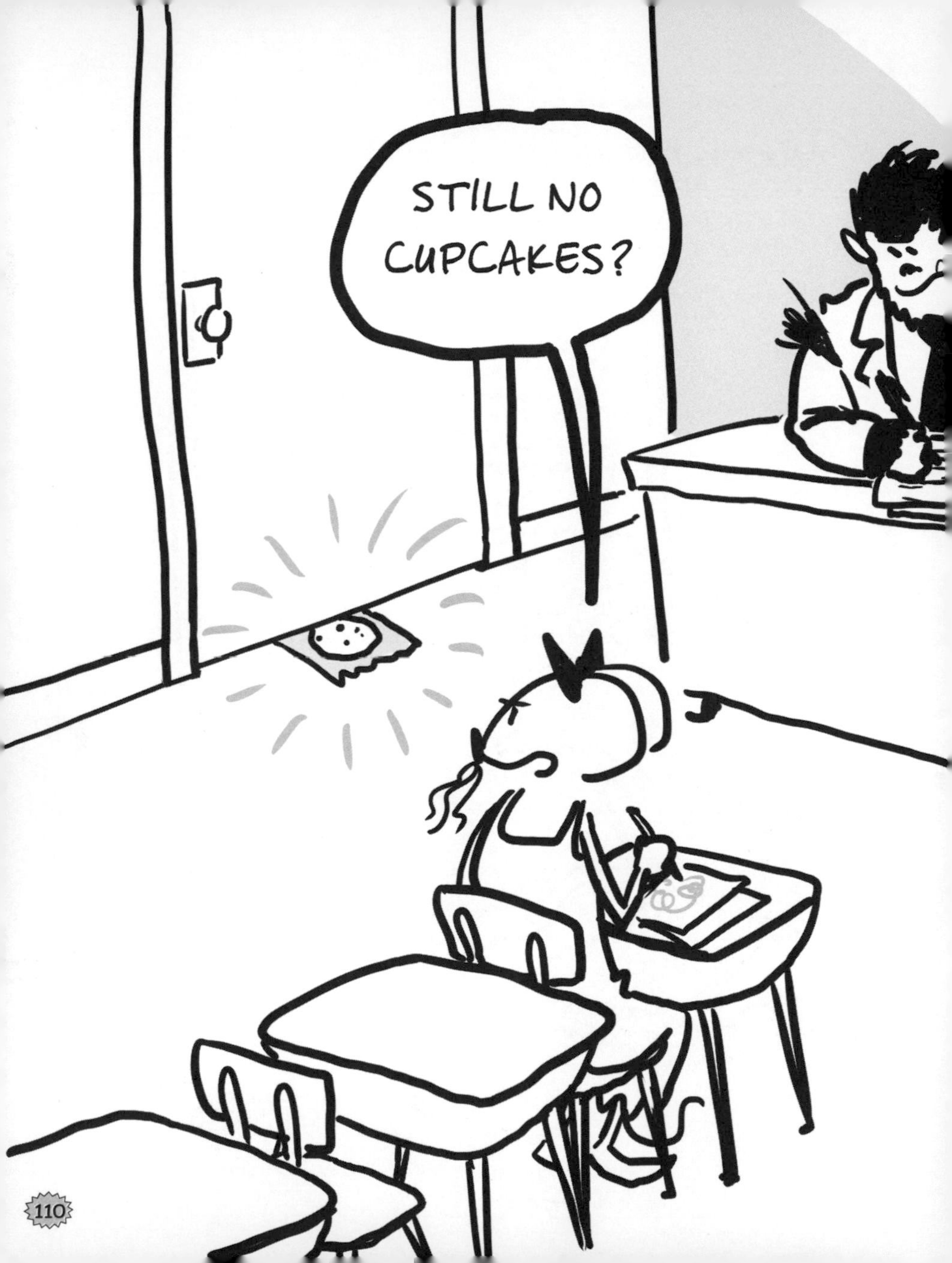
STILL NO CUPCAKES?

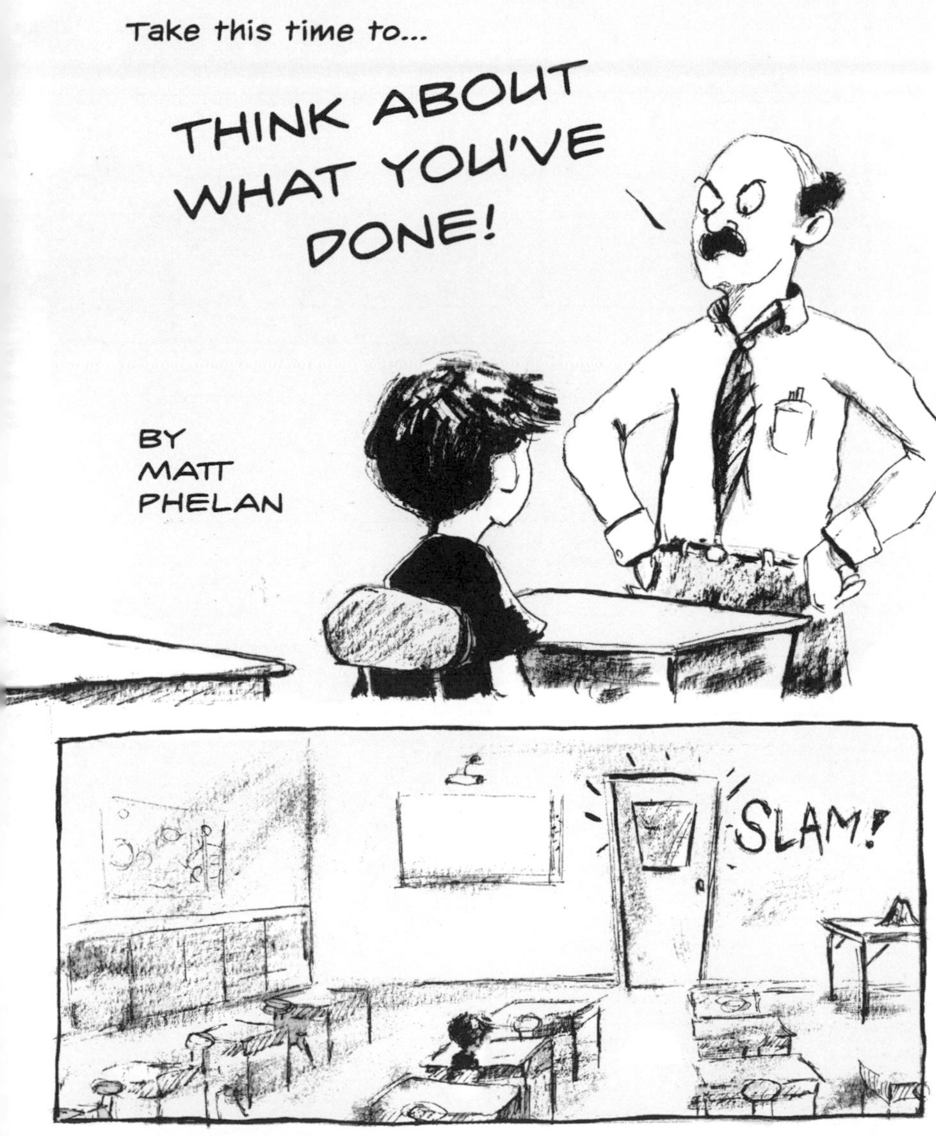
Take this time to...
THINK ABOUT WHAT YOU'VE DONE!
BY MATT PHELAN
SLAM!

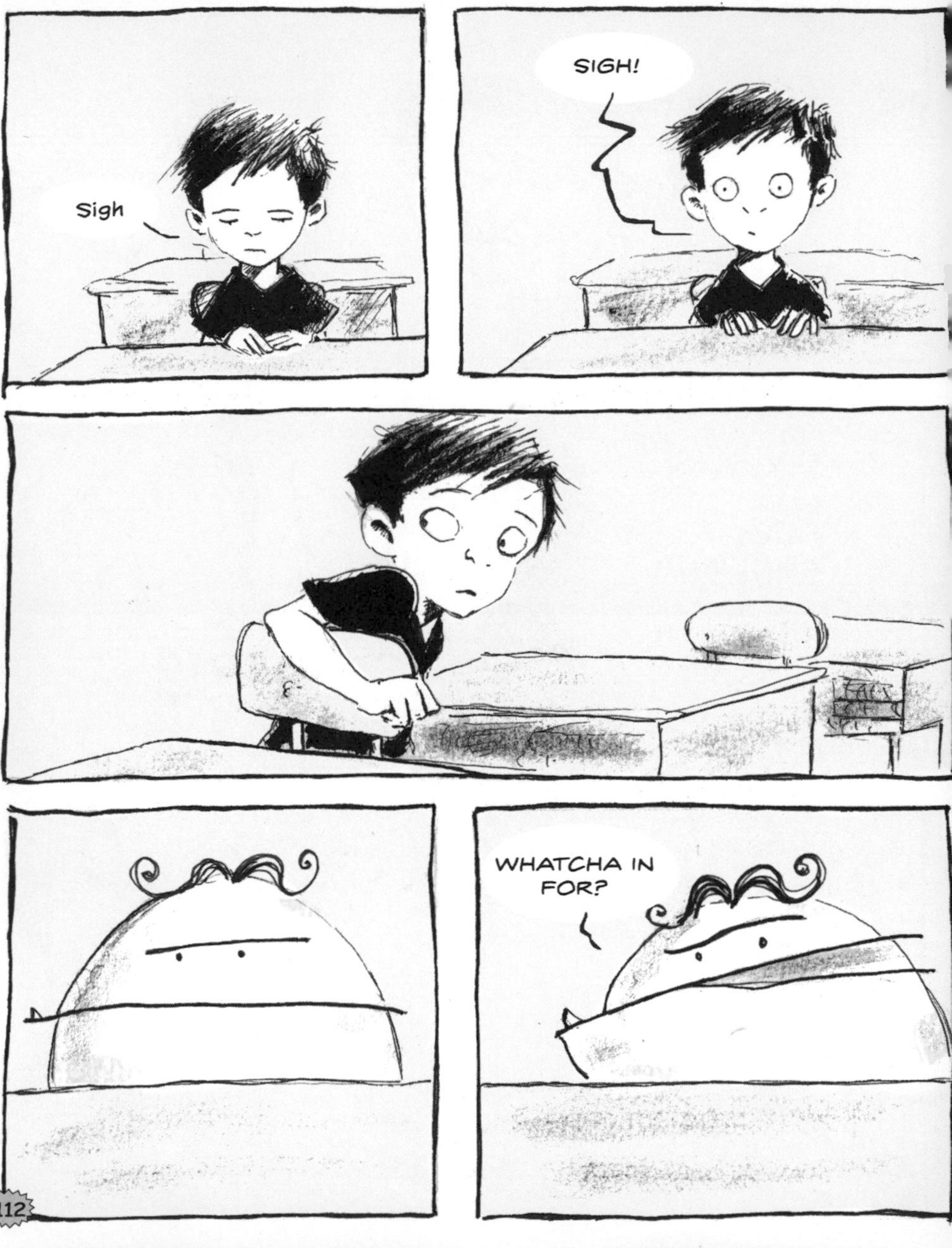
Sigh
SIGH!
WHATCHA IN FOR?

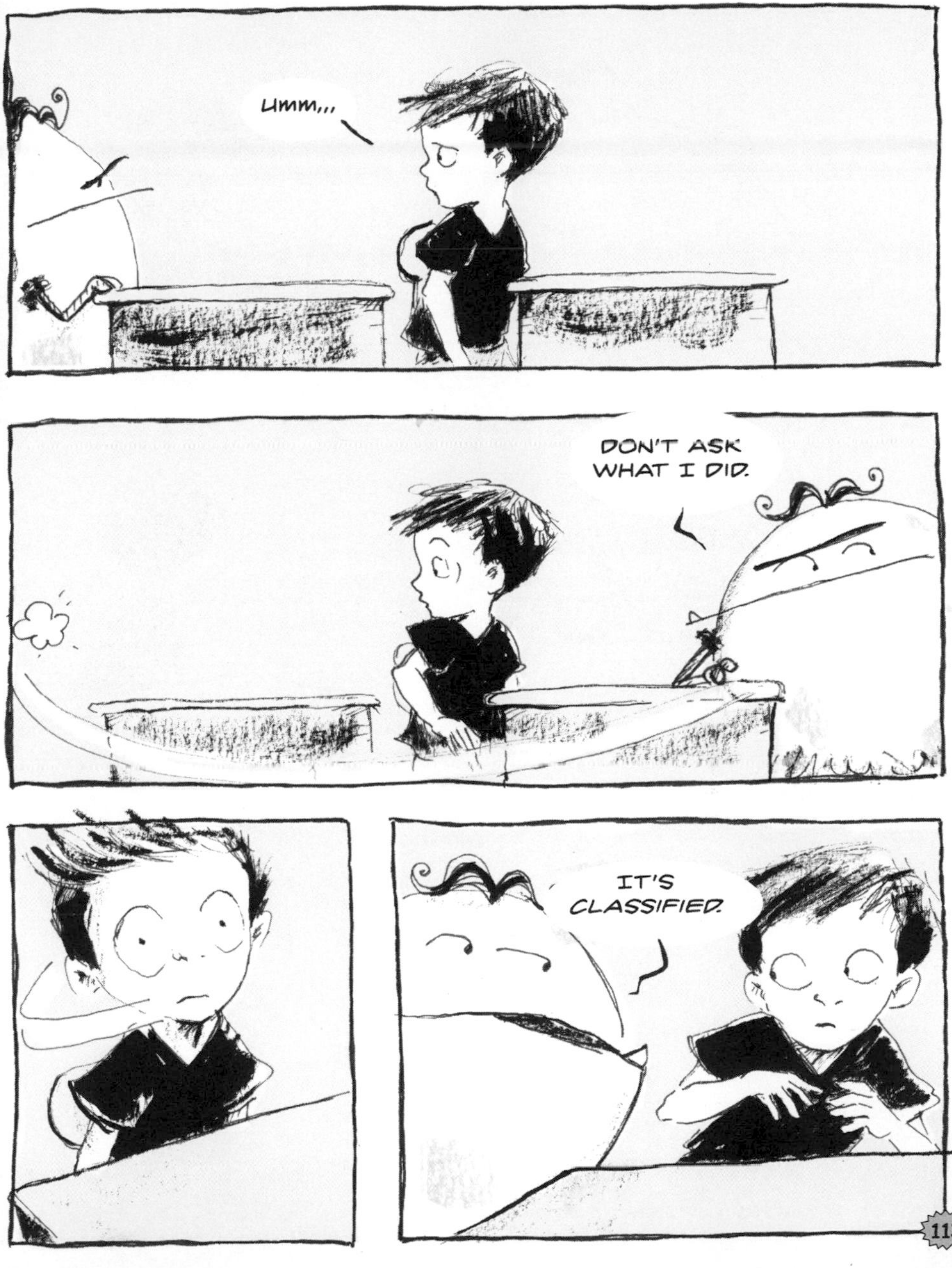
UMM,,,
DON'T ASK WHAT I DID.
IT'S CLASSIFIED.

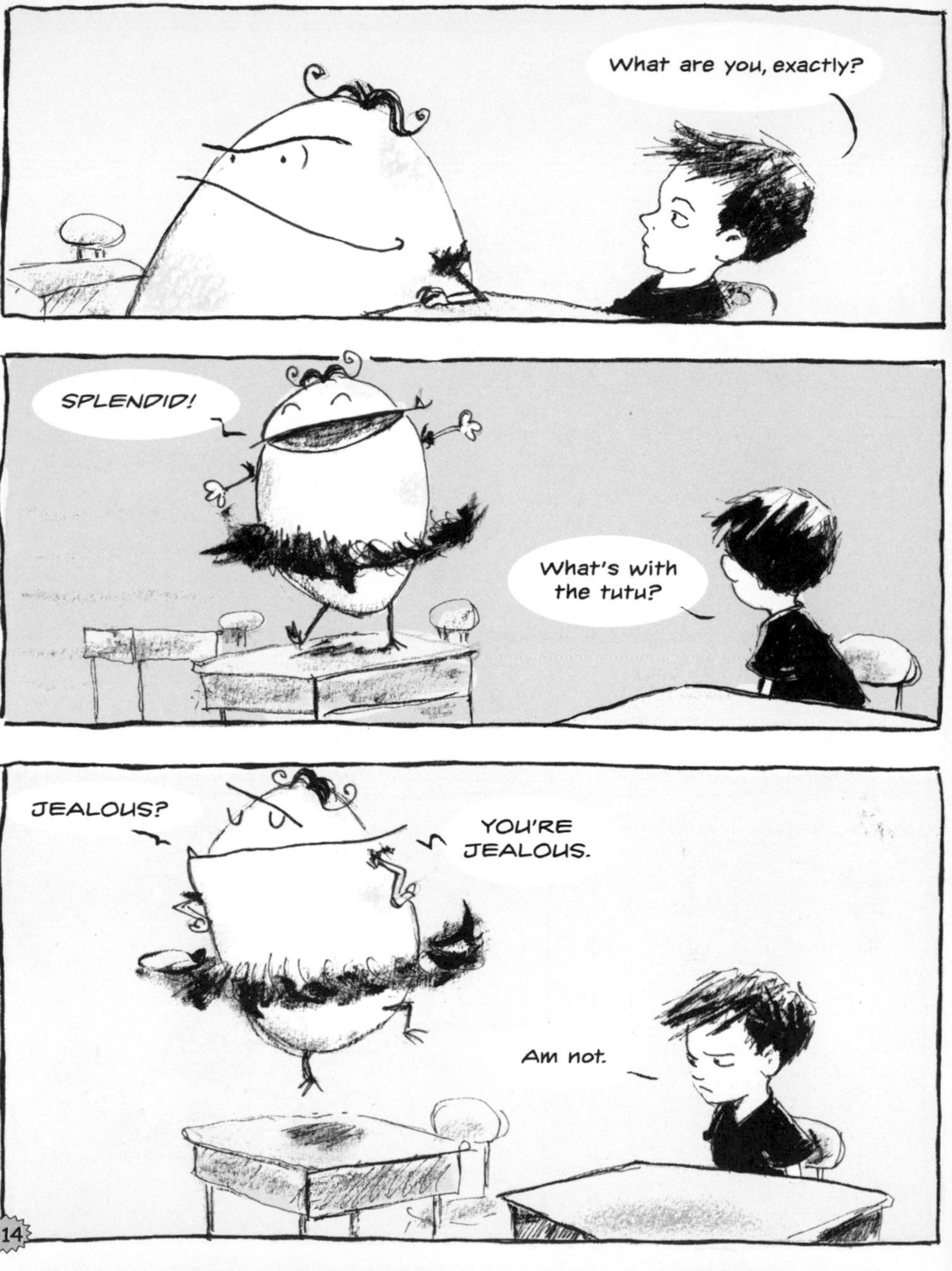
What are you, exactly?
SPLENDID!
What's with the tutu?
JEALOUS?
YOU'RE JEALOUS.
Am not.

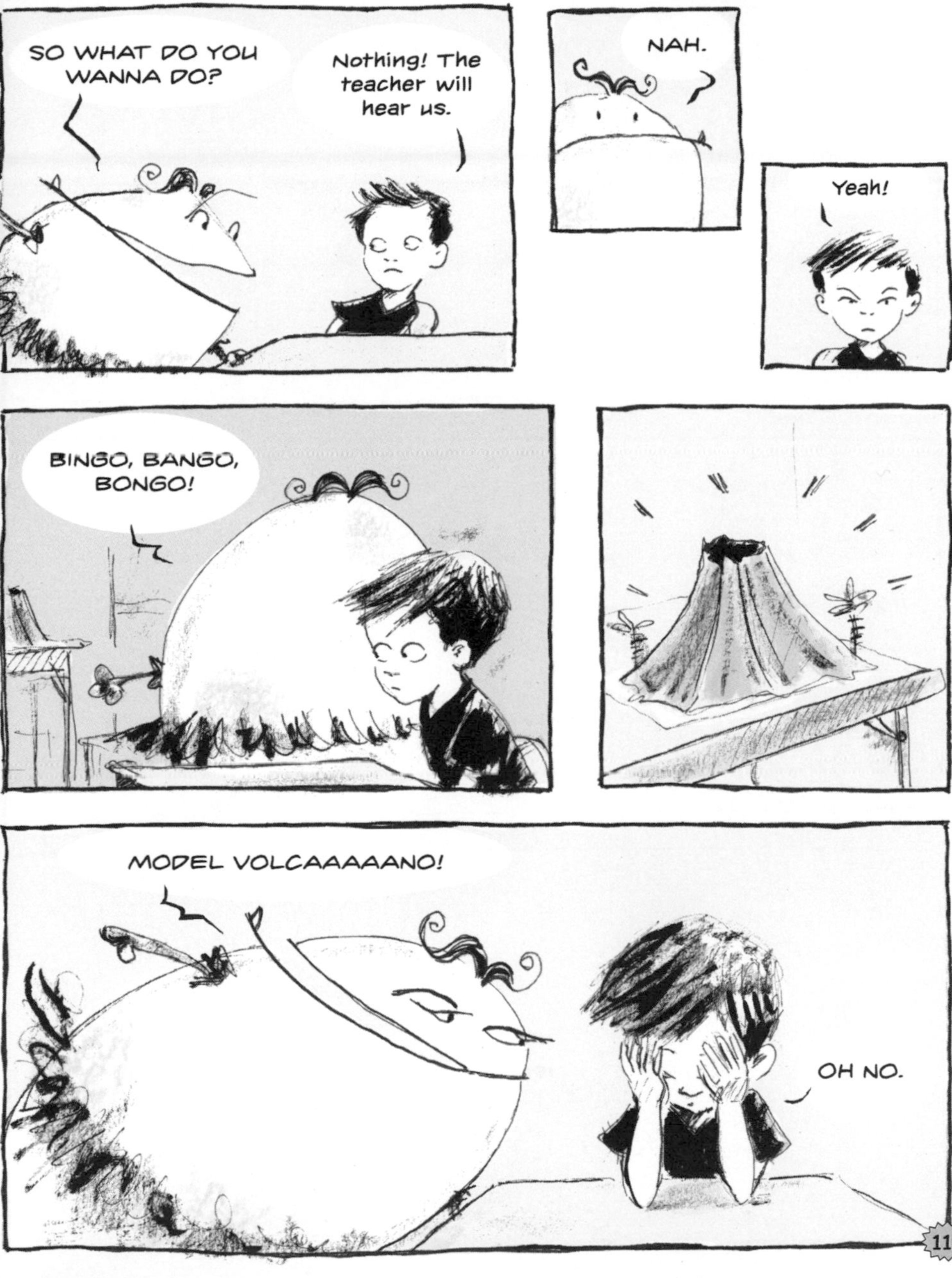
SO WHAT DO YOU WANNA DO?
Nothing! The teacher will hear us.
NAH.
Yeah!
BINGO, BANGO, BONGO!
MODEL VOLCAAAAANO!
OH NO.

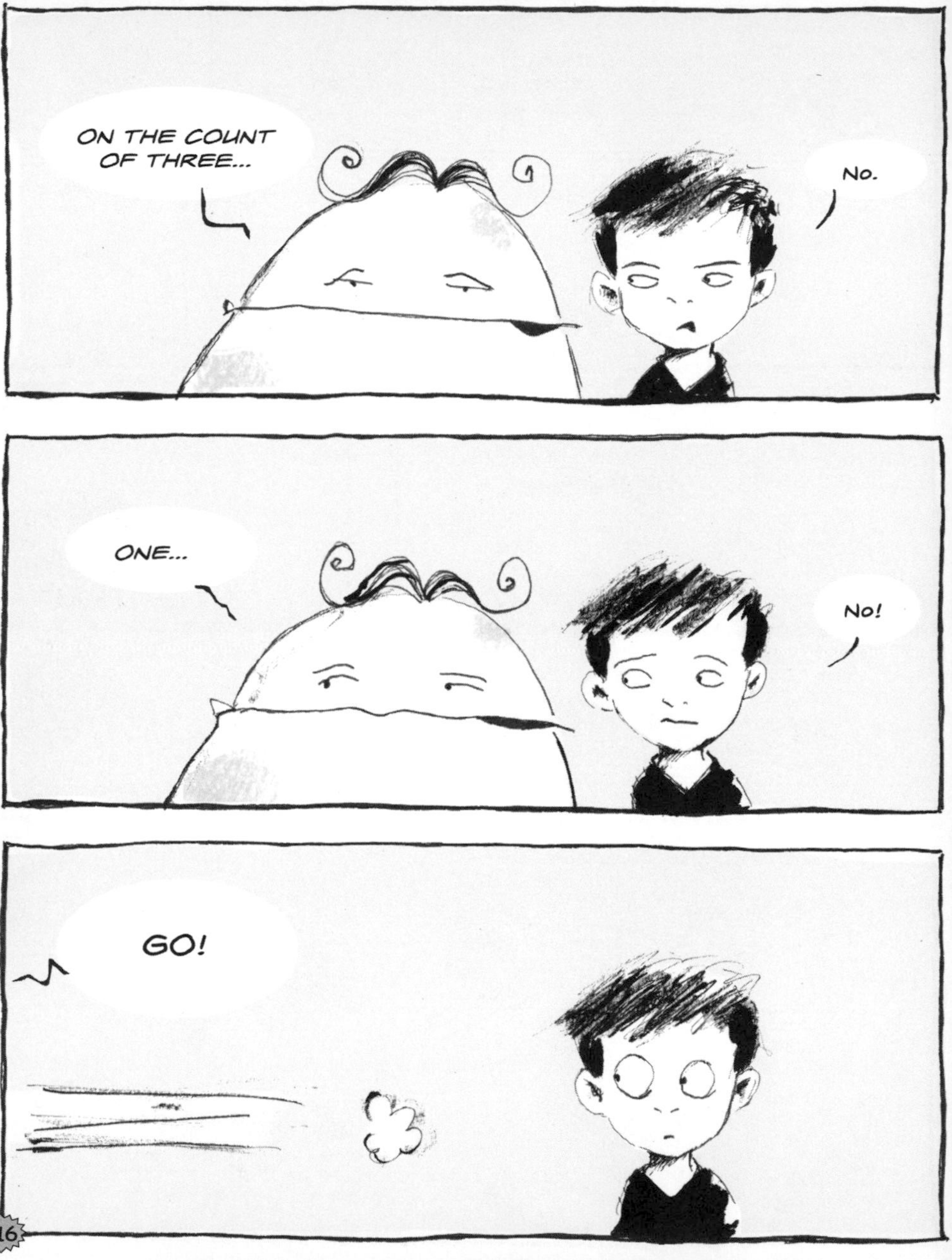
ON THE COUNT OF THREE...
No.
ONE...
No!
GO!

OKAY.
BAKING
SODA.
VINEGAR.

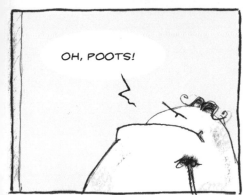

OH, POOTS!

CAN I GET SOME
HELP HERE?

LI'L ARMS!

117

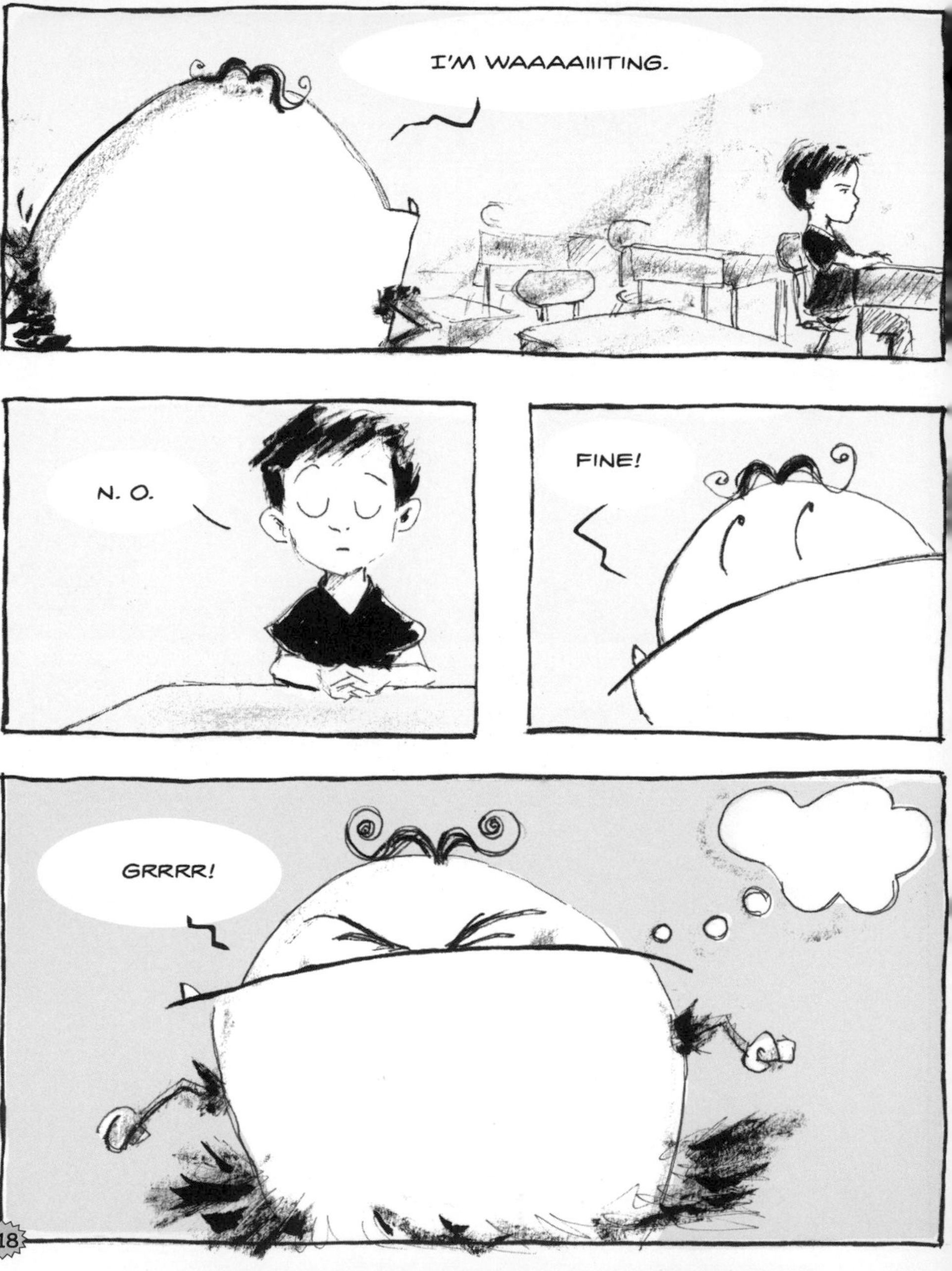
I'M WAAAAIIITING.
N. O.
FINE!
GRRRR!

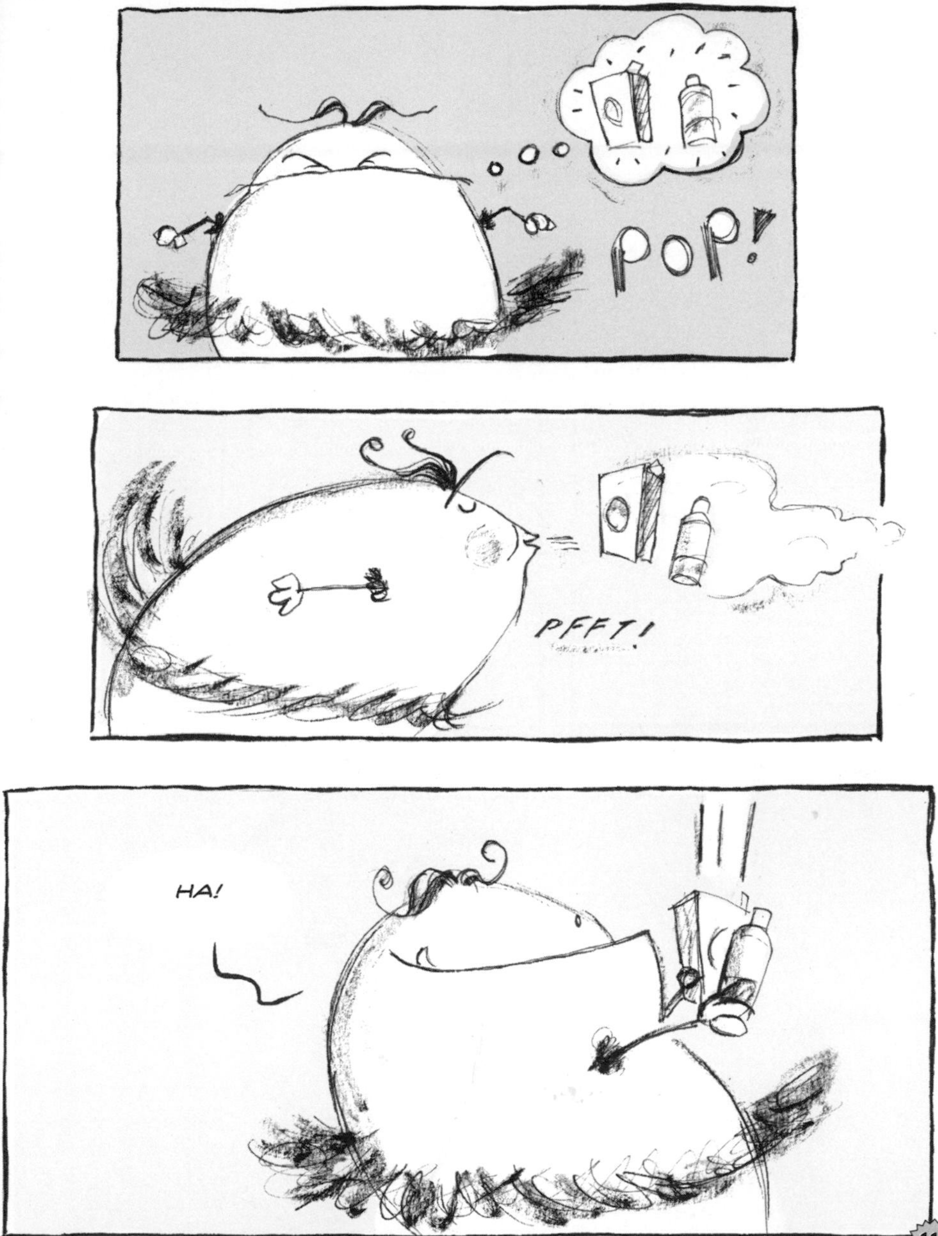
POP!
PFFT!
HA!

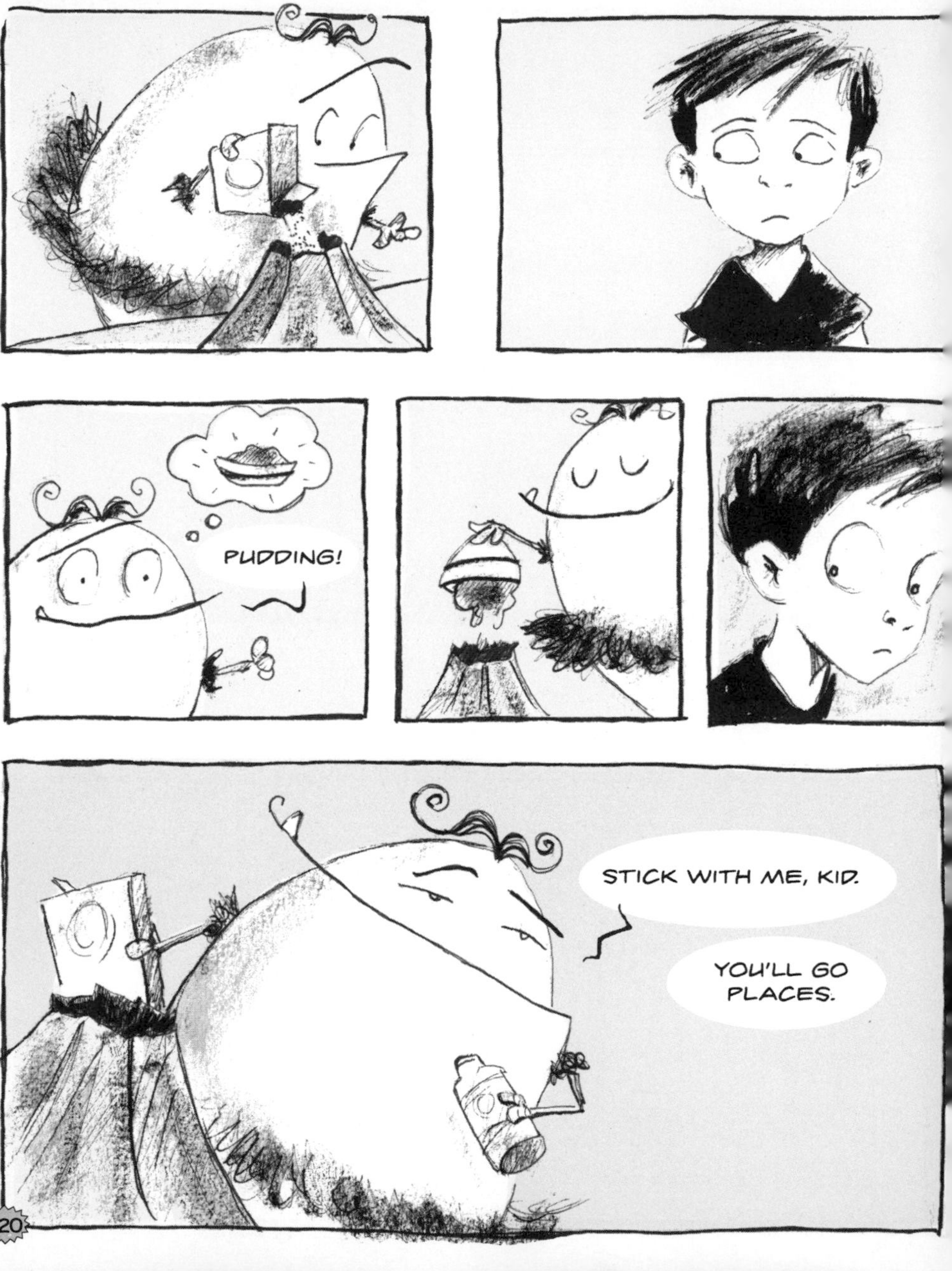
PUDDING!
STICK WITH ME, KID.
YOU'LL GO PLACES.

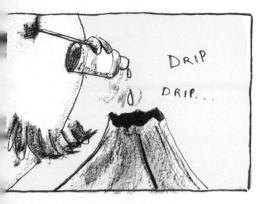

DRIP

DRIP...

BLOOP!

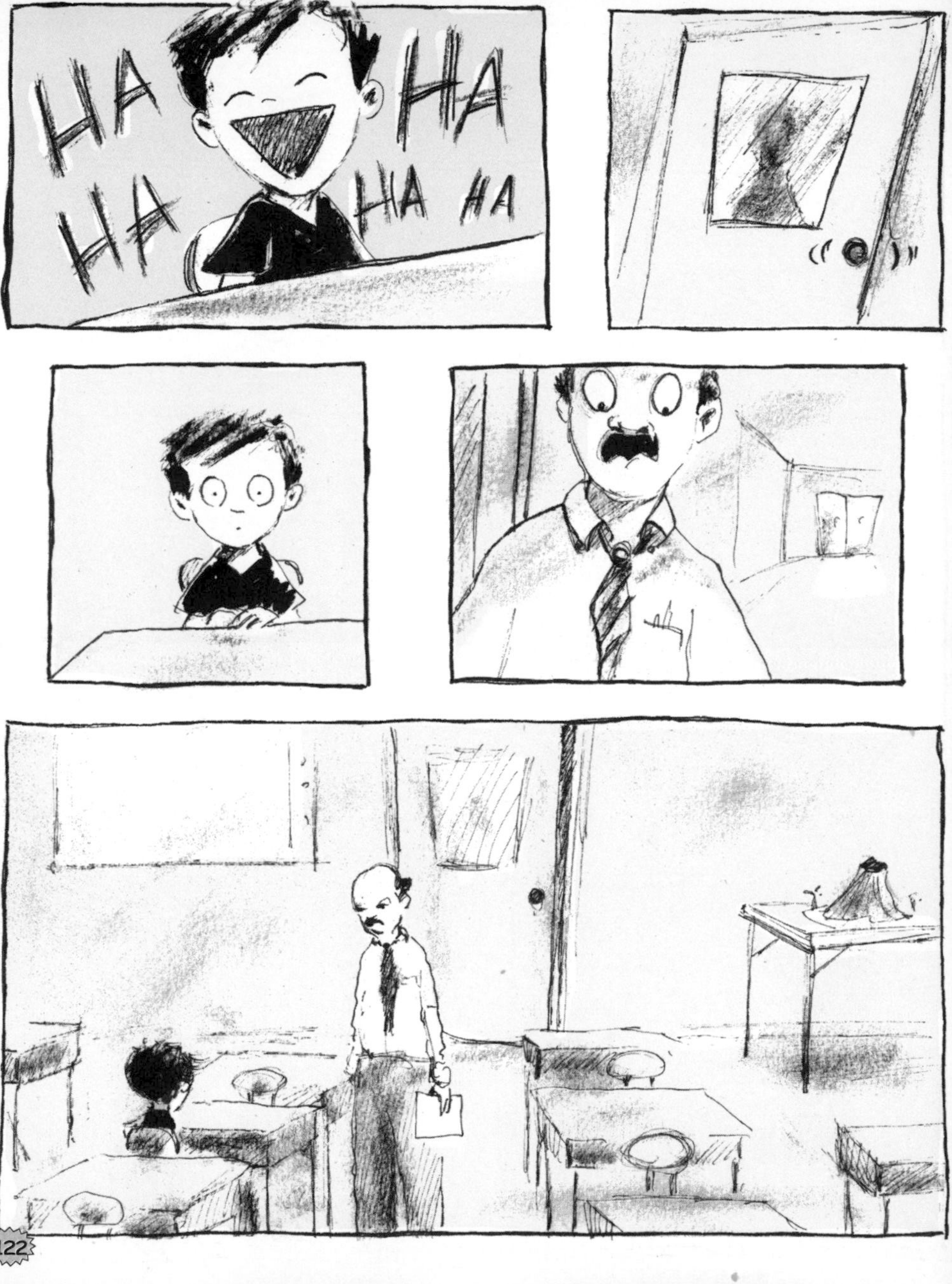
HA HA
HA HA HA HA

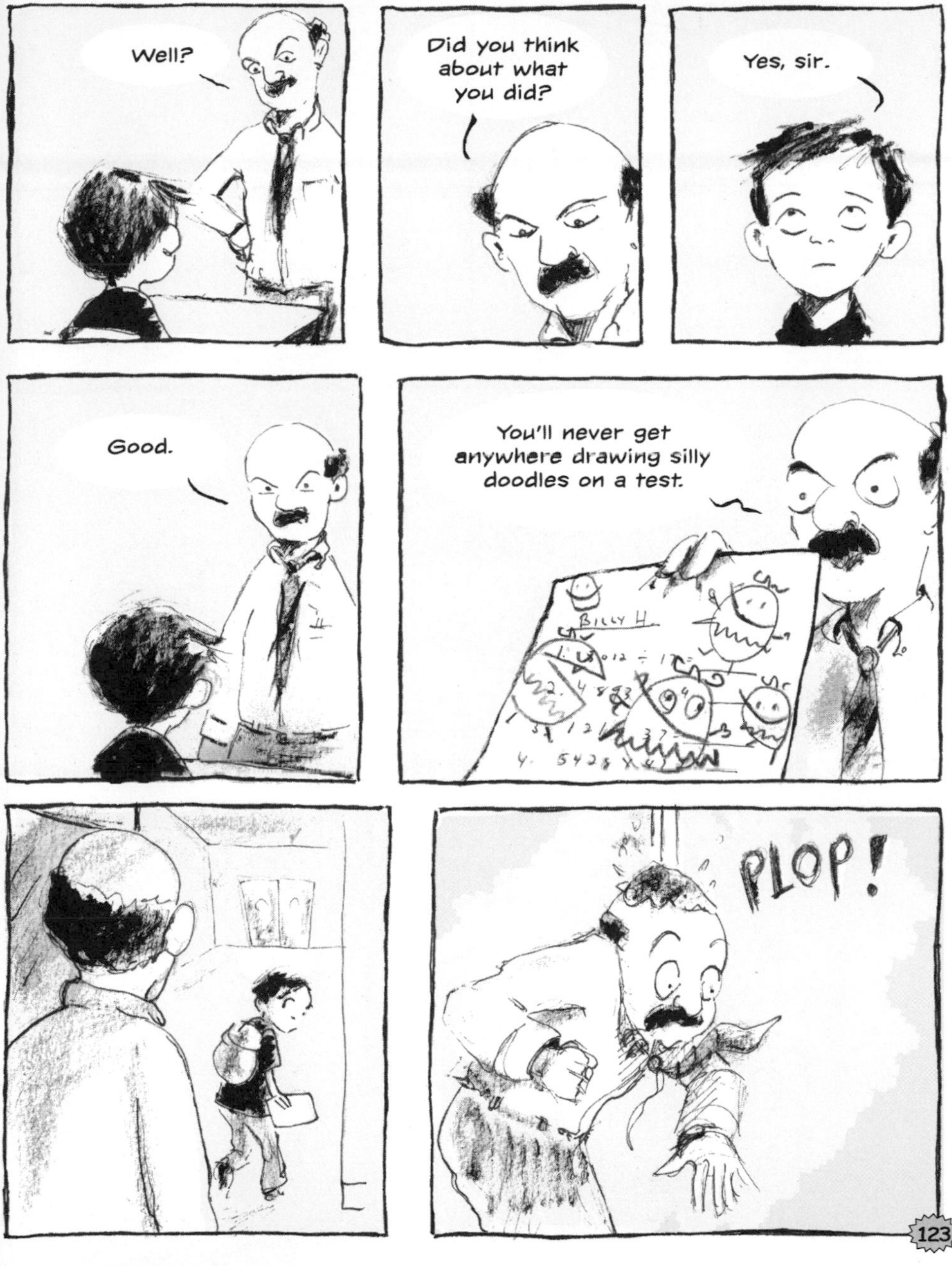

Well?
Did you think about what you did?
Yes, sir.
Good.
You'll never get anywhere drawing silly doodles on a test.
BILLY H.
PLOP!

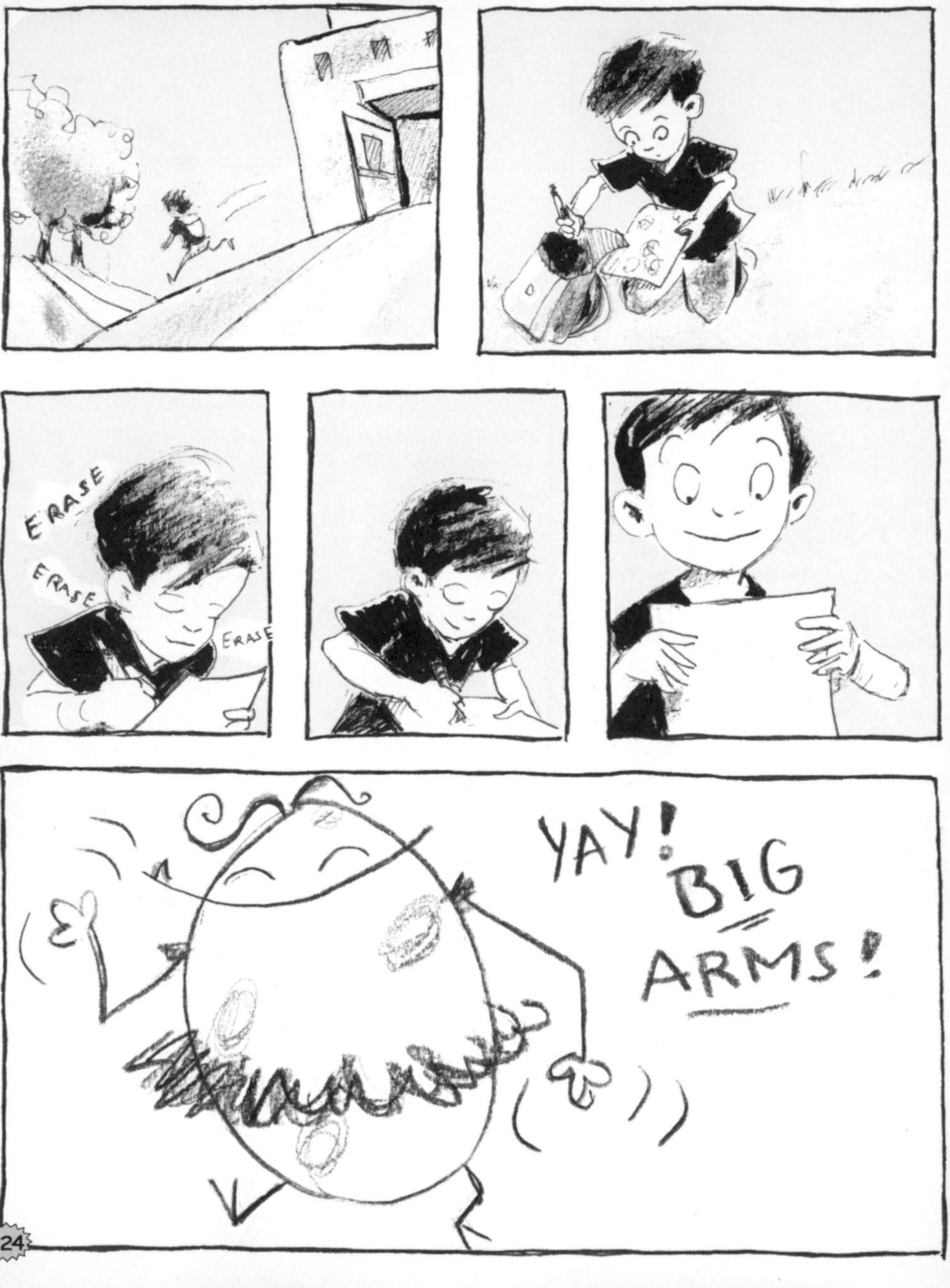
ERASE
ERASE
ERASE
YAY! BIG ARMS!

squish
LEAVE NO CELL BEHIND!

BY JENNIFER L. HOLM & MATTHEW HOLM

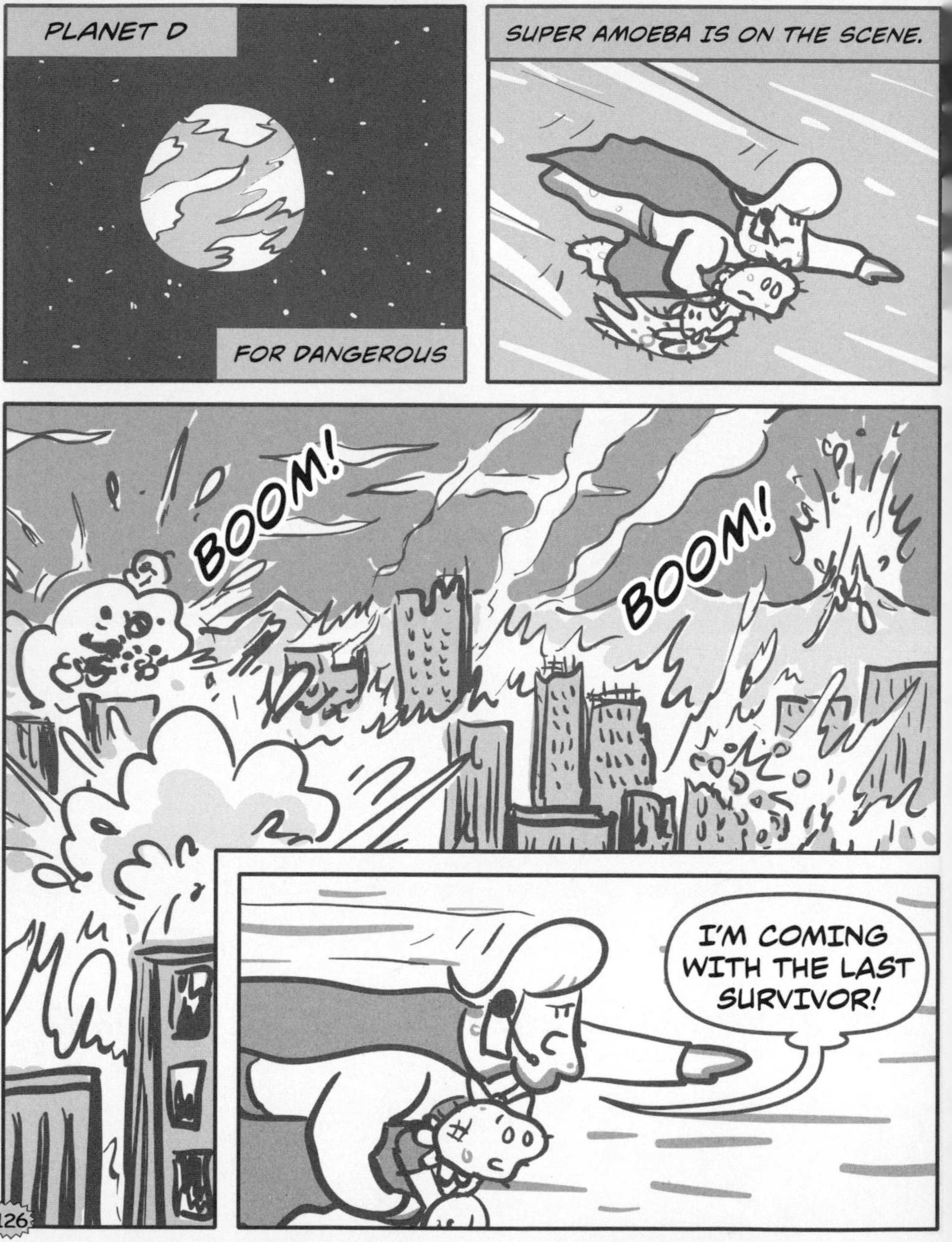
PLANET D
FOR DANGEROUS
SUPER AMOEBA IS ON THE SCENE.
BOOM!
BOOM!
I'M COMING WITH THE LAST SURVIVOR!

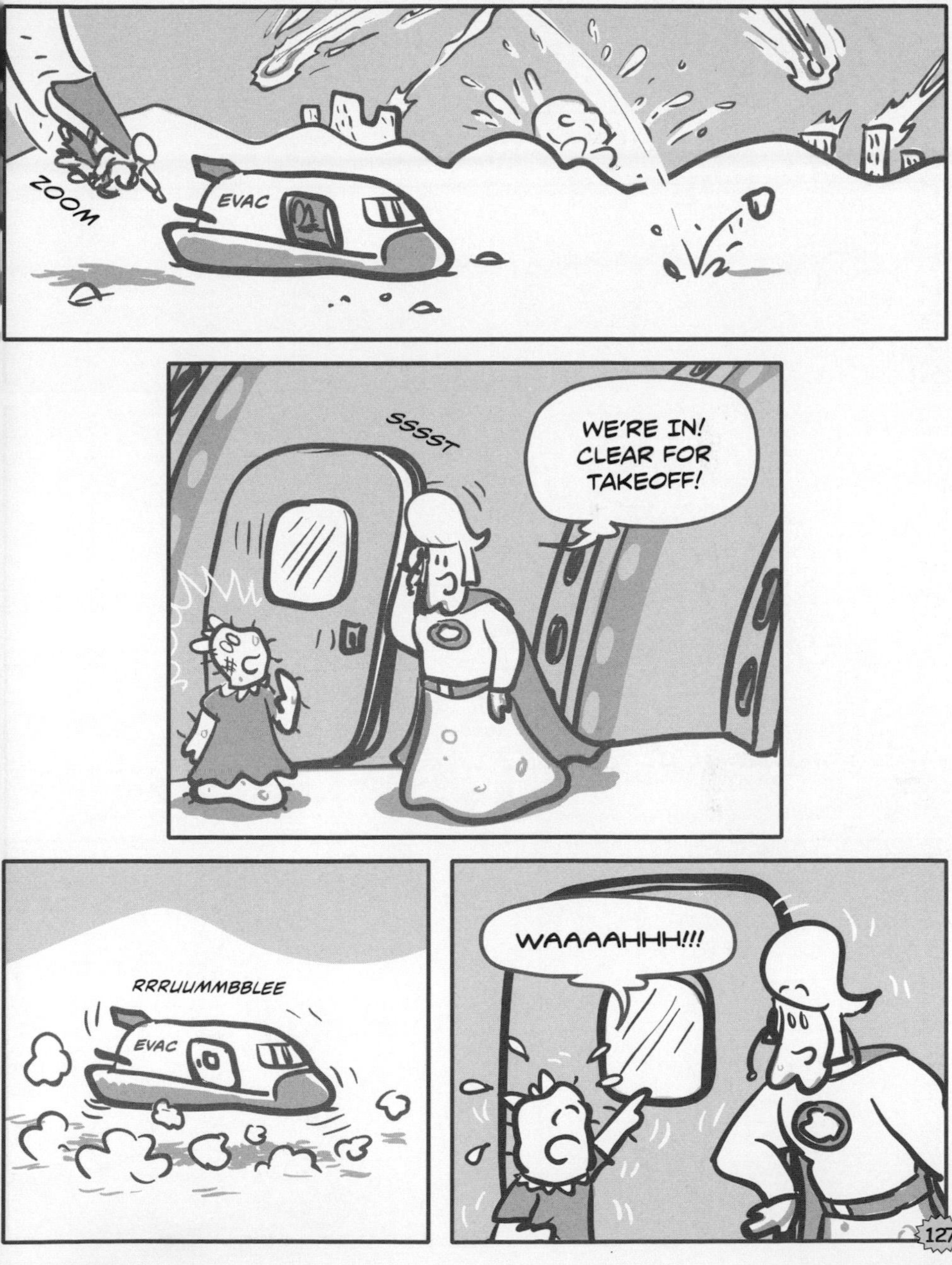
ZOOM
EVAC
SSSST
WE'RE IN! CLEAR FOR TAKEOFF!
RRRUUMMBBLEE
EVAC
WAAAAHHH!!!

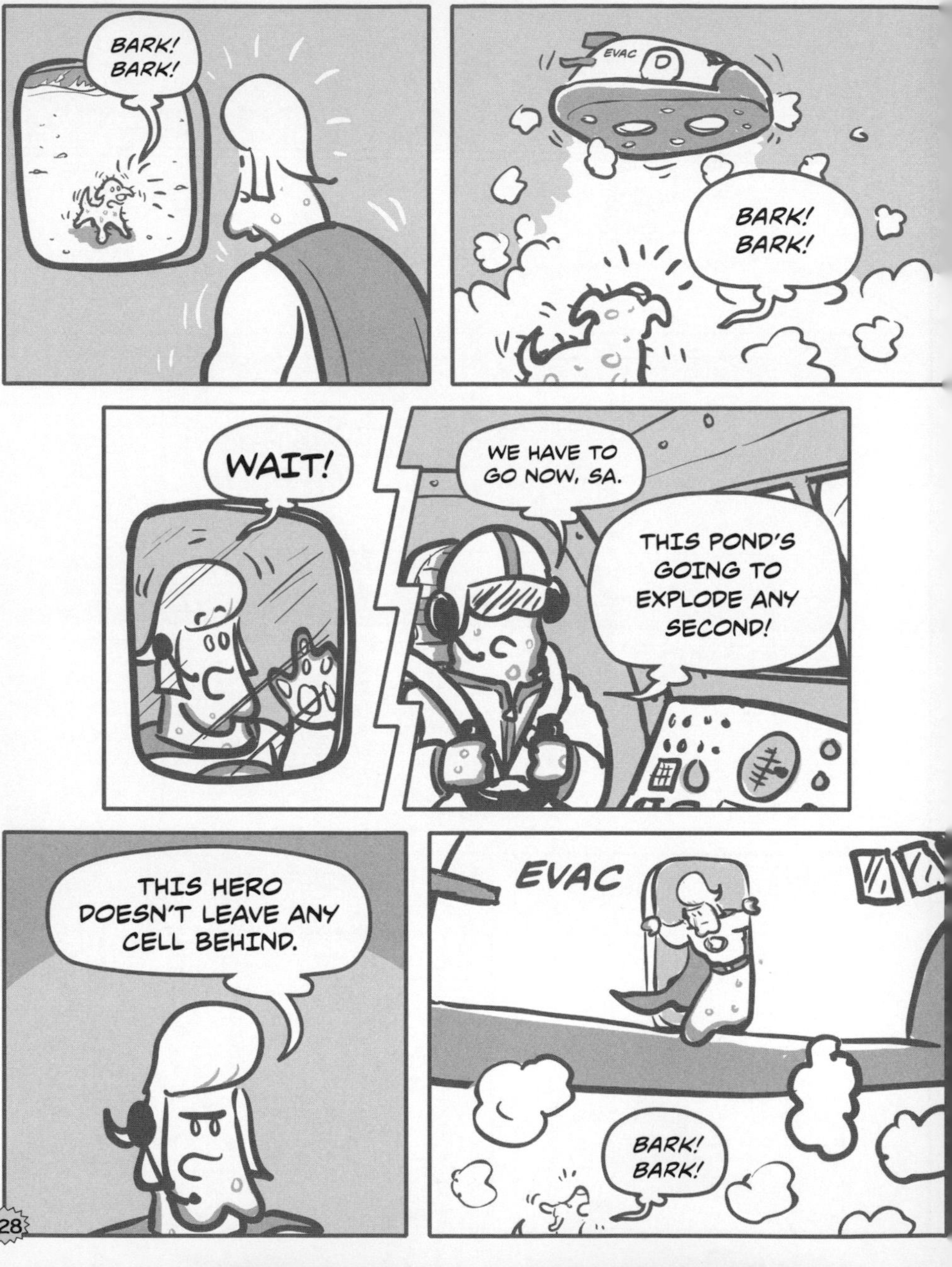
BARK! BARK!
BARK! BARK!
WAIT!
WE HAVE TO GO NOW, SA.
THIS POND'S GOING TO EXPLODE ANY SECOND!
THIS HERO DOESN'T LEAVE ANY CELL BEHIND.
EVAC
BARK! BARK!

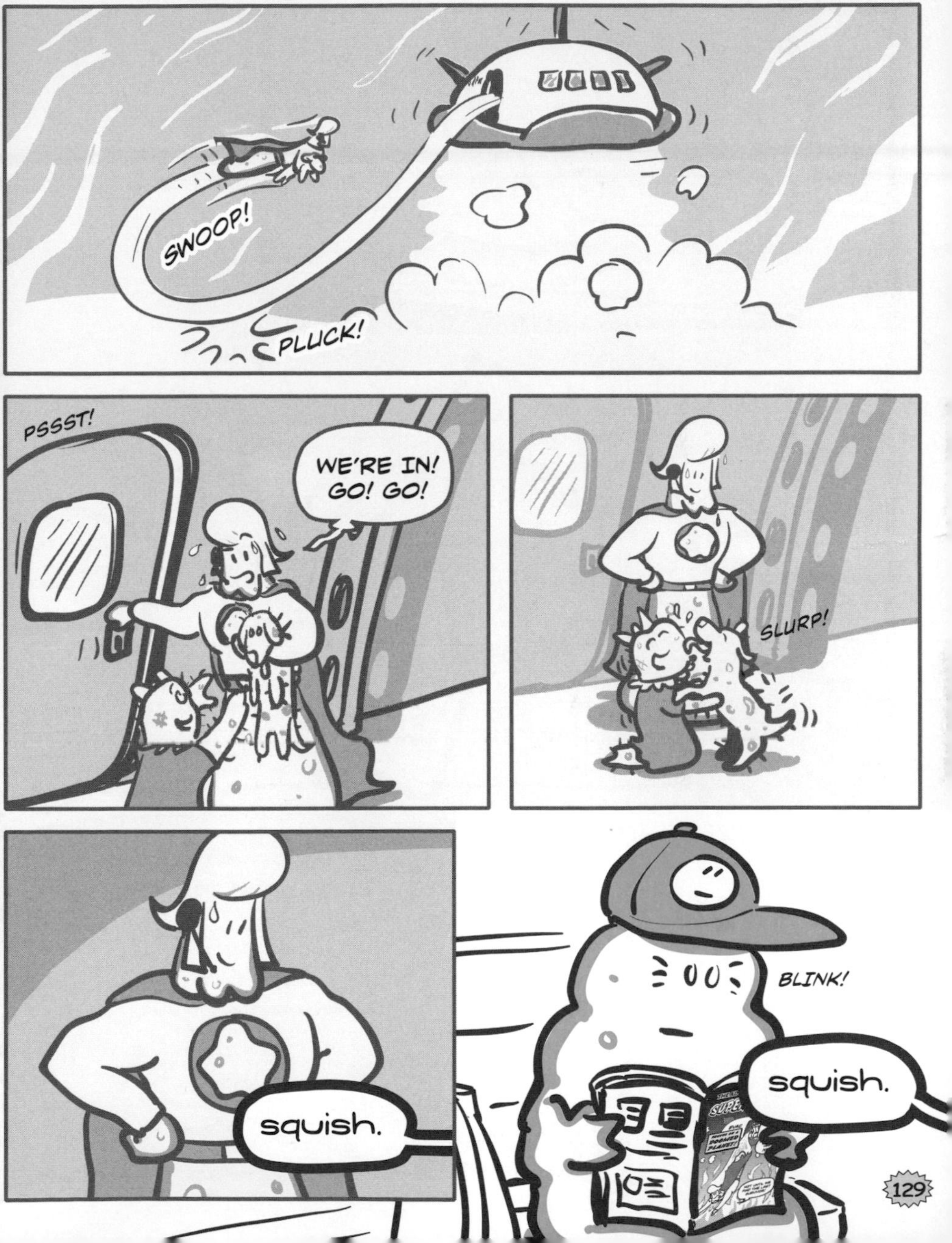
SWOOP!
PLUCK!
PSSST!
WE'RE IN! GO! GO!
SLURP!
squish.
BLINK!
squish.

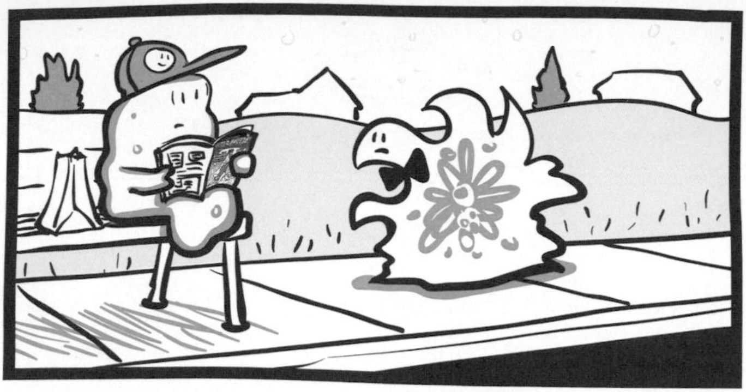

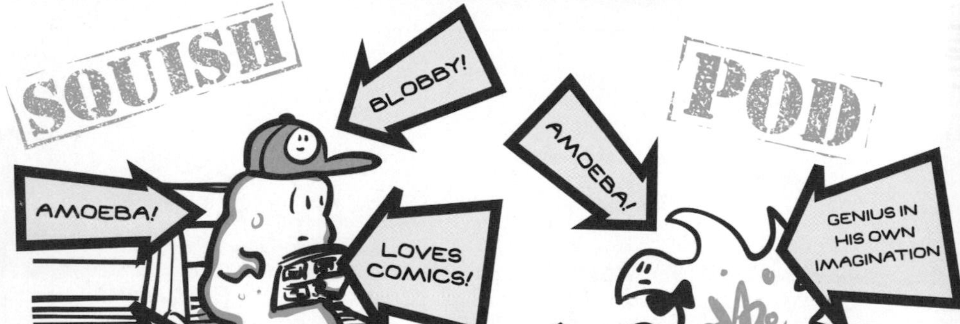
SQUISH
BLOBBY!
AMOEBA!
LOVES COMICS!
SINGLE-CELLED ORGANISM!
POD
AMOEBA!
GENIUS IN HIS OWN IMAGINATION
BEST FRIEND!
LOVES TO EAT SQUISH'S LUNCH

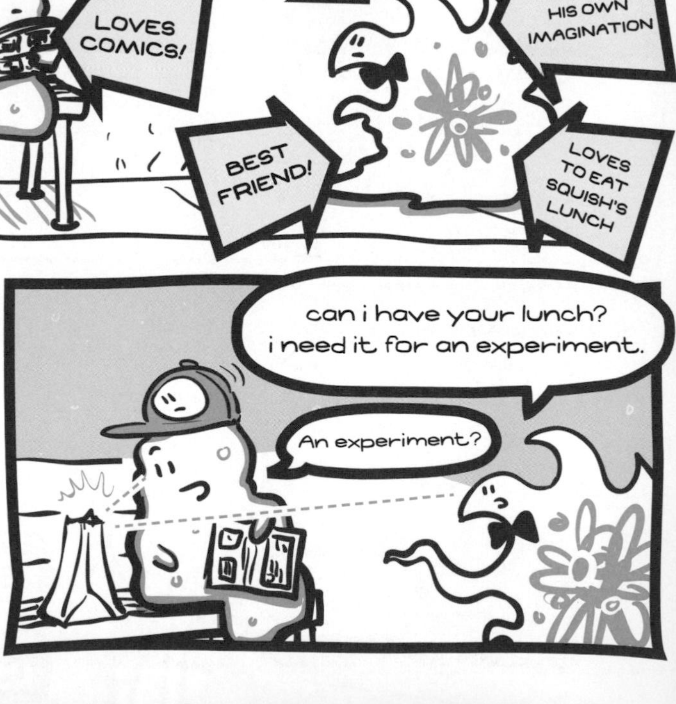
can i have your lunch? i need it for an experiment.
An experiment?

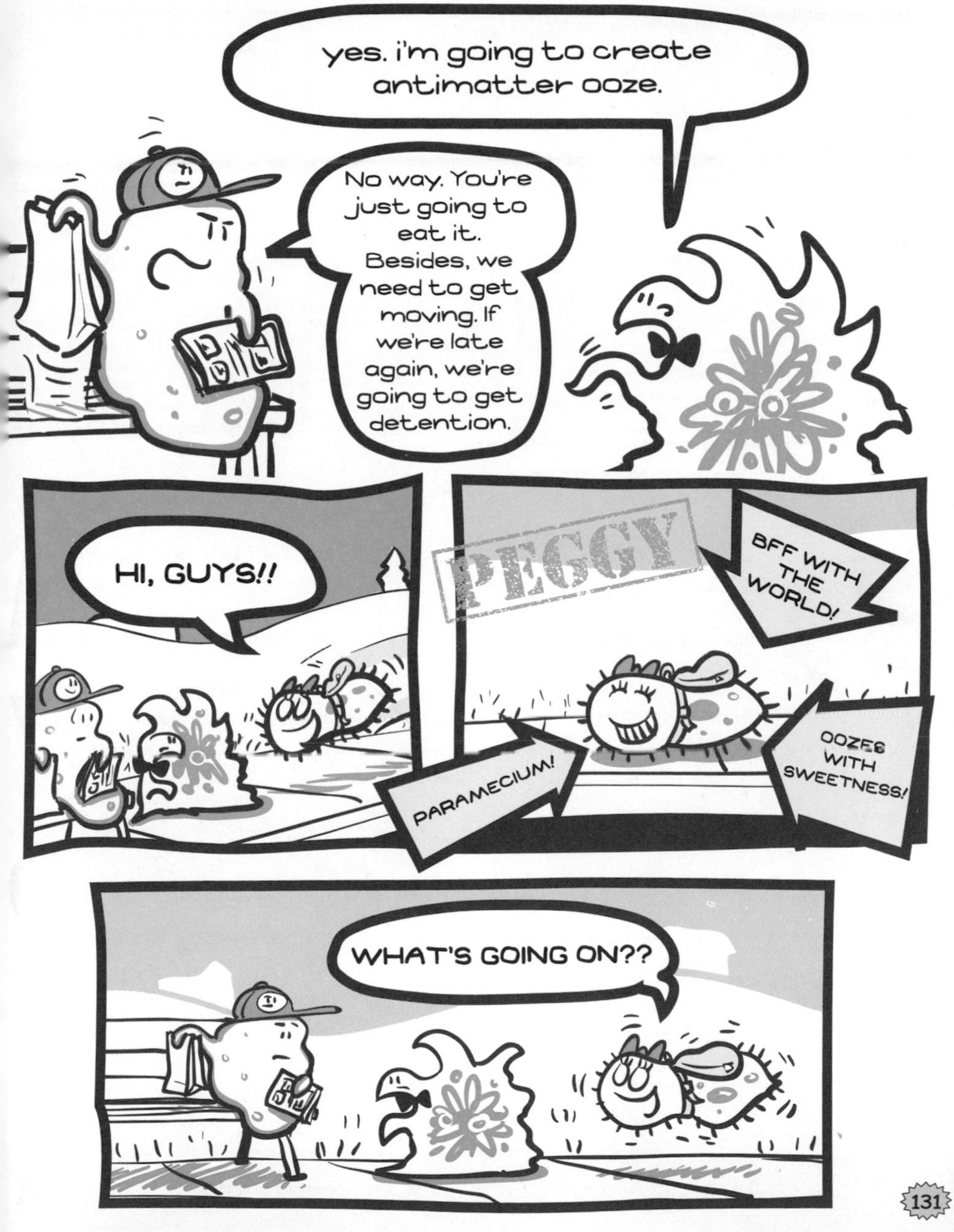
yes. i'm going to create antimatter ooze.
No way. You're just going to eat it. Besides, we need to get moving. If we're late again, we're going to get detention.
HI, GUYS!!
PEGGY
BFF WITH THE WORLD!
PARAMECIUM!
OOZES WITH SWEETNESS!
WHAT'S GOING ON??

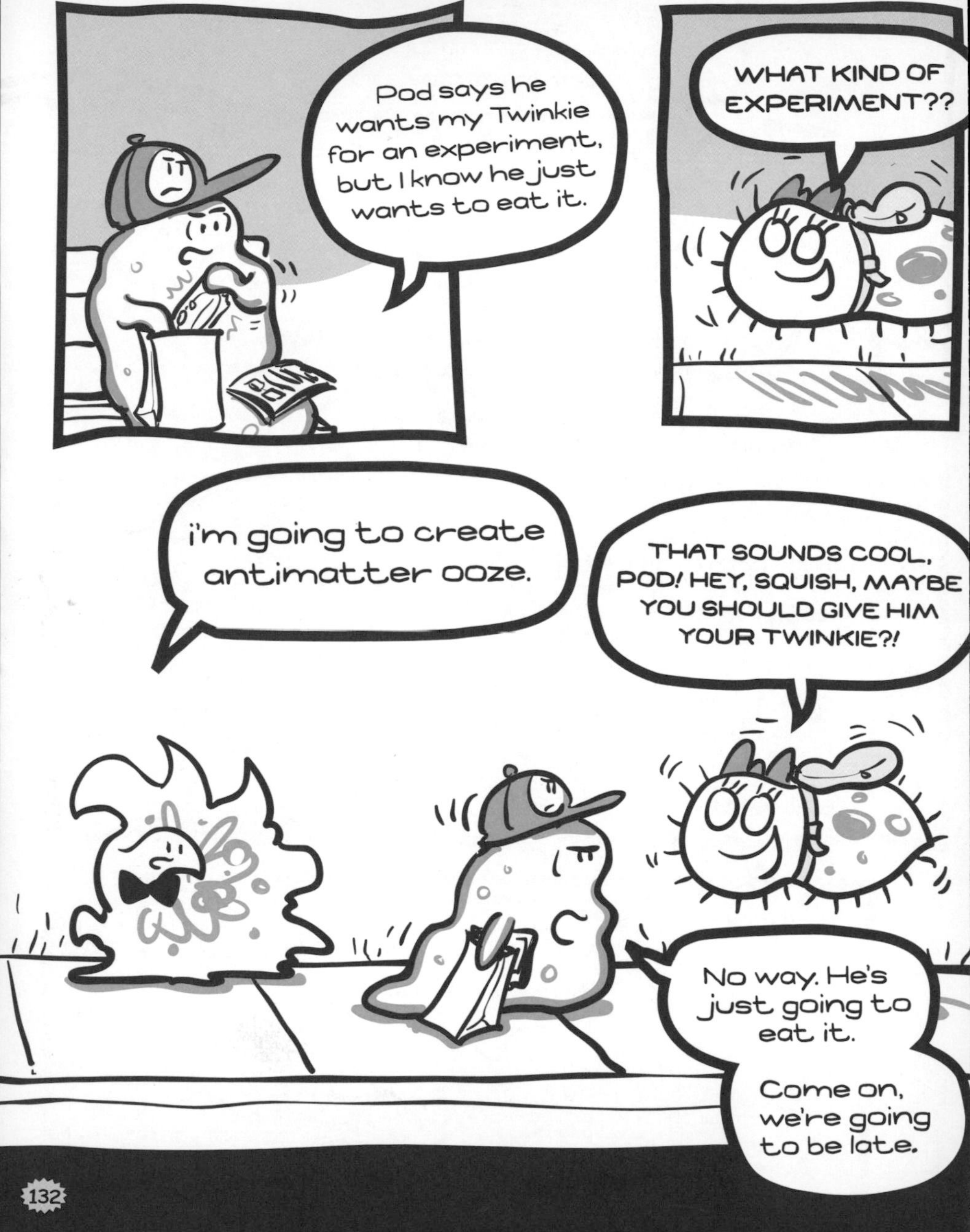
Pod says he wants my Twinkie for an experiment, but I know he just wants to eat it.
WHAT KIND OF EXPERIMENT??
i'm going to create antimatter ooze.
THAT SOUNDS COOL, POD! HEY, SQUISH, MAYBE YOU SHOULD GIVE HIM YOUR TWINKIE?!
No way. He's just going to eat it.
Come on, we're going to be late.

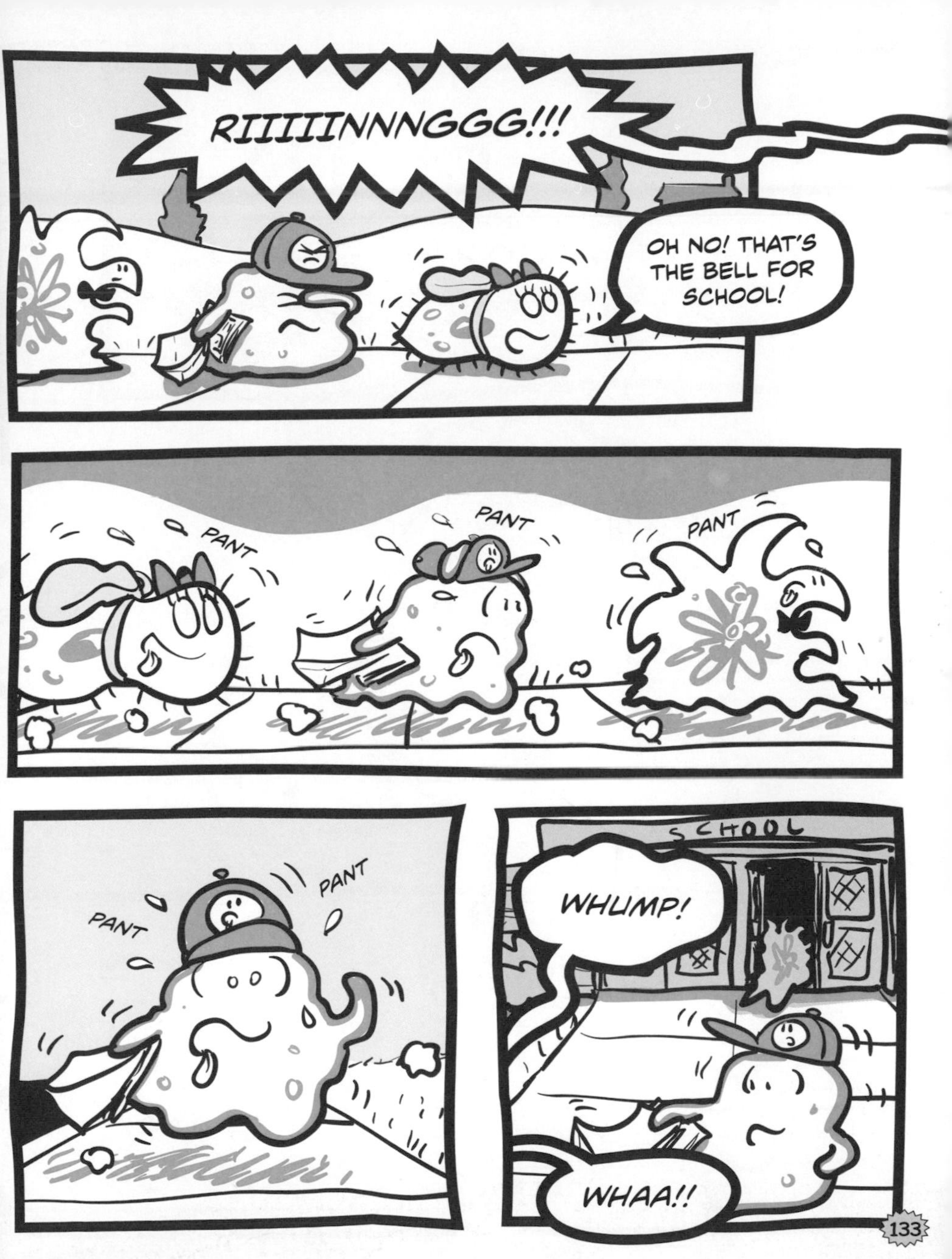
RIIIIINNNGGG!!!
OH NO! THAT'S THE BELL FOR SCHOOL!
PANT
PANT
PANT
PANT
PANT
SCHOOL
WHUMP!
WHAA!!

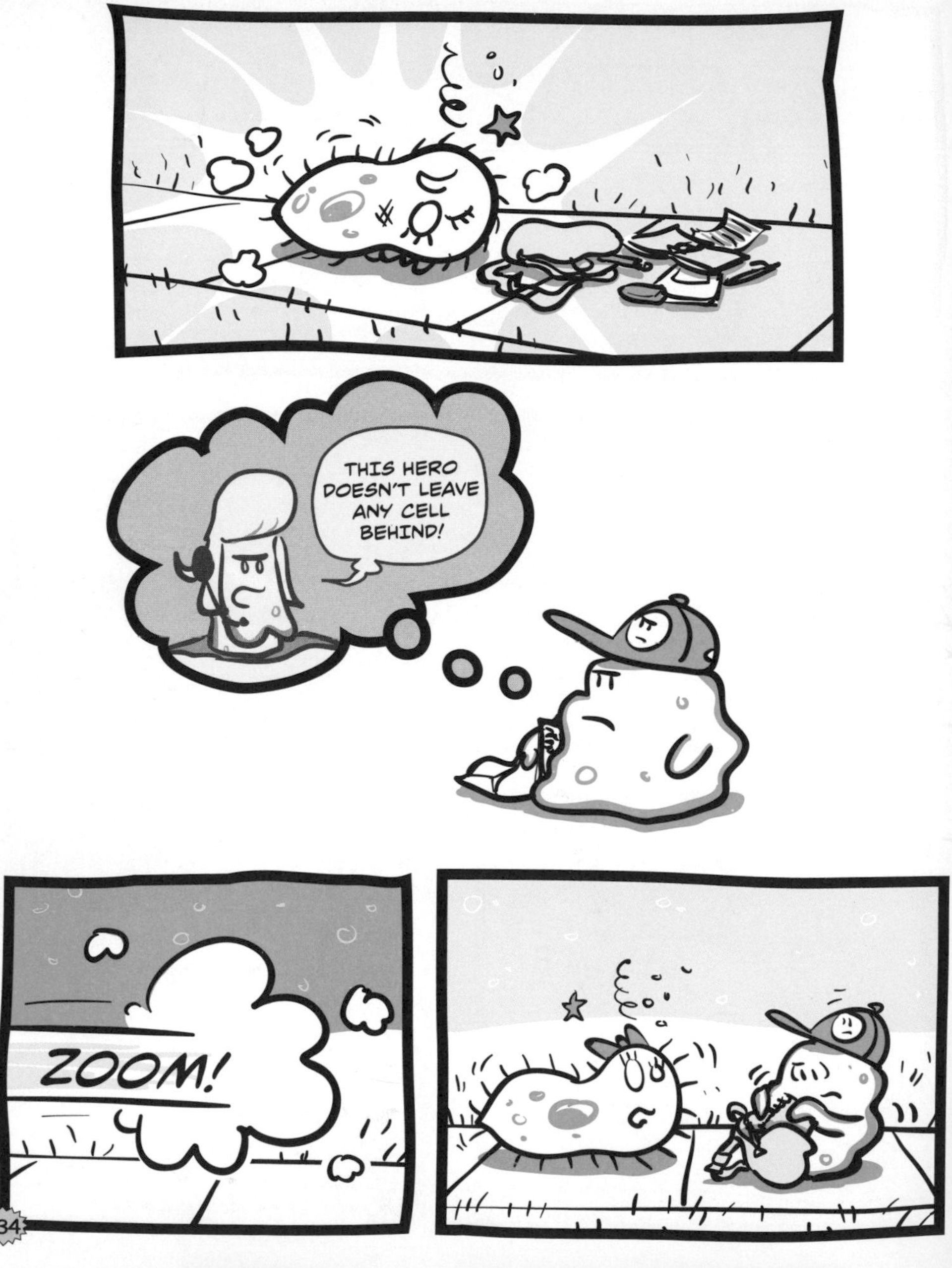
THIS HERO DOESN'T LEAVE ANY CELL BEHIND!
ZOOM!

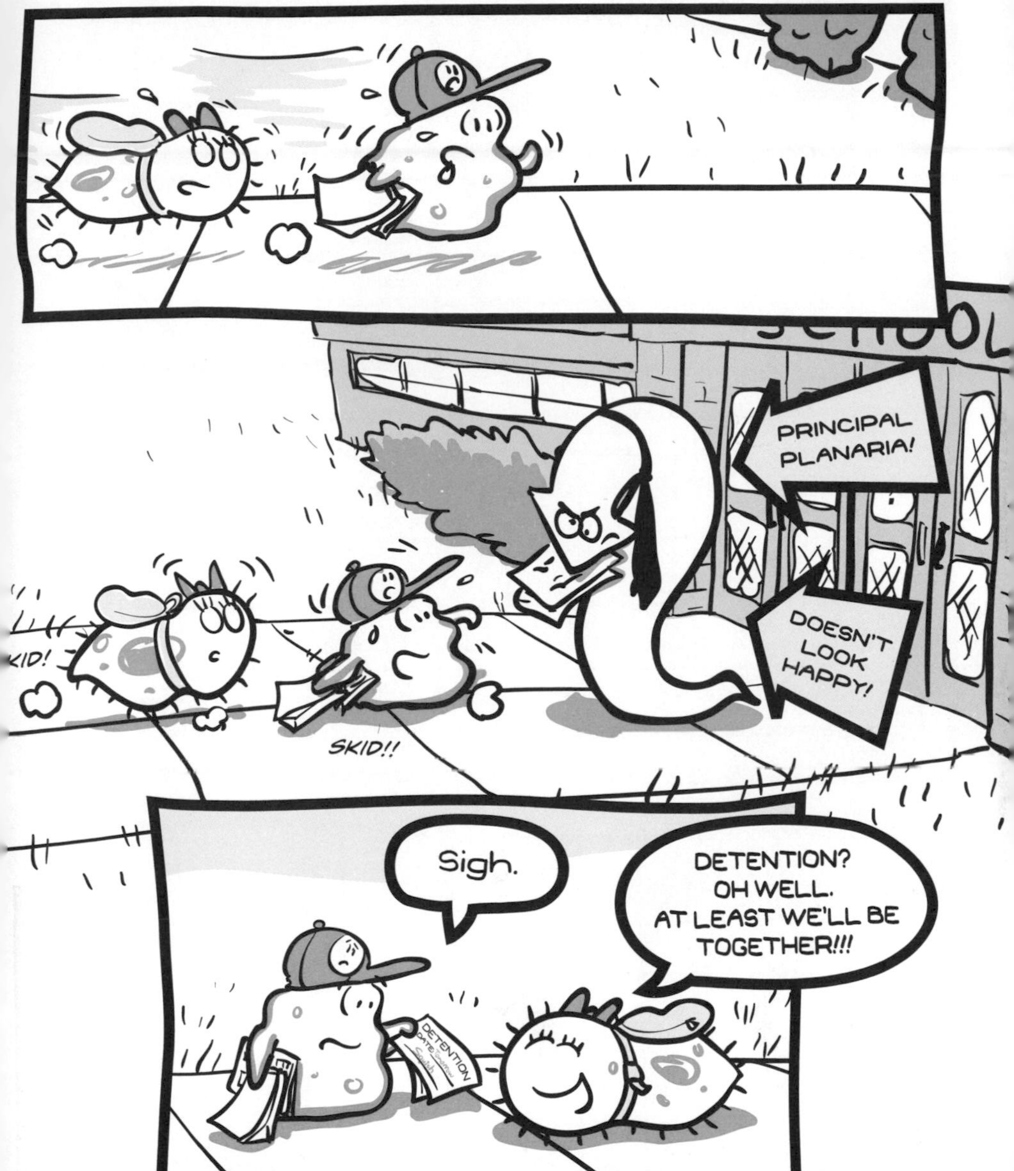
KID!
SKID!!
PRINCIPAL PLANARIA!
DOESN'T LOOK HAPPY!
Sigh.
DETENTION? OH WELL. AT LEAST WE'LL BE TOGETHER!!!

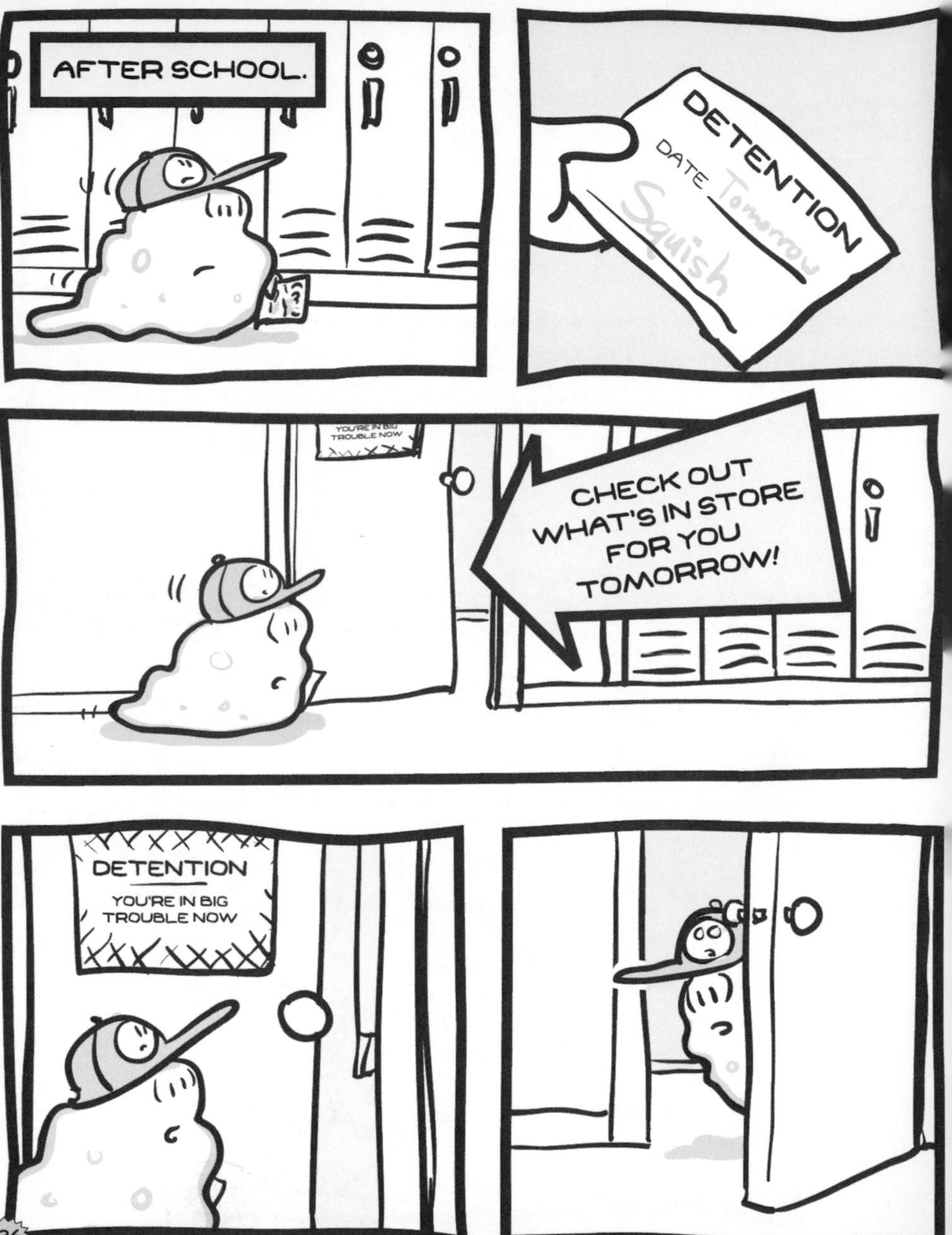
AFTER SCHOOL.
DETENTION
DATE Tomorrow
Squish
YOU'RE IN BIG TROUBLE NOW
CHECK OUT WHAT'S IN STORE FOR YOU TOMORROW!
DETENTION
YOU'RE IN BIG TROUBLE NOW

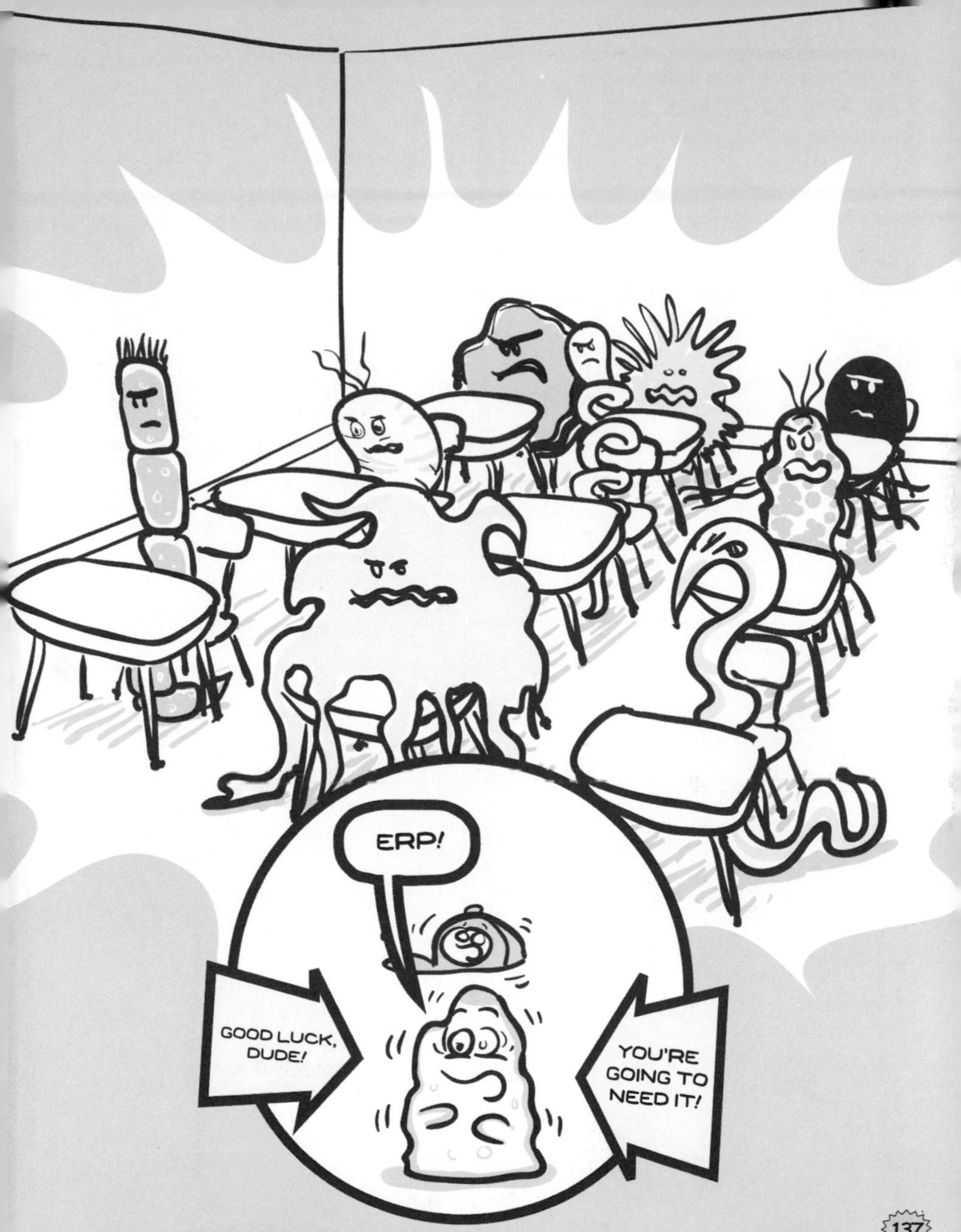
ERP!
GOOD LUCK, DUDE!
YOU'RE GOING TO NEED IT!

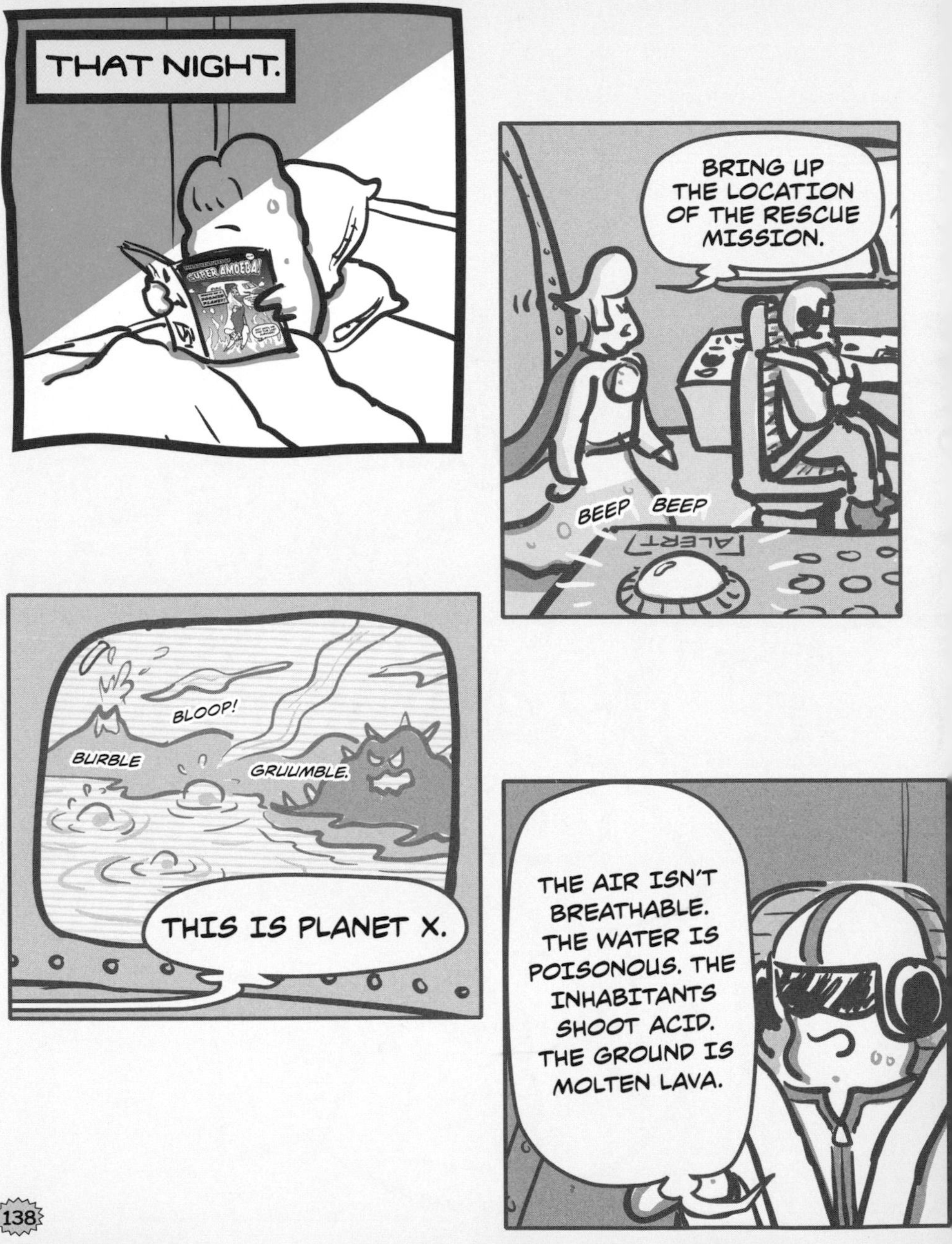

THAT NIGHT.
SUPER AMOEBA!
BRING UP THE LOCATION OF THE RESCUE MISSION.
BEEP BEEP
ALERT
BLOOP!
BURBLE
GRUUMBLE.
THIS IS PLANET X.
THE AIR ISN'T BREATHABLE. THE WATER IS POISONOUS. THE INHABITANTS SHOOT ACID. THE GROUND IS MOLTEN LAVA.

IS THERE ANYTHING *NOT* BAD ABOUT IT?
OH YEAH. NO BATHROOMS, EITHER.
SO DO YOU STILL WANT TO GO IN AND EXTRACT THE SURVIVORS? IT'S NOT GOING TO BE PRETTY.
WE DON'T CHOOSE THE MISSION.
THE MISSION CHOOSES US.
Hmm . . .
SUPER AMOEBA!

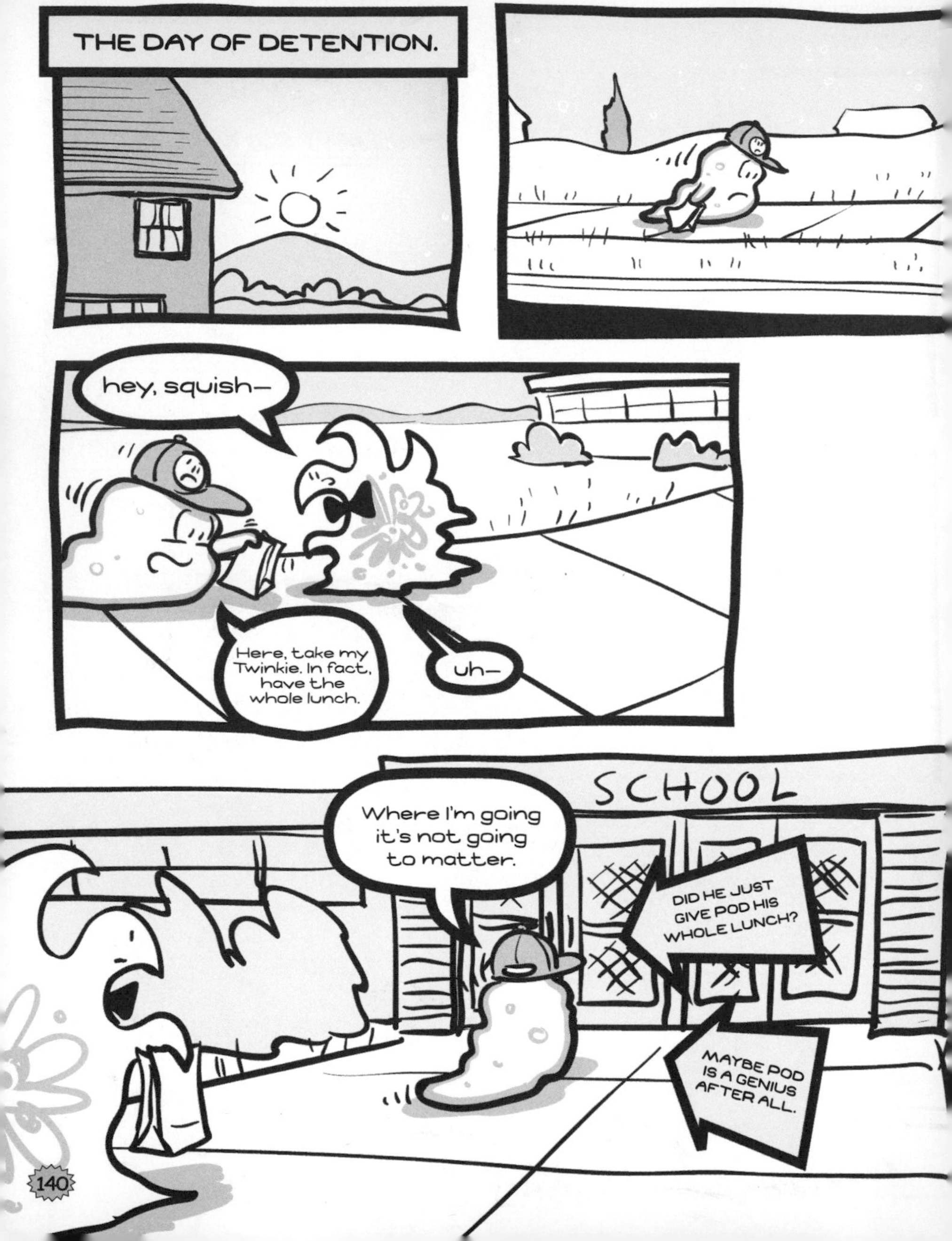
THE DAY OF DETENTION.
hey, squish—
Here, take my Twinkie. In fact, have the whole lunch.
uh—
SCHOOL
Where I'm going it's not going to matter.
DID HE JUST GIVE POD HIS WHOLE LUNCH?
MAYBE POD IS A GENIUS AFTER ALL.

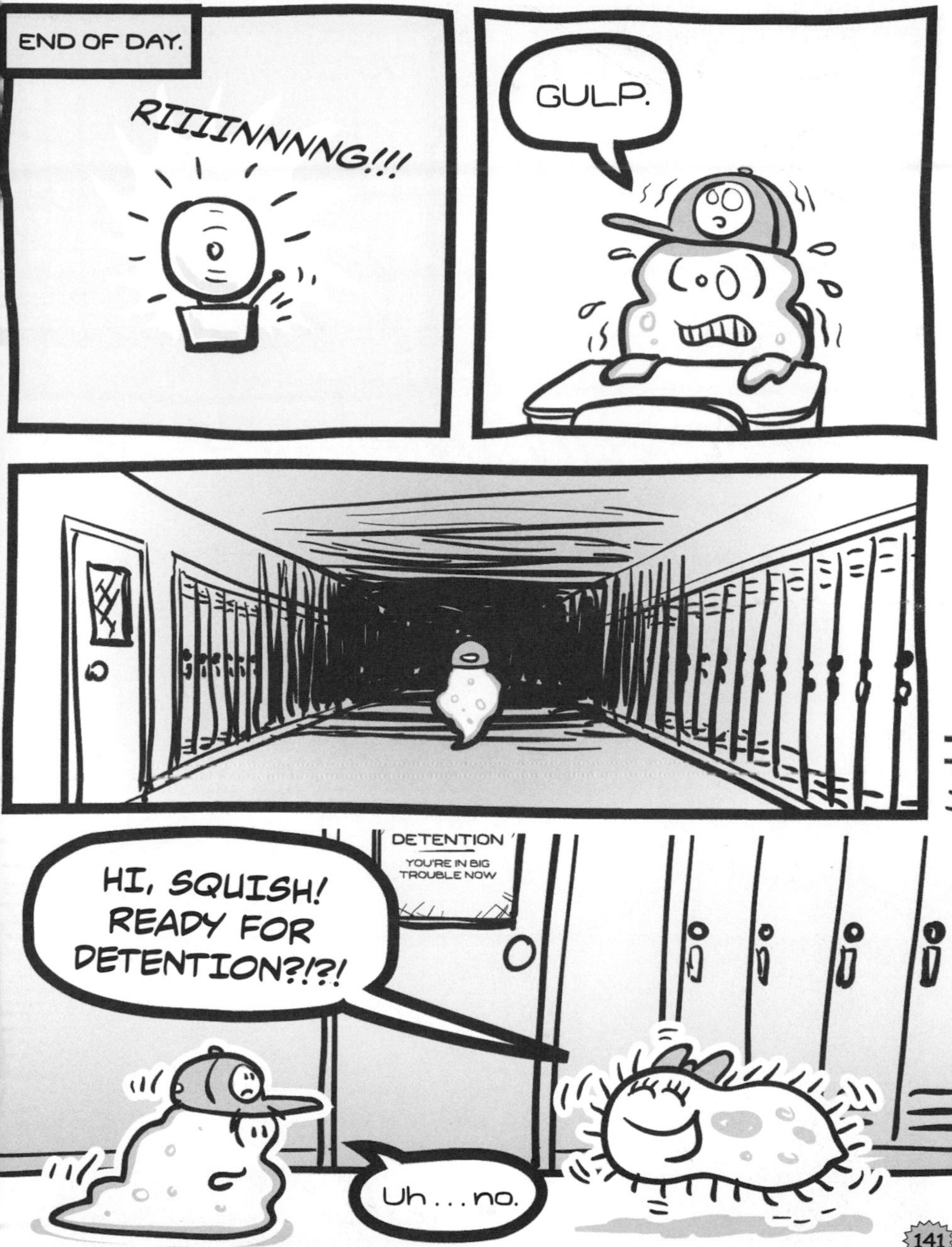

END OF DAY.
RIIIINNNNG!!!
GULP.
DETENTION
YOU'RE IN BIG TROUBLE NOW
HI, SQUISH! READY FOR DETENTION?!?!
Uh . . . no.

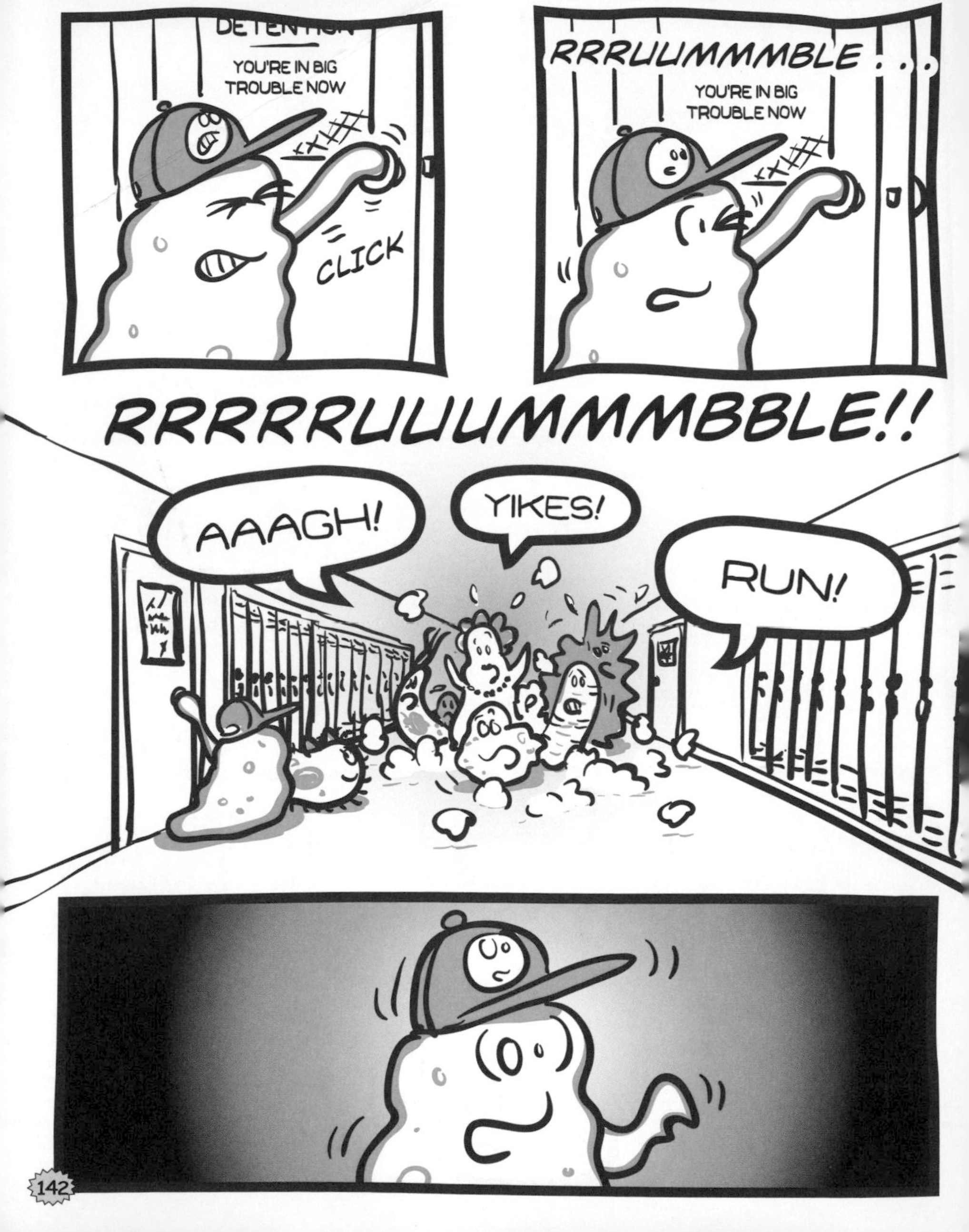

YOU'RE IN BIG TROUBLE NOW
CLICK
RRRUUMMMBLE . . .
YOU'RE IN BIG TROUBLE NOW
RRRRRUUUMMMBBLE!!
AAAGH!
YIKES!
RUN!

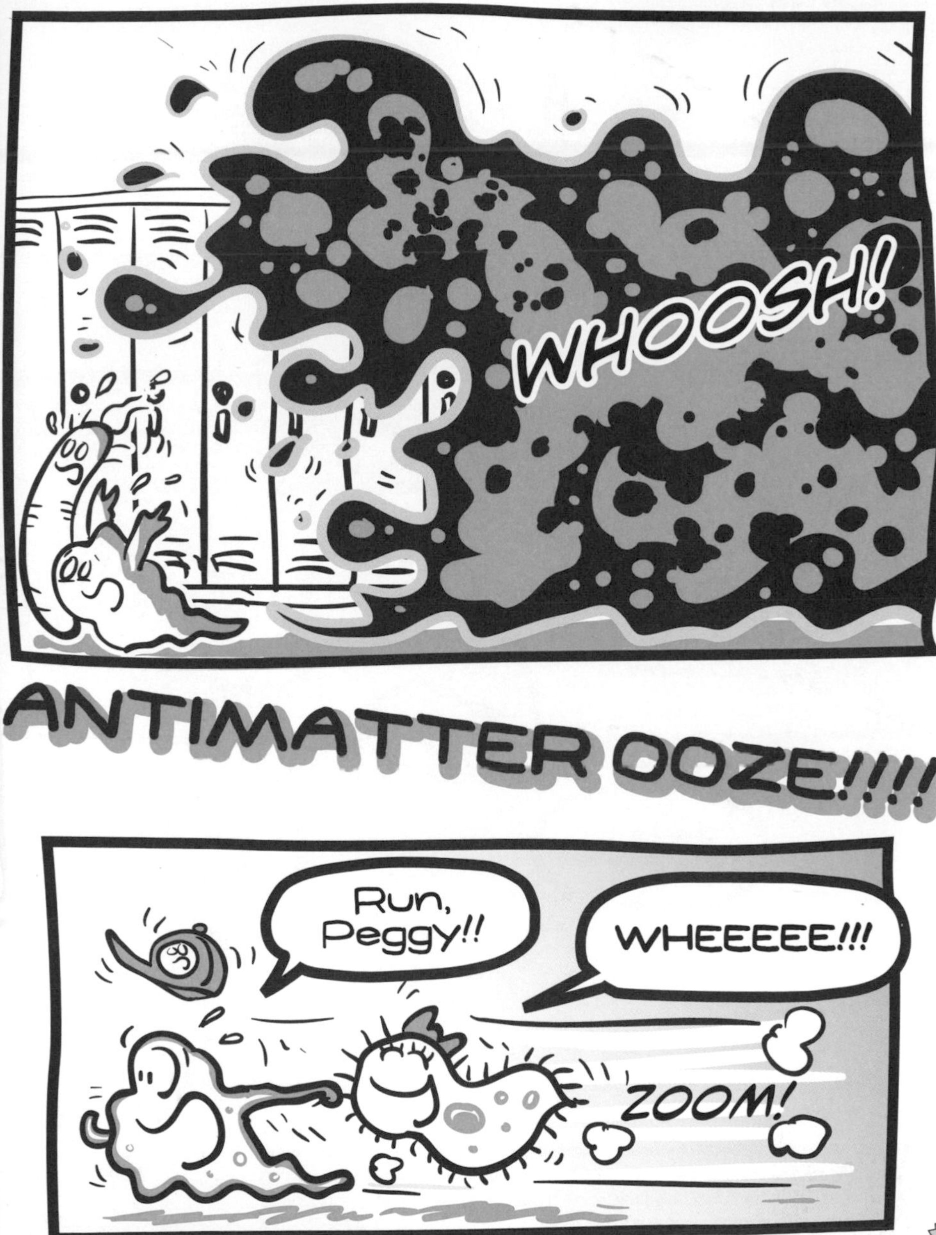
WHOOSH!
ANTIMATTER OOZE!!!!
Run, Peggy!!
WHEEEEE!!!
ZOOM!

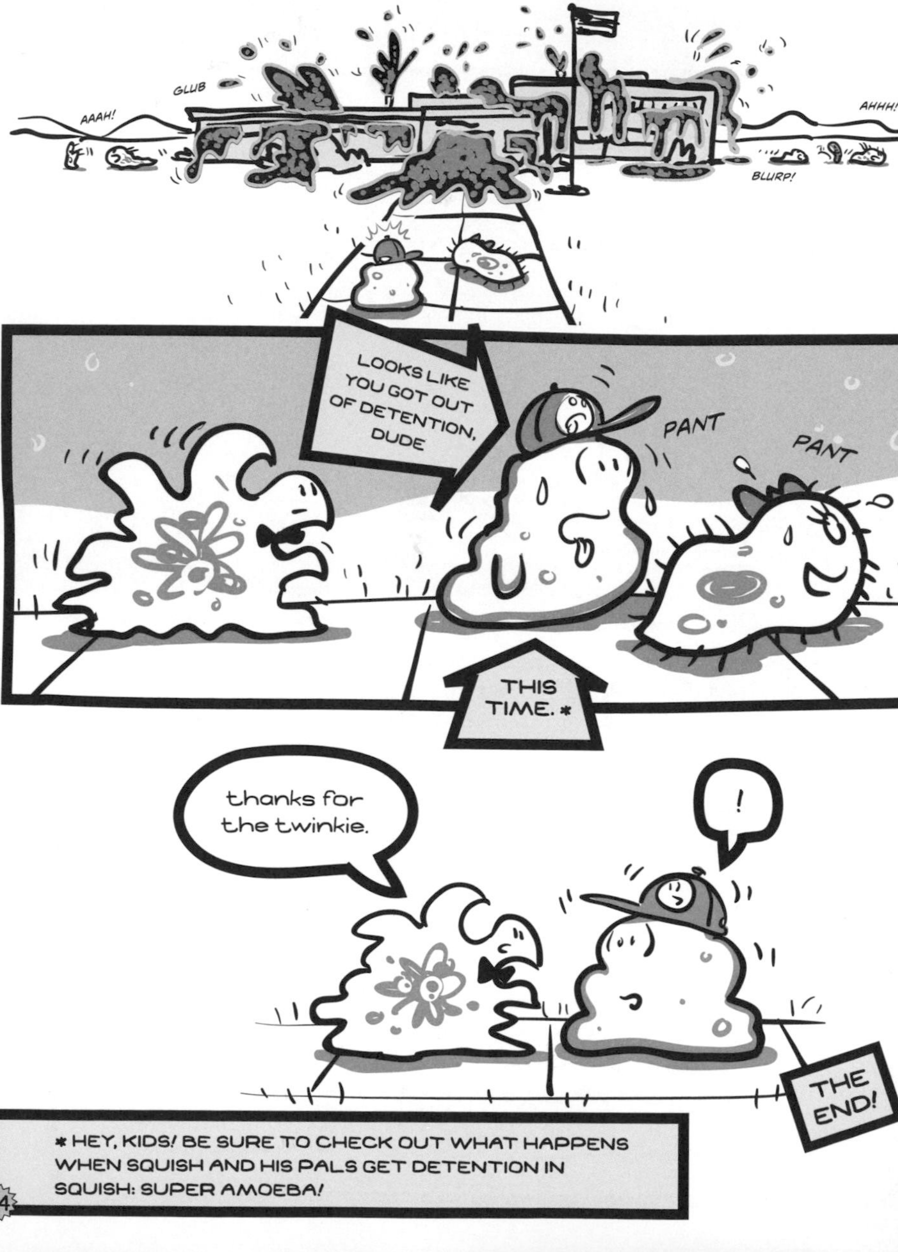
AAAH!
GLUB
AHHH!
BLURP!
LOOKS LIKE YOU GOT OUT OF DETENTION, DUDE
PANT
PANT
THIS TIME. *
thanks for the twinkie.
!
THE END!
* HEY, KIDS! BE SURE TO CHECK OUT WHAT HAPPENS WHEN SQUISH AND HIS PALS GET DETENTION IN SQUISH: SUPER AMOEBA!

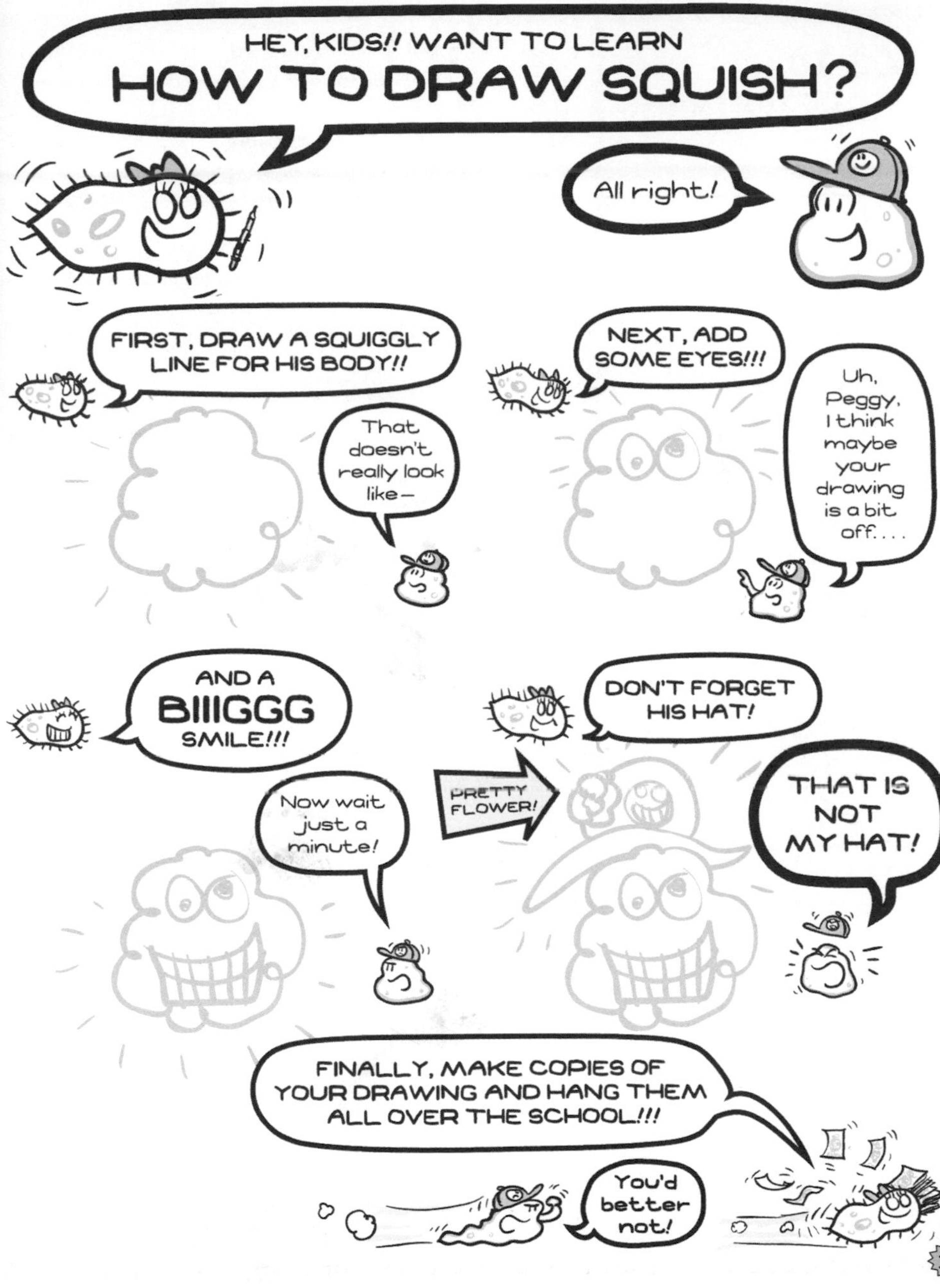
HEY, KIDS!! WANT TO LEARN HOW TO DRAW SQUISH?
All right!
FIRST, DRAW A SQUIGGLY LINE FOR HIS BODY!!
That doesn't really look like—
NEXT, ADD SOME EYES!!!
Uh, Peggy, I think maybe your drawing is a bit off. . . .
AND A BIIIGGG SMILE!!!
Now wait just a minute!
PRETTY FLOWER!
DON'T FORGET HIS HAT!
THAT IS NOT MY HAT!
FINALLY, MAKE COPIES OF YOUR DRAWING AND HANG THEM ALL OVER THE SCHOOL!!!
You'd better not!

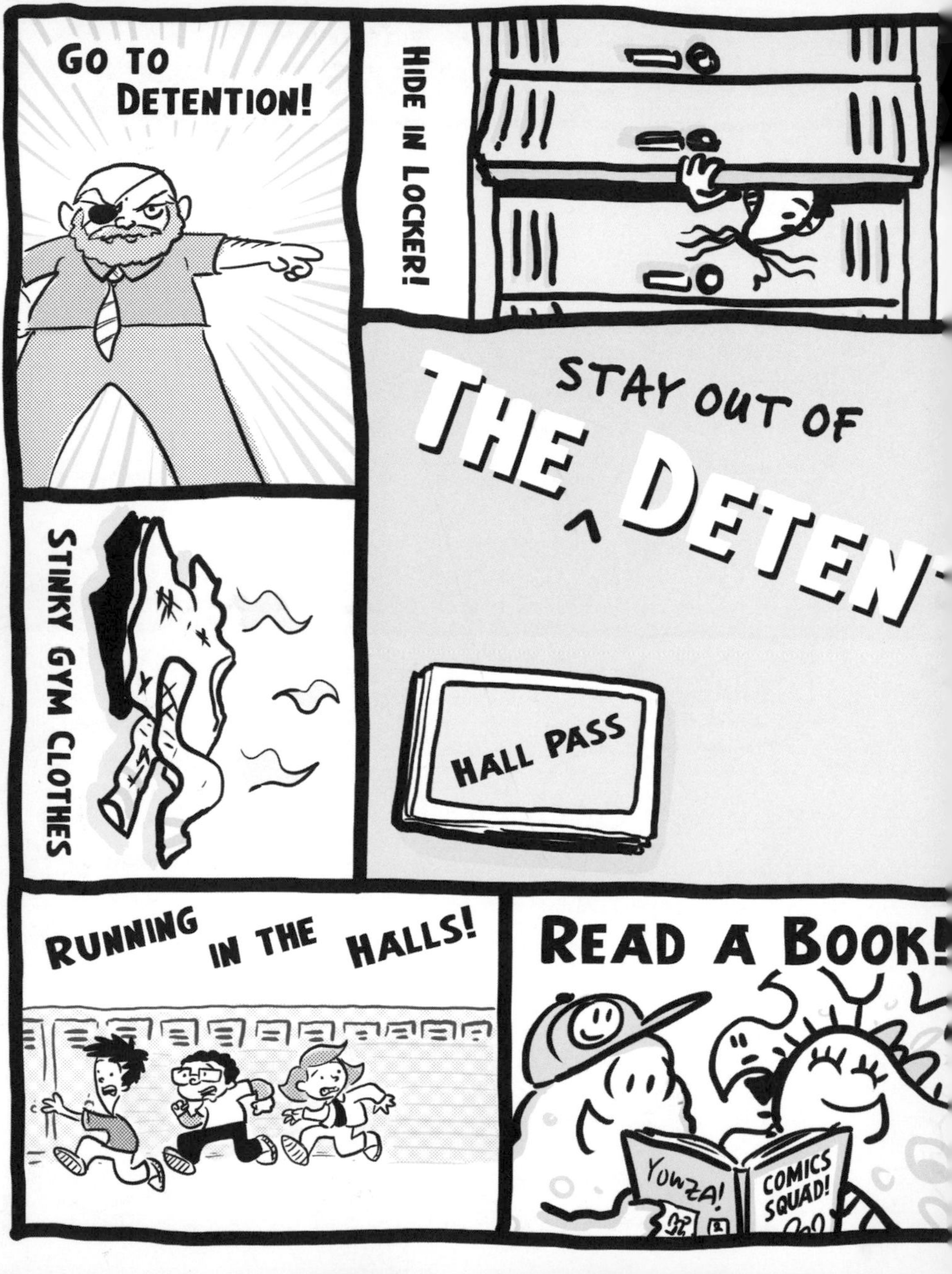

GO TO DETENTION!
HIDE IN LOCKER!
STAY OUT OF THE DETEN
HALL PASS
STINKY GYM CLOTHES
RUNNING IN THE HALLS!
READ A BOOK!
YOWZA!
COMICS SQUAD!

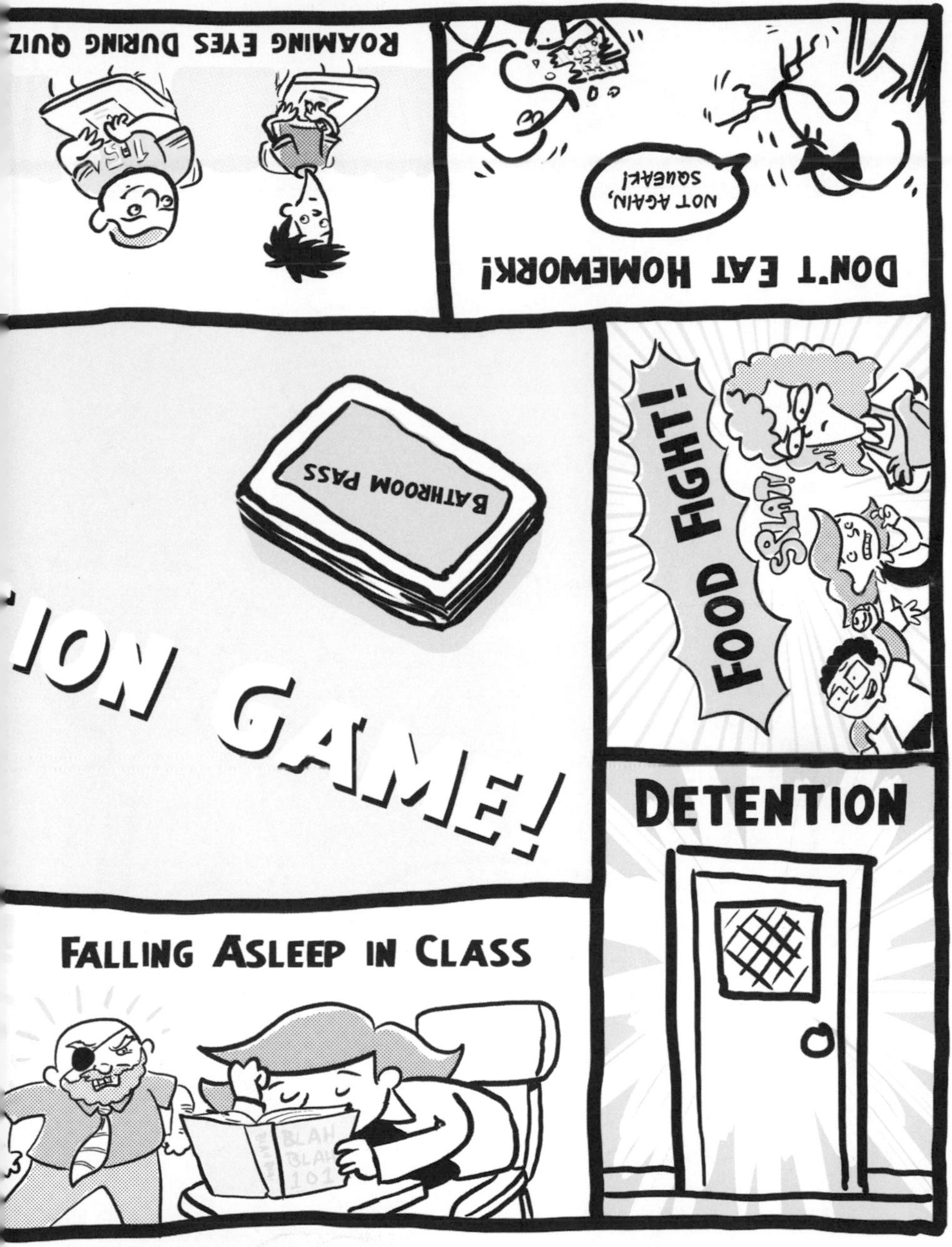

ROAMING EYES DURING QUIZ
TEST
DON'T EAT HOMEWORK!
NOT AGAIN, SQUEAK!
BATHROOM PASS
FOOD FIGHT!
SPLAT!
ION GAME!
DETENTION
FALLING ASLEEP IN CLASS
BLAH BLAH 101

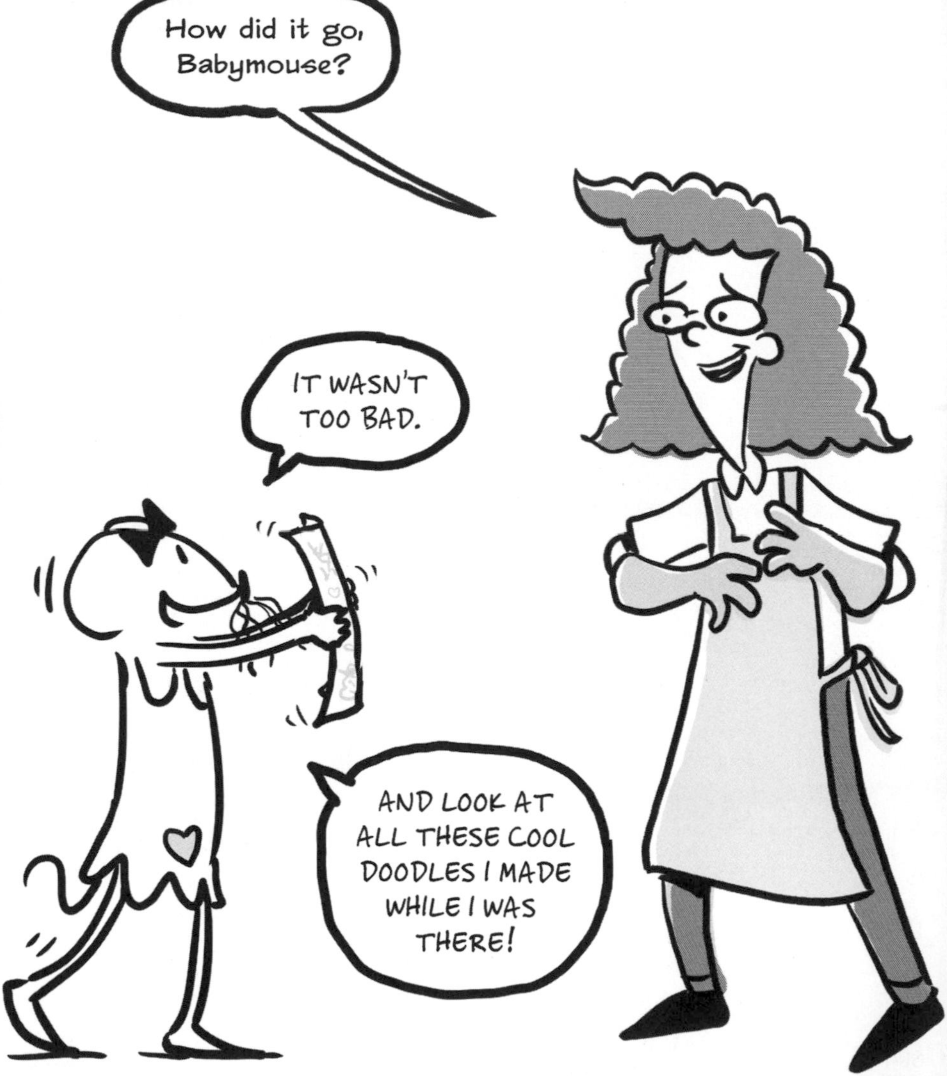
How did it go, Babymouse?
IT WASN'T TOO BAD.
AND LOOK AT ALL THESE COOL DOODLES I MADE WHILE I WAS THERE!

★ ABOUT THE AUTHORS ★

JARRETT J. KROSOCZKA

is the author and illustrator of more than thirty books, including the popular Lunch Lady graphic novels. He's delivered two TED Talks and can be heard weekly on SiriusXM's Kids Place Live. Jarrett is well-behaved; his pugs are not. (studiojjk.com)

GEORGE O'CONNOR

is the cartoonist behind the Olympians series of graphic novels. He never, ever had detention because he was always a very, very good boy. Totally. (olympiansrule.com)

VICTORIA JAMIESON

is the author and illustrator of the graphic novel *Roller Girl,* which won a Newbery Honor award. She lives in Portland, Oregon, with her family. She has only had one detention in her life, in driver's ed class in high school. Cause for the detention is still undetermined. (victoriajamieson.com)

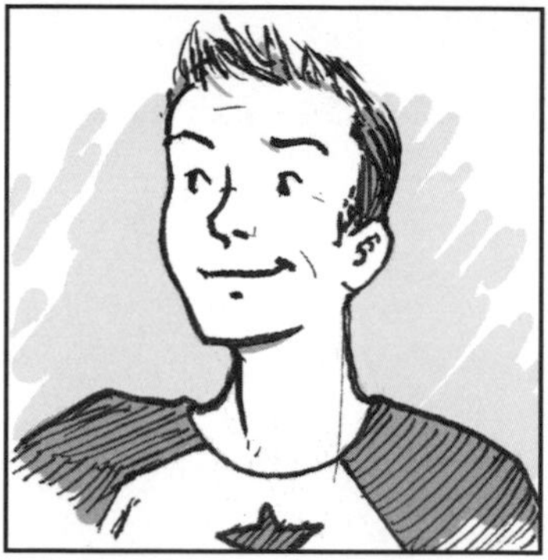

BEN HATKE

draws and writes both comics and picture books. He's particularly known for the Zita the Spacegirl trilogy. Ben dressed up as an eyeball once for Halloween. It was awesome. (benhatke.com)

RAFAEL ROSADO & JORGE AGUIRRE

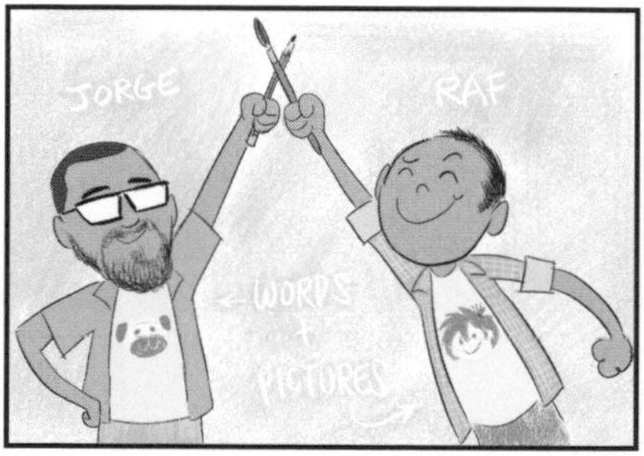
JORGE
RAF
←WORDS
+
PICTURES→

are the team behind the pint-sized hero Claudette (*Giants Beware, Dragons Beware,* and an upcoming third book). They became friends while at the Ohio State University. They have never been sent to detention together, but if they ever were, they'd probably spend the time making more comics. (dragonsbeware.com)

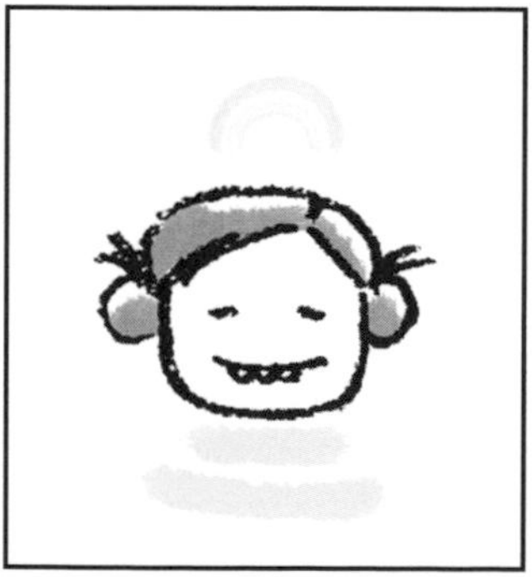

LARK PIEN

is the author of *Long Tail Kitty* and *Mr. Elephanter,* and the colorist of *American Born Chinese, Boxers and Saints,* and *Sunny Side Up.* Sometimes she is also a troublemaker!

MATT PHELAN

is the author-illustrator of *Bluffton* and three other graphic novels. This is the first comic he has set in the present day. Huh. Weird. (mattphelan.com)

JENNIFER L. HOLM & MATTHEW HOLM

are the brother-sister team behind two graphic novel series, Babymouse and Squish. They grew up reading lots of comics, and they turned out just fine. (babymouse.com)

★ DON'T MISS THESE OTHER GREAT ★ GRAPHIC NOVELS FROM RANDOM HOUSE!

BABYMOUSE

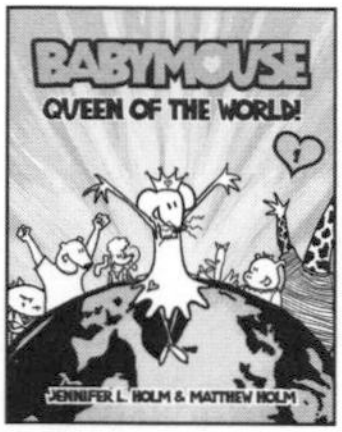
BABYMOUSE
QUEEN OF THE WORLD!
1
JENNIFER L. HOLM & MATTHEW HOLM
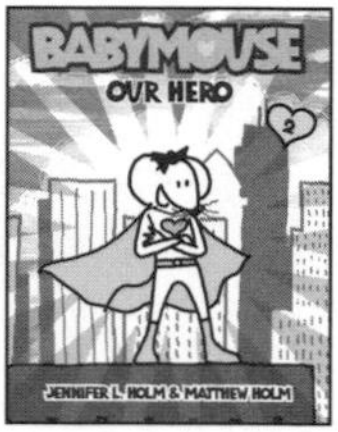
BABYMOUSE
OUR HERO
2
JENNIFER L. HOLM & MATTHEW HOLM
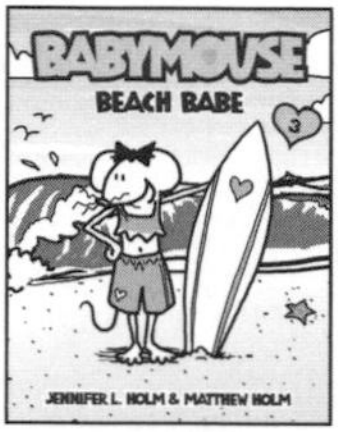
BABYMOUSE
BEACH BABE
3
JENNIFER L. HOLM & MATTHEW HOLM
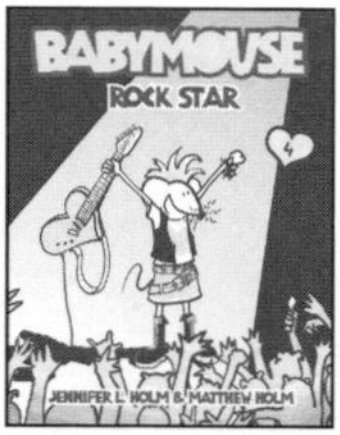
BABYMOUSE
ROCK STAR
4
JENNIFER L. HOLM & MATTHEW HOLM
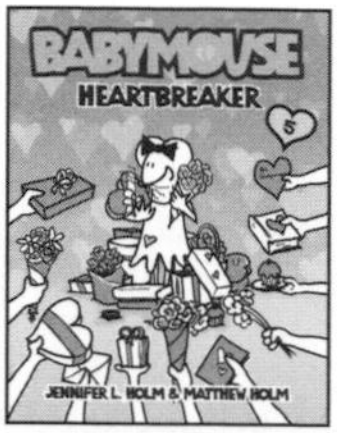
BABYMOUSE
HEARTBREAKER
5
JENNIFER L. HOLM & MATTHEW HOLM
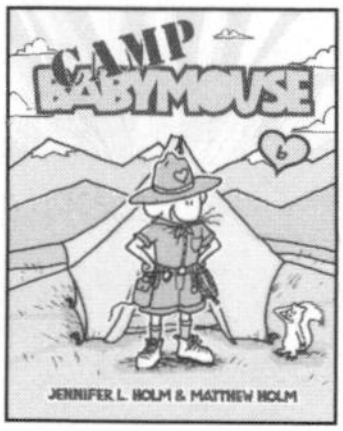
CAMP BABYMOUSE
6
JENNIFER L. HOLM & MATTHEW HOLM
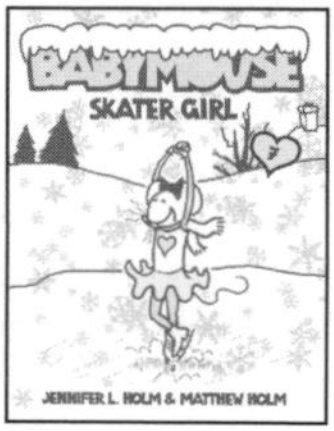
BABYMOUSE
SKATER GIRL
7
JENNIFER L. HOLM & MATTHEW HOLM
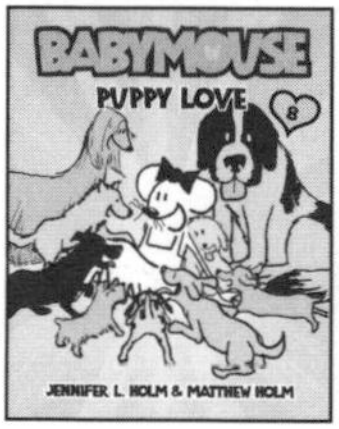
BABYMOUSE
PUPPY LOVE
8
JENNIFER L. HOLM & MATTHEW HOLM
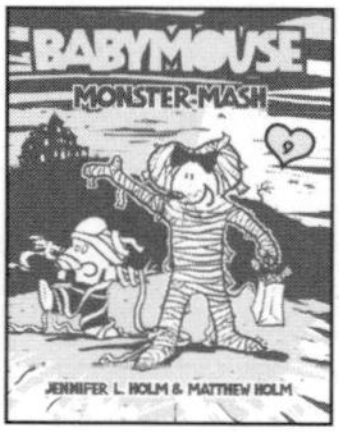
BABYMOUSE
MONSTER MASH
9
JENNIFER L. HOLM & MATTHEW HOLM
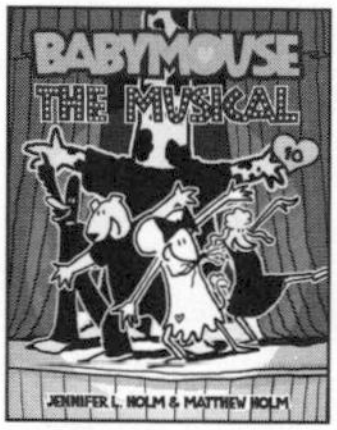
BABYMOUSE
THE MUSICAL
10
JENNIFER L. HOLM & MATTHEW HOLM
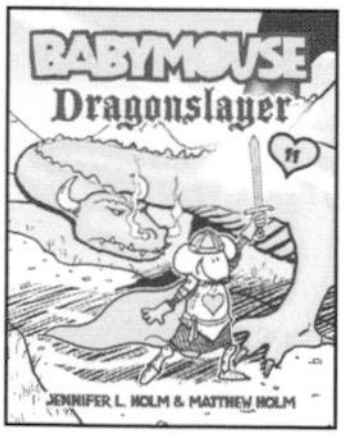
BABYMOUSE
Dragonslayer
11
JENNIFER L. HOLM & MATTHEW HOLM
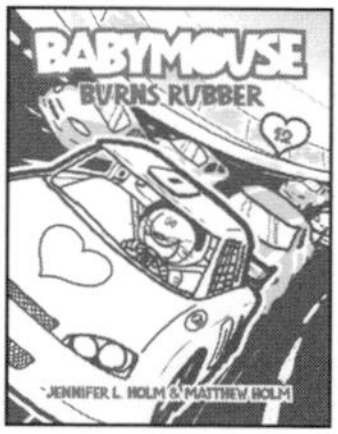
BABYMOUSE
BURNS RUBBER
12
JENNIFER L. HOLM & MATTHEW HOLM
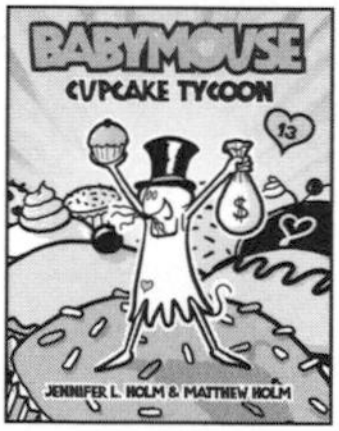
BABYMOUSE
CUPCAKE TYCOON
13
JENNIFER L. HOLM & MATTHEW HOLM
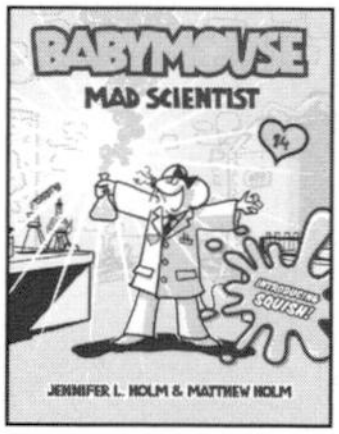
BABYMOUSE
MAD SCIENTIST
14
JENNIFER L. HOLM & MATTHEW HOLM
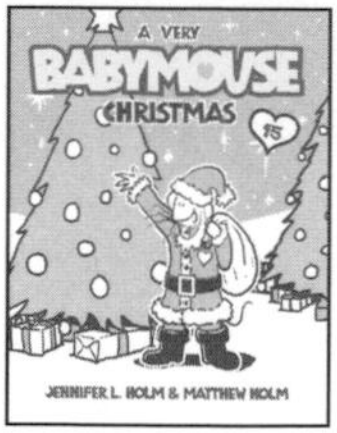
A VERY BABYMOUSE CHRISTMAS
15
JENNIFER L. HOLM & MATTHEW HOLM
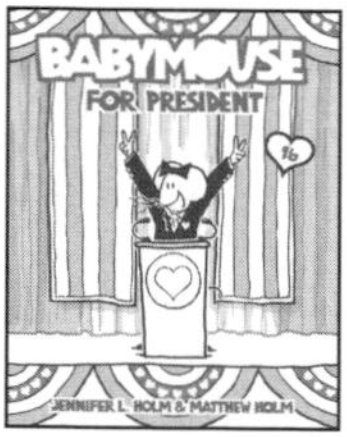
BABYMOUSE
FOR PRESIDENT
16
JENNIFER L. HOLM & MATTHEW HOLM
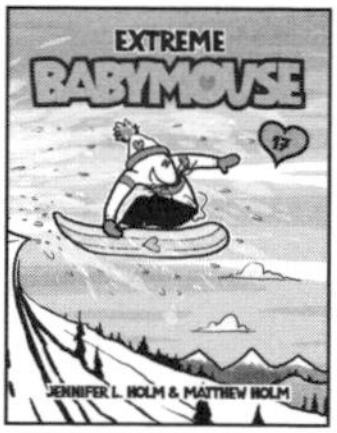
EXTREME BABYMOUSE
17
JENNIFER L. HOLM & MATTHEW HOLM
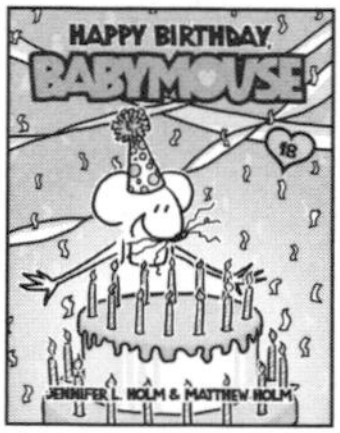
HAPPY BIRTHDAY, BABYMOUSE
18
JENNIFER L. HOLM & MATTHEW HOLM
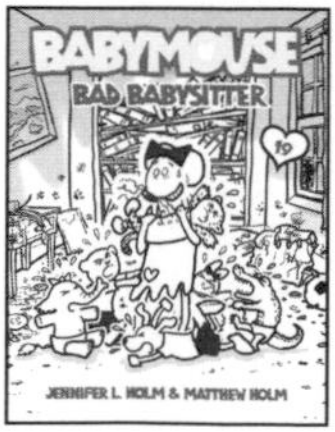
BABYMOUSE
BAD BABYSITTER
19
JENNIFER L. HOLM & MATTHEW HOLM
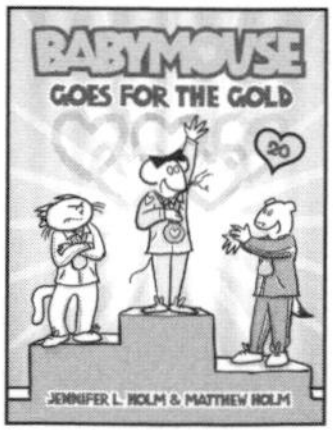
BABYMOUSE
GOES FOR THE GOLD
20
JENNIFER L. HOLM & MATTHEW HOLM

IT'S GREEN . . . IT'S BLOBBY . . .
IT'S GROSS . . . IT'S

squish

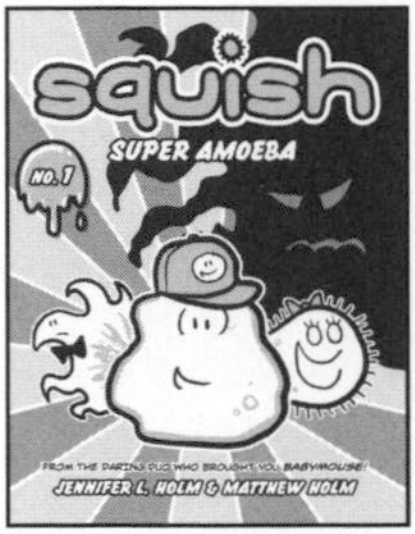
squish
SUPER AMOEBA
NO. 1
FROM THE DARING DUO WHO BROUGHT YOU BABYMOUSE!
JENNIFER L. HOLM & MATTHEW HOLM

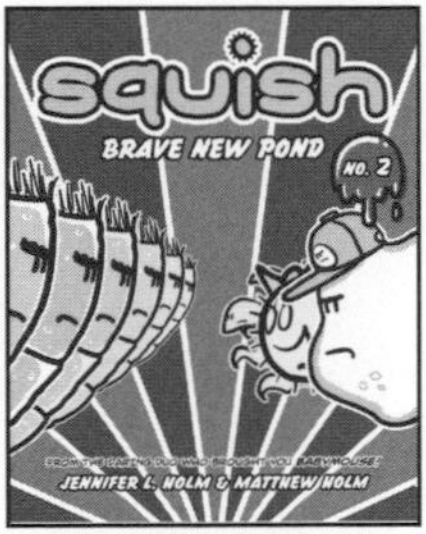
squish
BRAVE NEW POND
NO. 2
FROM THE DARING DUO WHO BROUGHT YOU BABYMOUSE!
JENNIFER L. HOLM & MATTHEW HOLM

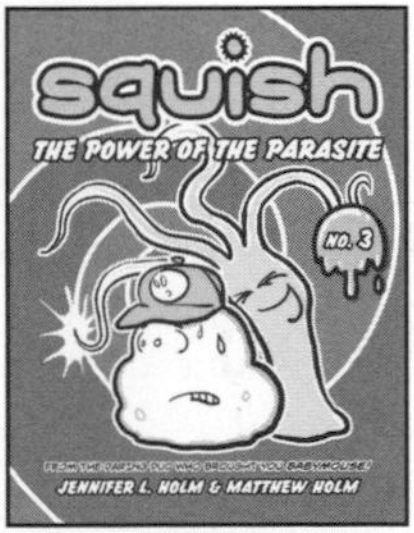
squish
THE POWER OF THE PARASITE
NO. 3
FROM THE DARING DUO WHO BROUGHT YOU BABYMOUSE!
JENNIFER L. HOLM & MATTHEW HOLM

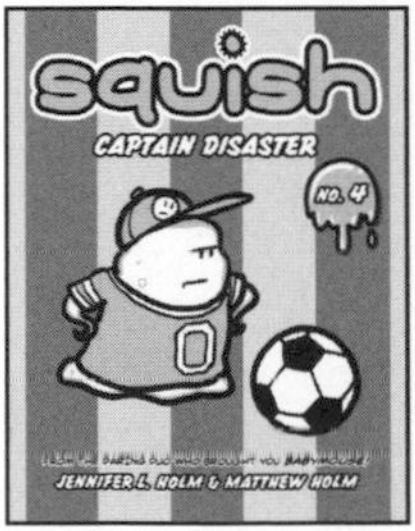
squish
CAPTAIN DISASTER
NO. 4
FROM THE DARING DUO WHO BROUGHT YOU BABYMOUSE!
JENNIFER L. HOLM & MATTHEW HOLM

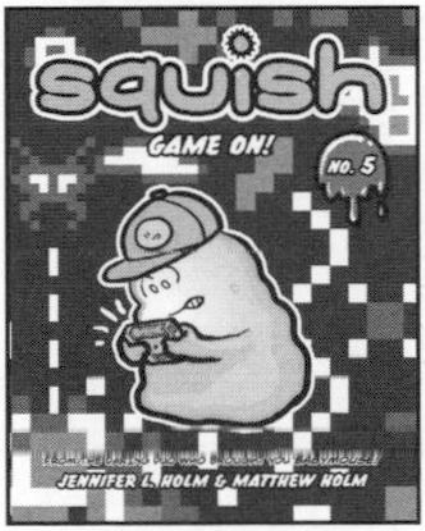
squish
GAME ON!
NO. 5
FROM THE DARING DUO WHO BROUGHT YOU BABYMOUSE!
JENNIFER L. HOLM & MATTHEW HOLM

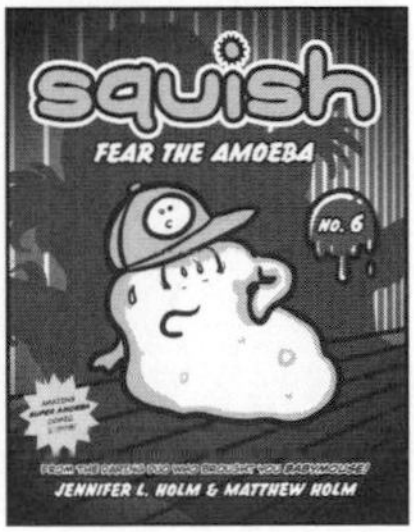
squish
FEAR THE AMOEBA
NO. 6
FROM THE DARING DUO WHO BROUGHT YOU BABYMOUSE!
JENNIFER L. HOLM & MATTHEW HOLM

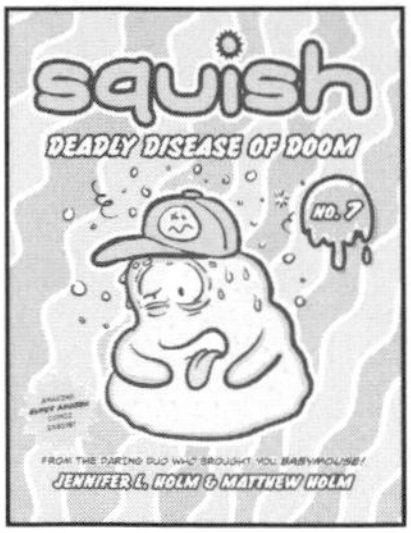
squish
DEADLY DISEASE OF DOOM
NO. 7
FROM THE DARING DUO WHO BROUGHT YOU BABYMOUSE!
JENNIFER L. HOLM & MATTHEW HOLM

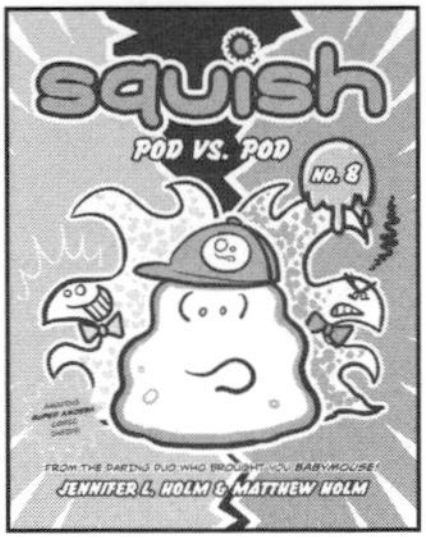
squish
POD VS. POD
NO. 8
FROM THE DARING DUO WHO BROUGHT YOU BABYMOUSE!
JENNIFER L. HOLM & MATTHEW HOLM

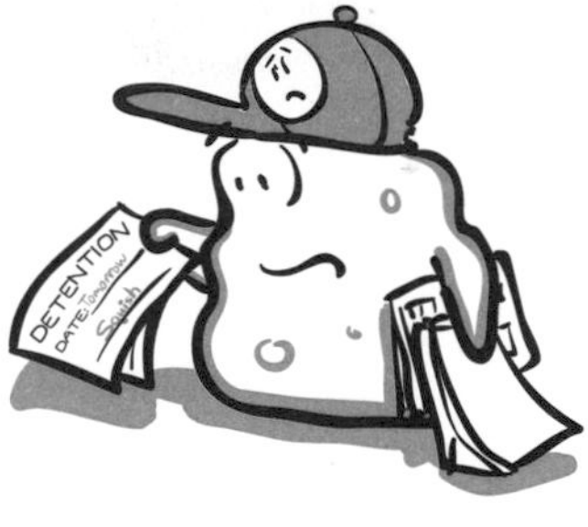
DETENTION
DATE: Tomorrow
Squish

LUNCH LADY

Serving justice! And serving lunch!

Jarrett J. Krosoczka
LUNCH LADY

© 2013 Jarrett J. Krosoczka